Praise for *New York Times* bestselling author Catherine Anderson

"[Anderson's] stories make you believe in the power of love."

> —#1 *New York Times* bestselling author Debbie Macomber

"An amazing talent."

> —*New York Times* bestselling author Elizabeth Lowell

"Count on Catherine Anderson for intense emotion."

> —*New York Times* bestselling author Jayne Ann Krentz

"Catherine Anderson has a gift for imbuing her characters with dignity, compassion, courage, and strength that inspire readers."
> —RT Book Reviews

"A major voice in the romance genre."
> —Publishers Weekly

Phantom Waltz

Catherine Anderson

JOVE
New York

A JOVE BOOK
Published by Berkley
An imprint of Penguin Random House LLC
penguinrandomhouse.com

Copyright © 2007 by Adeline Catherine Anderson
Penguin Random House supports copyright. Copyright fuels creativity, encourages
diverse voices, promotes free speech, and creates a vibrant culture. Thank you for buying
an authorized edition of this book and for complying with copyright laws by not
reproducing, scanning, or distributing any part of it in any form without permission.
You are supporting writers and allowing Penguin Random House to continue to
publish books for every reader.

A JOVE BOOK, BERKLEY, and the BERKLEY & B colophon
are registered trademarks of Penguin Random House LLC.

ISBN: 9780593437704

Signet mass-market edition / January 2007
Jove mass-market edition / July 2017
First Jove trade paperback edition / August 2019
Second Jove trade paperback edition / April 2021

Printed in the United States of America
1   3   5   7   9   10   8   6   4   2

Cover photo of hat and basket © Sandra Cunningham / Trevillion Images

To Steven Axelrod, my agent, who always goes the extra mile for me and has earned my gratitude and respect, and to Ellen Edwards, my editor, who has worked so hard behind the scenes over the years to make my books the very best that they can be.

Last, but not least, to Chris Jansen, Dr. Fred Black's nurse extraordinaire, who has been such a good friend to me. The world would be a much better place if every medical professional had as much heart as you do. Please know, Chris, that you are touching lives and making a difference. Also, by order of decree passed along to me by your brother, Jeff Fretwell, I wish you a belated, "Happy Birthday!"

Dear Readers:

Traditionally in romance, the heroes and heroines are physically perfect. That is not to say that those characters are unappealing. I have read hundreds of those books and loved them, I've written a few, and I hope to write and enjoy many more. However, as a novelist, I occasionally get a yen to write something different—a tribute, if you will, to those in our society who are, by birth or unfortunate mishap, left disabled. I have been so blessed as a writer to have an agent and editor, Steven Axelrod and Ellen Edwards, respectively, who have always encouraged me to break new ground. If not for them, *Annie's Song*, a book about a deaf girl, might never have been written.

So it is that, once again, I bring to you, my readers, a different kind of love story, this time about a young woman confined to a wheelchair. I invite you to cast aside all your preconceived notions about what constitutes a great love story and join me in Bethany Coulter's world, where hope for a normal life is only a memory and dreams of romance are long since forgotten . . . until magic comes knocking in the form of a tall, dark, rugged cowboy named Ryan Kendrick.

I would like to thank Dr. Fred Black and his nurse, Chris Jansen, for giving me information and direction in my research. I also salute the many paraplegics who have reached out to others with personal accounts of their disabilities and how paraplegia has affected their lives. I would also like to thank my wonderful husband, Sid, who has never failed to be my anchor in the storm and my bridge over troubled waters.

Catherine Anderson

Chapter One

F orget chewing nails. Ryan Kendrick was so mad he
could have chewed lug nuts. He had a broken-down
tractor, and the parts needed to fix it should have been delivered to the Rocking K day before yesterday. As of this
morning, they still hadn't arrived, and Ryan's follow-up
calls had gotten him nowhere.

With one shoulder, he butted open the door of The
Works, the largest ranch supply house in Crystal Falls. Harv
Coulter, a rancher who'd gone bust, had started the business
on a shoestring several years back, and the Kendrick brothers, along with many other ranchers in the area, had been pa-
tronizing the establishment ever since. Now the huge store
was a going concern, well stocked with everything from
heavy equipment to fancy western wear, the only problem
being that as sales increased, the quality of service seemed
to go downhill.

If Harv didn't get his employees whipped into shape,
he'd start losing accounts. Delays like this, smack-dab in the
middle of spring planting time, were intolerable. Due to late
snows, every farmer and rancher in the basin was already
behind schedule, and each day of downtime could mean
thousands of dollars in lost crop revenue.

Ryan headed for an overhead sign at the rear of the feed
section that read, "PARTS AND REPAIRS," his dusty riding boots
beating out an angry tattoo on the concrete floor. When he
reached a counter cluttered with parts and catalogs, he

shoved aside an air filter, rested his arms on the grease-stained Formica, and settled a blistering gaze on a slender young woman who sat at a computer station near the register.

A long, luxurious mane of sable hair partly concealed her face. Her slender, neatly manicured fingers flew over the keyboard with speedy efficiency. Ryan waited for just a moment. Being ignored did little to mellow his mood. The morning was half over. He glanced at his watch and set his jaw.

"Excuse me," he said. "Is it possible to get some help around here?"

That brought her head up. Ryan went still, his gaze riveted. She had the most beautiful eyes, large, outlined with thick, dark lashes, and so deep a blue they reminded him of the Johnny-jump-up violets that grew wild at the ranch. Normally, he scoffed at the sappy phrases men used to describe women. He'd looked into a lot of eyes and never felt in danger of drowning, or losing his heart.

"I don't usually work the floor, but I can try to help you," she said, her voice as sunny as her smile, which flashed an irresistible dimple in one cheek.

Ryan couldn't stop staring. Her face was small and heart-shaped, with sculpted cheekbones, a pointy chin with just a hint of stubbornness, and a soft, sweet mouth. The tip of her delicately bridged nose was shiny and sported a smattering of freckles, which told him her flawless complexion was natural.

"What seems to be the problem?" she asked.

He started to tell her, but for an instant, his mind went as empty as a wrangler's pocket right before payday, and he couldn't remember why the hell he was there.

He had the strangest feeling, dead center in his chest—a sense of recognition—as if he'd subconsciously been searching for her all his life. *Crazy.* Love at first sight was more his brother's style. Ryan shopped for women like he did for boots, trying them on for size before he settled in for a long-term relationship, and even at that, he'd yet to find a comfortable enough fit to last him a lifetime.

"I, um . . ." He rubbed beside his nose, a habit when he got nervous. A dull ache throbbed behind his eyes. "I'm Ryan Kendrick from the Rocking K," he offered stupidly.

The sweet curve of her lips deepened. "Hi. I'm pleased to meet you. And don't feel bad. I have days like this, only worse. At least you know your name."

He huffed with laughter. "You actually forget your *name*?"

The dimple flashed again. "What works for me is to back up. You're Ryan Kendrick from the Rocking K, and you came in here to . . . ?"

He snapped his fingers. "My parts."

"Your parts?"

He chuckled. "I want to know where the Sam Hill they are."

Pure devilment crept into her expression. "You've lost your parts and think *I've* got them? Most cowboys I know guard theirs like Fort Knox."

Ryan threw back his head and laughed. The tension that had knotted the muscles in his neck and shoulders all morning miraculously vanished.

"I hope you don't have a hot date lined up for Saturday night," she added. "A cowboy who's missing his parts could find himself in a very embarrassing situation."

He nudged up the brim of his Stetson. "Well, now, darlin', that all depends. What are you doin' Saturday night?"

It was her turn to laugh. The sound was rich and musical, and it warmed him clear through.

"I usually avoid cowboys who can't keep track of their parts."

"Go out with me, and I guarantee I'll find mine in damned short order."

"Maybe if you'll give me an order number instead of a hard time, I can help locate the little buggers for you."

Little buggers? Ryan almost corrected that misconception. But there were lines a man didn't step over, and he had a hunch this was one of them. Maybe it was the sweetness of her smile—or that innocent look he'd glimpsed in her eyes—but something told him she wasn't as worldly as she pretended to be.

As he fished in the pocket of his blue chambray shirt, he swept his gaze over her. She was a fragile, slightly built woman, which undoubtedly explained why those eyes seemed to be the biggest thing about her. But despite that, she was temptingly well-rounded in all the right places. *Perfection in miniature.*

Her brown shell top showcased a long, graceful neck, thin but well-defined shoulders, and creamy-white arms that looked surprisingly firm for someone with such a slight build. Beneath the brown knit, small, perfectly shaped breasts pleaded for a lingering look. Minding his manners, he flicked his gaze lower and bemoaned the fact that the counter concealed the rest of her. He was a leg man, and it was a woman's foundation that always swung the vote for him.

Wishing she'd stand up so he could get a look, he handed over the slip of paper on which he'd jotted his order number. While she scanned computer files and tracked down his parts order, they carried on a lively exchange, during which he learned she was twenty-six, had no significant other in her life except a feline named Cleo, and was the baby in a family of six kids. Her five rambunctious older brothers spoiled her rotten and kept things hopping at family gatherings.

Ryan enjoyed talking with her. Even with her attention divided between him and the computer screen, she kept him on his conversational toes. It wasn't often he ran across beauty, brains, *and* a great personality, all in one package.

"So . . . you gonna give me a name to put with the face?" he asked.

"Bethany." Finished with the computer, she leaned back in her chair. "Well, cowboy, time to eat crow. Guess where those parts of yours are."

"Where?"

"En route to the Rocking K. And it's not *our* fault they're late. This is the busy season. Those particular parts are in high demand right now, were on back order, and took two days longer to reach us than they should have."

Ryan had heard that one before, but coming from her, it seemed more credible. He tipped the brim of his hat back down to shade his eyes before returning outdoors. "Hmm. Lucky for me, I didn't raise too much sand, huh?"

"It takes more than a cantankerous cowboy to throw me. Five brothers, remember?" She propped her elbows on the chair armrests, her big blue eyes still smiling. "Have a nice day, and good luck fixing your tractor. Too bad you're not an employee. You could charge yourself time and a half."

By that, Ryan guessed she knew who he was. No big surprise. Practically everyone in Crystal Falls, Oregon, had heard of the Kendrick family. He tipped his hat to her. "Thank you, Bethany. It's been a rare pleasure."

"Any time," she called after him as he walked away.

He had nearly reached the door before he swung to a stop. To hell with walking out. He was thirty years old and hadn't come across a woman who interested him this much in a long time. *Bethany*. She was beautiful, sweet, and funny. The only other women he knew who could take him from pissed off to laughing in three seconds flat were his mom and sister-in-law. No way was he leaving without at least getting her phone number, a date if he could manage it.

"I know this may seem forward," he began as he returned to the counter.

Already back at work, she glanced up from the screen,

her thoughtful frown giving way to another warm smile. "You've lost your parts again *already*?"

Ryan chuckled. "Not on your life. I just—" He felt heat crawling up his neck. He hadn't felt nervous about asking a girl out since his early teens. "About Saturday night. I know we were only joking, but on a more serious note, I'd like to get to know you." At her startled look, he added, "Hey, I'm a nice guy. Your boss, Harvey Coulter, will vouch for me."

"Oh, I'm sure you're very nice, but—"

Ryan held up a staying hand. "How about dinner and dancing? We'll go out, have a fine meal, get to know each other a little better. Then we'll cut a rug. I'm hell on wheels at country western, and I know of a great band."

Her mouth curved in a wistful smile. "You like to dance, do you?"

"I *love* to dance. How about you?"

She averted her gaze. Ryan wanted to kick himself for coming on too fast. So much for that legendary charm his brother teased him about. Well, it was too late now. All he could do was go for it and hope for the best.

"I used to enjoy dancing very much." She tapped a pen on the work surface beside her computer, her small hand clenched so tightly over its length that her dainty knuckles went white.

Ryan shoved up the brim of his hat. He did his best convincing with his eyes. "Come on, sweetheart, take a chance on me. We'll have fun. I give you my solemn oath to be a perfect gentleman."

"It isn't that."

"What, then?"

To his dismay, he saw that all the laughter and mischief in her eyes had been eclipsed by shadows. He sensed he'd said or done something to cause that, but for the life of him he couldn't think what.

"If you're worried that you're too rusty to get on a dance

floor, I'm easy to follow. Give me ten minutes, and you'll think you've got wings on your feet."

She rolled her chair back from the computer station and folded her hands in her lap, gazing up at him with a prideful lift of her small chin. "Somehow I rather doubt that." Her strained, overbright smile was foiled by the flush of embarrassment on her cheeks. "Don't you?"

It took Ryan a full second to register what she meant. Then he saw that she was sitting in a wheelchair.

He felt as if a horse had kicked him in the gut—an awful, suddenly breathless feeling that made his legs threaten to buckle. It had to be a joke. She was so beautiful and perfect in every other way, the girl of his dreams. There was no way—absolutely no way.

But then his gaze dropped to her legs. The hem of her gathered black skirt came to just below the knees, revealing flesh toned support hose, finely turned ankles, and small feet encased in black slippers. The way her feet were positioned on the rests, one turned inward, was typical of a paraplegic's, and as shapely as her calves were, he could see that her muscles had begun to atrophy.

Sweet Christ. He felt like a worm. His first knee-jerk reaction was to make a polite excuse and get the hell out of there. To *run.*

The thought made him feel ashamed. Judging by those shadows in her eyes, she'd been down this path before and gotten badly hurt, undoubtedly by a long line of jackasses just like him who'd run when they saw her wheelchair.

He'd be damned if he'd do that to her. It was only one date.

Bethany fully expected Ryan Kendrick to make fast tracks or start stammering. That was usually the way it went. Watching his dark face, she had to give him credit; he looked stunned for a moment, but he quickly recovered. Flashing a wickedly attractive grin, he said, "Well, hell, I guess dancing's out. Unless, of course, I can come up with a set of wheels so we can do the wheelchair tango."

Usually men avoided mentioning her wheelchair, and while they groped for something to say, their eyes reflected a frantic need to escape. She always wanted to crawl in a hole when that happened, but Ryan Kendrick's reaction was even worse. If he felt an urge to run, he was a great loss to the stage.

"There are a number of things besides dancing that we can go do." He rested loosely folded fists at his lean waist, frowned, and then started naming off ideas, ending with, "How's dinner followed by a good movie strike you?"

It struck her as alarming. *Terrifying*. He was supposed to be heading for the closest exit. She flirted all the time. A girl had to have some fun, after all. But no man had ever taken her up on it. She didn't know what to say. Every time she looked into his gun-metal blue eyes, her mind went blank. He was *so* handsome, the epitome of tall, dark, and gorgeous. Chiseled features, a strong jaw, jet hair, and oodles of muscle. A dangerous mix. Crystal Falls was a large town, and Bethany had attended different schools than Ryan had. She'd also been a few years younger, so they'd never moved in the same social circles. But as a teenager, she'd seen him a few times at a distance, usually out at the fairgrounds during rodeos, and she'd thought he was handsome even then. He was even more attractive now. Little wonder his name was almost legend and half the women in town fancied themselves in love with him.

"I, um . . ." She shrugged, for once in her life at a total loss for words. If one of her brothers had been present, he would have marked the moment.

Her gaze fell to his mouth. His lips were long and narrow, mere slashes in the granite hardness of his face, yet beautifully sculpted with the muted shimmer of satin. At present, one corner of that hard mouth was twitching, as if he were suppressing a smile.

"Dinner and a movie isn't very imaginative, I know," he said apologetically. "I'll think of something more exciting next time around."

Next time? She wasn't sure how to deal with this. Why was he wasting his time with her? Because he felt sorry for her, maybe? She didn't want his pity.

She should have made certain he saw the wheelchair right away. Then this never would have happened. She couldn't go out with him. Her legs might not work, but her heart was in fine working order, and Ryan Kendrick was a little too charming. With those twinkling eyes and that sexy grin chipping away at her defenses, it would be all too easy to get in over her head.

She smoothed her hands over her skirt to make sure it covered her knees. There had to be a graceful way out of this. "Actually, Mr. Kendrick, the reason I hesitate is because I think I may be busy Saturday night."

He never missed a beat. "How about Friday, then?" He no sooner spoke than he snapped his fingers. "No, Friday won't work. I'm sponsoring a tractor in the mud pulls that night, and I really should be at the fairgrounds."

"Mud pulls?" Bethany immediately wanted to bite her tongue.

His gaze sharpened on her face. "Are you a mud-pull enthusiast?"

She pushed at her hair, then rolled closer to the counter to straighten the work area. "I used to enjoy them very much."

"I'm surprised. Mostly only men like the mud pulls."

She shrugged. "I had strange tastes for a girl, I guess."

"Why past tense? If you really enjoy the mud pulls, I'd love to take you."

He'd obviously never been around a paraplegic. "Oh, I couldn't possibly."

"Why not?"

"Between the parking lot and track, there's an acre of dirt and gravel."

"What's a little dirt and gravel?"

Her pulse started to pound. She swallowed, drew a deep breath, and tried to calm down. He wasn't interested in her that way; he was only being kind. She needed to focus on that, keep her sense of humor, and laugh this off. A little stark reality was called for, apparently. Who better to give him a dose?

"To a walking person, a little dirt and gravel is no big thing," she said slowly. "But my wheelchair tends to bog down on uneven ground, and getting it across deep gravel is difficult."

He gave her a measuring look. "Does it hurt you to be carried?"

"Pardon?"

"Does it cause you any pain when someone carries you?"

"You're kidding. Right? You can't mean to *carry* me."

"Why not?"

Why not? He really didn't have a clue. "The question isn't if it might hurt me, but whether or not your back can take the abuse." She shook her head. "It's very nice of you to offer. Really it is, Mr. Kendrick, but—"

"Ryan," he corrected. "Or Rye, if you prefer. I answer to both. And I'm not being 'nice.' I really want to take you."

"Ryan, then." Searching his gaze, which made her feel as if she'd just swallowed live goldfish, she said, "You're sweet to offer, but you've no idea what you'd be getting into. There are no walkways or bleachers down at that track."

"So? You have a chair, and I'll take a camp stool along for myself."

"No, you don't understand. It's not the seating arrangements that worry me, but that you'd have to carry my chair down there. It's very heavy and awkward to handle, and then you'd have to haul me down there as well." She shook her head again. "No. About the time you got me settled, it'd be my luck I'd need to use the ladies' room, which is clear up at the stadium. That's at least a quarter mile. There you'd be, carrying me and my chair all the way up there, then all the way back. By evening's end, you'd be wishing you never asked me."

"You can't weigh more than a hundred pounds. My back can handle it."

"A hundred and eleven," she corrected, thinking as she spoke that nearly half of that was dead-weight, which was heavier and more awkward to handle.

"All of that?" He chuckled, his steel-blue eyes dancing with amusement. "Honey, I lift twice your weight dozens of times a day."

"No, I—"

"It's a date," he insisted. Stepping to the counter, he reached over to push a notepad toward her. "I'll be on your doorstep to pick you up at precisely six o'clock on Friday night. Just jot down your address and phone number."

"I really—"

"Come on," he cajoled. "We'll have fun. It isn't often I meet a lady who enjoys the mud pulls. Where have you been all my life?"

She laughed and tried one more time to discourage him. "I'm really not much on dating. You don't have to do this. Honestly. You're off the hook."

In response to that, he narrowed an eye and shoved the notepad closer. "Full name, address, and phone number. If you won't give them to me, I'll play dirty and get them from Harv Coulter. The Rocking K is his largest account."

Imagining her father's reaction, Bethany smiled. "I should let you go ask him. It might prove interesting. I don't suppose you're a betting man?"

"Sometimes. What's the wager?"

"That my *boss* not only won't give you my address but may run you out of here with a shotgun. Daddy tends to be overprotective of his baby girl."

"You're Harv's daughter?"

"His one and only." With a sigh of resignation, she bent her head and wrote the information he'd requested on the slip of paper. "Don't say I didn't warn you. By evening's end, when you're popping ibuprofen and wishing you had a back brace, I don't want to hear any complaints."

"You won't."

As she tore the top sheet from the notepad and handed it to him, she added, "If something comes up and you need to cancel, Ryan, you can reach me here at the store during the day. I really would appreciate a call. For someone like me, getting ready to go somewhere is no easy thing."

He folded the paper and slipped it in his pocket. "I'll show. Count on it."

She shrugged, hoping to convey that she didn't care one way or the other. "I'll accept any excuse. Even 'my dog ate my homework' will work." She forced a bright smile.

"Friday," he said huskily. "Six o'clock sharp. I'll be looking forward to it."

As he walked away, Bethany heard footsteps behind her. She glanced over her shoulder to see her brother Jake approaching. Dressed in the same ranch-issue faded denim and blue chambray as Ryan, he looked enough like the other man to be related. Tall and lean, yet muscular, her brother had the tough look of a man who'd pitted himself against the elements most of his life.

Jake also had beautiful eyes—a deep, clear blue that was almost startling in contrast to his sun-dark skin and sable hair. At the moment, those eyes were fixed with glaring intensity on Ryan Kendrick's departing back. "What was that all about?"

"What was what all about?" she asked innocently.

Jake gave her a long, questioning look. "As I was coming downstairs, I saw the two of you talking, and it looked like he was flirting with you."

Bethany raised her eyebrows. "Flirting with me? How long's it been since you had your eyes checked?"

His jaw muscle started to tic. "You're paralyzed, Bethie, not dead. And you're a very pretty lady. I know men must flirt with you occasionally."

"So why the scowl?"

"Because that particular man is bad news. You steer clear of Ryan Kendrick, honey. The guy's got a reputation."

Still single at thirty-one, Jake had a bit of a reputation himself. Bethany refrained from pointing that out. "A reputation for what?"

"Loving them and leaving them." Jake stepped over to the counter, opened a parts catalog, and pulled a pen from his shirt pocket. "Don't do any toe-dipping in that particular pond. It's inhabited by a shark, and I don't want my little sister to be his next victim."

Chapter Two

By Friday evening, Bethany was laughing at herself. Ryan hadn't called to cancel, which meant their date for tonight was still on. Against her better judgment and despite all the lectures she'd given herself, she was excited about it—so excited she could barely stand it. For the first time in eight years, she was going out on a date. A *real* date. Not with a relative, not with some friend of her brothers', but with Ryan Kendrick, the most sought-after bachelor in town.

It was absurd to feel excited. It was only a onetime thing, and he had only insisted on taking her to be kind. But, hey. He was taking her someplace really fun, and she intended to enjoy every second of the evening.

Did her hair look all right?

She raced to her bedroom for a final inspection in the vanity mirror. Despite the extreme difficulty of stuffing her limp legs into tight jeans with only her dressing sling to assist her, she had decided to go with the cowgirl look tonight, which had been a little hard to pull off in a wheelchair, especially without a hat or riding boots. Hers were in her parents' attic, buried under a layer of dust.

She turned this way, then that, critical of her reflection. Did the red plaid and denim look silly? In Crystal Falls, most women wore snug Wranglers and western-style tops to events like mud pulls, but they weren't in wheelchairs.

Somewhere in the house, her cat knocked into something. The clattering sound nearly made Bethany part company with her skin. She flattened a hand over her chest and closed her eyes. *Enough.* She had to stop this.

She wasn't so foolish as to hope that Ryan was actually attracted to her. Just the thought frightened her. An evening out, simply to have fun, was one thing, an attraction quite another. That was a can of worms better left unopened.

Taking a deep breath, she opened her eyes and stared hard at her reflection, determined to see herself as others must. She supposed she was pretty, in an ordinary sort of way. Nothing about her was exceptional, though.

The one thing about her that was glaringly apparent was her wheelchair—the bane of her existence and always a part of her life. When Ryan looked at her, that wheelchair was what he would see, not the woman in it. She needed to remember that. She had believed in someone once, putting stock in dreams and thinking her paralysis didn't matter, but in the end, it had been all that mattered.

She would pretend he was one of her brothers. No big deal. She'd never see him again after tonight. She would thoroughly enjoy attending a mud pull again, and that's what she should be concentrating on. She rarely got to do things like this anymore because it was more trouble than it was worth, the hardship falling to friends or family members who volunteered to take her.

She returned to the living room, acutely conscious of the whirring sound her chair made as it rolled over the polished hardwood floors. Once parked, she glanced at the case clock on the mantel. *Six o'clock.* An achy feeling filled her throat. She straightened her shoulders, listening as the pendulum ticked away the seconds. He was just late. If he wasn't coming, he would have called.

And, hey . . . if he didn't show, no skin off her nose. She had a fantastic family, a great job, and interesting activities that kept her on the move from morning until night. She depended on no one for fulfillment or happiness.

Tick-tock—tick-tock. The pendulum mercilessly measured off the passing minutes, and each one seemed to last a small eternity. She leafed through a tole painting magazine, then tossed it back on the coffee table. *Twenty after.*

Oh, well. Like this came as a big surprise? Deep down, she hadn't really expected him to come. It would have been cold at the fairgrounds, anyway. Who wanted to freeze her buns off to watch tractors slide around in the mud?

She moved to a window and gazed out at the side yard where the deepening dusk and an icy chill hovered low over the nude deciduous trees. No buds had sprouted on the branches yet. Because of the high elevation, spring came late for the people in Crystal Falls.

And for some, it never came at all . . .

Bethany knotted her hands into fists and closed her eyes against a rush of scalding tears, hating Ryan for getting her hopes up and hating herself for giving him the power to dash them.

Never again. Maybe it was good that this had happened, serving as a reminder. No wishing on rainbows for her. Better to keep her feet—or in this case, her wheels—firmly rooted in reality.

Ryan glanced at his watch and cursed. Another red light. Why was it that everything slowed him down when he was in a hurry? *Damn.* That old lady in the Chrysler drove at one speed, slow. He smacked the heel of his hand on the steering wheel. Then he grabbed the cell phone out of the flip-down console beside him and punched redial again. No answer. Since they had a date, she was surely at home. Why the hell didn't she pick up? Maybe she had call waiting and was on the other line.

The light finally changed. Ryan rode the back bumper of

the Chrysler through the intersection. Then he gunned the accelerator, changed lanes, and swept past the car as if it were sitting still. The engine of the new Dodge hummed as Ryan opened it up on the straightaway.

He'd probably get a speeding ticket, but he didn't give a damn. *Bethany*. He kept remembering those dark, shifting shadows in her eyes when she'd told him she would accept any excuse to cancel. She had expected him to back out, and now he was running thirty minutes late. She would think he'd stood her up.

The doorbell pealed. Bethany wiped her wet cheeks. *Oh, God*. Her face was probably a mess. She considered not answering the door, but that was silly. Besides, it was probably only one of her brothers dropping in to check on her.

She rubbed hard under her lower lashes to make sure there were no mascara drips. Then she finger-combed her hair, giving it a fluff to fall around her shoulders. Not that she cared at this point if she looked nice, but she did have her pride. If, by chance, it was Ryan at the door, she didn't want him to know he'd made her cry.

Dumb. It was forty minutes after the hour. He wouldn't show up this late.

She raced down the hall, braking to a stop well back from the threshold. Leaning forward, she flipped on the porch light, unlatched the special dead bolt her brother Zeke had installed not far above the knob, and opened the door. The first thing she saw was a pair of dusty riding boots. Her gaze trailed up from there as she sat back in her chair, taking in an expanse of lean denim-clad legs.

"Oh!" she said, her heart skittering in a way that made her disgusted with herself. What was it about him, anyway? He put his pants on the same way other men did. He was nothing so special. "I thought it was one of my brothers."

"Nope."

He was taller than she remembered—broader through the

shoulders. Standing over her as he was and illuminated by golden light, he seemed to loom. Tonight he wore a faded denim jacket over the chambray shirt, the front plackets hanging open to reveal the muted wool plaid lining. The faint and not unpleasant smell of horses and hay rolled off of him. The black Stetson was in place, its brim tipped forward, shadowing his eyes. As before, those eyes glinted at her, only this time, instead of gunmetal, she was reminded of tarnished silver.

What was she thinking? Tarnished silver? *Brother*. He probably practiced that smoldering look in the mirror so all women within a mile would fall over like nine pins when he smiled. Well, count her out. He was mouthwatering to look at, but so was cheesecake, and cheesecake was a heck of a lot safer.

"You need a peephole," he said, his voice a deep rumble. "It's not safe to open up until you know who's out here, especially when it's almost dark."

He looked and sounded enough like one of her brothers to be a clone, which helped slow her racing heart.

"A peephole at my height? It's a little difficult to identify a man by his fly."

A startled laugh escaped him, the sound a gravelly "humph" that jerked his broad shoulders. "Not so difficult." He grasped the large silver buckle at his waist, tipping it toward the light for her to see. "Mine's flagged with my initials." He turned slightly to display the back of his belt, which was personalized as well. "You can tell who I am, coming or going."

She stared at the lettering on the ornate silver as he turned to face her again. "So I see."

He nudged back his hat, placed a hand on the door frame, and cocked a hip, his opposite knee bending with the shift of his weight. "I'm sorry I'm so late."

His voice rang with sincerity. Bethany steeled herself against it. "I'm sure you had a good reason." No excuse he gave her would be good enough. He was forty minutes late, he hadn't phoned. In her book, that was unpardonable.

He smiled slightly. "I tried to call. You didn't answer the phone."

"You did?" She'd had him pegged as more imaginative. "How strange. I haven't heard the phone ring, and I've got call waiting."

The long look he gave her made her feel as if her skin was turning inside out. She had a feeling he could tell she'd been crying. His lips tucked in at one corner, deepening the crease in his cheek. It wasn't really a smile, more just a quirk of his mouth, but his eyes came into play, crinkling at the corners to lend warmth to his expression.

"I know I wasn't dialing wrong. I double-checked the number."

An awful thought occurred to Bethany. She glanced over her shoulder. "My cat," she whispered.

"Say what?"

"Shortly before six, I heard her knock something over. I'll bet she bumped the guest room extension off the hook again."

"Ah. Mystery solved."

She started up the hall. "Please come in, Ryan. I'll only be a minute."

She imagined her brothers arriving en masse to check on her because she didn't answer the phone. The very thought made her cringe. It went without saying that Jake would not approve of Ryan's being there.

Once in the guest room, Bethany saw that the phone had indeed been knocked off the hook. As she returned it to the cradle, she lectured herself. Okay, fine. He had tried to call her, just as he claimed, and she'd jumped to conclusions, thinking he'd stood her up. It followed that he probably had a good reason for being late. But that didn't mean she had to let her foolish heart get the best of her again. He was taking her out on a date only to be nice. She would enjoy the evening. No hoping for anything more, no wishing for anything more.

She took a deep breath, feeling better almost instantly. When the evening was over, she'd have a nice memory to treasure, and perhaps he would as well.

This didn't have to be complicated unless she allowed it to be.

When she reentered the hall, he was still standing in the doorway. She saw that he was studying the tole paintings that hung on the entryway wall, compliments of her brother Hank because she couldn't reach that high to drive the nails. "That silly cat. She gets on the nightstand and knocks into things."

He hooked a thumb at the paintings. "You're very talented."

"Thank you, but not really. I've had lots of time to perfect my brushstrokes." She stopped a few feet shy of him and folded her hands. The touch of his gaze warmed her cheeks. "I hope my brothers didn't try to call. They're terrified I'll fall or something. I keep telling them it's silly to worry, that I managed just fine living alone in Portland for six years. I may as well talk to a wall."

"Protective?"

"Horribly. If one of them couldn't get through, he'd notify the others, and they'd all race over here."

He grinned and arched an eyebrow again. "Is that a warning?"

"You might say that. According to them, I'm too trusting."

"And are you?"

"I think my brothers greatly overestimate my appeal. Either that, or there aren't nearly as many wolves on the prowl as they seem to think."

Studying her upturned face, Ryan thought she was pretty damned appealing, and he didn't blame her brothers for being protective. It had been a while since he'd gone out with a woman whose expression was so open. She probably wasn't a very good judge of male character, and she could obviously be very easily hurt. Her eyes were red from crying, her dark lashes spiked with wetness. Knowing he'd been the cause of her tears made him feel like a skunk.

"I really am sorry I couldn't make it on time. I hope you're not mad at me."

"Not at all. I just figured something had come up."

He imagined her watching the clock, then finally giving up on him, convinced he hadn't come because he didn't want to spend the evening with her.

"It's been one of those awful days. Then, to top it off, one of my mares went into early labor. Her first foal, and she had a really rough time."

"Oh, *no*. Is she all right?"

The concern Ryan saw in her big blue eyes looked genuine. Most of the women he dated got their noses out of joint when they learned they'd played second fiddle to a horse or cow, a frequent occurrence in his line of work. "Yeah, she's fine now. Happy as a clam and proud as punch of her new baby."

"That's good. What was the problem?"

"The foal was large and got turned wrong."

"Oh, my. That can be tricky. Did you have to call out a vet?"

To Ryan's surprise, she seemed sincerely interested, yet another rarity. Most women only asked about the goings-on at his ranch to flatter his ego. "I called the vet out to be safe, but as it happened, I got the foal turned by myself. I really am sorry. The mare's sort of special to me. Shortly after she was born, her mama's milk dried up, and I had to bottle-feed her. We got pretty tight."

It occurred to Ryan that he seldom bothered to explain himself like this. He was a rancher, and things happened.

When an emergency came up, making him late for a date, that was just the way it was.

Looking into Bethany's gentle gaze, he found it difficult to take such a hard line. "She was really scared," he heard himself saying.

"Oh, of *course* she was, poor baby, which probably made giving birth even more difficult for her."

Ryan nodded. "I'm sure our ranch foreman, Sly, and the vet could have handled the situation, but I just couldn't bring myself to leave her."

"Please, don't apologize, Ryan. If you'd left her to keep a silly date, I'd feel awful. We assume a big responsibility with our pets."

Pets? Ryan supposed Rosebud was a pet to him, though it was something he never admitted. "She's a very expensive horse."

"Uh-huh, and that's why you stayed, because if something had gone wrong, you would have lost tons of money."

He chuckled and tugged on his ear. "Yeah, there was that, but mainly it was the apron strings tied to my belt loops. I'm her mama."

She laughed at that, her expression softening as if she understood exactly what he meant.

"Why do I get this feeling you like horses?"

"Probably because I do." She leaned forward in her chair. "I have to know. Was it a colt or a filly?"

"A colt."

"What color?" she asked, her eyes sparkling with interest.

"A little sorrel. Cute as a button, all gangly legs and knobby knees, with a big, bulbous nose. And his ears are so gigantic, I swear he's part donkey. But he'll pretty up in a few hours."

"Oh," she whispered, her smile wistful. "He sounds so *sweet*! I haven't seen a brand-new foal in so long, I can't remember when."

The yearning in her expression made Ryan want to scoop her out of that chair and take her to his ranch. As the feeling took hold, he wondered what was happening to him. No woman had tugged on his heartstrings like this in a good long while. Strike that. No woman, period, had ever made him feel like this.

Uncomfortable with the turn of his thoughts, he glanced at his watch. "Well, you about ready?"

"You're running really late, Ryan, and I'll slow you down even more. If you're one of the sponsors, you need to get there as fast as you can. It might be better if I just stay here. Maybe another time."

"Baloney. You aren't going to slow me down that much, and I won't have nearly as much fun without you."

As he said that, Ryan knew he meant it—maybe more than was wise. What was he thinking? There was no way in hell she could ever fit into his life.

"Where's your coat? It's gonna get chilly out there if the wind picks up."

Obviously eager to go, she wheeled around and buzzed across the entry to a coat tree. She lifted a blue parka from a lower hook and started to poke an arm down one sleeve.

Remembering his manners, he commandeered her jacket. It was more difficult to perform this courtesy with a chair getting in the way, but he tugged and stuffed until he got the garment on her. In the process, he accidentally brushed his hands over soft places. By the time he stepped around to lift her hair from under her collar, his guts were in knots. Those long, dark tresses slipped through his fingers like heavy silk, the strands still warm from her body.

She glanced back. "I need to get my purse. My keys are in it."

"Where is it?"

"I'll run and get it. Watch your toes."

A few seconds later when she returned to the entryway, Ryan scooped her from the chair. She gave a startled squeak and grabbed his neck. Her purse, dangling by its strap from her slender wrist, thumped his arm. "Oh, God, don't drop me!"

Ryan hadn't meant to frighten her. "Easy, sweetheart, I've got you." Even with the parka insulation as padding, he could feel her heart pounding where his left hand curled over her ribs. "Relax," he whispered, his breath stirring tendrils at her temple. "You weigh hardly anything, and I swear I won't let you fall."

Her voice quavered as she said, "I can't catch myself, you know."

He wouldn't have let go for anything. "If something happens and I go down, you'll think you're a basket of eggs. I'm not hurting you, am I?"

"No, not at all. I'm fine. Really."

She looked up, and he got lost in her big eyes. He had no idea how much time passed before he realized he was standing there like a dumbstruck fool.

"It really isn't necessary for you to carry me until we reach the fairgrounds, Ryan. My van's equipped with a lift, and I—"

"We're going in my truck."

"We *are*? Oh, I don't know. It's much less hassle to take my van."

"Sweetheart, trust me. I've got it all figured out. I'll lock up when I come back in for your chair. Is everything turned off, or should I do a walk through before I close up?"

"Everything's off."

He set off down the hall, his boots tapping on the waxed floors. As he turned to carry her out the front door, she cast an anxious glance at the wood ramp over the porch steps. "I hope you're surefooted. That indoor-outdoor tends to get slick on cold evenings like this."

"You'll think I'm a mountain goat. Are you sure I'm not hurting you? You're awfully tense." He flashed her a grin that he hoped might help her to relax. "Clutching my neck like your life depends on it."

"It *does*."

He chuckled at that. As he drew to a stop beside his truck, he executed a smooth maneuver, bending slightly at the knees to open the door, then nudging it wide with his arm. He heard her gasp as he swung her up onto the gray, contoured bench seat. She grabbed the handgrip above the door as if she was afraid she might pitch headfirst onto the concrete when he turned loose.

"I've got you," he assured her again.

Bethany could feel that he did. His hands were locked over her hips. Unlike many paraplegics, she had feeling there. The pads of his thumbs seemed to burn holes through her jeans.

"Steady on?" he asked, lifting a questioning brow.

She felt like a pea balanced atop a totem pole. Big man, big truck—a monstrous burgundy Dodge Ram. The seat seemed a long way from the ground. But then he settled her back so the contours embraced her, which made her feel safer. "Yes, I'm steady on."

He ran his hands under her knees, lifting to reposition her legs, which had flopped as they landed. Her cheeks went hot. That made warning bells go off. She wouldn't feel embarrassed if one of her brothers lifted her legs.

He reached behind her to tug the seat belt across her body. She was about to tell him she could buckle up by herself, but before she got the words out, metal rasped, and the next second, he was adjusting the strap to lie at an angle over her chest. The side of his hand grazed the peak of her right breast, making her nipple tighten. She thanked heaven for the concealing fluff of her parka and wondered, with some trepidation, if she was going to live through the evening.

*　　*　　*

She might not survive, Bethany decided a few minutes later. Ryan Kendrick was driving in the wrong direction. At the edge of town, he took an exit onto the freeway. The huge Dodge purred to life as he depressed the accelerator and opened it up to cruise at seventy. He turned up the heater to be sure she was warm. Then he flipped on the stereo, filling the cab with the honeyed voice of John Michael Montgomery. It was a lovely, comfortable ride. She just wished she knew where he was taking her.

It was absolutely absurd, but her mind chose that moment to remember every dire warning her brothers had ever given her. That abuse of handicapped women was alarmingly common, that there were sexual perverts who preyed on disabled females, and that she must never forget how helpless she was. Her brothers maintained that it would be sheer madness if she went anywhere with a man without first giving everyone in the family his name, his tag number, and a full physical description, just in case he happened to be a creep.

Typically of her, she hadn't listened to those warnings, and now here she was, going heaven knew where with a man she knew very little about. Even worse, she'd been so afraid of Jake's reaction, she'd told no one about the date.

As Ryan drove, he pulled a cordless Norelco from the console. A second later, the hum of the shaver filled the cab as he began removing his five o'clock shadow. "I hope you'll excuse me. I usually slick up before a date, but this evening I didn't have time. I know I must look like hell and smell like a horse."

He looked and smelled wonderful to her. He also seemed to grow larger by the moment. When he returned the shaver to the console, he drew out some aftershave. While steering with his elbows, he splashed some of the scented astringent into a cupped palm, rubbed his hands together, and then slapped it on his cheeks. She nearly jumped at the loud sound of his palms connecting with his jaws. She'd get a mild concussion if she hit herself that hard. The woodsy, masculine smell of the cologne drifted to her.

Still steering with his elbows and, she hoped, keeping one eye on the road, he returned the bottle to the compartment and removed his hat to finger comb his wavy black hair. After finishing his ablutions, all of which he performed without letting up on the accelerator, he settled the Stetson back on his head, glanced in the rearview mirror, and winked at her.

"This is as good as it'll get. Next time, I'll shower twice. How's that?"

There was that "next time" again. Bethany returned her gaze to the road, convinced that at least one of them should be watching it. A grin tugged at her mouth. If he had nefarious intentions, he was certainly going to a lot of trouble to smell nice before he attacked her.

"I'm not making you nervous, am I? I'm used to doing ten things at once."

"No, you're not making me nervous," she said, still struggling to suppress a smile. "I am sort of curious about where we're going, though."

He slanted her a look, the twinkle in his eyes evident even in the dim light. "It's a surprise."

Everything about him was a surprise. "That sounds fun. What kind of a surprise?"

"If I tell you, it won't be a surprise. What fun would that be?"

He had a point. She hadn't been adventurous in a long while, and no matter what her brothers might say, she meant to enjoy this evening with him. "What about the mud pulls? You're a sponsor, remember, and need to be there."

"I need to make an appearance. We'll still go—*after* the surprise. It's one of those things that just won't keep, and I think you'll enjoy it more than the pulls."

Bethany couldn't imagine what he had planned, but she instinctively trusted him—even when he drove with his elbows. She hugged her waist and stared through the windshield, her vision blurring on the yellow line.

He leaned forward to turn up the volume on the stereo. "Do you mind? This is my favorite song *ever*."

"You're joking. It's mine, too."

"You like Montgomery?"

She nodded. "I can barely sit still when a song of his is playing."

He swept off his hat, laid it on the console, and then, dividing his attention between her and the road, gazed across the cab at her as if she were the love of his life as he sang the refrain. The song was "I Swear," a beautiful outpouring of devotion in which the vocalist promised on the moon and the stars to be as steadfast as a shadow at his lover's side until death parted them.

Ryan Kendrick had a voice that made her bones melt. When he continued to sing to her, she couldn't resist joining in, even though she sounded like a toad croaking on a lily pad. She had never been able to sing worth a darn. Dancing had been her forte—once upon a memory, a lifetime ago. Now she could only feel the beat of country music and dream.

Just as she found herself dreaming right now that Ryan Kendrick really meant the words he was singing to her. *Idiocy*. What was it about him? Silly Bethany, spinning dreams. She supposed it was partly that Ryan was so handsome—the tall, dark, dreamy kind of handsome one usually saw only in the movies. That, coupled with the fact that he was so nice, made for a lethal package.

She was almost grateful that there would be only this one evening with him. Otherwise she might be in serious danger of getting her foolish heart broken.

Chapter Three

T he "surprise," as it turned out, was taking Bethany to see his new foal. The instant she glimpsed the sprawling brick house perched on a knoll overlooking Crystal Lake, she knew they were at his ranch. Moonlight shone through misty fog that wreathed the trees bordering the clearings, the shimmer of silvery illumination touching everything with magic. In the pastures they passed, she saw oodles of cows with spring calves at their sides, which made her laugh with delight.

"Oooh, aren't they *darling?*"

He stopped for a moment near an outdoor pole light so she could peer through the gloom at the babies. "See that little fella?" He pointed to a sweet baby Hereford with a snow-white face. "I call him Pig. He goes after the tit like you would not believe. Made his mama all sore and then started shoving other calves aside to hog their milk. For nigh on a week, I had to keep him in a pen and feed him with a titty bucket."

A funny look came over his face, and he scrunched his dark eyebrows in a frown. "Sorry," he said softly. "I forget sometimes that not everybody lives on a ranch and hears that kind of talk."

Bethany giggled. She couldn't stop herself. "I grew up on a ranch, Ryan. I'm not that easily offended."

He smiled and visibly relaxed as he shifted back into

drive. "You're a sweetheart. I'm sorry, anyhow, for not minding my manners."

As his truck bumped along the gravel road, Bethany gazed dreamily at the lake, which glistened like polished black glass, occasional patches of ice creating frosty islands in the vastness. She couldn't imagine waking up of a morning and being able to feast her sleepy gaze on such beauty while she sipped a cup of coffee. "Oh, my. How lucky you are, Ryan. It's beautiful here."

"I think so. But, then, I was raised out here so I'm probably biased."

She took in the expansive pastures nearer the house, which encircled countless outbuildings and were criss-crossed with white fencing. "You don't need to do this, you know. My chair doesn't handle well on muddy surfaces, and it's bound to be muddy in the stable. We had rain only a couple of days ago."

"If I wait to bring you out, there may not be any new foals. They're still cute later, but nothing beats seeing one right after birth." He flashed a grin, his teeth gleaming in the shadows. "In another hour, that colt's appearance will change." His voice dipped to a gentle, deep tone. "Just relax, honey. Have a good time. The mud won't be a problem."

On a ranch this size, there were probably mud wallows deep enough to swallow his Dodge. "I just don't want you to regret asking me out."

"I'm having fun. A lady who likes mud pulls, horses, *and* John Michael Montgomery. Where have you been hiding all my life?"

Oh, dear. He had no idea what he was getting into. She imagined her chair wheels dropping out of sight in the mud, and him, slipping and sliding as he wrestled to free them from the muck. She swallowed back further protests, though. This was a lovely gesture, and she didn't want to spoil it.

Even with outside lights blazing, she couldn't tell much

about his house—except that it looked big enough to hold three of hers. He parked the pickup as close to the stable entrance as possible, unloaded her wheelchair from the bed of the truck, carried it somewhere inside, and then came back to get her. She took a bracing breath when he opened the passenger door.

He quickly unfastened her seat belt and swung her up into his arms.

"Oh, my!"

"I won't drop you, sweetheart."

"What if you slip?"

He chuckled. "It'll be a first. I've carted struggling calves and foals through here when the mud was ankle deep, and I've never gone down yet. It might help if you'd be still, though."

She went instantly motionless, which prompted him to laugh again. "Why do I get this feeling nobody ever picks you up?"

"They don't usually. Not in ages and ages, anyway. I've worked hard to become self-sufficient. I hate inconveniencing people."

"And as a result, you haven't seen a new foal in so long you can't remember when? Forget about being an inconvenience."

He proceeded to carry her with apparent ease into the white clapboard building. As he picked his way down the well-lighted center aisle, he circled several muddy spots in the packed earth, which she eyed with growing dread.

"I wish you'd stop worrying," he told her. "I'm glad for an excuse to check on Rosebud. Sly, our foreman, will come over to look in on her, but it's not the same as doing it myself. Now I won't worry about her while I'm at the mud pulls."

He reached her wheelchair, which he'd left in front of a horse stall. Instead of lowering her into it, as she expected, he maintained his hold so she could look over the stall gate at the mare and newborn foal.

"Well?" His voice rang with pride. "What do you think of him?"

When Bethany saw the horses, she all but forgot the man who held her in his arms. Just as he had described, the foal was all gangly legs and knobby knees, and still so recently born that his nose and ears looked out of proportion to the rest of his body. She laughed in delight. "Oh, Ryan, he's *wonderful!*"

"I thought you'd like him," he said huskily.

"He's going to be gorgeous."

"His sire, Flash Dancer, throws some real beauties."

Rosebud whickered and left her foal to come welcome them. Bethany's heart melted the instant she looked into the mare's gentle brown eyes. "And you must be Rosebud. Aren't you *lovely*. No wonder your son's so handsome."

"Careful. Being a first-time mama, she's a little edgy, and you're a stranger. She tried to take a hunk out of the vet right after the foal was born."

Bethany reached over the gate. "I've never had a horse dislike me yet."

Ryan stiffened, prepared to block Rosebud if she made a threatening move, but the mare only sniffed Bethany's out-stretched fingers, then her arm. Apparently satisfied that this new human was no threat, the horse whickered again and moved closer to the gate, nudging Bethany's shoulder.

"I'll be. She does like you."

"Of course. Horses *always* like me." She shared her breath with the mare and stroked her muzzle. "I haven't any clue why, but it's been that way for as long as I can remember."

"Some people are just born with a gift."

"I think it runs in our family. My brothers are amazing with horses. Especially Jake and Hank. You know that movie about the horse whisperer? They're just that good.

When I was younger, I spent hours watching Jake work with them. My dad used to say he was like a horse charmer. Different name, same thing. He can work with a wildly uncontrollable horse and have it behaving beautifully in only a few weeks. It's uncanny, almost as if he actually communicates with them somehow."

Watching Bethany with Rosebud, Ryan could believe she had a special gift and that her brothers might as well. Her face fairly glowed as she admired the mare's finely shaped head. Ryan lifted her a bit higher so she could reach over the gate. Keeping one slender arm hooked around his neck, she twisted and arched up to scratch between Rosebud's ears. As a result, her parka drew apart and the plaid-covered peak of one softly rounded breast hovered a scant inch from his nose.

His breath hitched, and his throat closed off. She had no idea she was pressing her nipple so close, and he needed a swift kick for noticing. Even worse, he shouldn't imagine what it might be like if that nipple were bare.

Shouldn't, but did.

She fit comfortably in his arms, her weight so slight he barely noticed it. If they were lovers, he could nibble on that sensitive peak until she sobbed with yearning and begged him to nibble elsewhere. The sweetness of her scent worked on his senses like an intoxicant, the tantalizing mélange of baby powder, deodorant, well-scrubbed skin, and feminine essence making him want to taste every sweet inch of her.

Whoa, boy. What the hell was he thinking? She wasn't trying to entice him. Just the opposite. He recognized "hands off" signals when he saw them, and Bethany's eyes flashed the message every time she looked at him.

"You've spent a lot of time with horses, then?" he asked, forcing his gaze back to her face.

"You're looking at a three-time state champion in barrel racing."

He vaguely recalled that one of Harv Coulter's kids had

made a big splash on the rodeo circuit. For some reason, he'd always thought it was one of the boys. "Three-time *state* champion? You're kidding."

"Nope. I was phenomenal!"

He couldn't help but grin at her unabashed lack of humility.

When she noted his expression, she said, "Well, I *was*. No brag, just fact, cowboy. I practically lived in the saddle until I got hurt." Her eyes shimmered. "With five older brothers, I was the world's worst tomboy. I would have slept with my horse if Daddy hadn't put his foot down." She gave Rosebud a final scratch and then lowered herself back into the circle of his embrace to loop both arms around his neck. "Thank you so much for bringing me, Ryan. Even the smell of a stable seems heavenly after so many years. I've missed it."

Her breast now pressed against his collarbone, her nipple only a dip-of-his-chin away. "Don't a couple of your brothers still own horses?"

"Jake and Zeke do, and I'm sure Hank will again someday. On a much smaller scale now that we don't have a ranch, of course. They ride for pleasure. Isaiah and Tucker, my other two brothers, don't live here in town for the time being. They're both away right now, doing their internships."

"Doctors?"

"Vets." She smiled. "They hope to start a practice together here when they finish up. They're both horse lovers as well. Perhaps you can use them when they get their shingle up. It'll be tough until they build a reputation."

"I'll keep them in mind." Ryan frowned. "I'm sorry if it seems nosy, but I have to ask. If two of your brothers still keep horses, why is it you're never around them anymore?"

Her smile remained in place, but the radiance dimmed. "It upsets my mom if I even look at a horse." She glanced down at her wheelchair, clearly expecting him to deposit her in it. When she looked back up, she laughed and said, "Are you going to put me down, or have your arms frozen in this position?"

Ryan was loath to turn loose of her. *Oh, man*. He was in trouble here. He needed to back off, take a deep breath.

What the hell was the matter with him? He'd known men who took one look at a woman and went into Neanderthal mode, but he'd never been one of them. What was more, everything about Bethany's behavior told him she was wary and needed a slow hand. If he moved too fast, he'd scare her off.

The thought hung in Ryan's brain. If he moved too fast? When, exactly, had he gone from taking her out on an obligatory date to making moves on her?

He bent to set her in the chair, acutely conscious as his hands slid away from her soft curves. She felt *right*; there was no other word to describe it.

After she was settled, she leaned forward to grasp her left knee and lift her foot onto the rest. Ryan quickly helped with the other leg. As she sat back and he looked up, their gazes locked, and for a long moment he found it impossible to move or break eye contact. Unless he imagined it, she was holding her breath. He could breathe fine, but his pounding heart was about to crack a rib.

When he finally straightened, his throat had gone tight with an emotion he couldn't and didn't want to name. Judging by the look in her eyes, she felt it as well, and it scared her to death.

As he turned to unlatch the stall gate, he groped for something to say, anything to ease the sudden tension. "You hurt your back in a riding accident?"

It wasn't really a question. Why else would her mother get upset whenever she looked at a horse?

"While I was barrel racing." Her voice was shaky, and the brief silence afterward was brittle. "State competition, my fourth year. I had my eye on the nationals." A melancholy note laced her words. "My horse, Wink, stepped in a hole and went to her knees as she started into a turn. I went over her head, landed on my side over a barrel, and that was that." She brushed at a smudge of dust on her jeans, then pushed at her dark, glossy hair. His fingers itched to touch it. "I was very fortunate. When the barrel tipped, I fell directly in Wink's path and she couldn't stop. With all that weight crashing down on top of me, the injury to my spine could have been much worse."

Ryan glanced at her legs. Worse? Dear God, she was paralyzed from the waist down. It didn't get any worse.

By way of explanation, she added, "Most of the damage was to one side of my spinal cord, and unlike many paraplegics, I have some feeling here and there, which makes my life and daily routine much easier."

Ryan circled that, wondering how "feeling here and there" could make her life easier. Paralyzed was paralyzed. Right?

Apparently noticing the bewildered look on his face, she grinned. "That's a *polite* way of saying it. You'll have to ferret out the rest by yourself."

She was referring to continence, he realized, an ability many paraplegics didn't have.

She glanced around the stable. "How many horses do you have, Ryan?"

"Twenty-three in this stable, close to thirty over at Rafe's place. Working stock, some show. We breed and sell quarter horses on the side."

He moved her chair to swing the stall door wide. "Don't be nervous. Now that she's accepted you, Rosebud will be a perfect lady. I honestly believe I could lay a baby at her feet."

"I'm not nervous."

Eager for more petting, the mare exited the stall.

"Oh, Ryan, how sweet. She really does like me."

It was true; the mare headed straight for her. The new foal

wobbled in his mama's wake. Clearly delighted, Bethany leaned forward over her knees to pet him. Rosebud whickered and chuffed, almost as if she were giving permission. Watching the three of them together, Ryan frowned to himself, thinking what a shame it was that this young woman's affinity for horses was going to waste.

"You know, unless I'm mistaken, they have saddles for paraplegics."

In an oddly hollow voice, she said, "Yes, I know."

"Are you afraid to get back on a horse?"

"I honestly can't say. I haven't been on a horse since my accident." She went back to admiring Rosebud's colt. "Probably not. What happened to me, it was none of it Wink's fault. She was—*is*—the most wonderful animal on earth."

"She's still around?"

"Oh, yes. Bless my brother Jake's heart, he rescued the poor baby. Took her out to his place and sold her the following week to a local rancher who uses her to work cattle. She's only thirteen and has many a race left in her."

"You say Jake rescued her?"

"Daddy nearly shot her. Silly of him, blaming her." She ran her slender hands the length of the colt's ears. "Wink wouldn't have hurt me for the world."

"I know what you mean. My brother Rafe blamed a horse for the deaths of his first wife and kids, and he ordered the animal to be shot."

"I hear a story in there."

"An old story now, thank goodness. We'd gone north to pick up a stallion we'd purchased." He nodded toward the new foal. "Flash Dancer, this little guy's sire. Rafe took his wife Susan and their two kids along. We made a weekend out of it, took in a rodeo, treated the kids to a carnival, that sort of thing. On the way home a hailstorm struck, and the sound of the ice hitting the trailer frightened the stallion. Rafe was following along behind the truck and trailer in the station wagon, and he radioed me in the truck that maybe he and I should ride in the trailer for a while to settle the horse down before he hurt himself." The memories made Ryan's voice grow thick. "His wife Susan grew up here, and she was used to driving in snow and ice. It never occurred to either one of us that she might have a problem."

"Oh, no," Bethany whispered.

"Yeah." Ryan swallowed. "Only a couple of miles farther down the highway, she lost control in a curve, and the station wagon went over an embankment. She and both kids were killed instantly." He rubbed a hand over his face and blinked. "Rafe—he went berserk, trying to revive them. Afterward, he wasn't the same. It damned near killed him. One day he just up and left without a word. Vanished for over two years."

Bethany stared up at him, her eyes huge and stricken.

"Anyway . . . ." Ryan shrugged. "I didn't shoot Flash Dancer or sell him, and the story has a happy ending. Rafe met his second wife Maggie, it was love at first sight, and they've been together ever since, happy as clams." He forced a smile. "I know all about how people can react irrationally when their loved ones get hurt. In Rafe's case, I think it was easier for him to blame the poor horse than to blame himself, which was essentially how he felt, anyway— that it was all his fault."

"Maybe so. Daddy always fretted about me, worrying I might get hurt. Maybe he blamed himself for allowing me to compete. He still goes white around the lips at any mention of Wink."

"That isn't why he got rid of his ranch, is it? To keep you away from horses?" Ryan had heard Harv had gone bankrupt, but gossip was often wrong.

"Oh, no . . . he didn't get rid of the ranch by choice." A distant expression entered her eyes. "Although I'm sure keeping me away from horses was probably his reason for never buying another spread."

Rosebud nudged Bethany's shoulder, then lowered her head for a scratch. Bethany absentmindedly obliged, then finger combed the mare's mane.

"It's just as well since I can no longer ride. Horses used to be such a big part of my life. It was very difficult for me to adjust to the loss at first."

"You say he didn't give the ranch up by choice? What happened?"

"Medical bills." She shrugged. "At first, every doctor who examined me felt sure surgery might get me back on my feet. I was a three-time loser."

Ryan's heart caught at the pain he saw flicker across her face, whether for herself or her parents, he wasn't sure. Until she said, "Poor Daddy. He couldn't let it go, and he went broke, trying to work a miracle for me. A fourth-generation rancher, and he lost his family heritage."

"Some things are more important than keeping a piece of land."

"Absolutely," she agreed. "But we also need to be realistic." Her eyes clouded. "After the first operation, I knew in my heart that I might never walk again. I should have told Daddy and refused to have more surgery. But I was self-centered for a long time after the accident, blind to everything but my own misery. I wanted so badly to walk again, and it never occurred to me that my father was destroying himself trying to make it happen."

"You were awfully young, Bethany. I wouldn't be too rough on myself."

She smiled and threw off the gloom. "How did we get off on this? *Boring*. I don't like to think about those days, let alone talk about them."

That she didn't wish to dwell on it told Ryan more than she could know. Some people talked about their misfortunes to the exclusion of all else.

She cast a wondering glance around her. "This is quite some stable. All spiffy and clean and *huge*."

He followed her gaze. "My *house* is another story."

"A typical bachelor, are you?"

"Not really. Becca, the family housekeeper, comes over with a crew three times a week and supervises while they muck out the rooms. The buildup doesn't get too bad. It's more that I'm such a slob on the days in between. Dirty dishes, socks hanging off the lamp shades. I'm pretty bad."

"It must be nice to be so prosperous that you can afford housekeepers."

"Yeah, it is." Ryan saw no point in lying about it. "It's fantastic, actually." He smiled and rubbed his jaw. "It wasn't always like this. My dad built this ranch by the sweat of his brow. We saw lean years when I was growing up. Rafe and I had to fill in as ranch hands after school and on weekends. It was a family enterprise, and it took the whole damn family to make it back then."

"That's often the way of it. What happened to change things?"

"Rafe and I took over the place and damned near went bankrupt." Her eyes widened, making him chuckle. "Seriously. Dad was off in Florida, living the life of leisure, thinking he was set for old age, and then a string of bad luck hit, the worst of it a forest fire that wiped out over half our herd. Rafe's wife and kids were surviving on steak and milk, two things we had plenty of because we had cows. It was a hell of a mess. Right before we went tits up, we got the idea to sell off some of our land. We parceled off five thousand acres, divided it into lots, and sold sections to developers. We raked in over a hundred and fifty million."

Her eyes went even wider. "Did you say *million*? That's a lot. Is land really worth so much?"

"Yep. I know it sounds incredible, but it's not if you pencil it out. We could have doubled that amount if we'd sold directly to the public instead of to developers. As it was, we got fifty each for Rafe and me, and fifty for our parents, most of which we invested. We're all richer than Croesus now." He winked at her. "When I'm not working my ass off and wading around in cow muck, I count my money."

She laughed at that. "In other words, having a lot in the bank hasn't changed your day-to-day life very much."

"I don't worry about paying the bills anymore. That's a big change." He shrugged. "And I can blow money when the mood strikes. Mostly, though, I don't have time or inclination. It's a really weird thing, but at the south end of a cow, it's hard to think too ritzy. You know what I mean?"

She laughed again and nodded. "You're right. A cow's hind end has a way of putting things in their proper perspective."

She fell quiet, her face reflecting enjoyment and no small amount of yearning as she stroked Rosebud's velvety nose. Watching her, Ryan burned to get her back in the saddle again. He could almost see the expression that would light up her features.

She bent forward to kiss the mare's forehead. "This has been a wonderful treat, Ryan. I've enjoyed it so much, and I'm so glad you brought me out."

He glanced at his watch. "Speaking of treats, we'd probably better get cracking, or we'll miss the mud pulls completely."

After carrying Bethany back to the truck, he took her chair to a heavily graveled area at the front of the stables. Flipping a switch to activate the air compressor, he used the high-pressure hose at the front of the building to give the wheels a quick wash.

When he joined her in the Dodge, she said, "Okay, confess. You have a paraplegic relative you haven't told me about."

"No. What makes you think that?"

"For a man who's never been around someone in a

wheelchair, you're amazingly competent at seeing to my every need."

Glancing over at her as he started the truck, Ryan searched his memory for the last time he'd enjoyed a woman's company so much. He came up blank, which led him to wonder if he was seeing to her needs—or satisfying his own.

Chapter Four

B*ethany*.
    Ryan had been to countless mud pulls, but never had he enjoyed one so much. Because he was sponsoring a tractor, he and Bethany were allowed to sit in the pits, she in her wheelchair, he on a camp chair. They dined on hot dogs, Coke, and cotton candy, not exactly haute cuisine, but she acted as if it were, saying, *"Yum,"* and wiping drips of relish from her chin every time she took a bite.

Despite the bursts of deafening noise, she made everything seem exciting and special. At one point a tractor lost traction, broke loose, and skidded across the mud toward them. Ryan's heart shot into his mouth. He leaped from his chair, scooped her into his arms, and ran behind the fence. It wasn't until he felt certain she was safe that he realized he'd not only spilled her soft drink all over them, but squashed what remained of her hot dog between their bodies.

Instead of being frightened or upset, Bethany laughed until she was limp.

"Oh, what *fun*!" She shook mustard from her fingers, then glided her tongue over her lip, leaving a sheen on the rose-pink softness. "The *look* on your face when you saw that tractor coming toward us! Oh, if only I'd had a camera."

He didn't know what possessed him, but he dipped his head and licked a blob of relish off her chin. For an instant, she froze, her big blue eyes suddenly filled with wariness.

He wanted to say there was nothing to be afraid of, but

maybe there was. He was drawn to her in a way he couldn't understand, and it was happening far too fast. It made no sense. Off the top of his head, he could list a dozen reasons why a relationship between them would never work. But despite that, he felt the pull and was quickly losing his resolve to resist it.

Hoping to make her laugh again, he growled low in his throat, licked at a smear of mustard on her cheek, and said, "Yum. I must still be hungry."

It broke the tension. She laughed and swiped at another spot on her cheek. "Probably! My brothers can eat six hot dogs without even shaking a leg."

"I'll go buy more food, I guess. You're an expensive date, lady."

"Ha. You're a millionaire and getting off cheap."

Ryan was in complete agreement. She deserved better than this, that was for sure. Filet mignon and expensive wine, candlelight and music.

She splayed a fine-boned hand over her chest and groaned as if she were in pain from having laughed so much. In that moment the sounds of the mud pull faded, and he became entirely focused on this woman he held in his arms. Even smeared with condiments, she was so damned beautiful.

He tried to take a mental step back. She couldn't possibly be as lovely as all that. But she *was*. Her nose was small and tipped up slightly at the end, begging to be kissed. A touch of rose accentuated her daintily sculpted cheekbones. Her dark brows formed perfect arches over her eyes, which were big and so incredibly blue, they reached right out and grabbed hold of him.

From the chin down—*don't go there, you jackass*—she was delectable, slightly built but delightfully round in all the right places. Whenever his gaze strayed in that direction, he thought of long nights on silk sheets, the soft glow of candlelight casting an amber sheen on her ivory skin. The image was so clear in his mind that he could almost see her—eyes dark and unseeing with passion, lashes sweeping low, breathing quick and shallow.

Ryan jerked himself back to the moment, disgusted with the way his thoughts were running. After a quick cleanup job with napkins from the refreshment stand, he carried her back to the pits, bought them each more food, and then settled beside her to watch the pulls. Fearful that another tractor might break loose, he nearly moved their chairs behind the fence, where he knew Bethany would be safe, but she would have none of that.

"I don't get a chance to live dangerously often. Sitting down here is fun."

Ryan didn't want anything to happen to her—not on his watch. But he also wanted her to have a good time. He'd swept her out of harm's way once; he could again.

Seeing the sparkle in her eyes made him ache with sadness for her. What must it be like to have been physically active as she'd been, and then end up confined to a wheelchair? He couldn't imagine it.

During intermission, he pumped her for information. He learned that she'd once loved the wilderness and had frequently gone in by horseback with her brothers to camp at high-mountain lakes, an activity he enjoyed himself.

A dreamy expression came over her face as she shared memories of those rides. "For me, the wilderness was a spiritual experience. I *know*. That sounds really corny, but for me, it was like church. The beauty at daybreak, the muted glow of first light peeking over a ridge, the fantastic colors, the first song of a bird to greet the new day—it's surely God's way of saying good morning."

As if she feared he might laugh, she wrinkled her nose and grinned. He had no urge to laugh, for he felt exactly the same way. "I know what you mean. Nothing makes me feel closer to God than being on a mountaintop. Seeing the sunrise or a gorgeous sunset. An eagle in flight or a deer with a fawn."

Hugging her waist, she sighed and nodded, her expression wistful. Once again, Ryan found himself wishing he could get her on a horse again.

"And *campfires*!" she said softly.

He forced his mind back to the conversation. "Pardon?"

"Campfires. Is anything tastier than coffee boiled over an open flame?"

Her skin—just there, under her ear—would taste pretty damned good. "Nope. Nothing beats camp coffee."

"And, oh, how I loved to huddle around the fire with my brothers at night. We sang songs, ate trout we'd caught for dinner, and then they scared me to death, telling spooky stories about Big Foot and ghosts until we all went to bed."

"And then the fun was over."

"No, that's when it really got lively. They all had one-man pup tents, which are barely big enough for one person, and someone had to make room for me."

"You didn't have your own tent?"

"Yes, but after the stories I was too scared to sleep alone. It became a ritual—the argument about who got stuck with 'the twerp.' They drew straws, and poor Jake always lost. On purpose, I think. He felt responsible for me."

Rafe's wife Maggie had a twelve-year-old sister who lived with them. Heidi thought of Ryan as her older brother—when she wasn't entertaining the notion of marrying him someday. He had taken her on a couple of wilderness rides and knew exactly how it went when a young girl got scared at night. Like Bethany's brothers, he'd grumbled, but he hadn't really minded sharing his tent. He wouldn't mind making room for Bethany, either, for entirely different reasons.

"If you took up riding again, maybe you could still take occasional wilderness jaunts," he suggested.

She considered the possibility for a moment. "No, it just isn't feasible."

"Why?"

A blush flagged her cheeks. "I have too many special needs. Most ordinary wheelchairs are terribly heavy, unsuitable for rough ground and much too bulky a burden to take in on a packhorse. There'd be no room left for supplies. On top of that, there are no handicapped facilities in the wilderness."

Handicapped facilities? He hid a smile when he realized she was referring to rest rooms. She amused him and kept him guessing, this woman, sassy and outrageous one moment, then painfully shy about silly things the next.

As Ryan watched her talking, one thought entered his mind repeatedly. *Perfect for me*. She was the lady of his dreams in every way except one; she could no longer walk.

"So what do you do for fun now?" he couldn't resist asking.

"*Tame* stuff. My family is so protective of me since my accident. Anything that involves an element of risk is out." She caught her lower lip between her teeth, yet another gesture he was coming to realize was habitual. "I suppose it sounds pathetic, a grown woman allowing her family to dictate to her."

Ryan hadn't been thinking that at all. He couldn't fault her for being considerate of people's feelings, though he did wonder at the wisdom of it in this particular instance.

"It's just that I hate to worry them. While I lived in Portland, it wasn't as bad. I lived in this totally cool apartment complex for handicapped people. I had oodles of friends, and we all checked on each other all the time. We were always planning group activities, which were a lot of fun because everything there was universally designed, even the swimming pool. When my—"

"Whoa. Back up. What's universally designed mean, exactly?"

She quickly described the complex—how all the bathrooms were spacious to make room for special equipment for paralyzed residents, how all the doorways and halls were wider than usual. "And you should have *seen* the kitchens! Low, extended counters with tons of knee room and accessible work areas so that even someone in a wheelchair could easily cook and reach appliances. I *loved* it. Where I'm renting now, nothing is especially designed for me. My brothers and dad have built me ramps, and I just make do. Everything has to go in the bottom cupboards. Daddy installed turntables so I can reach everything. Even at that, it's inconvenient. All the appliances have to be at the front edge of the counters. The top shelves in my refrigerator are bare. Jake built me a little ramp I can roll onto that makes me tall enough to reach the sink, and Zeke made me a pullout cutting board that's low enough for me."

Ryan had never stopped to think how difficult it must be for someone like her to do things in a regular house.

"Anyway . . . I'm sure that's boring. What were we talking about?" she asked with a laugh.

"How it was easier dealing with your family while you were in Portland."

"Oh, yes. And, boy, was it. I just fielded their questions when they telephoned or came to visit, but the rest of the time, my life was my own. A bunch of us even went skydiving once. I did a buddy jump, of course, so I was in very little actual danger."

The thought made him cringe. He suppressed his dismay and quizzed her about how she'd ended up in Portland, so far from family.

"After my accident and surgeries, I went to outpatient rehab there, decided to take some college courses in my spare time, and ended up going for a bachelor degree in computer science. I landed a good job in Beaverton after I graduated." She shrugged and smiled. "My family urged me to move home, but I was settled in by then."

"So . . . how did you end up back in Crystal Falls after all this time?"

"Daddy has a heart condition. A few months ago, the doctor ordered him to cut back on his work hours, and Jake had to take over the business. When he called and said he needed help, I couldn't very well say no." She rolled her eyes. "In truth, I think he invented a job for me just so I'd come home, but that's neither here nor there. So far, it's worked out fairly well—except that my brothers sometimes suffocate me by hovering."

That explained why the customer service at The Works had been suffering lately. Her brother had taken over. Ryan knew firsthand how that went. It hadn't been so long ago that his dad had retired. As for her brothers hovering, Ryan could easily picture himself doing the same thing. She did have a disability that made her more vulnerable than other women who lived alone.

"What one hundred percent *safe* activities do you enjoy?" he asked.

"I paint like a fiend." She narrowed an eye. "Sit still long enough, and I may paint you."

He'd seen evidence of her artistic bent. Usually Ryan didn't care for clutter, but Bethany had a flair for making it look nice. Her paintings and doodads, stamped with her sunny disposition, added warmth and charm to her surroundings.

"What else do you enjoy?" he asked.

"Tennis."

"Tennis?" he repeated incredulously.

Her eyes danced. "I have one paraplegic friend so far in Crystal Falls. I met her at the 'Y,' a totally cool lady named Jenny Nelson. We roll around the court together three mornings a week. Mostly we serve to each other and miss. We get a lot of exercise, chasing the balls, and we have fun, ribbing each other about our completely deplorable lack of skill." She thought a moment. "I also swim two evenings a week. I *love* to swim. It gives me an incredible sense of mobility. And occasionally when I visit my folks, I sneak next door to play basketball with the neighbor boys. They're teenagers and think it's totally cool, playing basketball with a crazy lady in a wheelchair."

"Basketball?" Ryan couldn't imagine how she managed.

"My chair's self-propelled. I can press the controls with one hand and bounce the ball with the other. It took practice, but I've gotten pretty good. Good enough that I've won a few games." She cast him a mischievous, sidelong glance. "I run over their toes. While they're jumping around on one foot, I race to the hoop and do my wheelchair version of a slam dunk." At his horrified look, she giggled and said, "All's fair when you're playing with a handicap."

"You'd never run over anyone's toes on purpose, you little liar."

"I'm ruthless in competitive situations."

"Uh-huh." Ryan doubted she had a ruthless bone in her whole body.

She gazed at the tractor being hitched to the sled. "I've got ten dollars that says this one wins the competition."

Ryan grinned. "I'd hate to take your money. The winning tractor will be the one I'm sponsoring."

"Want to bet?"

His grin broadened. "You're on," he agreed.

When the mud pulls were over, he owed the lady ten dollars, which she accepted and stuffed in her pocket while grinning at him mischievously. "I did tell you I'm ruthless," she said with a laugh.

By evening's end Ryan had decided he definitely wanted to see Bethany again, as friends if nothing more. Big problem. She apparently liked him and seemed to enjoy his company, but he could tell that she still felt uneasy around him. He'd tried to keep the mood light to help her relax, but there'd been moments when the chemistry between them had taken over, turning a casual glance into a long searching look, a quick touch into a lingering caress. Each time, she'd grown quiet and tense.

What if he asked her out and she said no?

After he parked the Dodge in her driveway beside her gray van, he said, "I can't remember the last time I enjoyed anyone's company so much."

She sat with her arms hugging her waist. In the moonlight slanting through the windshield, he could see a dark splotch on her jacket from the hot dog mishap. "Thank you for inviting me. I had a fantastic time."

Ryan curled his hands over the steering wheel, his grip tightening as tension coiled inside him. Usually after a date, he said, "Hey, this was fun. I'll call you, all right?" And that was it. He couldn't be that casual with Bethany.

He started to speak, then stopped and coughed. Great start. "I, um—" He looked into those big, luminous eyes, and his brain went blank. *Damn.* What was it about this girl that made him bungle everything? He never got nervous or tongue-tied. And he sure as hell never got in a sweat.

"I'd really like to see you again, Bethany," he heard himself say and then immediately wanted to kick himself for sounding so—God, what was the word?—*stupid*, he'd sounded stupid.

In the moonlight her eyelashes cast clongated, spiked shadows onto her cheeks. "That would be nice. Give me a call sometime, and if our schedules jive, I'd love it."

Watching the fleeting expressions that crossed her face, Ryan realized she thought he was just being polite. An awful, sick feeling twisted through his stomach. "I'll do that," he assured her.

When he had her comfortably resettled in her wheelchair in the entryway, he told himself not to complicate matters by kissing her good night. Only there was that sweet mouth, calling to him, and he couldn't resist just one taste. She gave a startled leap when he hooked a finger under her chin. Her eyes went wide when he lifted her face. He searched her gaze for a long moment, trying to read her expression. She looked more surprised than actually afraid. That was a good sign. Right?

He had a feeling she hadn't been kissed in a good long while, a suspicion that was proved correct when their mouths connected. She was so tense and uncertain of how to hold her head that her nose bumped the underside of his. She also had her lips pressed tightly together. With a determined exploration of his tongue, he discovered that her teeth were clenched shut as well.

He drew back, arched his brows, and said, "You straining out bugs?"

"What?"

He immediately wanted to call back the words. She obviously wasn't in the habit of doing this, and making wise cracks wasn't the right tack. He didn't want to embarrass her.

Feeling unaccountably nervous himself, he nudged his hat back and crouched in front of her chair. She watched him as if he were a strange insect she feared might bite. He rubbed his jaw, swallowed, and met her gaze. He tried to remind himself that he kissed other women all the time and thought nothing of it, that he was so well practiced in the art, he could damn near do it in his sleep. Somehow that didn't help. She wasn't another woman, and it was suddenly extremely important to do this right. Perfectly right.

She was too sweet to give her anything less.

"Been awhile, has it?" he asked softly.

She laughed and rolled her eyes, her cheeks turning a pretty pink. "Eight years."

"Eight *years*?" he repeated.

"Isn't that pathetic?" She pushed nervously at her hair, took a deep breath, and then met his gaze again. "Maybe we could just skip this part."

Ryan chuckled. "Not on your life. I've been burning to kiss you all evening."

She rolled her eyes again. "I seriously doubt that you—"

He cut her short by grasping her chin. She was so damned beautiful. He knew she thought that all he saw was the wheelchair, but he was far more aware of the woman in it. The front of her jacket lay open, teasing him with glimpses of her figure, the shape of her small but full breasts showcased in the V. Her scent, a simple blend of soap, shampoo, talc, and feminine sweetness, worked on his senses like an intoxicant.

As had happened earlier in the stable, he wanted her, and his thoughts veered off track, making him yearn to peel away the parka and explore the woman hidden underneath it. He didn't know what it was about her. *Something*. He'd felt it the first time he saw her, been unable to chase her from his thoughts all week, and now the feeling had grabbed him by the throat.

He moved in, determined to show her just how hotly he burned. Taking control in a way he never found necessary with other women, he tipped her face to an accommodating angle. When her mouth remained closed, he applied gentle pressure to force it open.

Her lips trembled beneath his—a shy, startled, uncertain surrender, her lungs grabbing convulsively for breath. He shared his own, angling his head to deepen the kiss, dipping into the recesses of her mouth for a taste. *Sweet*. That one word kept circling in his mind. Wonderfully, incredibly sweet. He felt the jolt clear to his boot heels.

Damn. Was he saying good night or hello? He no longer knew or cared. She had the most fantastic, intoxicating little mouth, and her shyness only prodded him, making him want to delve deeper, to taste every honeyed recess. Silk on silk. He brushed his lips lightly over hers, nibbling, coaxing with flicks of his tongue, urging her to relax.

Finally she sighed raggedly, and her breathing changed,

the intakes shallow and urgent. He felt her slender fingers grasp the front of his shirt. She sank against him, no longer counting on the chair to support all her weight. She was a welcome burden—a soft, delicate burden that seared his skin at every pressure point. Oh, God. He couldn't believe this, had never experienced anything like it.

He slipped an arm around her, drawing her even closer. All that prevented him from lifting her out of the chair was a purely instinctive reluctance to rush her. Her lips went malleable beneath his. Her mouth opened for him. Her tongue engaged with his in a shy, hesitant dance of touch and retreat. Ryan's head swam.

She moaned, the sound a hushed throb of pleasure at the base of her throat that inflamed him. He moved his hand from her chin to curl it over the back of her head. He needed to be in complete control—to orchestrate her movements, to thrust more deeply, male into female, the urge as old as mankind and so primal, so compelling he was powerless to restrain it. *His*. He wanted to possess her. Learn the feel of her. Lay claim.

His thoughts swirling in a molten eddy, he barely realized what he was doing when he slipped his left hand beneath the parka and settled his palm at her waist. *Softness*. He explored the shape of her, gently probing the thrust of her hipbone through the denim of her jeans. Then he skimmed his fingers upward over her blouse, tracing the line of each fragile rib. She jerked with every pass of his fingertips, her breath catching and becoming a mewling sound in her throat, the soft cries telling him she was as lost to the sensations as he was. One fine-boned hand slipped into his hair, made a fist, clinging to him, the urgency in her transmitting itself to him through every pore of her skin.

Ryan ran out of ribs to trace. His fingertips nudged the underside of her breast, the swollen heat and softness calling to his hand. He imagined the generous softness of her cupped in his palm, knew it belonged there and that the weight of her would feel right, absolutely right, filling the emptiness in him that suddenly clawed at his guts. *Bethany*.

Only by supreme force of will did he resist the temptation. Anchoring his palm on her side, he allowed only his fingertips to touch the beginning swell of her breast—light, coaxing glides that made him yearn to do more. She moaned into his mouth and pressed closer, the invitation explicit, her nipple thrusting forward until he felt the hardened tip graze his shirt, tracing lines over his skin like a red-hot pointer.

With each pass, a jolt went through her, making her slender body jerk. Oh, God, she ached to be touched there. He wanted to take over, to do it for her and do it right, to give her what she so obviously needed. Only when he started to move his hand higher, warning bells went off. He didn't know why, couldn't think clearly enough to examine his reasons for holding back. It would only be a touch, after all, and through the layers of her blouse and bra, which didn't constitute a daring intimacy.

But, no . . . Not now, not yet. He remembered in a flash how this had begun, with her mouth closed against him. In years and life experience, she was a grown woman and a fair mark, but when it came to sex, she was obviously a novice, and he should take it slow.

Ryan knew his limits. One more pass of that throbbing nipple over his shirt, and he was going to lose it. He tried to end the kiss, drawing back marginally. Her hot, eager mouth clung to his, the still shy and inexperienced forays of her tongue gliding lightly over his bottom lip. His guts clenched. He reached up to grasp her face between his hands and forced their mouths apart.

Gazes locked, they stared at each other, both of them breathing raggedly, the reality of how they both felt and what they might have done—what both of them still wanted to do—rising around them like an electrical field. Her eyes were cloudy and confused, the pupils large and liquid black.

Looking into those eyes, he knew the exact instant when awareness began to return to her.

Her first reaction, which he also read in her eyes, was shock, quickly followed by dismay that brought an embarrassed flush to her cheeks.

"Wow," he whispered, bending to kiss the tip of her nose, a tender smile playing over his lips as he tried to bring her down gently. She was such an enigma, an intriguing blend of maturity and inexperience. Kissing her had aroused him yet made him feel protective of her as well, forcing him to slow down when what he really yearned to do was speed forward. "That was—something else."

She made an odd sound in her throat. He curled his hands over her shoulders to prevent her from falling because she'd leaned so far forward in the chair. Holding her breath, she stared at him. His own breathing was ragged. He could see the pulse at the base of her throat, a telltale sign that she was as aroused as he was.

She gulped for breath, sat back in her chair, and said in a strained voice, "I think you'd better go now, Ryan." Hugging her waist, she gazed at him with accusing eyes. "Thank you for a wonderful evening. I'll never forget it."

Just like that, he was supposed to leave? After what had occurred between them? He'd never felt like this. Never. There was something very special at work here. Something he'd never even imagined might be possible. How could he turn away from that, no questions asked, and simply walk out?

He rocked back on one boot heel. Still crouched at her eye level, he stared hard into those beautiful, expressive eyes. She was angry, her polite thank-you only a smoke screen. She had enjoyed the kiss, no question there, so he knew that wasn't the problem. He'd lost it for a second, but nothing had happened, so that couldn't be it, either.

"Bethany, I—"

She shook her head and held up a silencing hand. "Don't say anything. Just go. Please."

He pushed to his feet. No mistake. That was definitely anger in her eyes. Over the years, he'd made his share of mistakes with women and been on the receiving end of their anger a few times, but he usually knew what he'd done, at least.

"Honey, I'm—"

"Just *go*," she whispered, her tone fierce. "I mean it, Ryan. I want you to leave. *Now*."

He went. What else could he do?

Once in his truck, he sat in the darkness with his forehead resting on the steering wheel. *Just go.* Oh, God. She was royally pissed, and he hadn't a clue why. Granted, he'd gotten a little carried away, but he'd stopped. You couldn't hang a guy for thinking about it.

He lifted his head and dragged in a steadying breath. *Whew*. The suddenness of it was what had gotten him in trouble. He'd started out trying to refresh her memory on the fine art of kissing, and the next thing he knew, she had been teaching him a few things—like how it felt to lose his head over a woman.

Badly shaken, Ryan drove home, lecturing himself the entire way. He needed to think and be damned sure what his intentions were before he took this an inch farther. A girl like Bethany couldn't be tried on for size and then tossed aside if there was a pinch.

Bethany ripped off her parka and threw it with all her strength. The zipper tab hit the wall with such force that the sound reverberated like a rifle shot. She covered her face with her hands, her chest aching with stifled sobs, her stomach lurching. *Oh, God.* Never had she been so humiliated.

Thinking back over the kiss, she remembered how he'd tried to pull away and how she'd clung to him, begging for more with her mouth and body. She had never felt like that before, had never even allowed herself to get in a situation where she might feel like that. Why put herself through the unnecessary heartache? According to the specialist in Portland, she shouldn't try to have children, and chances were, she'd be unable to enjoy sex. There was also the inescapable fact that most men took one look at her wheelchair and ran in the other direction. Why explore that side of her nature, why open up all those feelings and be forced to deal with them, when she knew they'd probably never have an outlet?

Now, without half trying, Ryan Kendrick had jerked the lid off the Pandora's box of her sexual awareness, making her want things she could never have. No, *want* wasn't the word. He'd made her *ache*, damn him, leaving her aware of needs and yearnings she'd tried to ignore or pretend didn't exist.

She rubbed furiously at her mouth, trying to get the taste of him off her lips. It clung tenaciously, a bitter reminder of how she'd behaved, moaning and trembling and throwing herself at him. She still trembled with yearning. The feeling had hit her like a bulldozer, obliterating her sense of self, sweeping aside her pride.

Never again . . . *never.* If he hadn't pulled away, putting a stop to the madness, there was no telling what might have occurred. He might even have done her the ultimate kindness and made love to her, not because he really wanted to, not because he'd been planning to, but because he felt sorry for her. The poor paraplegic who never got any, so needy that just a kiss had her panting for it. What was a guy to do but give her what she wanted?

Tears stung her eyes. Her face twisted as she fought not to shed them. Just the thought that it could have gone that far made her feel sick. This was exactly why she'd always avoided this kind of situation. Given that she wasn't even sure she was functional in that way, what was the point? She'd only end up getting hurt. Sex was the number one priority for most men, barring all. Her boyfriend Paul had taught her that lesson well, and if she allowed herself to start hoping otherwise, she deserved whatever she got.

She wiped her cheeks. Eight years ago, she'd sworn that no man would ever have the power to make her cry again, and now just look at her. Well, she'd never cry over one again, mark her words. The next time a man—any man— asked her out on a date, her answer would be an unequivocal *no*.

Chapter Five

A night hawk cawed somewhere along the lakeshore, the sound lonely on the icy wind that blew in off the water. Sitting with his back braced against a lone pine that grew on a slight knoll, Ryan hunched his shoulders inside the lined denim of his jacket. He smelled a storm moving in, though he guessed it might be a couple of days yet in arriving, and his instincts told him it would bring snow. *Typical*. Officially, it was spring, but that meant diddlee squat at this elevation.

He sighed, not really caring if old man winter dumped more white stuff. In Crystal Falls, the occasional late blizzard was expected. The crops were in, but this early on, even a hard freeze wouldn't do that much damage.

The sound of pounding hooves drew his attention. He turned and peered through the moon-silvery darkness. After a moment he made out the silhouette of a horse and rider. Glancing at the luminescent dial of his watch, he saw that it was ten after eleven, late enough to make him wonder who was out riding.

"Howdy-ho!" a feminine voice called.

"Mom? What the Sam Hill are you doing out here?"

Her mare, Sugarplum, decreased speed and fell into a trot, throwing up sandy lake soil with her shod hooves. "When I looked out my kitchen window and saw you under your thinking tree at this time of night, I figured something was up. I thought maybe you needed to talk."

Ryan sometimes wondered if his mother had some sort of maternal telepathy. "What did you do, scan the lakefront with an infrared scope? It's dark. You couldn't have seen me from your window."

"The outside lights are all on up at your place. I could see your silhouette. A man in a Stetson casts an unmistakable outline."

Ryan knew that the ranch foreman, Sly, had been stopping in every hour all evening to check on Rosebud. "How'd you know it was me and not Sly or one of the hired hands?"

"Process of elimination. No one else would be fool enough to sit out here in the freezing cold."

She drew up in front of him and swung off her horse. Leaving the reins to dangle, a method referred to as ground tying in their neck of the woods, she stepped to her saddlebag. Ryan heard glass clink. He narrowed his gaze. As his mother came up the incline, he saw that she was carrying a half-gallon bottle of wine and two goblets.

"Want to share a nip or two with me?"

He ran a thoughtful gaze over her slender figure. Petite and blond, she was still a beautiful woman, even at sixty. "You and Dad fighting?"

She laughed as she sat beside him. Moonlight played over her face, the gentle glow concealing her few facial wrinkles. The gray of her eyes shimmered and shifted like quicksilver. "Your dad gave up fighting with me years ago." She handed him the wine bottle and a corkscrew. "He never wins."

Ryan chuckled as he set himself to the task of opening the bottle. "Only because he pulls his punches, and you don't."

"He also has difficulty articulating when he's furious, which I've learned to use to my advantage. In answer to your question, no, all is fine on my home front."

She braced her forearms on her upraised knees, a waiting goblet clutched loosely in each hand. Ryan popped the cork and filled the glasses she extended.

"That bottle is going to be a dead soldier before I leave," she announced.

"Uh-oh. You feeling a need to tie one on?"

"No, but I think you are. You've been a bit distracted the last few days."

"Distracted?"

"As in staring off at nothing and not answering when we yell your name three times. Tell your mother what's eating you."

Ryan knew he had been preoccupied. Since first meeting Bethany, he'd been unable to get her off his mind. "Nothing's eating me. What makes you think that?" He took a sip of wine, swallowed, and nearly choked. "*Jesus!* What *is* this shit?"

Ann took a taste and grimaced. "It's Hazel Turk's homemade plum wine. Dad says it's got the kick of a sawed-off double-barrel shotgun." She thrust a hand toward him, palm up. "That's twenty you owe to the college fund."

"Ah, Mom, come on. Jaimie's at home in bed asleep."

"Pay up. Two cusswords, ten apiece. Those are the rules. If you don't follow them when he's not around, you'll slip when he is. My grandson is not going to be expelled from preschool for using bad language. Only 'damn' and 'hell' and a few other bywords are allowed, end of subject."

Ryan handed her his wine while he dug in his pocket for his money clip. He peeled off a hundred-dollar bill and traded it for the return of his goblet.

She squinted to see. "This is way too much."

"I'm not finished yet. That gives me eight on account."

"*That* bad?" Ann laughed and stuffed the bill in the pocket of her Wranglers jacket. "Okay, spit it out. I knew you were upset about something."

Ryan took another sip of wine, shuddering as he swallowed. "This stuff tastes like cough syrup."

"I understand that Hazel's wine can give you such a case

of the squirts, you don't dare cough. I suppose it could do double duty as a cough remedy."

He gritted his teeth, curled a lip, and stared at the dark liquid.

Ann took a big gulp. "Be brave. Hazel's a dear. Sunday night at the ranchers' association dinner, I want to tell her I drank this and enjoyed it."

Ryan groaned at the reminder of the dinner. He was required to go as well. He'd meant to line up a date, had become distracted by a certain brunette, and completely forgotten. "How drunk do you plan to get? That's what it'll take to enjoy this crap. Besides, if you tell Hazel you like it, she may give you more."

"Oh, my, I hadn't thought of that. Ah, well, I'll just come visit you."

"Thanks." He took another sip. "It tastes better after the first shock."

They both fell to gazing across the lake. While they sipped the wine, they talked about the weather, decided they both smelled snow on the air, and then chatted about Rafe's family.

Ryan was on his second glass and started to feel the tension flow from his body when he finally said, "I met her this week, Mom."

"Ah," Ann said knowingly. Then, "Her, who?"

"*Her*. Miss Right. The girl of my dreams, the one I've been waiting for. I took her out on a date tonight."

"Oh, Ryan, that's *wonderful*. I told you it would happen, sooner or later." She twirled her goblet, watching the crystal sparkle. Then, frowning, she said, "If you just took her out, and she's Miss Right, why on earth the long face?"

"I kissed her, and everything went wrong. She got upset and told me to leave."

"What happened to make her upset?"

Ryan rubbed a hand over his face. "Well, now, there's a question. I was just going to kiss her good night, an old-fashioned, first-date kiss, the kind of thing a guy does on the doorstep. Only things got a little out of hand." He felt a flush creeping up his neck. He and his mother were close, but even so, there were some subjects he felt uncomfortable discussing with her. The particulars about his love life ranked near the top of that list.

Ann's eyes widened. "Wow. It must have been some kiss."

"Yeah, *wow*. I lost it, she lost it." He clenched his jaw, shook his head. "After all the women I've dated, I ask you, what were the chances that I'd run across a half-pint girl with big blue eyes who kisses with her mouth closed, and she'd blow my socks off?"

"One in a thousand, maybe?" Ann studied him, her expression thoughtful. "She kisses with her mouth closed? How old is she?"

"Twenty-six."

"Is she religious or something?"

"No, Mom, not fanatically or anything." Ryan propped his elbows on his knees. "She's just—it's been a while for her, and I suppose you could say she's also a little green."

"At twenty-six?"

"Yeah. I should have handled the situation with more finesse." He drained his glass of wine, then refilled both their goblets. "I sensed that she was wary."

"Wary of you?"

"Yeah, sweet and friendly, but a little standoffish. I think she's been through a bad relationship, gotten hurt. That's my guess, anyway."

"Hmm." Ann shook her head, her expression bemused.

"I think she's as attracted to me as I am to her," Ryan added, "but she's afraid of getting hurt again."

"Ah," Ann said knowingly. "How'd you come up with that?"

"Because when I kissed her, she was right there with me until I pulled away, and then, bang, she looked at me like I'd punched her." He sighed. "Sometimes I think men and women come from different universes. I don't suppose you have any insight to share on the female psyche?"

Ann smiled. "Sweetie, we aren't all designed by the same blueprint." She raised the toes of her boots and slowly lowered them to point downhill again. "Is your bewildering puzzle pretty?"

"Beautiful," he whispered. "She's got the prettiest blue eyes I've ever seen. I swear, they're the biggest thing about her—so brilliant a blue, they put me in mind of Johnny-jump-ups."

"Uh-oh. That's as close to poetic as I've ever heard you get. A bad case, huh?"

He sighed and said, "I just—*yeah,* a bad case. The first time I saw her, I felt thunderstruck. And it's not just her looks. Pretty women aren't scarce in a town as large as Crystal Falls. It was something else—almost a sense of recognition, like I'd been waiting to find her all my life, and there she was. I can't explain it."

Ann smiled sympathetically. "Honey, no one can explain the mystery of love." She grew thoughtful again as she sipped her wine. "You say you think she's been through a bad relationship? How on earth did she manage that without learning how to kiss?"

Ryan's jaw muscle knotted. He stared sightlessly across the lake. "I didn't say she doesn't know how, but that she's out of practice and a little green. I'm only guessing, but I think she was very young at the time she had the relationship and probably a bit of a tomboy. Seventeen, maybe eighteen years old. The sort of thing that never went much farther than handholding and clumsy kissing with a boy who had little more experience than she did."

"And she's never been involved with anyone else since?" Ann asked incredulously.

"She's a cripple."

"A what?"

"A cripple." The word came hard, catching at the back of Ryan's throat. "Not the politically correct term, I'm sure. Paralyzed, Mom, a paraplegic. She was injured eight years ago in a barrel-racing accident."

Silence.

A bitter taste washed over Ryan's tongue. "I don't think men have been standing in line to date her since then. A wheelchair has a way of dampening the male ardor. I don't know who the guy was that hurt her, but he was probably some immature little jackass she knew in high school."

"Oh, *Ryan*." Ann's eyes darkened in the moonlight, looking like splotches of charcoal in her suddenly pale face. She frowned thoughtfully and gazed across the lake for several seconds. "Not saying you aren't right," she said softly, "but having worked in a rehab center, I'd say it's just as likely that she has faced so many rejections and restrictions since her accident that she's become wary and distrustful. When a woman is found to be lacking countless times by the opposite sex, she protects herself in any way she can, and that might make her seem wary."

"Could be," Ryan conceded. "Going by things she said, I got the feeling that most men run the other direction when they realize she's in a wheelchair." He shrugged. "Hell, to be honest, when I first realized she was a paraplegic, I wanted to run myself, only I'd already asked her out, and I didn't want to hurt her feelings. If I'd started crawfishing, it would have been obvious why." He swallowed and closed his eyes for a moment. "So I took her on a date, thinking it'd only be for an evening, and that afterward I could do a graceful fade-out."

Ann said nothing, which prompted him to continue.

"I got to her house late," he said gruffly. "Rosebud went into labor, and when I tried to call her to explain, her phone was off the hook, and I couldn't get through. She thought I'd stood her up, and I could tell she'd been crying. I felt like a skunk. When I told her I'd been held up by a horse, I expected her to be pissed. Instead, she was a real sweetheart about it."

"That's a nice switch," Ann said with a smile. "Most times, don't your dates get miffed if you're late because a horse requires attention?"

Ryan grinned. "You could say that, yes. As in livid. It was an even nicer switch that I had a fantastic time with Bethany. She's bright and funny and interesting. I've taken women out, dropped two or three hundred, and been bored to tears. I took her to the mud pulls, fed her a hot dog, and had more fun than I remember having in ages."

Ann laughed incredulously. "The mud pulls and a hot dog? She must be a very special young lady."

"Yeah, there's just something about her, you know? I've got this feeling. I can't describe it." He flattened a hand over his chest. "This bone-deep feeling. I'd like to explore the possibilities, see if—well, you know—if we can find common ground to build a lasting relationship, but now I doubt she'll give me the chance."

Ann said nothing for a long time, her gaze trailing slowly over his face in a way that had made him squirm when he was a teenager. "I see," she finally said, her mouth twitching as she suppressed a smile. "You're worried about the sex."

Ryan's throat felt as if a cruel hand had closed over his larynx. He swiped at his nose and looked away. "Damn, Mom. Cut right to the chase, why don't you? There are some things a man doesn't feel right discussing with his mother."

Ann laughed. "Since when do we beat around the bush in this family? There are no taboo subjects."

"I can speak frankly with you about almost anything, but this is—well, for me it *is* a taboo subject."

She chuckled again. "So I'm right. You *are* worried about the sex." She bumped him with her arm. "Come on. Loosen up. I may be your mother, but I'm also a retired nurse. You can't hit me with anything I haven't heard a hundred times before, and you may discover that my input is enlightening."

He nodded. "I don't doubt that. It's just that—all right, yes. I am worried about the sex." He felt her gaze on him. "Don't look at me like that. I'm a bastard, and I know it."

"I wasn't thinking that at all."

"Yeah, well, it's what I'm thinking. She's so *sweet*, Mom."

"Good sex is a major concern to most men, and I believe you're normal in that respect." She took another sip of wine. "There's nothing wrong with that."

Ryan relaxed slightly. "I have to admit, it's right up there with oxygen when I'm considering the things I absolutely can't live without. It's definitely enough to make me step back and think twice before getting involved with a woman."

Ann laughed and leaned sideways, bumping him with her shoulder again. "Where did you get the idea paraplegics can't have sex?"

"That's obvious, isn't it? She's *paralyzed*, Mom. No sensation from the waist down. Maybe some men wouldn't care, but I like partners who enjoy that particular activity as much as I do."

"You're making an idiotic assumption. A common one, but it's dead wrong. I know about these things. Whether or not she has feeling in certain places depends on the location and severity of her injury. Some paraplegics, especially women, enjoy normal intimate relationships."

"Really? Are you positive?"

Ann arched an eyebrow. "Is this young lady special enough to continue this discussion?"

He narrowed an eye. "Yeah, you could say that."

"Then, yes, I'm positive. A lot of paraplegic women enjoy active sex lives, not always attaining satisfaction in the same way an able-bodied woman does, but everything being relative, who's to say they enjoy it less? For instance, some of those who can't climax in the usual way experience a phenomenon called 'phantom orgasm.'"

" 'Phantom orgasm?' "

"I liken it to an amputee who can still feel the missing limb. A paraplegic sometimes feels intense pleasure in another part of the body at the point of orgasm."

"That's a far-out concept."

"Factual," Ann corrected. "The body is a marvelous mechanism and compensates when it can. What difference does it make, honey? As long as the girl feels fireworks of some kind, do you really give a hang where they go off?"

Ryan chuckled and rubbed beside his nose. "No. I don't guess I do. Fireworks are fireworks. You *sure* about this, Mom?"

"Absolutely. Do you think I'd say so if I weren't? Even if normal or phantom orgasms are absent, I've heard that paraplegic women are usually fantastic lovers. Because they're handicapped, they're often more willing than an able-bodied woman to go that extra mile to please their partners." She raised her eyebrows and smiled. "When two people care deeply for each other, they aren't afraid to be creative if necessary, and sometimes that's the very nicest kind of love—not perfect in the usual sense, but beautiful because it's extraordinary."

"Hmm."

"It sounds to me as if you're on the verge of falling hard for this young lady."

"Teetering," he admitted. He took another swallow of wine. "Phantom orgasm." He thought about it for a moment. "It'd sure be hell if it happened in her appendix, and she had to go under the knife."

Ann burst out laughing. "Only a man would think of that."

"It's *important,* Mom."

"And you males have a corner on that?" She shook her head. "Back to your young lady. I know it's difficult, but try to be analytical for a moment. You say she really got into it when you kissed her?"

Ryan nodded.

Ann smiled knowingly. "Strange, that. She must have been experiencing a strong physical reaction somewhere. In her elbow, perhaps?"

He chuckled and then grew sober as he recalled the sweet way Bethany had melted against him and trembled with desire when he nearly touched her breast. She had been every bit as aroused as he was. He would have bet his entire financial portfolio on that. "Damn, Mom, you're right. Fireworks were going off somewhere."

"Probably in the usual places. It's a very good indication, at any rate."

Ryan nodded.

"As for her asking you to leave? This is just your mother's take, all right? But I think I know why."

"Why?" Ryan fixed a piercing gaze on her.

"You say you only meant the kiss as an old-fashioned, first-date kind of thing?"

He nodded.

"I'm sure she must have realized that," Ann said softly. "If we're right, and she's already been rejected a number of times, just think how she must have felt, responding that way to you, if it wasn't apparent to her that you were feeling the same way."

Ryan winced and swore under his breath.

"If she hasn't been kissed very many times—which is a fair assumption—then she may not have realized you became aroused as well. When you pulled away, she may have been mortified. I know I would have been." Ann sighed. "I can't say for sure. But if I'm right, she probably hopes she never sees you again."

"Oh, *Christ*."

"It isn't the end of the world, dear heart. Fences can be mended."

"How?"

"You're your father's son. Trust me, you'll think of a way. If you want to, that is. Unless you're very serious about this girl, Ryan, perhaps you should just stay away from her." She reached over to pat his back. "On the other hand"—she leaned forward to peer at his downcast face—"if she's really the girl you've been searching for, you'd be the biggest fool on earth to let her slip through your fingers. Don't let a wheelchair stop you. If you've got that once-in-a-lifetime feeling, there's nothing—and I do mean *nothing*—that's so great an obstacle it can't be overcome. How's that song go that you like so well? If you have love in your heart, you can move a mountain. Love can make miracles happen, honey."

Ryan exhaled a ragged, pent-up breath. "Do you think I'm nuts, Mom? To be feeling this way about a girl I just met?"

Ann tossed out the remainder of her wine and used his shoulder for leverage as she gained her feet. Her wine goblet dangling loosely from her fingers, she gazed toward the mountains where the Rocking K sprawled farther than the eye could see.

"I think you're a Kendrick," she said softly. "If the tendency to fall in love, hard and fast, is crazy, it's an inherent trait, so why fight it?"

"How does a guy know if it's love?"

Ann frowned thoughtfully. "You just do. It's not something you can explain to someone else—or even to yourself. You just know." She splayed a hand over her heart. "A feeling, way down deep." Her eyes began to dance with twinkling laughter. "Of course, sometimes it's only acid indigestion. So be careful."

"You're a big help."

"You're on your own. Only you know how you feel. Let that guide you."

Ryan watched as she picked her way down the bank. "Hey, Mom?"

"Hmm?" She stopped and looked back.

"Have I mentioned lately how much I love you?"

She smiled and resumed her pace. After stowing her goblet in the saddlebag and remounting Sugarplum, she sat there for a moment, her hands braced on the saddle horn, her head tipped back to stare at the sky. "What did you say this girl's name is?"

"Bethany," Ryan said huskily.

"Ah, Bethany. I like that. It has a very nice ring, coupled with Kendrick."

"I haven't decided to *marry* her yet, Mom. I have a lot of thinking to do before I even decide to see her again."

"Yes, you do," Ann agreed, all trace of levity gone from her voice. "It's entirely unnecessary to say this, I know, but I'll say it anyway. A young woman like that has endured heartache enough. You could hurt her so very easily." She drew sideways on the reins to turn Sugarplum. "Sometimes it's better to simply never know where a feeling may take you than to find out and have regrets."

Ryan gazed after her as she rode off, his mouth tipped in a sad smile.

Chapter Six

I t was nine-thirty the next morning, and Ryan had a dozen things to do. Instead he stood at the breakfast bar, staring at the telephone. A glance at his watch told him he'd been at this for twenty minutes, long enough to work out a routine. He picked up the receiver, started to punch in Bethany's number, hung up, and then grabbed the pen by the Rolodex to doodle.

This was a waste of time. He either wanted to call her or he didn't. A fairly simple decision. So why was he standing here acting like a lovesick teenager and getting a crick between his shoulder blades?

Turning to leave the kitchen, he nearly stumbled over the yellow Lab sprawled on the floor near his feet. Because the dog was so often underfoot, Ryan had dubbed him Tripper two years ago when he had appeared on the doorstep, bedraggled and starving. The name had stuck, and so had the dog.

Tripper whined and rolled onto his back for a belly scratch. Smiling, Ryan bent to accommodate him. "I've got to put you on a diet," he said affectionately. "You're getting fat."

Tripper arched his spine to rub his shoulders on the floor. Ryan sighed when he saw how many hairs were coming off on the burnt-umber tile. It seemed that Tripper's fur multiplied as soon as it fell from his coat. Ah, well. Without a dog, life was barely worth living.

He patted Tripper's head and gave the phone a last look. Then he turned away, determined to get on with his day. Moving across the family room to the coat tree, he collected his Stetson, settled it on his head, and stared out the sliding glass door at the large deck, where he loved to relax on summer evenings.

Damn. The slight drop to the deck would be a precipitous barrier for a woman in a wheelchair. If he started dating Bethany and brought her out for visits, he'd have to build ramps and rearrange the furniture to provide wider traffic paths. There were also the bathrooms to consider. They were spacious enough, and because he often housed sickly newborn critters in the bathrooms while he had them on medication, the doorways were plenty wide, but he needed to install bars, at least.

He sighed and rubbed his aching eyes. Tension. If he picked up that phone, there'd be no backing out later. He couldn't do that to her. If he pursued this, he had to know beyond a doubt that what he felt for her was real and lasting.

After grabbing the cell phone and his jacket, he whistled for Tripper and left the house. There was tack to repair, a horse that needed shoeing, and various other chores to eat up his day. He didn't have time to stare at the phone.

Once inside the stable, Ryan approached Rosebud's stall to say good morning. The mare whickered in greeting and came to the gate, flaring her nostrils and looking past Ryan's shoulder as if expecting to see someone else.

Ryan smiled knowingly. "You really took a liking to her, didn't you?" he whispered as he rubbed the horse's nose. "Me, too."

Rosebud nudged his arm and sniffed his jacket. Ryan fished in his pocket for the expected sugar cube. As the mare nibbled the treat from his palm, he petted her, thinking how much Bethany would enjoy this morning ritual.

"You're rotten, you know it?" he whispered to his horse.

"Why are all my critters so spoiled, huh? I've got to stop pampering you."

Rosebud chuffed and blew, as if she were telling him what she thought of that idea. Ryan gazed past her, recalling how Bethany's eyes had sparkled last night when she saw the foal.

His throat went tight at the image. When he tried to remember the faces of other women he'd dated, they were all a blur, eclipsed by pixie features and huge, pansy-blue eyes. He couldn't seem to get her out of his head.

He glanced over his shoulder at the depressions left in the dirt by her wheelchair. Farther up the aisle, there were muddy places where she would get stuck if he didn't lay asphalt, and if he did that, he might as well go the whole nine yards with cement pads and walkways outside the stable. Such an undertaking would be costly. But, then, it wasn't as if he'd ever miss the money. He could almost see her buzzing up the aisle, her smile lighting up the gloom. A man couldn't put a price tag on that.

Bethany. He sighed, exhausted. There was no understanding the feelings he had for her. It didn't seem to matter that they made no sense. They simply existed and gained a stronger hold with each passing second.

Bethany dabbed her brush in greenish-black paint to add shadows and definition to the trees in her mountain scene. It was as close as she came to the wilderness these days, re-creating it on canvas. As she painted, she recalled trips she'd taken with her brothers. The scenery, the smells, the sound of laughter on the wind. Oh, how she ached to experience those things again.

Ah, well. This was almost as good, and staying home had its advantages, a hot bath each evening ranking high on the list. Her new bathing sling was wonderful, lowering her into the tub in a reclining position so she could soak.

She added some shading to a drooping fir bough, thinking how lucky she was to have all morning to paint. Other than work and the occasional family obligation, little happened in her life to interfere with her leisure time. She could do what she wished, when she wished, and she liked it that way. She didn't need a man in her life, that was for sure. Why complicate things? She enjoyed living alone with only her cat Cleo to demand her attention. If she wanted to read all weekend, she usually could. If she decided to watch television, she didn't have to fight with an overbearing male over the remote control.

The phone rang. Bethany always brought the portable with her into the hobby room. She leaned sideways to grab it off her craft table, a makeshift work surface Jake had thrown together with shortened sawhorses and a ripped sheet of plywood.

"Hello?"

A deep voice replied, "Good morning, beautiful. You still mad at me?"

Ryan. Bethany's hand tightened on the phone, and her heart climbed into her throat. A flush of humiliation seared her cheeks. Every time she thought about last night, she wanted to die.

"Good morning right back at you," she managed to say cheerfully. "And I was mad at myself, not you. It was a lovely evening, and I had a fantastic time."

He was silent for a moment. "It really was a great evening, and I'd like to do it again."

Bethany squeezed her eyes closed. "I'd love to. Give me a call one of these times, and we'll see if we can't do that."

"This is the call." His voice was laced with amusement. "I'd like to see you tonight."

Tonight? *Why?* So she could throw herself at him again and make a fool of herself? "Gosh, Ryan, I'm sorry," she said tautly. Lying, for any reason, had never come easily to her. "Remember, I told you last week, I'm busy tonight."

"Oh, that's right." He sighed. "What about tomorrow?"

"Church and family things."

"You busy tomorrow night, too? I've got a big do I have to attend. I'd love to take you as my date."

"I'm busy then, too, I'm afraid," she said, vastly relieved she needn't lie about that as well. The annual Crystal Falls Ranchers' Association dinner was tomorrow night, and as owners of The Works, her parents were still members. She fleetingly wondered if that was the big "do" Ryan had to attend, then told herself not to borrow trouble.

"Not a problem," he assured her. "I'll take what I can get. What night next week do you have free? I'll juggle my schedule."

Bethany stared sightlessly at the window. "I'm sorry. Monday I have store errands to run that'll keep me busy until late. Tuesdays and Thursdays are my swim nights at the 'Y.' It'll be one thing or another all week."

"Why don't you come out here Tuesday night to swim? I've got a heated pool. Afterward we'll have dinner. I grill a mean steak."

"I swim with my mother. She helps me get dressed afterward. When I'm away from home and all my equipment, I require assistance."

"Ah." Silence again. Then, "What kind of equipment?"

She couldn't imagine why he asked. "All different kinds, mainly transfer gadgets."

"Transfer gadgets?"

"Devices to lift me from my chair and deposit me elsewhere. I can't motivate on my own. Out of my own environment, I find it very difficult to manage."

There, she thought. If that didn't make him turn tail and run, nothing would.

"I'm a great transfer gadget," he informed her silkily. "I'm also multifunctional and come real cheap. All I charge is a smile."

"I would never trust a blind man to pick me up and move me around."

Brief silence. "I'm not blind."

"If you come anywhere near me while I'm dressing, you'd better be."

He laughed. "Ah, I see your point. I guess I need to do some shopping."

Bethany's throat closed off, and her pulse began to hammer in her temples. "Why are you doing this, Ryan?" she asked shakily.

"I think that's obvious." She heard a horse whinny, then the sound of water running. She imagined him in the stable, talking to her over a cell phone while he cared for his stock. "I've developed an incurable fascination for a certain lady with huge blue eyes. What're you doing next Friday night?"

"Next Friday?" She reached over to rustle some papers on the table, hoping he'd think she was checking her calendar. "Gosh. I'm busy, I'm afraid."

"How about Saturday?"

"The same. My calendar seems to be full for the next several weeks."

"I see. A brush-off. A very sweet one, but a brush-off, all the same."

Bethany touched her fingertips to her mouth, remembering how it had felt when he kissed her—how she'd all but melted and then clung to him when he tried to pull away. She also recalled Jake's warning, that Ryan Kendrick had a reputation for loving and leaving them. She didn't want to become another name on his list. There was something about him that penetrated all her defenses and left her far too vulnerable. This might be only another flirtation to him, but it wouldn't be for her. She'd end up falling in love with him, and it would devastate her when he decided to move on.

"It's not a brush-off," she assured him. "I really appreciate your thinking of me. I had a wonderful time last night,

I'd love to do it again, and I'm very sorry my schedule is so full right now."

"I'll keep in touch. Maybe I'll catch you some evening when you aren't already booked."

"I'd like that. Good-bye, Ryan."

"I hate the word good-bye, especially with a beautiful lady I'm determined to see again. I'll catch you later, how's that?"

"Right. Catch you later."

Bethany broke the connection and let the phone drop to her lap. She bent her head and sat there for a full minute, silently chiding herself. It was so silly to wish for more than she already had, so silly to want more. She had so very much to be grateful for. What was it about Ryan Kendrick that made it all seem so meaningless and empty?

Besides, realistically, what did she have to offer a man who already had it all? She should be grateful that he'd been a gentleman last night. It had been a narrow escape. To put herself at risk again would be foolish. She knew from experience that broken hearts took a very long time to heal.

When Ryan got off the cell phone, he turned from Rosebud's water trough to see his older brother Rafe standing outside the stall. After turning off the faucet, Ryan stepped out, swung the gate closed, and secured the latch.

Arching one jet eyebrow, Rafe regarded Ryan from under the brim of his tattered black Stetson, his mouth tipped in a bemused grin. "That sounded like a no score, little brother. You losing your touch?"

"I sure as hell struck out with that one." Ryan tucked the phone back in his pocket. "It would appear she's going to take some convincing."

"And you'll bother? You usually just move on to better grazing."

"Not this time."

"Hmm. That doesn't sound like you."

Rafe stepped to the stall gate, the lazy shift of his lean but well-muscled body deceptively languid for a man who could move with lightning speed when he chose. Dressed in blue chambray and denim, he stood with his arms resting on the gate, one booted foot bearing most of his weight.

Just then Ryan saw his nephew run up the aisle toward them. In tiny Wrangler jeans, Tony Lamas boots, and a denim jacket, Jaimie was the very image of Rafe except for his big brown eyes, which he'd gotten from his mother. Given the fact that the child wasn't actually Rafe's, the resemblance never ceased to amaze Ryan.

As the two-year-old tried to dart by, Ryan scooped him up in the crook of his arm. "What have I got here? A peck of trouble?"

"Jaimie!" the child chortled.

Ryan lifted the little boy's black hat to see his face better. "I'll be, it *is* Jaimie. What's your mama feedin' you, hotshot? You've grown a full inch since I saw you last."

Always on the run, the child giggled and squirmed to get down. Ryan kissed his chubby cheek, getting a whiff of peanut butter breath, which made him grin as he swung the toddler back to the ground.

Rafe watched the boy run deeper into the stable. "Where's he off to, I wonder?"

"Looking for Sly, no doubt. That old codger attracts kids like honey does bears. Remember how we used to pester him?"

Tripper barked and fell in behind the little boy.

"I remember." Rafe shook his head, his gaze still riveted to Jaimie. "He is growing fast, isn't he? Before I know it, he'll be asking to borrow my truck keys."

Ryan chuckled. "We've got a few more years before that happens, thank God. What brings you over this way?"

Rafe and his wife Maggie lived in the main ranch house

on the opposite side of the lake, not far as a crow flew, but a distance of about three miles by vehicle.

Rafe inclined his head at the stall. "I thought I'd come see the foal. Maggie was painting her toenails. I thought I'd give her a break. Mom's there, playing with the baby. It's not often these days that Maggie gets any quiet time."

"Mom's there, huh?" It went without saying what that meant. "Then you've heard all about Bethany."

Rafe pretended intense interest in Rosebud's colt. "I heard some."

"Some? In her entire life, when has our mother ever been reticent?"

"Okay, I heard a lot," Rafe admitted with a shrug. "I thought maybe you'd like to talk."

Ryan didn't like the sound of that. He joined his brother at the gate. "There's really not all that much to tell. Her name's Bethany Coulter."

"Any relation to Harv Coulter?"

"His daughter. I met her last week when I went into the store. Asked her out, she said yes. I took her to the mud pulls last night, and we really hit it off."

"You forgot to add that her eyes remind you of Johnny-jump-ups."

Ryan laughed. "There are some things in life you can always count on. The sun will rise of a morning, it'll set at night, and our mother will be talking nonstop every second of daylight in between."

"That's Mom, dependable." Rafe turned to regard Ryan with solemn, steel-blue eyes that seemed to miss nothing. "She says this girl's a paraplegic."

"Yeah. She got hurt barrel racing eight years ago."

A muscle rippled in Rafe's cheek. "How do you feel about that?"

Ryan mulled over the question. "I'm okay with it."

"You're *okay* with it? From what Mom says, you're serious about this girl, little brother. You'd best do better than that."

"I'm a big boy, Rafe. I know what I'm doing."

"I hope so. I'd hate to see you screw up your life."

"Meaning?"

"Meaning you're too tenderhearted for your own good." Rafe swung his hand to encompass the ranch. "All the damned bulls we've got on this place bear testimony to that. If you nurse a sick calf, you develop an attachment, and when it comes time to castrate, you hide it from me."

"I've never hidden a calf from you."

"You most certainly have. Two years back, it was Boomer. You couldn't bear the thought of him ending up on a styrofoam tray, and you locked him in a horse stall. I knew it then, I know it now. I don't know why you keep denying it."

"That is such bullshit. He just wandered in there."

"Oh, yeah? We sure have a lot of calves that accidentally *wander* into enclosures on castration day. Last year it was T-bone." Rafe held out a hand. "Pay up. 'Bullshit' isn't allowed."

Ryan clenched his teeth and fished in his pocket for his money clip. If he didn't get his mouth cleaned up, he'd go broke. As he peeled off a ten spot, he said, "There must be enough in that fund to send the kid to Harvard by now."

"Don't change the subject."

Ryan sighed. "Who in his right mind would name a pet calf T-bone?"

"A softie who was trying to distance himself and not love the damned thing, that's who." Rafe tucked the money into his shirt pocket so he wouldn't forget to put it in the ginger jar when he got home. "And don't tell me you didn't hide him. How else did he wind up in the tack room?"

"He must've followed someone in there, and that person shut the door."

"Someone." Rafe grinned. "You, maybe?"

"Could've been. He was always following me around, if you'll remember."

"All I know is, he never went under the knife."

"He's gonna be a fine-looking bull. Even you can't deny that."

Rafe sighed and bent his head to scuff his boot in the dirt. "No, I can't. He's turned out real nice. Probably all that special feed you give him."

"What special feed? You're letting your imagination get away with you."

As if on cue, T-bone wandered into the stable just then. When the half-grown black bull spotted Ryan, his vacuous brown eyes lighted with eagerness, and he lumbered toward them, chuffing and mooing for his grain.

"Christ," Rafe said.

"That's ten you owe to the college fund." Ryan was still laughing as he went to the feed room to get T-bone his breakfast. When the bull was happily munching grain from a trough, Ryan rejoined his brother at the stall. Rosebud ambled over for petting. Rafe scratched her nose and smoothed her mane.

"You running a ranch around here, or a spoiled-critter shelter?" Rafe asked. "Here's another one of your projects. Hadn't been for you, she never would've survived."

"Nope, and isn't she a beauty?"

After petting the horse a bit more, Rafe smiled. "I wouldn't change you, Ryan. You're a good man. There's no crime in having a big heart. All I'm saying is, just because you feel sorry for someone, you needn't marry her."

"The way I feel about Bethany has nothing to do with feeling sorry for her." Ryan tried to think of a way to explain. "She's fun and interesting, not at all the sort of person who inspires pity. And I haven't said I'm planning to marry her."

"No, but you're thinking about it. I know you."

Ryan bumped the gate with the toe of his boot. "I just met her, Rafe. Don't go jumping the gun."

"Famous last words. With the men in this family, when has time ever played into it? You're talking to the world's fastest operator, remember. What was it before I asked Maggie to marry me, three days?"

"And look how happy you are. I've never seen a man so dopey over a woman."

"Yeah, well, this dope is worried about you, little brother."

"Don't be. I've been around the track a few times. I won't do anything stupid. Trust me on that."

"No one needy has ever gotten a tether on you. I know you, Ryan. You can't walk past a bird with a broken wing. Tie up with a lady in a wheelchair, and you'll never slip free of the rope."

"Needy?" Ryan chuckled and shook his head. "I can't wait until you meet her. What are you picturing, a pale and wan invalid? She has a smile to light up a room and a sense of humor that won't quit. You barely notice the wheelchair."

"You'll remember it fast enough when you're stuck at home, playing nursemaid," Rafe warned. "For some guys, marriage to a paraplegic might work, but I'm not sure it would for you. Physical activity is your whole life."

"And my life is so frigging great, God forbid that I should make some changes? You're so wrapped up in Maggie and the kids, you don't know what my life is really like. Maybe I'm the needy one. Did you ever think of that?"

"You?" Rafe gave him a long look. "What's that mean?"

Ryan gestured at the stable. "You kid me about the spoiled-critter shelter I'm running over here. Maybe I'm just lonely." Until that moment Ryan had never focused on his emptiness, let alone tried to articulate the feeling to someone else. Now that he had, it seemed to intensify. "Maybe these spoiled critters are all I've got."

"Mom and Dad live a few minutes away, and Maggie and I are the other direction. You can come over any time you want. You also date regularly. How the hell can you be lonely?"

"Because none of that counts." Ryan hooked his arms over the gate and gazed solemnly at the horses. "You rib me about T-bone. Well, laugh all you want, but that dumb bull, bawling for a carrot at the kitchen window, is sometimes the social highlight of my evenings."

"You're making me feel terrible."

Ryan laughed. "I don't want you to feel bad. I'm just trying to explain. You and Maggie invite me to dinner, and—" He broke off and shifted his weight. "I appreciate being included. And I know you ask me more often than most brothers would, so please, don't think I'm finding fault. It's just that as nice as it is and as much as I enjoy your company, afterward I go home to an empty house. Sometimes the silence is—hell, I don't know—loud is the only word. And I get up in the morning to more of it. I work my ass off, from dawn till dark, and then I work a little longer to put off being alone again. You know what I'm saying?"

A stricken look came over Rafe's face. "Damn, Ryan. Why haven't you said something? We'd love to have you over at our place more often."

"It's a loneliness you can't fill, Rafe. I need a life of my own, a family of my own. And not with the first woman who comes along. I want it to be with someone really special, someone who'll love me as much as I love her, someone who'll need me as much as I need her. Does that make any sense?"

"Of course it makes sense." Rafe bent his head and puffed air into his cheeks. "I've been there. I know exactly what you mean. Before I stumbled upon Maggie and Jaimie,

I felt lost. I didn't care if I lived or died—didn't have any reason to care. All I did was worry about how I'd buy my next bottle of booze."

"It's not quite that bad for me," Ryan admitted. "I haven't lost a wife and kids like you did, and I haven't turned to alcohol yet. I'm just lonely. Like at Christmas. I watch you and Maggie, shopping and whispering and hiding Jaimie's presents. That's what it's all about to me—that sense of family and having a greater purpose, and when I see how empty my life is by comparison, I just . . ."

"Feel lost?" Rafe said with an understanding smile.

"Yeah. I guess that word does say it best, *lost*. At heart, I'm a family man. It's what I was raised to be, what I've always imagined I'd be someday, but for the life of me, I've had no luck finding the right lady. Someday has come and gone. I'm thirty years old, I'm not getting any younger, and I was starting to think it might never happen for me."

"Until now?"

Ryan hesitated for several seconds before responding to that question. When he finally spoke, his voice had gone gruff. "Yeah, until now."

Rafe cocked an eyebrow. "You sure, Ryan? You only just met this girl."

"If you're asking me to explain it in rational terms and reassure you, I can't," Ryan admitted. "It doesn't make a lick of sense. I know that." He half expected Rafe to agree with him, but instead his brother only frowned thoughtfully. "One look was all it took. I walked into that store, wanting to take someone's head off. The last thing on my mind was meeting the love of my life. And there she was." A flush of embarrassment crept up his neck. "I know it sounds crazy, but that's how I felt the second I saw her."

Rafe took off his hat and raked his fingers through his hair. Letting the Stetson dangle from his loosely fisted hand, he said, "Maybe we're both crazy, because that makes more sense to me than anything else you've said."

"What does?"

"That you felt something the first instant you saw her." Rafe fixed his gaze on nothing, his expression distant. "I felt exactly that way the first time I clapped eyes on Susan, way back when I was just a kid. Remember that?"

Ryan smiled. "Like anyone in our family will ever forget. You never looked at another girl all through high school and college."

Rafe nodded. "When she died, I didn't believe I'd ever feel that way about a woman again. In fact, I *knew* I wouldn't. That kind of love—the way I felt about Susan—it's a once-in-a-lifetime kind of love, and very few men are lucky enough to find it even once. Then, out of the blue, there was Maggie. I came out of a drunken stupor and stared through the shadows at her, telling myself no woman on earth could be as sweet as she looked. And then that feeling plowed into me. I resented it. I felt as if I was being unfaithful to Susan's memory, even *thinking* along those lines, but I couldn't shake the feeling no matter how I tried. I guess God thought I'd suffered more than my fair share and decided to send me a miracle, because Maggie and Jaimie were exactly that for me, a reason to sober up, two people who needed me as much as I needed them. I think I fell Stetson over boot heels in love with her the instant I clapped eyes on her."

"Did you wonder if you were out of your mind?"

Rafe grinned. "I *was* out of my mind. Remember? I went at courtship like I was killing snakes. The poor girl never had a chance."

"You came to your senses eventually, and it's worked out nicely."

"Yeah. We're happy. Very happy."

"Maybe you should take it on faith that it'll work out just as nicely for me."

Rafe smiled and nodded. "Maybe so."

"One thing's for sure. I've never felt like this before, and it sure as hell wasn't for want of exposure. I've dated so many women, I can't remember them all, and never once did I go over the edge like this. Only with Bethany."

"If this girl is what you want, Ryan, I'll support your decision all the way."

"Good, because she is what I want. I can't explain it. I only know I can't shake it, and it's right. Now I just have to convince her of that."

Still frowning, Rafe said, "Being in a wheelchair, she can't be dating all that often. I'd think she'd jump at the chance to go out with you again."

Ryan huffed and said, "Yeah, well, she's not. Once burned, and all that. She's one blanket-shy filly."

"Blanket shy?"

"You know what I mean. As long as I kept it light, we had a lot of fun, but the instant I let on that I felt a physical attraction, she went all icy."

Rafe mulled that over. "Seems to me there's your answer, little brother."

"What is?"

"Keeping it light. Pretend all you've got on your mind is being good friends. No matter what the cause, skittish women take a slow hand. Trust me to know. I went through the same thing with Maggie. Friendship won't spook her."

"I have a lot more than friendship in mind. Pretending different would be sneaky and—I don't know—it seems sort of underhanded to me."

Rafe chuckled and shook his head. "Man, do you have a lot to learn. Be too direct and honest with women, and they run the other way."

"How do you figure?"

"That's just how it is. Me and Maggie, for instance. We take a walk along the lake nearly every night. Every step of the way, I'm usually thinking about sex. Not her. Last night, it was kitchen tile—which color and pattern would look best when we remodel. Earth tones are coming back in. Should we go with yellows and golds? Whites and greens? On and on. Like I give a rat's ass? I'll love the kitchen however she does it just as long as she's standing in it naked after it's done."

Ryan snorted with laughter. "You are so bad."

"Maggie'd think so, too, so I pretend I'm interested in color choices. I rub her arm and tickle her ear and tell her I'd like tile the same color as her eyes. She's happy as a clam, and once I get her home, I'm happy, too. Call me sneaky and underhanded if you like, but if I were honest, where would it get me? Besides, what's wrong with being friends with Bethany before you become lovers? All really good relationships begin with a strong friendship, so it's not as if you're blowing that much smoke. You want to be friends with her. Right?"

"Sure."

Rafe grinned. "Well, then?"

At a little after seven that evening, Bethany had just completed her bath when the doorbell rang. Thinking it was one of her brothers stopping by to check on her, which they did regularly, she tightened the sash of her pink terry robe, quickly wrapped her wet hair in a towel, and went to answer the summons. To her surprise and intense dismay, Ryan Kendrick stood on her porch.

"You definitely need a peephole," he informed her dryly. "Then you wouldn't make the mistake of opening up to someone you'd rather not see."

His steel-blue eyes glinting with amusement, he nudged his hat back, placed a boot over the threshold, and leaned a shoulder against the door frame. Whether he intended it or not, he had effectively scotched all possibility of her closing the door. Dressed as he had been last night in faded Wrangler jeans, a wash-worn blue shirt, and a lined denim jacket, he looked both wonderfully familiar and dangerous.

Bethany gazed into his eyes, aware of each chiseled feature of his dark countenance. She felt a shiver sluice down her spine. Though she'd just finished brushing her teeth, her mouth went suddenly dry.

He held a white business envelope in one hand which he tapped against his thigh. "I intended to leave this on your door, but your van was in the driveway and the lights were on, so I figured you might be home."

Given the fact she'd told him just this morning that she had plans for tonight, Bethany groped for an explanation. It was, she decided with panicky confusion, a classic case of a lie coming home to roost.

She tugged on the sash of the robe again, reached down to make sure the front was overlapped to cover her knees, and pushed at one end of the towel, which had fallen over her face when she bent her head. "I, um . . . yes. I'm home."

"Is this your idea of a hot date?" He arched an ebony brow, his thin lips tipping in a slight smile, his eyes as sharp and relentless as honed steel. "Taking a bath and washing your hair?"

She hugged her waist, trying without much success to gather her composure. "It was a *hot* bath."

He gave a low laugh. "Well, that's something at least." Without being invited to do so, he stepped in and closed the door. "I wouldn't want you to get chilled," he said by way of explanation as he extended the envelope. "These are pictures of Rosebud's colt right after he was born and a couple that were taken this morning. I thought you might enjoy having a set."

Pasting on a smile, Bethany accepted the offering, her mind screaming one question. *Why is he here?* At a loss for anything to say, she lifted the flap of the envelope. When she drew out the photos of the foal, the uppermost one was so darling she momentarily forgot her concerns.

"Oh . . ." she said softly. She glanced at the next picture down and laughed out loud. "He's so cute. What a struggle, standing up that first time!"

Ryan leaned around to look as well, and chuckled. "I like that horrified expression on his face. Every time I see it, I wonder if he was looking at me."

She came to the third picture. "Oh, my! Crash and burn. He nearly did splits with his little front legs." She sighed and lowered the pictures to her lap. "Thank you, Ryan. How thoughtful. These are a lovely memento."

"Of the evening—or me?"

The faintly challenging note in his voice took her by surprise. Her gaze jerked to his, and the determination she saw there alarmed her.

The distinctly masculine scent of him surrounded her—a tantalizing blend of leather, fresh air, horses, and spicy cologne. He hunkered down, nudged up the brim of his hat, and gave her a long, solemn perusal that made her stomach feel as if she were riding a roller coaster.

"I think we need to talk," he said, his voice a silky rumble.

"About what?"

"About you and me—and what happened between us last night."

His straight-to-the-point manner unnerved her. He was a man on a mission, and she had a bad feeling she was it.

She remembered last night with brutal clarity—how he'd crouched down just this way and kissed her. *Never again.* He was too potently attractive, too charming, too *everything*. She'd be lost if he touched her. Even worse, she had a feeling he knew it as well.

She just wanted him to go away and leave her alone.

As though he guessed her thoughts, his eyes began to twinkle. "That's exactly why we need to talk. I really screwed up last night, and I'd like to mend my fences if I can."

He had screwed up? The way she saw it, she'd been the one who botched it all by getting turned on by a silly kiss and throwing herself at him.

"I, um . . ." He jerked his hat off, raked a hand through his black hair, and scratched above his ear. When he met her gaze again, his eyes reflected heartfelt sincerity. "I had such a good time with you at the pulls. We just clicked. You know what I'm saying? That so rarely happens, finding someone I can laugh with like that. I don't want to muck that up with the other. You know?"

"The other?"

He nodded. "Yeah—you know—the physical thing. I, um . . ." He puffed air into his cheeks. When he met her gaze again, he smiled. "I won't lie and say I'm not strongly attracted to you. That kiss knocked my socks off. But physical relationships are a dime a dozen, and a friendship like the one I sense we can have doesn't happen every day. If I have to choose, and I think it's obvious you want no part of the physical thing, I'll take the friendship."

Bethany's heart clenched. "You want to be friends?"

"You got something against friendship?"

"No, of course not. I just—"

"You just what?"

"I just don't see how that can work."

"Why not?"

A searing heat flooded into her cheeks. How could she tell a man that being around him made her want a whole lot more than an occasional friendly pat on the shoulder? "I'm very attracted to you," she settled for saying.

He smiled again and rubbed his jaw. "Yeah?"

"Yeah. That being the case, friendship becomes a tad difficult to pull off."

"Not true. If we both agree from the start that a wonderful friendship is our focus, and neither of us steps over the line, we can pull it off very easily."

For some people, caring wasn't a decision. If she was around him very much, she was bound to fall in love with him.

"I, um—I'm not so sure I can keep it on a friendship basis," she admitted ruefully. "I'd muddy up the water before we ever waded in, and I can't take that chance. I don't want to get hurt, Ryan."

"I'd never hurt you, honey. You don't hurt your best friend."

The husky sincerity in his voice was nearly her undoing. *His best friend.* A tight sensation banded her chest. "Oh, Ryan, I know you wouldn't mean to. It's just—sometimes things just happen. You may have good intentions, but everything goes wrong. I'd be one of those things. You make me feel so vulnerable."

He sighed and smoothed a hand over his hair. "If that happens, we'll just go with the flow and see where it takes us."

"It can't take us anywhere," she said. "That's the whole problem."

"Why can't it?"

Looking into his eyes, Bethany realized he honestly didn't know. Tears rushed to her eyes, and an acidic burning slid up the back of her throat. With hands gone numb from nervousness, she jerked the towel from her head and lay it on her lap. She knew her hair must look a fright. She didn't care. Let him see her at her worst.

She carefully returned the photos to the envelope, her fingers trembling as she folded down the flap. Wishing with all her heart she could avoid this conversation, she swallowed a lump in her throat that she felt fairly certain was her pride and forced herself to look him in the eye. "I have no feeling in certain parts of my body. You could jab a pin in the calf of my leg, and I wouldn't feel a thing."

His gaze flicked to her terry-draped knees, then returned to her face.

Before she lost her courage, she went on to say, "I'm not sure I can have a normal physical relationship with a man. Chances are, probably not."

"And on the strength of that iffy prognosis, you'll turn your back on life?"

"I haven't turned my back on life. I've just learned to accept that some things may no longer be possible for me. Maybe it's easy for you to go with the flow and see where something takes you. It isn't for me. Chances are, I'll only disappoint you and get hurt in the process. I'd just as soon pass."

"Who did this to you?" he asked so unexpectedly she couldn't school her expression. His lashes swept low, and his smile became a clench of white teeth. "You're so . . . *controlled*. Do you realize that?"

She stared bewilderedly at him. "Controlled?"

"Reasonable. *Calm*. It's not natural, and it sure as hell isn't healthy. Somebody hurt you. It's written all over you. I see it in your eyes every time you look at me. And you know what else I see?"

She shook her head. "No, but I have a feeling you're about to tell me."

"Damn straight. It's worrisome." He leaned closer to peer into her eyes as if there were a crystal ball inside her head. She knew he was teasing, but even so, she had the feeling her heart had become an open book. "I see anger. Deep down where you can't reach, you're so pissed you could take something apart."

A tearful laugh nearly strangled her. "Really. You can see all that?"

"Oh, hey. That and more. You're smoldering and churning like a little volcano about to erupt."

"Has anyone ever told you you're crazy?"

"A few people have made noises to that effect. I ignored them."

"Most women get hurt somewhere along the way, and they don't erupt later in life like volcanoes," she pointed out.

"They don't usually get hurt the way I suspect you did," he countered. "Maybe they get dumped a couple of times before they find the right guy, and maybe they get their hearts broken. But it's not usually over something quite as devastating."

She formed a steeple with her fingers and touched the tips to her lips.

"And you know what else? I'll bet they scream and cry and get angry and unload all the hurt and anger on someone, their moms or best friends. *Someone.* Otherwise, nine-tenths of the female population would be certifiably nuts."

"Are you saying I'm certifiably nuts?" she asked teasingly.

He searched her gaze. "No, honey. Just that you're hurting, and that it'll never go away if you don't talk to someone about it."

"I can't allow that one incident to affect the rest of my life."

"So there *was* an incident." He winked. "Caught you with that one."

"So? My last observation stands. You don't let one incident affect the rest of your life. You move on."

"You shouldn't move on, pretending it never happened, though. Venting and getting it out of your system is the far better choice. You ever try it?"

"Of course, I—" Bethany broke off and stared at him as she remembered back.

"Did you scream and cry?"

"No," she whispered.

"Did you throw things and call him a few vile, filthy names?"

She laughed again, the sound ringing hollowly. "It happened right after the first surgery, and I wasn't supposed to move much. My family was hovering all around me. I couldn't vent, as you call it. Not without upsetting everyone who loved me."

"That sucks." He shifted his weight onto the ball of his other foot and settled his crossed arms on the opposite knee. "I got hurt once. Back in high school."

"You did?"

"Oh, yeah. Like you say, practically everyone gets hurt at least once. It happens to guys, too. Not on the same plane as you did, of course. But at that age, you aren't very philosophical and don't think of how much worse it could be. It just hurts like hell."

For some reason Bethany had never pegged Ryan Kendrick as the type who might have gotten his heart broken. He struck her more as the heartbreaker type.

"Did you vent?" she asked.

He narrowed an eye at her. "If I hadn't, would I be encouraging you to? Of course, I did. And I felt a world better afterward, too." He leaned closer to whisper, "You wanna go find the little creep? I'll smack him for you."

She laughed again and shook her head. "That won't be necessary. It's been eight years. I really am over it."

"Liar." All trace of humor fled from his expression. "Name me one thing you've done to get over it."

She shrugged. "I handled it in my own way. Paul was—"

"Ah-ha. Now we're getting somewhere. The rotten little bastard has a name."

She couldn't handle this. He looked too deep, saw too much. She felt as if she couldn't breathe. She ran shaky hands over the envelope.

"Yes. Paul." The name stuck at the back of her throat and became a huge, dry lump she couldn't swallow. "And he wasn't really rotten, just a nice young man who wanted to have a normal life, and there were no guarantees he could ever have one with me."

"So the nice young man walked out on you."

The memories hurt. Even though she no longer had any feelings for Paul, the sense of betrayal was still razor sharp. She bent her head and flicked a fingertip over a snagged tuft of terry. "Yes."

"And you say he was a nice young man?"

"He really was a nice boy, and he was also only eighteen, which is really young to handle that sort of thing. Looking back on it now, I don't blame him for ducking out." She shrugged and tried to smile. "A lot of grown men might not have handled it as well."

"Don't make excuses for him. You're not his mama."

She rolled her eyes.

"Well," he scolded. "When you've been hurt, you don't make excuses for the jerk who hurt you. That's his mama's job."

"We've gotten a little off track. I was trying to explain to you why I—"

"Not necessary. I can see you're not ready for anything but friendship, honey, and that's fine by me."

"I'm not sure it's fine by me."

"I'm not talking about a steamy affair. Just friendship. Where's the risk in that?"

She brushed at her cheeks. "Maybe. Let me think about it. Maybe."

He touched a fingertip to the end of her nose, then thumbed a tear from under her eye. "What's there to think about? Everyone can use another friend. We could have so much fun together."

She clenched her hands on her lap, so tense that her nails dug into her flesh. Her heart skipped a beat. She feared he might see the longing in her eyes. She searched for something else to focus on and found herself staring at his shirt button.

The front door swung open just then. She looked up to see Jake standing there, his long, denim-sheathed legs braced apart, his eyes a piercing blue as he glanced first at Ryan, then at her. When his gaze came to rest on her face and he saw the tear tracks on her cheeks, his expression went from surprised to furious in one second flat.

"What the hell's going on here?" he demanded, his voice vibrating with rage.

Bethany jumped with a start. Her brother was nobody to mess with when he got his dander up, and nothing got Jake's dander up quicker than a threat to her, real or imagined. She hoped Ryan would have the good sense to stay crouched down. At least then she could be sure Jake wouldn't hit him.

But no. Ryan pushed slowly to his feet. The two men were well-matched physically, both of them tall, bulky through the shoulders and arms, yet lean enough to be lightning quick. Bethany glanced worriedly at her hand-painted terra-cotta flower pots on the floor in the corner of the entry. Then she could only wonder where her head was at. Her brother and Ryan would half kill each other before one of them went down. And she was worried about her pots?

"Hello, Jake." Ryan extended his palm for a handshake. When Jake didn't reciprocate, Ryan kept his arm extended and said, "In answer to your question, nothing's going on. Bethany and I were just talking."

Through teeth clenched so tightly she was surprised he could speak, Jake snarled, "Talking about *what*?"

"The feasibility of our being friends."

Bethany's heart dropped. At that moment she would have tapped Ryan with her toe to get his attention if she'd been able to. *Not the truth,* she wanted to cry. *Don't tell him the truth.*

"Our personalities really click," Ryan said. "We have a great time together."

"That'd better be all that's clicking," Jake said softly.

Ryan finally lowered his arm. He glanced down at Bethany as he returned his hat to his head. The man clearly didn't realize how volatile Jake's temper could be. Either that, or he didn't have the good sense to recognize danger when he saw it. He actually *winked* at her.

"Don't come sniffing around my sister," Jake ground out. "If I can't kick your ass, I've got four brothers who'll be standing in line behind me. Nobody makes her cry and gets away with it."

Bethany wiped frantically at her cheeks. "I'm not crying, Jake. I got a lash in my eye. Ryan was just trying to get it out."

Both men raised their eyebrows and looked down at her incredulously. Okay. So it wasn't the most believable lie she'd ever told. She didn't want 450 pounds of testosterone wreaking havoc in her house.

As if she'd never spoken, Ryan looked back at Jake and said, "As bad as it may look, I did nothing to make her cry. We were talking. That's all. I'll also remind you that she's a grown woman. If she doesn't want me sniffing around, I guess she'll tell me."

"Don't press your luck," Jake said silkily.

"If telling you the unvarnished truth is pressing my luck, one of us has a problem with his temper, and it sure as hell isn't me."

Bethany fully expected Jake to punch him then. To her surprise they just eyed each other stonily, both of them eking every inch they could from their considerable heights, their bodies taut. She finally decided it was a man thing—some mysterious sort of silent communication that took place between bristling males that gave quailing females heart attacks.

Ryan tipped his hat to her, gave Jake another long, smoldering look, and sauntered out the door. Bethany had seen cold molasses move faster.

"Good night, Bethany," he said before pulling the portal closed. "I'll be in touch."

She wanted to say, "Just *go*. Hurry!" Instead she shakily said, "Good night, Ryan. Sorry about this."

He flashed her a grin, winked again, and said, "Hey. Not a problem."

Chapter Seven

Bethany was so angry with her brother she wanted to shake him. "I can't *believe* you acted like that!" she cried. "You've got no business barging into my house and treating my friend that way."

Standing over her with his fists resting at his hips, Jake scowled thunderously. "Your *friend?*"

"Yes, my friend. I am allowed to have friends, aren't I?"

"Friendship is *not* what that guy has in mind." His gaze dropped to her bathrobe, then jerked back to her face. "Why were you crying? Did he get out of line with you? If he did, I swear to God, I'll break him in half."

Just the thought of Jake and Ryan getting into a fight made her blood run cold. "Ryan Kendrick didn't get out of line with me. Get that thought straight out of your head. What makes you think he'd even want to?"

"Why wouldn't he want to? And if he didn't, why were you crying?"

"Not over anything Ryan did."

Bethany wheeled around and started up the hall. Jake fell in behind her, his boots thumping loudly on the bare wood floor. She stopped to lay the photographs on the hall bookshelf.

Jake spotted the envelope. "What's that?"

"Nothing important." She tossed the damp towel in the general direction of the bathroom hamper as she passed the open doorway. "Just some snapshots he brought over for me."

"Of what?" he asked suspiciously as he snatched up the envelope. A befuddled look came over his chiseled features when he withdrew the photos. "Whose foal?"

"Ryan's." As she continued up the hallway, she explained about their date the previous evening. "He brought me the snapshots as a memento."

"You went out with him and didn't tell me? How many times have I told you never to do that? I also warned you to stay away from him."

"Yes, well, I'm in the habit of making my own decisions. Why don't you do me a big favor, Jake, and get married? That way, you'll have someone to fuss over besides me. If this keeps up, I'm going to move back to Portland, where I can have some peace."

Jake followed her into the kitchen, looking comically disgruntled, his sable hair ruffled into furrows from his long fingers. "You can't move back to Portland. I need you at the store."

"Baloney. The computer field is flooded with qualified people."

"It's dirty pool, using that as a threat. Think how disappointed Mom and Dad would be if you moved away again."

"It's not a threat, Jake, it's a promise. You have to give me some breathing room. I'm not a child. I don't need you to look after me."

"You're in over your head with Kendrick."

While she put on a pot of coffee, using the ramp that Jake had built her to reach the sink, he rattled off reasons why she should steer clear of Ryan.

She finally broke in to ask, "Do you know that for a fact?"

"Know what for a fact?"

"That he changes women more often than most men do

their neckties? Just how often do most men change their neckties, anyhow?"

Jake narrowed an eye. "You're not taking anything I've said seriously."

She flipped on the coffeemaker, then returned the coffee to a lower cupboard. "On a personal basis, do you know anything at all about Ryan?"

"I've done business with him down at the store plenty of times. Judging by the things I've heard, that's as personal as I want it to get."

"Hearsay, in other words." She sighed in exasperation. "Jake, nine times out of ten, gossip isn't true. Forgive me for pointing it out, but you've had a string of girlfriends yourself. Does that make you a heartless womanizer?"

"Don't compare me to Ryan Kendrick. We're nothing alike."

Bethany thought they were very much alike in many ways, but now wasn't the time to argue the point. "True. Ryan's family is very wealthy, and yours isn't. If he even breathes wrong, everyone notices and makes a big deal out of it, whereas with you, no one pays much attention."

"Your point?"

"That maybe he isn't a bad person at all, but a victim of vicious tongues."

Jake pinched the bridge of his nose. "Okay," he said more calmly. "I get the point. I don't know him very well, and there's a possibility all the stuff I've heard is a pack of lies. By the same token, you must admit that you don't know him very well, either, and that the stories may be fact."

"I hate it when you reason with me. I'd much rather fight with you."

He made an odd sound, a sure sign he was about to lose his temper.

"All right, all right," she inserted. "I don't know him well. It's just hard, you know? He seems like a very nice man."

"He's charming, I'll admit, but there's a difference. Some men have no respect for women, Bethany. All they care about is getting them in the sack, and they draw the line at nothing. I don't want you to be his new flavor of the month."

She closed the cupboard door with a bit more force than she intended. "He isn't like that."

"Oh, yeah? And how would you know?"

Before Bethany could stop to consider the ramifications, she said, "Personal experience."

The words cut the air like a knife.

"What do you mean?" Jake asked softly.

Searing heat flooded into her face. She wished she could call back the words, but it was too late for that. "Just what I said. When he brought me home, all in the world he did was kiss me good night. That isn't exactly a hanging offense."

"So why were you in tears, then?"

"Not over anything he did. The rest was entirely my fault."

"The rest?"

She brushed a hand over her eyes. Not for the first time, she found herself thinking that life might have been much simpler if she'd been born with a zipper on her mouth. "It was nothing, Jake. Just a simple, polite kiss at the end of the evening, like I said. It just—well, it got a little out of hand. He's very attractive, I like him, and I haven't been out on a date in a good long while." Exasperated, she threw him a meaningful look. "Is it really necessary for me to spell it out?"

Jake's brows knitted in another scowl. "What are you saying, that you were interested in more, and he passed on the offer?"

"I wouldn't put it exactly like that." She tried to think of a better way to say it, but couldn't think of one. "Sort of, I guess." She sighed and closed her eyes. "In the nicest possible way, yes, he passed on the offer. Are you satisfied now that you've ferreted out all the sordid little details?"

Silence fell over the kitchen, an awful, brittle silence, broken only by the sputters of the coffeemaker and the tick of the wall clock. While she waited for Jake's reaction, she held her breath, not entirely sure what to expect. Even so, she was taken off guard by the huff of sheer outrage that erupted from him.

"He *passed* on the offer? Who the hell does he think he is?"

Bethany nearly strangled on the startled laugh that escaped her. *Jake.* Oh, how she loved him. Of all the reactions she might have predicted, indignation wasn't one of them. She fixed a horrified gaze on his taut face.

"He turned you *down*? I'll kill him. I swear to God, he's a dead man."

She laughed again, this time a little hysterically. "I don't believe you. First you want to break him in half because you think he's trying to take advantage of me. Now you're threatening to kill him because he didn't?"

"Oh, honey." The husky note of sympathy in his voice caught at her heart and brought a rush of tears to her eyes.

In two strides he was across the kitchen. Squatting down next to her chair, he gathered her close. It felt absolutely wonderful to feel his arms around her again, calling to mind countless times in her childhood when he'd held her just this way. *Jake.* He'd always been there to set her world aright. Unfortunately, now that she was older, her hurts ran too deep for easy fixes.

"Oh, God," she whispered raggedly against his shirt. "I never meant to tell you such a thing. I'm really not in the habit of throwing myself at men. Now what'll you think of me?"

"That you're human," he replied, his voice gravelly with affection. "And a very foolish girl for casting your pearls to swine."

"I think that's supposed to be pearls of wisdom among swine, and trust me, wisdom had nothing to do with my behavior."

"Whatever. He's a pig. How *dare* he turn you down. What is he, blind?"

"Oh, Jake, I love you."

"I love you, too, sweetie. You'll never know how much."

She tucked her cheek against his collar to hide the contorted twist of her mouth. As if crying would solve anything. The turmoil of the last twenty-four hours had worn down her defenses, she guessed, and all her feelings lay perilously close to the surface.

He made a fist in her still damp hair and hauled in a shuddering breath. "Ah, Bethie. I told you to stay away from him, and for just this reason. I knew you'd end up getting hurt."

Smiling through tears, she said, "Believe it or not, it isn't really his fault, Jake. Please, don't be mad at him."

"I never get mad, I just get even."

"There's nothing to get even for. Honestly there isn't."

"It just pisses me off that he kissed you in the first place. If he wasn't prepared to take it further, why start something? There's nothing that hurts more than being rejected."

"He didn't reject me. Not really. I thought so at the time, but now I'm beginning to realize it wasn't like that. It was just a good-night kiss that mushroomed out of control, taking him as much by surprise as it did me. He could have been a jerk and taken advantage of the situation, but he didn't."

Jake's hand relaxed, his hard palm and long fingers curling warmly over her scalp. Little wonder she was in perilous danger of falling in love with Ryan Kendrick, she thought. He was very like her brother—big and rough-edged, but disarmingly gentle and wonderful as well. No matter what misfortunes befell her, she would always be rich beyond measure in her family.

"He's really gotten under your skin. Hasn't he?" Jake whispered.

"I'm afraid so," she admitted. "I know it's not smart, that it simply can't be, but my foolish heart isn't listening."

"So what are you going to do now, Bethany?"

She sighed. "Stay away from him. What else? He stopped by this evening to suggest that we be friends and nothing more. On the surface, that sounds really good. We had a fantastic time together last night, and I think we could have a lot of fun. But I'm way too attracted to him for it to work. I'd end up falling in love with him. I know I would."

Jake framed her face between his palms. "Falling in love doesn't always lead to heartbreak, honey. With the right man, it can be a one-way ticket to paradise. If the two of you hit it off that well, who's to say he isn't the right man?"

"Aren't you doing an awfully sudden about-face?"

He cocked a dark eyebrow. "I didn't know the whole story before. The guy takes you out, you have a fantastic time. Then he brings you home, has you where he wants you, and passes on the chance?" He shrugged. "That says a lot for his character, in my book."

"Yes," she agreed wistfully.

"Maybe you should give him a chance. Guard your heart. I'm not saying you shouldn't. But at least get to know him a little better."

"To what end? There are so many counts against me, Jake, so many possible problems. I can't even have children."

"Isn't that a little premature? You work your way up to the kid thing."

"Not me. I couldn't just *sleep* with him without the kid thing and forever being part of the package. That isn't how I'm made."

Jake stared hard into her eyes for a moment. She could almost see his mental wheels turning. "No. Of course not. I don't know where my head went." He sighed. "I don't want you to try to have kids, anyway. Too dangerous. What about those damned blood thinners you take? They'd probably take you off of them while you were pregnant, and you could get another clot."

As if. According to what Doctor Reicherton had told her, she would probably miscarry before clots became a worry. "Oh, Jake. As important as it is, the baby thing is only part of it. He's a *rancher*. His whole life revolves around outdoor activities. Rough ground, fences. How does a wheelchair fit into a world like that? I'd be a big lump, just sitting there in a chair."

"His world can be modified," Jake pointed out. He gestured at the sink ramp. "With all his money, he could remodel his whole house."

"His house, yes. But you can't modify thousands of acres. I couldn't be a real part of his life. And what about— you know—the really big issue?" she asked hollowly.

"Sex, you mean?" Jake's eyes filled with pain for her. "Sweetie, you can't know for sure how that'll go until you give it a try."

Bethany felt as if a hand was squeezing her larynx. "No. But if it went badly, which it very well might, he'd be trapped. Stuck with me."

"You wouldn't be trapping him. He'd be making the decision, not you."

"It'd never work," she whispered, "not in the long run. A guy like Ryan Kendrick? He could have anyone he wanted." She threw up her hands. "It's just *everything,* Jake. No matter what angle I look at it from, all I see is problems. It makes me tired just thinking about it."

"Ah, Bethie," he whispered. "If you really like the guy, why not lay it all out on the table and let him decide? If he cares about you, all the stuff you're worried about won't matter a whit to him."

Managing a strained smile, she sat back and rubbed her cheeks. "I can't believe you're encouraging me to pursue this."

He chuckled and rumpled her hair. Then he rested his hands on her shoulders. In a low voice he said, "Don't take every man's measure by Paul. That's all I'm saying."

Twenty minutes after Jake left, Bethany's phone rang. She raced over to answer. Then, just before she picked up, she thought better of it and let the machine take the call.

"Hello, Bethany, this is Ryan."

She sat back in her chair.

"I just wanted to make sure everything's all right. Your brother was pretty steamed. I hope my being there didn't stir up too much of a hornet's nest. Normally I would've stayed to lend moral support, but he was so upset, I figured that might only make things worse." He paused and cleared his throat. "I guess maybe you're away from the phone right now." Another silence. Then he sighed, and she heard a tapping noise. She envisioned him striking a hard surface with a pencil or pen. "I'd really like a chance to finish our conversation. How's about calling me tomorrow when you have a few minutes? I'll be in and out most of the day, but I can check my messages."

He left her both his home and cell phone number. Then in a husky tenor that tugged at her heart, he ended by saying, "I know you're nervous about seeing me again. Let's talk about that. All right? There's nothing we can't work out, Bethany. *Nothing*. Take a chance on me. That's all I'm asking. I promise you'll never regret it." He hesitated, then said, "No good-byes. Catch you later."

When he broke the connection, Bethany released a pent-up breath, unaware until that moment that she'd even been holding it. *Ryan*. She closed her eyes, his words replaying in her mind. *Take a chance on me.*

*   *   *

Ryan was opening a can of soup for supper when a knock sounded at the side door. Glancing at the copper-framed kitchen clock, he saw that it was after nine. Wondering if there were problems with one of the brood mares, he quickly wiped his hands and went to answer the summons. He couldn't have been more surprised when he saw that his caller was none other than Jake Coulter.

Standing with his booted feet spread apart and his hands shoved in the pockets of his brown leather jacket, Jake stared hard at Ryan for a moment before he stated his business. "We need to talk."

Ryan opened the door wider and stepped back, gesturing for the other man to enter. After moving over the threshold, Jake panned the great room with brilliant blue eyes that reminded Ryan strongly of Bethany's, the only difference being that hers reflected gentleness and sweetness while her brother's were sharp as razors. Jake's attention lingered on the newspapers lying on the ivory carpet beside the teal recliner.

"I was fixing a bite to eat," Ryan said, leading the way into the large adjoining kitchen. "Can I offer you something to drink?"

"What'cha got?"

"Coke, carbonated spring water, beer." Ryan thought about offering some of Hazel Turk's wine as a purgative for what ailed the man, but he resisted the urge. "I've got some hard stuff as well. Name your poison."

"A beer suits me fine." Jake slung his jacket over the back of a chair, then sat down at the oak table. Glancing from Ryan to the adjacent brick wall encompassing the kitchen fireplace, he said, "This isn't what I expected."

"Oh, and what did you expect?"

"Fancier digs, I guess. Nice place, but it's not elaborate like I pictured."

Ryan opened the refrigerator. "We're ranchers, knee deep

in cow dung every day. Fancy is for fancy folk or church on Sunday."

Tapping his boot on the tile, Jake said, "Just a good old boy, is that it?"

Ryan took two beers from a shelf and elbowed the door closed. After handing one bottle to Jake, he sat down across from him. Twisting off the cap, he said, "Did you drive clear out here to take shots at me, Jake?"

Jake flipped his bottle cap in the air, palmed it on the descent with a quick snap of his wrist, and then lay it on the table. He took a slug of beer, whistling as he exhaled, and then settled back, his eyes glittering as he met Ryan's querying gaze. "I'm here to talk to you about my sister."

Expecting to be told to stay away from Bethany, Ryan tensed. "So, start."

Jake thoughtfully eyed the gold lettering on the bottle label. "She'll kill me when she finds out I came here. I interfere in her business more than I probably should, and this is definitely sticking my nose where it doesn't belong."

"Nothing you say is going to keep me away from her. Only she can make that call, and I'll do everything in my power to change her mind, even if she does."

A muscle moved in Jake's cheek. "And friendship's all you have in mind."

The man's eyes were a hell of a lot sharper than mere razor blades, Ryan decided. They cut through him like laser beams. It was one thing to tell Bethany that all he expected was friendship and quite another to get her brother to buy it. "No, friendship isn't all I've got in mind," Ryan admitted. "Just for the record, however, if you tell her I said that, I'll deny it."

"So you flat out lied to her."

"Whether I lied depends entirely on one's definition of friendship."

"Don't play games. Friendship and intimacy are two different things."

"In your opinion. I'm from another school and believe all relationships need a strong foundation, and the strongest foundation is friendship. This will give Bethany and me something solid to build on later, later being the keyword in that statement. She needs time. I understand that, and I'll give it to her."

"Bottom line, you intend to have an intimate relationship with my sister, and you're using the friendship ploy to lull her into a false sense of security."

"That pretty much covers it." Ryan half expected Coulter to come up off the chair when he made the admission.

Instead Jake just nodded. "And then what?"

"I'm sorry? Exactly what is the question?"

"After you seduce her, then what? I don't want her getting hurt, Kendrick. She isn't the kind you can just use and dump, not if you have any decency."

Ryan touched a fingertip to a droplet of condensation on his beer bottle. "I have no intention of using her and dumping her, Jake. I'm in for the long haul."

Jake laughed sourly. "The long haul? Tell me, does that include vows and forever after? Or will you scat when you start to feel bored?"

"Vows and forever after."

Jake didn't attempt to conceal his surprise. "Just like that."

"No, not 'just like that.' I'm in love with her."

"You only just met her a week ago."

"I know exactly when I met her, and it hasn't been quite a week. Time doesn't play into it." Ryan shrugged and sighed. "I can't explain what I mean by that, so don't ask. I just know, is all."

"It's called physical attraction."

"I know what physical attraction feels like. This is more. Laugh your ass off if you want, but this is it for me."

"Are you always so quick to make decisions about women?"

"I never have before. Bethany's different."

"How?"

"She just is." A picture of her face swept through Ryan's mind, and he smiled slightly. "Any man with eyes can see that she's different, Jake." He arched a brow. "Why else would you be here? You know exactly how vulnerable she is. And it scares the holy hell out of you."

"Yeah, it does. I'm afraid you'll hurt her."

"I won't."

Jake relaxed on the chair. "You're really taken with her, aren't you?"

"You could say that. I know you're worried. I sympathize with that. But you've got my personal guarantee it's unnecessary. She'll be in good hands."

"There are things you don't know, things that may change your mind."

"I doubt it."

Jake leaned forward, bracing his arms on his knees. "Humor me and listen. If nothing I tell you in the next few minutes throws you off course, fine by me, but just in case it goes the other way, do her a favor and turn tail right now—before you break her heart. She's been badly hurt once already, Ryan. It took her nearly two years to get over it."

"She still isn't over it. Trust me on that. She still isn't over it."

Jake conceded the point with a nod, took a sip of beer, and then swore under his breath. "So she told you about him, did she?"

"No. Just his name, and only that because I insisted."

"Shortly after the accident, he took up with a girl who'd been Bethany's best friend since kindergarten."

"Sweet Christ." Ryan's stomach clenched. "Her best friend?"

"That's right. In terms of betrayal, it was a double whammy. Before Bethany was transported to Portland for surgery, the two of them went to see her every night at the hospital, acting as if they cared while they were having a thing on the side. Nan got pregnant, and Paul married her in Reno without telling Bethany beforehand. Shame and cowardice. The little son of a bitch did a real job on her. He couldn't bear to look her in the eye and admit what a jerk he was. She had to read about it in the paper. There she lay, trapped on that damned bed, still wearing the promise ring he'd given her, and she came across the marriage announcement in a paper from home. I was there when she found it. She turned as white as a sheet."

"Her best friend? Some friend."

"Exactly. Someone she'd trusted and loved all her life. The worst of it was, the marriage didn't last three months. I'm not sure which hurt Bethany more, Paul's defection or Nan's betrayal. I only know it was the kind of hurt that ran too deep for tears. She just stared off into space with an awful look in her eyes and took off the ring. After that, she seemed—hell, I don't know the word for it. Diminished, somehow, like the life went out of her."

Silence. Ryan pictured Bethany's face again and those big eyes that revealed her every thought and feeling. He sincerely hoped he never ran across good old Paul. He'd plant a fist in his teeth. "I'm not going to break her heart again, Jake. If that's all that's worrying you, rest easy. I'm not perfect and I'm bound to make mistakes, but hurting her that way will never be one of them."

Jake gave him a searching look. "I honestly believe it'd destroy her."

"If there's one thing I can say with absolute certainty about Kendrick men, it's that we're loyal. We don't step out on our women, and we sure as hell don't run like scalded dogs when the going gets rough."

"It doesn't worry you that she may be unable to enjoy a normal sex life?" Jake asked bluntly. "She has no sensation in certain parts of her body that are more or less vital to a woman's enjoyment."

Ryan took another swallow of beer before answering. "I was a little worried about the sex at first. I'll admit it."

"And now?"

"Now I'm not." At the vague answer, irritation flared in Jake's eyes. Ryan struggled to suppress a grin. "My mom's a nurse. I learned some very interesting things from her, namely that lack of sensation isn't a death knell. There's good chemistry between Bethany and me, and that's more than lots of people begin a marriage with. If problems crop up, we'll work our way through them. I'm willing to be inventive if it's necessary."

"Inventive." Jake curled his lip. "And you'll be content with that?"

Ryan sighed. "We're both unattached males around thirty. Can you sit there and tell me good sex with someone you don't love leaves you feeling content and happy afterward, or that you don't wish for more?"

"No, of course not."

"Me neither, and I'm sick to death tired of wishing for more. I feel content and happy when I'm with your sister. Does that make any sense?"

"Yeah, it makes a lot of sense," Jake said.

"The way I see it, if certain things about our personal life don't fit the usual mold, will I really give a shit? If we're happy together and we can please each other, what difference does it make *how* we do it?"

"None, I guess." Jake smiled slightly. "What if she can't carry a child to term? There is a big possibility of that. Her spinal surgeon told her in no uncertain terms she shouldn't have kids."

That took Ryan by surprise. He'd read about brain-dead women who'd carried children to term, and a woman couldn't get much more paralyzed than that. "She can't have kids?

Paralysis doesn't interfere with fertility. I've been reading up on it on the Internet. I never saw any mention of that."

Jake shrugged. "Reicherton, her spinal surgeon, said she'd probably miscarry. Special problems of some kind. The point is, that's a possibility. How do you feel about it?"

"I can live with it."

"I'd think a man with all your land and money would want kids of his own."

"Naturally I'd love to, but I'm prepared to adopt if it's necessary."

"Don't pay this lip service. My sister may never have children. If I've got a vote, I'd just as soon she never tried. After her last surgery, she got a blood clot in one of her legs. A real humdinger that left the vein permanently narrowed with residual fibers from the clot that interfere with some little valves in there. They'd probably take her off her medicine while she was pregnant, increasing the risk of a second clot. We could have lost her with the last one."

"I certainly won't get her pregnant if a doctor tells me it's dangerous. But I have to point out that exercise and good muscle tone will greatly improve a condition like that. If she gets on a good program, she probably won't need medicine."

"Exercise?" Jake sighed and rolled his eyes, the gesture reminding Ryan so sharply of Bethany that he nearly smiled. "Right. I'll get her started tomorrow. Jogging, do you think?"

"Go ahead. Be a smart ass. I've been reading stuff, like I told you. Did you know there are treadmills equipped with special harnesses so even quadriplegics can walk regularly and keep their legs muscles toned?"

"Yes, and they carry price tags equal to the national debt."

"I can afford it," Ryan said softly.

Jake sighed wearily. "So you've thought of everything and still mean to pursue this."

Ryan chuckled. "Is that what this is about? You were hoping to scare me off? Save it, Coulter. You're not going to hit me with anything that will throw me that bad, nothing I won't find a way to deal with. I'll also remind you I've got money out the kazoo. One of the main reasons handicapped people can't lead more normal, active lives is because their insurance peters out on them, and they've got no financial resources with which to modify their environment."

Jake narrowed an eye. "What if the state won't approve her as an adoptive parent?"

"There are private agencies, and as I just pointed out, money isn't a problem. We'll be able to adopt children, guaranteed."

"How will your family feel about that? Will they accept an adopted kid?"

"My kids will be loved, adopted or not."

"You really are serious about marrying her," Jake mused softly.

"Hell, yes, I'm serious."

After searching Ryan's gaze for a long moment, Jake finished off his beer. "You got another one of these hiding in there?"

"It's a long drive back to town. You sure you want another one?"

"My limit's two when I'm driving. Yeah, I'll have another one."

Ryan fetched them both a second round. When he was settled back on his chair again, Jake said, "It appears you've done your homework and know what you're getting into."

"That's right."

"That being the case, there's only one more thing I want to say to you, Kendrick. Once it's said, maybe we can take a shot at becoming friends."

Ryan shrugged. "So far, I don't much like you, but stranger things have happened."

Jake grinned. "I don't much like you, either, but my sister does. I guess her vote carries the day. I'll back off. No more interference. You'll have an open playing field all the way. Just understand one thing." His smile faded and a dangerous glint crept into his eyes. "If you hurt her—if you cause her to shed so much as a single tear—you'll answer to me. And I promise you, when I'm done kicking your ass, you'll rue the day your daddy looked at your mama with a twinkle in his eye."

Chapter Eight

It had been nine years since Bethany had last attended a Crystal Falls Rancher's Association dinner, but the event proved to be much the same as she remembered. It was still held at the Ranchers' Co-op Grange, a cavernous hall at the edge of town in which countless tables were set up around a central dance floor. During the meal, the association president competed with the din of flatware clinking on china to give a long speech peppered with microphone whistles and bad jokes that elicited polite laughter from his audience.

While Bethany ate, she exchanged amused glances with her twenty-eight-year-old brother, Hank. Jake's date, a new acquaintance named Muriel, was a novelty. The redhead was pretty in a flashy, voluptuous way, which was undoubtedly what had caught Jake's eye, but her taste in clothes was appalling. Tonight she wore a tight sequin dress that showcased her generous curves in emerald green. The neckline plunged so low that her bosom threatened to spill out onto her plate every time she leaned forward to take a bite.

The Coulter males and Bethany's mother watched in horrified fascination. Bethany could barely keep a straight face. *Poor Jake*. She doubted he'd ever invite a woman to be around his family on the first date again. Bethany and her mom wore dark, modest dresses: Bethany's a jersey, Mary's a lightweight wool.

"Ohmigawd!" Muriel fairly bounced on her chair when she saw the band setting up. "I just *love* live music. Are we gonna dance, Jake?"

Jake's gaze shot like a bullet to his date's jiggling bosom, and his face turned an interesting shade of burnished brown with burgundy undertones. "I think they play mostly country western. That probably isn't your cup of tea."

"Oh, I like all kinds of dancing. Fast, slow, and everything in between."

Jake's smile was strained. "Fantastic."

"Save at least one dance for me, Muriel," Hank inserted, his blue eyes twinkling.

Jake's return glare could have pulverized granite. In that moment Bethany could see why so many people in Crystal Falls believed that her oldest brother was a horse whisperer. His eyes were such a vivid blue in contrast to his dark skin tone, his gaze had a cold fire that almost burned.

Bethany bent her head and pretended intense interest in her steak. The moment Jake looked away, she elbowed Hank in the ribs. "Behave yourself."

"So, tell us, Muriel," Bethany's mother, a matronly brunette with gentle blue eyes and a warm smile, said politely. "How did you meet our son?"

Muriel batted her caked black lashes. The bleary, vacuous expression in her pretty green eyes clearly wasn't entirely due to contact lenses. "Which one?"

Mary cast a bewildered look at her big, dark-haired husband, who sat beside her. Amusement danced in Harv Coulter's azure eyes. He shrugged his broad shoulders, his sharply hewn features softening in a smile as he poured his wife more wine.

"Me, Muriel," Jake whispered. "You just met Hank and my folks tonight."

"Oh." Muriel smiled blissfully and glanced back at Mary.

"Jake and I met each other at Safeway. He was squeezing the avocados."

"Ah." Mary cast her eldest son a questioning look. "I see."

"I've never been able to pick out good avocados," Muriel elaborated. "So I asked him to show me how. The next thing we knew, the whole pile came toppling down. Avocados everywhere! When we were finished picking up the mess, one thing led to another, and he asked for my phone number." She winked at Jake. "I doubted he'd really call me. But he did, so here I am."

"I wonder what she was wearing," Hank whispered to Bethany. "I've got twenty that says Jake went blind every time she leaned over."

Bethany touched her napkin to her lips, doing her best not to giggle. "Behave yourself," she whispered again.

"You're no fun anymore," Hank complained.

By the time their meal was cleared away and the band began playing its first number, everyone at the Coulter table was relieved to hear Jake ask Muriel to dance. As the couple moved onto the crowded dance floor, Harv chuckled and said, "I'll bet Jake thinks twice before he goes near a produce section again."

"She's a nice enough girl," Mary said with her typical Pollyanna sweetness. "A bit of a dim bulb, perhaps, but that isn't her fault."

Harv grinned and winked at Hank. "She definitely doesn't hide what little brilliance she has."

Hank, who'd come without a date, excused himself and went to ask a blonde at a nearby table to dance. After watching his tall, dark-haired son walk away, Harv glanced at Mary. "Well, honey? You want to polish my belt buckle?"

Mary frowned. "Are you sure you're up to dancing?"

"The doctor says it's stress that'll kill me, not a little good old-fashioned exercise. I work out every morning. Where's the difference?"

Mary smiled and glanced at Bethany. "Will you be all right, darling? I hate to leave you sitting here all alone."

Bethany waved a hand. "Don't be silly, Mom. I enjoy just watching."

As her parents moved onto the floor, Bethany allowed her smile to slip. She glanced at the empty chairs around the table, resigned to another boring evening. She would have preferred to stay home with her brushes and paints.

Ah, well. She turned her chair to have a better view of the dancers, her fingertips tapping in time to the music. The hall suddenly grew dark and a rotating sphere sprang to life overhead, casting multicolored spirals of light onto the floor. She scanned the crowd. Her folks had vanished, but Jake was as easy to spot as if he were dancing with a beacon.

As the next number began, she saw a tall, dark-haired cowboy stepping onto the floor with a brunette tucked under his arm. The way he moved struck a chord, his loose stride and the fluid shift of his broad shoulders familiar. *Ryan.* Dressed in black with his shirt open at the throat to reveal a V of bronze chest, he cut such a handsome figure that her heart rapped against her ribs.

His hair glinting in the light like polished onyx, he leaned down to catch something the woman said. His face creased in a grin that flashed white teeth. Then he threw back his head and laughed, swinging her in the circle of his arm to face him as they began to dance. They made an attractive couple, he so tall, muscular, and dark, she so dainty and beautiful. The lively western beat required fast footwork, which they executed flawlessly, his black dress boots dwarfing her sassy high heels as he cut a circle around her, then twirled her back into his arms. Bethany knew they had danced with each other many times before.

She concentrated her gaze on the woman, taking in her burgundy silk blouse and skirt, the latter full and swirling gracefully around her shapely legs. When Ryan settled a hand low on the woman's back, Bethany couldn't help but notice how the splay of his fingers stretched to the curve of her hip. Her dainty build accentuated his muscular bulk, the two of them a study in contrasts.

She couldn't believe how it hurt to see him dancing with another woman. And, oh, how that rankled. She curled her hands into fists, then relaxed them when she realized what she was doing. What difference did it make to her if he had come with someone else?

A very beautiful someone else.

An awful, achy sensation filled her chest. She tried to look away and watch the other couples, but her gaze remained fixed on Ryan. Oh, how she wished she were the woman in his arms. She would have given almost anything to have two functional legs so she might dance with him until dawn.

When the song ended and he turned to guide his partner off the floor, he scanned the tables, his gaze gliding past Bethany, then jerking back to settle on her with glittering intensity. Even in the dim light, she saw his jaw clench. He veered toward her, drawing the woman along as he cut through the crowd.

The last thing Bethany wanted was to meet Ryan Kendrick's date for the evening. She considered wheeling away to hide in the ladies' room, but such behavior struck her as being childish. Instead, she forced herself to smile.

"Hello!" she called as they drew closer.

Ryan's firm mouth twitched at the corners then slanted into a grin that made her bones feel in danger of melting. He kept his arm around the woman's slender shoulders as he drew to a stop near the table. "Bethany." His gaze moved slowly over her. "I had no idea you were going to be here tonight."

The woman, who was even more beautiful up close than she'd appeared to be at a distance, beamed a friendly smile, her big, liquid brown eyes revealing no hint of animosity. She glanced expectantly at Ryan.

Catching her look, he said, "Maggie, I'd like you to meet a very good friend of mine, Bethany Coulter. Bethany, my brother Rafe's wife, Maggie."

Heat flagged Bethany's cheeks as she shook hands with Ryan's sister-in-law. "It's a pleasure to meet you, Maggie."

"The pleasure's all mine." Maggie's eyes sparkled with warmth. "Ryan mentioned that you enjoy going to the mud pulls."

"Yes, very much."

"Me, too. Maybe the four of us can go together sometime soon."

Bethany glanced at Ryan. "I'll look forward to it," she settled for saying.

"It's a date, then? That'll be fun. I'll get Rafe's mom to watch the kids, and we'll make an evening of it. Do you like Mexican?"

It took Bethany a moment to register what she meant. "I love Mexican, the hotter the better."

Maggie nodded decisively. "I'm going to like you. Another bean and tortilla fanatic! We found the greatest restaurant. The atmosphere there is absolutely wonderful, very relaxed and friendly."

"Give Maggie a generous helping of greasy tortilla chips with a huge bowl of fiery hot salsa, and she thinks the place has great ambience," Ryan said.

Maggie elbowed him in the ribs. "Don't listen to him, Bethany. The truth is, he wouldn't recognize authentic Mexican or delightful ambience if they ran up and bit him on the leg."

Ryan groaned and splayed a hand over his stomach.

"Poor baby." Maggie's eyes twinkled with mischief. "There's nothing sadder than seeing a big strong man quail with dread at the thought of eating an enchilada."

She grinned at Bethany. "He'll take on a thousand-pound bull bare-handed, but a bottle of hot sauce sends him running."

Bethany couldn't help but laugh. Maggie was delightful, and Bethany was completely charmed by the pair's teasing banter. It reminded her of the way she and her brothers needled each other.

Maggie turned and lightly touched Ryan's shirtsleeve. "I'm off to grab my husband before the next song. He promised to dance with me." She turned back to Bethany and extended a delicate hand. "It's been great meeting you, Bethany. Please, make Ryan bring you out to the Rocking K for a visit soon. We'll run off the guys and have a good old-fashioned coffee klatch."

"I'd enjoy that very much," Bethany replied, and sincerely meant it. Maggie Kendrick was an easy person to like.

As she walked away, Bethany looked questioningly at Ryan, who grinned lazily and straddled a chair facing her, his crossed arms resting loosely on its back. After staring at her until she wanted to squirm, he said, "Hi," his voice a husky caress that seemed to wrap her in warmth. "Fancy meeting you here."

"It's a small world, after all, I guess." She thought that sounded stupid and wished she'd said something else. Only what? When he looked at her like that, her brain seemed to freeze.

He nodded, his gaze teasing hers as his mouth slanted into another slow grin. "Too small for you to avoid me. Is that what you're thinking?"

At the moment she had difficulty holding onto a thought.

"Do all men make you so nervous?" he suddenly asked.

"Nervous?"

His gaze dropped to her hands, which were clenched and white-knuckled on her lap. "I don't bite." A heated gleam slipped into his eyes. "Never hard enough to hurt, anyway." He reached out to touch a fingertip to the end of her nose. "What are you doing, sitting here all alone?"

"They'll be back soon. Right now, they're all out dancing."

He glanced at the empty table. "This can't be much fun."

"I'm fine." She shrugged. "My dancing days are over, but that doesn't mean everyone else can't enjoy themselves."

He studied her thoughtfully. "I'll bet you loved it."

"Loved what?"

"Dancing."

Memories. Bethany tried never to dwell on things she could no longer do, but dancing was a tough one, especially when she found herself sitting at the edge of a dance floor. "Yes, I did love it," she admitted. "My dad taught me to waltz when I was about seven, and from that moment on, I was hooked. Whenever we went to a function with music, I drove him and my brothers crazy, begging them to dance with me. I liked all kinds, fast or slow, it didn't matter."

He turned his hands palm up and gazed solemnly at the lines etched there. When he met her gaze again, he said, "Do you miss it terribly?"

Normally Bethany told polite lies, but she found it difficult, if not impossible, to tell him anything but the truth. "Yes, very much." She tried for what she hoped was a bright smile. "There are a number of things I miss a lot."

"Does friendship have to be one of them?"

She laughed. She couldn't help it. "Has anyone ever told you that you're as tenacious as a pit bull once you sink your teeth into something?"

"My mom's words, almost exactly." He let his hands dangle, his broad shoulders lifting in a shrug. "What can I say? I made you a proposition, and you haven't given me your answer yet. Is the friendship on or not?"

"I'm still mulling it over."

"While you mull, can I campaign?"

She laughed again. "You're impossible."

"Just think of all the fun we can have."

The twinkle in his eyes was full of promise. "Doing what?" she couldn't resist asking.

"The possibilities are endless."

"That's a cop-out if ever I've heard one."

"Hey, if all else fails, you can teach me to paint."

At the suggestion, Bethany laughed until tears filled her eyes. She would almost regain her composure—*almost*—and then she'd look at his huge hands and start laughing again.

"I'm offended."

She wiped under her eyes. "I'm sorry. Really. I'm sure you could learn. It's just—" Her voice went thin with suppressed giggles. "Somehow you just don't strike me as the type who'd have the patience for it."

Ryan grinned, thinking to himself that it would all depend on what he used as a canvas. Her flawless ivory skin would sure as hell hold his interest. He'd start by painting the petals of a daisy around her navel and move on from there.

"Honest answer," he said, leaning forward over the chair to hold her gaze. "Right now, this very instant, aren't you having fun?"

Her smile winked out, and a dark, worried look came into her eyes. "Yes."

"Point made. Doing nothing, we have a great time. Just think how much fun we can have if we set our minds to it."

"Probably a lot."

He nodded and pushed to his feet. "Hold that thought."

She was frowning bewilderedly, not to mention looking abandoned and a little lost as he walked away. Knowing he'd soon be back, Ryan smiled as he shouldered his way through the milling crowd toward the bandstand.

*   *   *

Everyone in her family had returned to the table and then left to dance again when Bethany saw Ryan striding back through the crowd toward her. His silver belt buckle flashed in the dim light with every shift of his lean hips. He was so handsome that she allowed herself a brief moment of fancy, pretending he was a stranger who didn't know about her paralysis and was heading her way to ask her to dance. Scotch that. If she was going to dream, why not go all out and dream that she could actually walk?

He sauntered to a stop, gave her a slow, crooked grin that made her pulse skitter, and said, "May I have the next dance, Miss Coulter?"

For just an instant, Bethany felt as if he'd punched her in the solar plexus. Didn't he realize how much she would love to dance with him? Sometimes, if she allowed herself to think about the years of confinement that stretched ahead of her, she felt like a rat in a cage.

"I'd love to," she said flippantly.

"I was hoping you'd say that."

He stepped around to grasp the handles of her chair. As he set off for the front exit, Bethany glanced over her shoulder at him. "What are you doing?"

He flashed her another grin and winked. "Wait and see."

Once in the vestibule, which served double duty as a cloakroom, he started rifling through the coats and wraps hanging on the rod along one wall.

"Are we going outside?" she asked.

"Yep."

"Did you misplace your jacket?"

"Nope."

"Well, if you're looking for mine, it's way down at the other end."

He came up with a heavy black sweater, gave it a long look, and said, "A little big, but it'll do." He turned, advanced on Bethany, and started stuffing her arms down the sleeves. "Your coat would be too bulky for what I have in mind."

"But—this isn't mine."

"I know," he said as he tugged the garment up onto her shoulders.

"Whose is it?"

A mischievous glint entered his steel-blue eyes. "Beats the hell out of me, but we'll have it back before she ever misses it."

"Ryan!" she cried as he wheeled her toward the front doors.

"What?"

"I can't swipe someone's sweater."

He chuckled. "You're not swiping it."

"I'm not?"

"Nope. I swiped it, you're just wearing it."

"Either way! I'm not taking someone's sweater."

"Yeah, you are." He leaned over her to shove open the doors and push her outside. "Relax. What can they do, arrest us for short-term sweater theft?"

Bethany was grateful for the sweater when the frigid night air wrapped around her. "You're crazy. And you'll freeze out here without a coat. Where are we going, anyway?"

"You'll see, and trust me, I won't freeze. I spend so much time outdoors, I'm inured to the cold."

" 'Inured?' Cowboys aren't supposed to know such words."

"Beg pardon, ma'am. I'll work on it. Get me a wad of chew, spit between sentences, and scratch where I shouldn't. Goin' to college flat ruint me."

"I didn't know you attended university. What was your major?"

"Animal husbandry and ag. Got degrees in both." He turned left to push her along a cement walkway that circled to the back of the building. "Never did figure out why any man in his right mind would wanna play husband to a bull. Got good marks in female anatomy 101, though."

She laughed at that. "I'll just bet you did."

"When I came home with my pigskins in hand, I could guess a woman's measurements at a hundred yards. After all the money he'd forked out for tuition, the old man was flat impressed."

Bethany grinned, imagining a younger Ryan fresh out of college. With his looks, he must have been as close to lethal as a young man could get. "What school did you attend?"

"Oregon State. Most goat ropers go there so they can strut around campus in their Stetsons and spit fancy. It's a requirement, knowin' how to spit, and it takes a real knack. Sly, our foreman, can nail a fly at ten feet."

"I was raised on a ranch, remember. I know all about you cowboys. It has been my observation that you're all full of bull."

"That's right. You have been around cowboys. I guess that means I should cut the crap?"

"Good plan."

"I never took female anatomy 101. The rest is fact. I have an eye for female curves that won't quit. You, for instance. I could buy you a wardrobe, from the skin out, and everything would fit perfectly. Any bets?"

"Oh, puh-leeze."

"Women. Why is it they're never interested in seeing a guy show off?"

"Because we're seldom impressed."

"Thirty-two, B. Twenty-one inch waist. You impressed yet?"

He was amazingly accurate, and knowing that he'd looked at her that closely made her skin tingle. "If you like treading on thin ice, you're doing well."

He chuckled and fell quiet. To their right was a parking lot. In the moonlight the cars and trucks resembled shiny-shelled beetles. Above them, the moon hung like a china supper plate against a backdrop of midnight-blue velvet sequined with stars. The cold breeze carried the essence of fir and pine, drawing Bethany's gaze to the mountains that ringed the basin.

She sighed. "It's a beautiful night. Just look at that sky."

"Nothing quite like it, is there? I've heard Montana referred to as sky country. I figure those folks have never been to Oregon on a clear night."

He wheeled her to a covered breezeway at the rear of the grange. The back doors were propped open, and they could hear the music almost as clearly from there as from inside. The band was finishing the current number. Before they began the next song, Ryan stepped around her chair and leaned down, coming almost nose to nose with her.

"Put your arms around my neck, sweetheart."

"Whatever for?"

He grasped her wrists and lifted her arms himself. "Because," he whispered, "we're going to dance."

"Oh, no, I—"

Before she could complete the protest, he slipped an arm around her waist and plucked her from the chair. Left with no choice, she gave a startled squeak and grabbed onto him. *"Ryan!"*

"It's all right. I swear I won't drop you." He shifted her against him, cupping one big hand over her posterior. "Hold tight. You hanging on?"

For dear life. "Yes, and so are you. No funny business. I can feel that, you know."

"You can?" He slipped his arm from around her waist and moved his other hand down to her rump. Intertwining his fingers, he formed a seat of sorts to hold her hips snugly against his. "I thought paraplegics were totally numb from the waist down."

"Not me. My spinal injury is at L2 and didn't damage all

the—" She jumped and gave him a look. "What are you doing?"

He grinned and winked. "My thumb was in a crick. You really *do* have feeling there."

She narrowed an eye. "Yes, and if you do any more wiggling, you'll pay."

"No more. I promise."

"This will never work. I appreciate the thought. It's very sweet, but—"

"Shut up," he whispered.

The first notes of the next number drifted to them, and she realized it was the band's rendition of Montgomery's hit song, "I Swear." Tears sprang to her eyes, for the instant she recognized the tune, she knew Ryan had requested it.

"Dance with me," he whispered.

"I feel foolish."

"Who'll see? Only me, and I'm your best bud, so I don't count. Besides, why should you feel foolish?"

"My legs are dangling. My feet will thump your shins."

"Those soft slippers won't hurt my shins," he assured her.

And with that, he swept her into a waltz.

Bethany expected it to feel awkward. As he executed the first few steps, she was rigid with tension, afraid he'd stumble and drop her, or that she was too heavy and he'd exhaust himself.

Instead, it was glorious, and she felt as if she were floating, his strength her buoyancy. *Dancing.* It wasn't really dancing, of course. She kept telling herself that. But it seemed as though it was. *Dancing.* Oh, God. She'd yearned to do this a hundred times over the last eight years, and now she actually was. It gave her the most incredible feeling. Free and light as a bird, caught in the arms of a tall, dark cowboy.

Bethany straightened her arms, let her head fall back, and closed her eyes, wishing the feeling would never end. "Oh, Ryan."

"Good?"

"Oh, yes. Oh, *yes*. You just can't know."

Watching the expressions that crossed her face, Ryan thought he had a fair idea. How must it feel, he wondered, always to be trapped in that damned chair, and now, suddenly, to be swirling in the moonlight?

Damn, she was sweet. Holding her like this was as close to heaven as he ever hoped to get. *Bethany*. A dreamy smile curved her mouth, conveying pleasure so intense he doubted she could put it into words. He imagined making her smile exactly that way while he made love to her, hearing her sigh like that when he kissed her.

Someday . . .

For now it was enough just to hold her like this in the moonlight and see her smile, to know she was happy and that in some small way, he was responsible for that.

By the end of the second number, Ryan's energy was starting to flag. She didn't weigh a lot, but dancing ceaselessly while he supported an extra one hundred and ten pounds took its toll. He hated to return her to the chair, and he wished with all his heart he didn't have to.

Unfortunately, even good things had to end. He made it through a third dance, and then his legs started to give out on him.

She blinked when the music ceased, and he drew to a reluctant stop. The dreamy, slightly befuddled expression in her eyes told him just how much she had enjoyed the dances and that she would cherish the memory long after the evening was over.

"Oh, Ryan." She bestowed a glowing smile on him, her eyes shimmering with gladness and tears. She said nothing more, but those two words conveyed so very much, far more than she probably realized, a gratitude that ran too deep for words, and a bewildered incredulity because he had done something so completely unexpected, simply to give her pleasure.

It was her expression of incredulity that touched him the most. It had been such a small thing, really, lifting her from that chair and taking a few turns around the breezeway. He'd worked harder countless times, and with far less reward. Could there be a sweeter gift than seeing Bethany smile?

She would never spend another evening sitting alone at a table while everyone else danced and had a good time, he promised himself. Never again.

He gently returned her to her chair, which he was quickly coming to realize was a prison without bars. Leaning low, he thumbed a tear from beneath her eye and whispered, "Hey, what's this? I meant for it to be fun, not make you cry."

"Oh, it *was* fun," she said. "I just—" She shook her head and wiped her cheeks. "I'm sorry. This is silly. It's just that I've wanted to dance so many times, and I didn't think I could. That was as close to dancing as it gets. I can't tell you how wonderful it felt." She smiled tremulously. "Thank you, Ryan."

Resting his hands on the chair arms, he held her gaze for a searching moment. "We can have a lot of fun together, you and I. No risks, no expectations, just friendship. I can make it work if only you'll give me a chance."

"I'm tempted," she said with a wet laugh. "You make it so hard to say no."

"Then don't."

She caught her bottom lip between her teeth, her eyes reflecting hesitation and uncertainty. "Let me think about it."

"What's to think about?"

"If I'm around you very much, I'm afraid I'll do something ill-advised and totally dumb, like fall in love with you," she admitted shakily.

Ryan was counting on it.

Chapter Nine

The following afternoon on her way home from Bend, where she'd gone to pick up an order of custom-made saddle blankets for the store, Bethany ran into bad weather. Initially, she couldn't quite believe her eyes when a blob of white struck the windshield. The weather forecast hadn't predicted snow.

Within seconds, visibility was reduced to almost nothing. She flipped the windshield wipers onto high and peered at the veil of white ahead of her. Gusts of wind buffeted the stands of fir and pine that bordered the road and swept across the pavement to form shallow drifts on each shoulder.

This couldn't be happening. It was the last of April, for pity's sake, far too late for snow. She slowed down and tightly gripped the steering wheel. She was at a high elevation right now. In a matter of minutes, she'd probably drop out of this into heavy rain. Rain, she could handle. Just as long as she didn't need snow chains, she'd be all right.

Approximately ten minutes passed. The windshield wipers went *swish-thunk—swish-thunk,* the rhythmic sound seeming to mock her as the blades pushed aside the thick buildups of snow. The highway was covered now. *Oh, God.* Her van didn't handle well on ice. Just yesterday over Sunday dinner, her brothers had been talking about getting her a four-wheel drive SUV before next winter. A fat lot of good that did her now.

After turning on the stereo and switching from CD to

FM, she tried to pick up a Crystal Falls radio station. When she located her favorite spot on the dial, a country-western channel that played only hit songs, she listened to the disc jockey's comments on the weather front with growing unease. *A freak snowstorm.* He advised against driving, even in town, unless people had a bona fide emergency. Several multi-car accidents had already occurred on the outskirts of Crystal Falls.

Nervous sweat beaded her face. She felt the rear end of the van lose traction and slip toward the shoulder. She needed to put on traction devices. Big problem. It would be sheer madness to get out of the van. If the vehicle was slipping and sliding, her chair would do the same.

Swish-thunk—swish-thunk. She turned off the stereo to listen. An occasional whining sound told her the back tires were losing their grip and spinning to grab hold again. Squinting to see up ahead, she could detect no letup in the downfall, only snow as far as she could see, forming a white wall. If she lost control and went off the road—well, it didn't bear thinking about.

Positive thoughts, she told herself. If she drove slowly and hugged the center of the road, she'd probably make it fine. It was silly to worry about things before they happened. Right?

Just as she thought that, the van fishtailed on a slight incline. She tried to steer into the skid and regain control, but the vehicle went into a spin. For a crazy instant, the world became a blur, the forested slopes at either side of the road whizzing past the windows like video images on fast-forward. Trees, snow, rocks, and sky. She clung hard to the steering wheel, her only anchor as she was flung sideways by the force of gravity.

Oh, God. The half-formed prayer was cut short when, with a sudden lurch, the van dove off into the ditch with such force that the front bumper plowed into the frozen earth. Bethany's teeth snapped together. The nylon strap that held her in her chair bit into her shoulder. She screamed and tried desperately to regain control of the vehicle, but the hand brake wouldn't work.

The undercarriage of the van jounced over the rough ground. Each time metal struck rock, the noise seemed to explode in the air around her. Through the swirling downfall, she glimpsed a looming blur of gray and white ahead. Still holding hard on the brake, she tried to stop, but the conditions were too slick. The van sped onward, unchecked, until it hit the obstacle, the resultant crunch of metal so deafening that it seemed to reverberate inside her skull.

Her head snapped forward, her face almost hitting the wheel. For a moment afterward, she just stared in befuddlement at the windshield, her one clear thought that the wipers were still working. With each pass, the left blade caught on a spray of gritty mud, making a *swish-scritch* sound that would soon drive her mad. She reached to turn off the wipers and then hesitated, imagining how claustrophobic she would feel, trapped and unable to see out.

And what was she thinking? That was the least of her problems. She'd just had a wreck. A *wreck*. There could be gas pouring from a crack in the tank—or she could be bleeding to death from a cut she didn't know she had. She sniffed the air. If the tank was ruptured, she'd surely smell fuel.

An absurd urge to laugh came over her. She found that vaguely alarming and wondered if she was in shock. The van was tipped at a crazy angle. Her purse and coat, which had been on the passenger seat, now lay on that side of the floorboard beyond her reach. A fine pickle, no question about it.

A rock, she decided. The van had crashed into a rock. Strike that. Any stone that large qualified as a boulder. Craning her neck to see over the dash, she tried to assess the damage. Through the swirl of snow, all she could tell for certain was that the hood looked crunched.

Oh, God—oh, God. She had to *do* something. Only what?

All that kept her chair anchored in place were the restraints. If she dared to unfasten the straps, she might topple out of her chair.

Trembling with nerves, she checked her person, paying special attention to her legs because an injury there would cause no pain. As near as she could tell, she was unharmed. *Thank heaven.* She had seen no traffic for at least thirty minutes, so she couldn't count on a passerby to stop and help her.

The van was still running. That was good. Perhaps she'd be able to back out of the ditch and limp on home. The thought no sooner passed through her mind than she heard a hissing sound and saw a cloud of steam shoot from under the van's mangled hood. The engine gave two coughs, sputtered, and died.

Silence. It settled around her with unnerving thickness, broken only by the faint snapping sound of cooling metal.

"Wonderful!"

She rubbed a peephole on the fogged glass to peer out. The snow was already so deep, she could see no asphalt, not even in her skid marks.

"Stay calm." She took a deep breath and slowly let it out. "No major catastrophe here. Just a fender bender and a damaged radiator. No big deal."

Only for someone like her, it *was* a big deal. Like menacing specters looming from the mist, the huge, snow-laden trees that grew along the road bore witness to the remoteness of her location. The woods stretched for miles in all directions. For the first time in her life, she felt intimidated by the wilderness.

At the edges of her mind, panic mounted. An able-bodied woman would be able to climb over the console to get her coat, at least. Without a functional heater, she could very easily freeze to death out here.

With trembling hands she groped in the console, the contents of which were now tossed every which way. Where was her phone? She always kept it in there when she traveled. She cast a worried glance at her purse. After finishing her business in Bend, had she forgotten to return the cell phone to the console?

Yes. Of all the stupid, idiotic, *mindless* things to do.

She thought of all the times she'd harangued her brothers for being overprotective of her. *I'm a grown woman. I don't need anyone to watch out for me.* Those words came back to haunt her now. *I don't need anyone—I don't need anyone.* Pride talking, nothing more. At times like this, her helplessness was pounded home.

Well . . . there was no way around it. If the purse wouldn't come to her, she had to go to it. That cell phone was her only link to help. She couldn't just sit here until someone finally happened along and found her.

Heart in throat, she reached down to disengage the restraint straps that anchored both her and her chair behind the steering wheel. The hasp slipped free. For an instant, nothing happened. Bethany was about to breathe a sigh of relief. Then, with a suddenness that caught her by surprise, her chair flipped sideways, the right arm crashing against the console.

She fell sideways and forward, smacking the dash with her chest. The next instant she lay in a twisted heap on the floorboard, her head wedged against the passenger door, her neck in a painful crick, her useless legs sprawled and anchoring her lower body. *Oh, God.* She pushed and shoved, trying to right herself. The force of gravity fought against her, the van tipped at such a sharp angle that she was almost standing on her head.

Quickly out of breath from her struggle, she rested for a moment, horribly aware that she lay on top of her purse and coat. When her breathing evened out, she ignored the angle of her neck to tug on her purse. What seemed like a small eternity later, she finally wrested it free. She plucked out the phone and stared at it in concern, afraid she had damaged it in her fall. It looked intact.

She dialed the state police, praying as she did that the call would go through. When she heard a female dispatcher's voice, she went limp with relief. She quickly explained her dilemma.

"There are several accidents out that way," the woman said. "In some places, the traffic is backed up for miles both directions. Where are you, exactly?"

Bethany tried to recall the last road signs she'd seen and gave it her best guess. "I can't see a milepost to pinpoint my exact location."

"That's close enough. You're right on the highway, not all that far from town. The problem will be getting a car out there. It may take an hour or more, depending upon officer availability and how long it takes to clear the road. We're dealing with several emergency situations right now, the most urgent ones first."

Bethany stared at the fogged window above her, thinking that her situation was pretty urgent. "I understand. It's just that I'm in a rather difficult spot. You did hear me say I'm a paraplegic? I've fallen on the floorboard, and I'm lying on my coat. I'm not sure I'll even be able to cover up."

"Are you injured, ma'am?"

Bethany was tempted to say yes, just to get some help. It was no fun, lying in a twist with her neck bent sideways. But then she thought of the other people out on the road who'd been involved in accidents, people who might be injured and need assistance they might not get if she lied. "No, I'm not hurt," she admitted. "Just extremely uncomfortable and getting very cold."

"I'll get a car out there as quickly as I can," the dispatcher replied, her voice laced with concern. "Can you hold on for an hour or so?"

Bethany was loath to break the connection. "I'll be right here," she said, forcing a laugh.

After ending the call, she went back to staring up at the passenger door window which, because it was partially shielded by the angle of the vehicle, wasn't completely covered with white. Looking at the falling snow from this angle was dizzying, making her feel as if she was inside an all-white kaleidoscope. Before long, her van would be completely covered. She just hoped the ditch wasn't so deep that a highway patrolman driving by would fail to see her.

A shiver racked her body. *Cold.* It seeped through the floor, its icy fingers curling around her. She had poor circulation in her legs, which didn't help. She tended to chill more easily than other people.

She set herself to the task of dragging her coat out from under her. *Impossible.* Her rump anchored the wool to the floorboard, and the downward tilt of the vehicle made it difficult to elevate her torso. She pushed and strained and twisted about, all to no avail. In the end, the stupid coat remained under her butt.

Blinking away tears of frustration, she settled for tugging one corner of the wool over her right leg. She told herself that at least the garment protected part of her body.

The seconds dragged. To see her watch, she had to wipe condensation from the crystal face. The dispatcher had said it would be an hour, possibly longer, before an officer could reach her. Judging by how badly she was already shivering, she hated to wait that long.

Ten minutes passed, and Bethany went from shivering to shuddering. She had no idea what the ambient temperature was. Her wool skirt and blouse provided adequate warmth in a heated room, but out here, she may as well have been wearing nothing.

She glanced at the phone. Jake would be at the store. She knew if she called him he'd move heaven and earth to reach her, which was exactly why she hesitated. Her situation wasn't so dire that she wanted her brother to put himself at risk, driving in these conditions.

In the space of five minutes, Bethany felt like a vibrating icicle. She recalled Ryan's swiping the sweater for her to wear last night and wished she had it now. On the tail of that thought, she remembered how strong and wonderfully warm his arms had felt, curled so firmly around her.

Ryan. Bethany blinked and stared at the snow-covered windshield above her. His ranch wasn't far away. Maybe the highway wasn't blocked between here and there.

She grabbed the phone, then hesitated. If she made this call, it would be an irrevocable step. *Friendship.* Normally she wouldn't find that frightening. As Ryan said, no one could have too many friends. But how many women had male friends so handsome that a mere grin could give them heart palpitations?

Stupid, so stupid. It wasn't as if the man was angling for a steamy affair, after all, or even hinting at one. Recalling the gentle way he'd held her last night and the aching sincerity she'd seen in his eyes when he'd spoken to her of friendship, she instinctively trusted him.

Decision time. She could be a total idiot and lie here, freezing to death unnecessarily, or she could take Ryan up on his offer of friendship.

She tried to remember his telephone number and couldn't, so she dialed information. A moment later she was punching in the number to his residence. *Please, be home, Ryan. Please, please, be home.*

Ryan was laying a fire when the phone rang. He brushed his hands clean on his jeans and stepped to the end table to grab the portable from its base. Thinking it was his mother calling again, he bypassed saying hello. "No, I don't want to join you and Dad for snow ice cream," he said with a chuckle. "I'd have to be nuts to go out in this."

"Ryan?" a shaky feminine voice said. "This is Bethany."

She sounded awful, and his heart caught with sudden fear. "Bethany? Honey, are you crying?"

"No, no. I'm just shivering."

The hair stood up on the nape of his neck. "Shivering?"

"From cold. I'm so sorry to call you like this, but I've gotten myself into a bit of a pickle."

She went on to describe her predicament. Ryan tightened his grip on the phone. He glanced out the sliding glass doors at the blizzard in progress. "Dear God, you're stranded in this?"

Her voice quaking in a way that alarmed him, she said, "I'm not hurt or anything. Please, don't get all upset. It's not that big a deal. I think my radiator is bashed. The engine coughed and quit, so I can't run the heater." He heard her take another shivery breath. "I'm sort of—lying in a heap on the floorboard." She laughed shakily. "On top of my coat, of course. Murphy's Law, and all that."

Ryan started to pace. Long, heel-stomping steps muffled by the carpet, his body taut with alarm. "Son of a bitch. Where are you, honey?"

The picture that formed in his mind of her lying on the floorboard sent sheer terror coursing through him. She could be bleeding to death from a cut on her legs and not even know it.

"Have you checked yourself for cuts?"

"Oh, yes. Not a mark that I could find. I'm fine, honestly. Just chilly."

Chilly? She sounded as if she was lying on a vibrating bed. "Where are you?" he asked again.

"You know the Eagle Ridge turnoff? I remember seeing the sign just before I went off the road. That isn't a terribly long way from you, is it? I mean—if it is, the driving conditions are so awful I can just wait for the police. There are wrecks between here and Crystal Falls, but they're working to get the roads cleared and can be here in an hour or so."

There was no way on earth Ryan would let her lie on a cold floorboard for an hour. He knew exactly where she was, and traveling as a crow flew, he could reach her in twenty minutes. "No worries. I'm used to getting around in snow."

"I just—" She broke off and sighed, the sound shrill, shaky, and conveying such weariness, he wished he were already there with her. "Do be careful, Ryan. I'll never forgive myself if you have a wreck, trying to reach me."

"You just hold tight, honey. I'm on my way. I've got blankets in the storage compartment of my snow horse. Rafe and I are members of Search and Rescue. You'll be snug as a bug in a rug before you know it."

After breaking the connection, Ryan left the house at a dead run, tugging on his jacket as he went. Seconds later, he threw open the doors to the snowmobile shed, thanking God and all His angels that he and Rafe were always ready for an emergency. He kept a heavy plastic storage trunk on the back of his snowmobile stocked with blankets, emergency food rations, and an extensive first aid kit. He grabbed some bungee cords from a hook on the wall and stuffed them in with the rescue supplies. Then he filled the tank with fuel.

In less than five minutes, he was headed for Eagle Ridge, traveling cross country over snow-covered pastureland and through heavily wooded areas where the winter snowpack still hadn't melted.

Bethany huddled as best she could on the floorboard, shivering so hard her teeth clacked. It seemed to her that hours went by before she heard the distant sound of an engine. Her heart leaped with gladness. She craned her neck, trying to see out the window above her, but the snowfall was so thick, visibility was no more than a few feet.

Finally she heard what could only be Ryan's snowmobile approaching the highway to the north of her. The rumble grew faint, telling her the driver had turned the opposite way. Soon the sounds drifted into silence.

What if he failed to find her? She could no longer see out

the windshield. What if her van was no longer visible to someone on the road?

Minutes later she heard the snowmobile returning. "Ryan!" she cried. "Ryan, I'm down here!"

When the vehicle finally rumbled to a stop somewhere near the van, she nearly wept with relief. The engine sputtered and went quiet. Then she heard boots crunching on the snow.

"Bethany?"

His voice sounded so wonderful. Before she could reply, the passenger door opened and she nearly slid out of the van onto her head.

"Whoa, girl. I've got you."

"Ryan!"

Never had anyone felt so good. Just as she had imagined, his strong arms gathered her close. Bethany clung to his warmth, shuddering uncontrollably.

"Oh, Ryan."

She felt him run a hand over her hip. "I'm sorry, honey, but I've got to check you myself to be sure you're not hurt."

She blinked and peered over her shoulder, the oddest feeling of separateness coming over her as she watched him hike up her skirt and run big, brown hands the length of her twisted legs. His long fingers prodded the flesh-colored nylon of her support tights, and she realized he was searching for bone fractures. Normally she would have been humiliated beyond bearing. Her legs lay in an immodest sprawl at awkward angles to her body. Only this was Ryan. Not just any man. Watching the careful way he touched her, she couldn't quite muster a feeling of embarrassment.

He sighed, the sound conveying his vast relief. "You seem okay." He drew her skirt back down, then gently rearranged her legs, keeping one hand cupped over her knees as he lowered them to the floor. "Thank God for that. Huh?" He hunched his shoulders around her and tightened his embrace, pressing his face against her hair. Melting snow dripped off the brim of his Stetson and plopped on her sleeve. She felt the tension ease from his body. "Damn, honey. Talk about scaring the hell out of a fellow. I was so afraid you might be hurt."

Through chattering teeth, Bethany said, "I t-told you I wa-wasn't."

He abandoned his grip on her knees, and she felt him twisting at the waist. The next instant, his heavy jacket settled around her shoulders, the lining still warm from his body. The heat felt sublime.

He reached around her to get the phone and dialed the state police. An instant later he was speaking to a dispatcher. He quickly explained that it was unnecessary now for an officer to be sent out. After ending the call, he tucked the phone into a pocket of the jacket he'd wrapped around her. Then he smiled and gathered her close again. He looked strong and capable, the collar of his shirt flapping in the wind. The ever-present black Stetson was caked with snow.

"I can wear my own coat, Ryan," she protested. "You'll freeze."

"I'm inured to the cold. Remember? And my jacket's already warm. Maybe it'll help to chase the chill off you. We'll use your coat to cover your legs."

As he spoke, he lifted both the coat and her into his arms. Bethany hugged his neck, so glad he was there that for once it didn't alarm her to be picked up.

"One question. What in the *hell* are you doing out on these roads today?"

Against his wet collar, she said, "The weather report didn't predict snow. I went to Bend to pick up an order."

"This is Oregon, remember? And high in the mountains, no less. Never, and I do mean *never,* take a weather report as gospel in this country. The storm front was supposed to pass over north of us, but it changed direction. I've been smelling snow in the air for the past two days."

"You have?"

He struck off up the bank. When he reached the snow-mobile, he set her on the saddle seat, then covered her legs with her coat. Bethany grabbed hold of the handlebars to maintain her perch while he dug through a plastic storage compartment behind her. He dragged out two heavy lap robes and a silver insulated blanket, all three of which he wrapped around her, the silver sheet going on last to block the wind.

The entire time he was tucking the blankets around her legs, he lectured her. "The next time you take off on a long trip, you call me, and I'll go with you. There are maniacs out on these roads. What if you get a flat?"

"I can always call for road service."

"Like hell. I've got a friend who's a cop. He lectures women's groups on highway safety. Even if you call for road service, it's dangerous to remain with your vehicle. Psychos look for easy targets, and a lone woman who has car trouble along a deserted highway is one of the easiest targets on earth. You've heard people say to just put a flag on the antenna and lock the doors?"

"Yes."

"Well, that's the worst thing you can do. You're virtually sending out signals to anyone who drives by that you're all alone, broken down, and helpless. Some creep grabs a tire iron, bashes in the glass, and you're next."

"Oh, my."

"Yeah, 'oh, my,' is right." Snowflakes gathered on their faces as his steel-blue eyes met hers. In their depths, Bethany saw more fear than anger. "I don't want anything to happen to you. No long trips by yourself anymore. Agreed?"

"Sometimes I need to go places," she said weakly.

"From now on, you just holler, and I'll go with you. I can always juggle my work to take a few hours off." He sighed, closed his eyes for a second, and then hooked a hand over the back of her head and pressed his forehead against hers. "Damn. I'm sorry, I don't mean to yell. Driving here, I kept thinking of all the things that could happen and praying no one else stopped."

Before she could reply, he was gone. She watched as he collected her keys and purse, then wrested her wheelchair from the van, locked the doors, and climbed back up the bank.

"Is there anything else you'll need tonight?" he asked.

"Surely the road will be cleared before dark."

He put the chair in a carry rack at the rear of the snow-mobile and secured it with bungee cords. "Take a gander at that snow coming down. The highway will be closed until they can get it plowed, and even after they do, it'll be slick. Where's the point in taking you home when you're welcome at my place?"

"All I've got with me that's important is in my purse. I didn't plan to be away overnight."

"You have enough medication to last you?"

"No. I didn't think I'd be gone overnight and haven't got it with me."

"What all do you take?"

"Just Coumadin, a blood thinner, and a muscle relaxant at bedtime to prevent leg spasms."

He thought a moment. "A couple of glasses of wine will keep your blood thin, and it should work as a muscle relax-ant as well. I'll double-check with my mom, just to be sure."

After stowing her things in the storage compartment, he mounted the snowmobile behind her. Sitting sideways as she was, her shoulder butted his chest as he drew her close. After telling her to hug his waist, he started the engine.

"You steady on?" he asked.

"I think so."

"Hold tight, honey. I'll take it easy."

Bethany burrowed her face against his shirt, comforted by the solid warmth of him radiating through the wet cloth. After he got the snowmobile shifted into gear, he locked a strong arm around her. The vehicle surged powerfully beneath them, and they were off.

Oddly, she felt perfectly safe even when the snowmobile leaned sharply and she slipped on the seat. Ryan had a firm hold on her. The noise of the engine made talking difficult, so she simply hugged him tightly and relaxed. It was heavenly to feel at least marginally warm again.

Traveling cross-country instead of by road, Ryan was able to cut off several miles, and it didn't take long to reach his ranch. For that, he was thankful. However, he could feel Bethany shivering violently. He needed to get her warmed up—and fast.

His dog Tripper came bounding through the falling snow to greet them when Ryan pulled up near the house. He spoke softly to the mutt, but didn't give him the expected ear scratch and pat, choosing instead to gather Bethany up in his arms and hurry inside. He carried her directly to the great room where he'd been about to light a fire when she called. After depositing her on the sofa, he grabbed the portable phone and dialed his parents' place.

His mom answered on the third ring. Ryan quickly related the situation to her. "I need to get her into a hot bath," he concluded. "Can you come over?"

Ann sighed theatrically, the sound drifting faintly to Ryan over the phone line. "Dear heart, have you looked outside? Those are blizzard conditions."

"I realize that, Mom. Just hop on the snowmobile."

"Not when it's snowing this hard. I could drive off into the lake."

His mother could drive the lakeshore with her eyes closed. "Take it slow. I really need you, Mom. Another woman, you know?"

Ann sighed again. "Ryan, dear. This *is* Bethany, the girl who's had your tail tied in a knot for the last week?"

"That's right."

"I see. The same Bethany you've been searching for all your life who has eyes like pansies?"

"What's your point?"

Ann chuckled. "I think a wise man would handle this emergency himself."

Ryan thought she was teasing and laughed himself. "I appreciate the thought, Mom, but there's a time and place for everything. This ain't it."

"Use your head for something besides a hat rack," Ann said with a smile in her voice. "Opportunity knocks. You said you were going with a friendship tack."

"Right."

"So . . . get friendly."

"Mom, I rea—"

"Oops. My timer is going off. I have to run before the cookies burn."

"Mom! Don't hang—"

The line went dead. Ryan stared down at the phone, resisting the urge to cuss a blue streak.

"What's wrong?" Bethany asked, chattering with cold.

Ryan put the portable back in its base. His mother had lost her mind, but somehow he didn't think he should tell Bethany that. Smiling with his teeth clenched was a shade difficult. "Nothing, honey. Just the snow. With the visibility so poor, Mom's afraid to ride over."

"Oh." She huddled inside the blankets, gazing up at him with big, worried eyes. "I see." She waited a beat, shivered, and then said, "I really don't need a hot bath, anyway, though it was nice of you to think of it."

"You're freezing. With such poor circulation in your legs, it'll take hours for you to warm up without one."

"I'll manage."

"Manage?" Ryan scooped her up off the sofa. "We'll manage, all right."

"I can't take a bath, not with only you here to help me."

"Sure you can. I can be a very inventive fellow when I set my mind to it."

Sitting in his upholstered rocker by the fire, Keefe Kendrick studied his wife with narrowed eyes. She was grinning like Lewis Carroll's Cheshire cat as she hung up the telephone. "Annie, are you up to mischief?"

She flashed him a startled look, her gray eyes shimmering. "Mischief?"

He bit back a smile as she walked toward him. "You're not afraid you'll drive off in the lake, and if you've got cookies in the oven, I want some."

She lifted a slender shoulder in a shrug, her rounded hips displayed to mouthwatering advantage by her snug jeans. Even at sixty, his Annie was a looker, with gorgeous legs and perfectly shaped breasts that filled out her red sweater just the way he liked. "Sometimes Ryan needs a push to get moving."

She plopped her plump fanny on his lap and looped her arms around his neck. Keefe knew when his wife was trying to sidetrack him. He cocked an eyebrow. "What're you up to?"

"Hmm." She nibbled his lip. "It's snowing outside. I think snow is *so* romantic. Don't you?" She wiggled her bottom, making a certain part of his anatomy turn hard. "Let's open some wine and make love by the fire."

Keefe seized her bottom lip between his teeth and put just enough force into his bite to let her know he wasn't as dimwitted as she might think. "Annie girl, are you interfering in your son's love life?"

She kissed him, using her tongue with such expertise he nearly forgot his question. "Never. I'm just being a good mother and completely resisting the temptation to interfere. That's Bethany over at Rye's place. *The* Bethany."

Keefe trailed questing fingers up her rib cage. His Annie

was one sweet armful. "The girl with the incredibly blue eyes?" he asked huskily.

"That's the one. She got stranded in the storm, and Rye went to fetch her. She's frozen half to death and needs a hot bath. He wanted me to go over and help. Silly boy. Like I'd dream of it. Though a hot bath has interesting possibilities."

Keefe pushed suddenly to his feet. She bleated in surprise as he headed for the bathroom. Keefe's mind was brimming with images of her, rosy from hot water and slick with scented soap. "A bath definitely has interesting possibilities," he agreed with a low growl. "Sometimes, Annie girl, mischief can backfire."

Chapter Ten

Bethany sat in the bathroom, her gaze fixed on the vanity mirror, lighted by an oak bar of globes that cast glaring brightness over her and everything else. Studying herself in the glass, she decided she resembled a shuddering stick baby with huge eyes and a mop of straggly hair. No wonder Ryan was worried. She couldn't flex her leg muscles like most people to get her blood moving, which meant that half her body had an inefficient temperature-control system.

She rubbed her arms but continued to shiver. Lifting the hem of her wool skirt, she touched her knee and found it was ice cold, even through the nylon mesh of her tights. Oh, how she wished she were at home in her familiar bathroom with all her trusty bathing equipment.

A light tap came on the door. The sound startled her so that she jumped. "Come in," she managed to say in a halfway normal voice.

Her bath attendant entered—all six feet plus of him. Snow-drenched denim skimmed his long, well-muscled legs. With each step he took, his boots rapped the earth-brown tile, the sounds sharp and decisive as he advanced. He'd thrown on a dry shirt, which he hadn't buttoned. The gaping front plackets revealed an expanse of rippling bronze chest, lightly furred with black hair that narrowed to a triangular swath as it descended to his flat, striated stomach.

Her mouth went as dry as dirt, and all she could think to say was, "Hi."

"Hi," he replied, his voice deep and vibrant. The sound made her skin feel as if it were humming. "All ready?"

She'd never be ready. Her mother had helped her dress and undress enough times for her to know he couldn't do this without getting an eyeful.

His gaze as sharp as honed steel, he gave her a thoughtful once-over. From the waist down, she was still fully clothed. From there up, though, all she had on was an oversize T-shirt he'd lent her. Her blouse and bra lay in a neatly folded stack on the vanity, the bra at the bottom so he wouldn't see it.

The only bright spot in this entire, miserable mess was that he'd lent her a blue T-shirt instead of a white one. She knew from experience that white T-shirts became transparent the instant they got wet.

"Is it still snowing?" she asked.

"Yeah, it is. Sorry. No let up at all so far. I called Jake, by the way. I didn't want your family to be worried about you. He said he'll go over to feed and water your kitty." He startled her by suddenly hunkering down in front of her. His firm mouth tipped slowly into a grin as he reached up to push a damp tendril of hair from her face. "Honey, I hope all that shivering is from cold and not nerves. You're not afraid of me, are you?"

"Heavens, no." She laughed shakily and then clamped her teeth together to keep them from chattering.

"You sure?" He trailed his fingertip along her cheekbone, coming to a halt at her chin, where he spent a moment tracing the slight cleft with the back of a knuckle. "I've been trying to put myself in your shoes. It's a little difficult. I know this has to be tough, though."

"I'm fine, Ryan. Honestly. I just wish a bath wasn't necessary."

"I have it all figured out."

Uh-huh. He obviously hadn't taken into account that without support bars or a dressing sling, she couldn't even get her panties and tights off without help. At home, she managed by herself with her equipment, and even then, it was no easy task.

"Trust me," he said softly. "Good friends don't embarrass each other."

"I just wish I were h-home, is all. I have everything I need there."

"I'm sorry I don't have everything you need here. I will have soon."

"Oh, no. You mustn't start buying stuff for me."

"Why not?"

She knew there were a dozen good reasons, but she couldn't readily think of one. "Because?"

He chuckled. "One of the advantages of having so damned much money is being able to buy things for my friends whenever the mood strikes. Have you any idea how much fifty million earns annually in interest? My tax obligation looks like the national debt."

Bethany couldn't conceive of having that much money. "You poor thing."

He narrowed an eye. "I'm running a business out here, and anything I buy to accommodate the handicapped, namely you, will be a much-needed write-off."

"I see."

"We do have handicapped buyers come out to look at our horses. If I want to buy stuff to make you more comfortable at my ranch, I'll do it, no arguments. All right?"

"All right."

He smiled slightly. "We are going to pursue this friendship thing. Right?"

"I d-don't part with my clothes for just anybody, so I think it's safe to say I consider you to be a very good friend."

That elicited a chuckle from him. "So I can rest my case?"

"Please, don't. The longer you talk, the longer I can put this off."

"There, you see? The situation we have right now is awful. You need a hot bath, and getting you in the tub is a major production, with you all nervous and upset. I'd like to be set up so it's as comfortable for you here as at home. That way, when you need a bath, you can get in the tub by yourself."

"Are you a clean freak?"

"A what?"

"If you're given to sniffing armpits, I may have to reconsider this friendship thing."

He sighed and shook his head. "A smart ass when you're nervous. I should have known."

Guilty as charged. She did tend to crack jokes when she felt uneasy, and right now she felt extremely uneasy.

"Out here, being able to grab a quick bath is a necessity. You've been around animals. Get slapped by a muddy horse tail, and you'll be glad I planned ahead for the eventuality."

Bethany rubbed her arms. "I just wish you were set up for it now."

"I know."

His voice dipped to a husky tenor, and by that she knew he understood how unpleasant this was for her. Somehow, that helped.

She took a bracing breath that shuddered in and out because she was shaking so hard. "Okay," she said, trying to inject some confidence into her voice. "I'm ready. Let's do it and get it over with."

"Will it make you feel any better to know that I called our foreman, Sly, and he's already at work in the welding shop, whipping together some makeshift bathroom bars?"

"He is?"

"When we're finished here, I'll go over to help him. What we come up with won't be fancy, but you'll be halfway comfortable here until morning, anyway."

Bathroom bars? Bethany almost hugged him. She resisted the urge to glance at the commode. Makeshift was fine. Makeshift was *wonderful*. She didn't care if the bars they fashioned were pretty as long as they enabled her to manage that necessity without help.

Still hugging her waist and shivering, she said, "I hate to put you to so much bother, Ryan."

"It's not a bother, honey. We do a lot of welding here on the ranch, and I've got tons of pipe lying around. We'll have something thrown together in just a few minutes." He pushed back to his feet and leaned down. "Hug my neck, sweetheart. Let's get you in that tub. I'm starting to feel cold, just watching you."

Oh, how she dreaded this. There was no way around it, though. "Maybe you could just wrap me in an electric blanket. That'd chase the chill away."

"I don't have one. I'm sorry. I have down quilts on all the beds."

"I could just sit close to the fire."

Much as he had last night, he grasped her wrists and put her arms around his neck himself. "Feel how badly you're shaking? You're going in the tub. You're not catching pneumonia on my watch. Jake would never forgive me."

Jake. Oh, how she wished Jake were there.

"Have a little faith in me," Ryan whispered.

She envisioned him trying to hold her erect with one arm and tugging clumsily at her clothes with his other hand, her body smashed against his the entire while. *Oh, God . . . oh, God.* Her face went hot with shame.

"This will be over before you can yell, 'Hallelujah.'"

She fully expected the usual ordeal she experienced with her mother on swim nights, with him grunting and straining, and her legs flopping every which way like limp noodles.

She should have known better. After catching her around the waist with one arm, Ryan straightened as if she weighed scarcely anything. The next thing she knew, she was clasped to his chest, her lower body dangling.

"Oh, God!"

"It's all right, honey. I won't drop you."

He groped under the T-shirt to unfasten her skirt. That accomplished, he divested her of the garment, her tights, and her panties in one fell swoop. She felt his fingertips graze bare skin at the small of her back, but otherwise he executed the maneuver without touching her intimately. The next thing she knew, he was tugging down the hem of the T-shirt and putting her back in the chair.

"There, you see?" He crouched in front of her again to tug the elasticized stockings down her calves. "No fuss, no muss. That wasn't so bad, was it?"

It hadn't been bad at all, and the very fact that it hadn't been made her feel trembly.

He grasped her by each ankle to remove her black doeskin slippers and then swept her clothing aside. "Damn, honey, your feet are like ice." He skimmed a hand up her calf. "No wonder you're shaking."

Bethany tugged at the hem of the T-shirt, trying to keep her knees covered. "I can't believe it was so easy. It's always a struggle when Mama helps me."

He slanted her an amused look. "I saw your mom at the grange last night. She's not much bigger than a minute, so that comes as no surprise." After setting her slippers aside, he stood. "Now I'll just pick you up and put you in the tub. If you'll make a fist on the hem of the shirt, it won't float up as I put you in. I brought a clothespin to do anchor duty once I get you situated."

A clothespin? He truly had thought of everything.

As he bent over her, Bethany braced herself, visually aware as he caught her behind the knees with one arm, sensually aware when his left arm slipped between the chair and her back. A big warm hand curled over her side, strong fingers splaying on her ribs just beneath her breast.

"Easy, sweetheart," he said as he lifted her. "I've got you."

He had her, all right. She felt surrounded by vibrant, male strength. Heat radiated through the T-shirt from his bare chest, and coarse, springy black hair rubbed against one of her elbows. He felt so marvelous, she almost took a taste of his sturdy neck. It was the color of caramel, which was right behind chocolate as one of her favorite flavors on earth.

He went down on one knee beside the tub, lifting her over the edge and then gently lowering her into the water he'd already drawn. He kept one arm hooked under her knees to carefully position her legs.

As he had suggested, she grabbed a handful of T-shirt hem so the cotton wouldn't float up. "You're very good at this."

"It seems to come naturally." He flicked her another smiling glance as he drew a clothespin from his breast pocket. Brushing her hand aside and grasping the hem of the T-shirt, he gave it a twist to draw the cotton snug around her thighs, then secured it with the pin.

Bethany watched as he turned on the hot and cold water, then shoved a broad wrist under the stream to check the temperature. As he adjusted the valves, he said, "We'll have you warmed up in no time flat."

She sighed in appreciation and sank a little lower in the water. "Oh, this is lovely." The warm water he was running from the tap curled around her hips. "Thank you so much. I'm sorry to be so much work."

"You're no work. I'm glad to have you here."

The heat was helping her to stop shivering, and her jerking muscles began to relax. Ryan started massaging her legs, his sun-burnished hands striking a sharp contrast to her pale skin. As she watched, she found herself wishing she could feel his touch. She imagined his palms would be slightly rough, the grip of his long, thick fingers wonderfully warm. *Don't go there, Bethany. Friendship. No more, no less.* She couldn't allow her silly female heart to start spinning fantasies and risk ruining what promised to be a good friendship.

He caught her staring at his hands and said, "I thought I might get the blood moving. I'm not hurting you, am I?"

"No. If only you could."

He gave her a bewildered look. Then he winced. "Right. I'm sorry. Stupid question. I just thought—hell, I don't know what I was thinking." He worked his way up to just above her knee, "You can't feel anything at all? Not anywhere? That's so hard for me to fathom. Intellectually, I know it, but on a more instinctive level, I automatically think in terms of having sensation."

Bethany managed a strained smile. "Don't apologize. I'm the abnormal one, not you. And as it happens, I do have a couple of live spots." She touched a fingertip to the inside of her left thigh. "One right there."

He stared at the spot she indicated as if he were committing the location to memory. "Just there?"

"A couple of other places, too. Nerve damage is a weird thing, especially in my case, where the worst damage occurred on one side of the spine. I have sensation in places I shouldn't, and none in places I ought to. Right after I got hurt, our family doctor and a local specialist stood over me, frowning and scratching their heads a lot. I didn't conform to the textbooks and journals."

He frowned thoughtfully. "So you're not completely numb in your legs?"

"Not completely. The numbness is spotty from the point of injury down to the tops of my thighs and grows worse from there until I'm completely numb." She lowered her voice to a conspiratorial whisper. "I have very good feeling in my derriere, for instance, and can detect wiggling thumbs."

She expected him to laugh. Instead, his gaze darted to the juncture of her thighs. "Don't grab me by the hair and shove my head under water for asking. Okay? One friend to another. Are you numb there?"

Bethany wasn't sure how her face could turn so hot when she was still so cold otherwise, but somehow it did.

He immediately backtracked. "I'm sorry. Inappropriate question." He returned his attention to the water faucets, then checked the bath to see how hot it was. "Just curious, is all. You seem convinced you may not be able to have a normal physical relationship. If you've got any sensation at all there, I was just wondering why."

"For starters, I've been told flat-out by my doctor that I probably can't."

"Doctors can be wrong."

"I know, but given his reputation as a spinal specialist, his opinion carries a lot of weight. He's one of the best on the West Coast." Bethany trailed her fingertips over the surface of the water, keeping her gaze carefully averted. "Nerve damage is a strange thing. One nerve may work fine, but another nearby that's vital to the operation may be a dud. A bell with no ding, in other words?"

He chuckled. "Now, there's a way to put it."

"However one puts it, who can say what I'll be able to feel or experience? I can only go by what Doctor Reicherton told me, which wasn't encouraging."

He arched a dark eyebrow. "So you've never—you know—tried a solo flight to check things out yourself?"

Her gaze flicked back to his. "No, I, um—" She shrugged, feeling suddenly uncomfortable. How could she explain that she'd chosen to keep a lid on her sexuality? It made little sense to kindle physical needs and yearnings she might never be able to satisfy. "I haven't dated since my accident, and I guess I never saw much point in checking out the possibilities." She flashed him an impish smile. "Besides, one of my brothers nearly went blind from doing stuff like that."

He huffed with laughter. Then a ruddy flush crawled up his neck. It was his turn to avert his gaze. "I'm sorry. I shouldn't have asked." He tested the water again. "I think that's about hot enough for now. What do you think?"

She thought he felt as uncomfortable with the conversation as she did, which had the odd effect of making her feel more relaxed. "It feels wonderful."

He shut off the faucets, then turned to sit on the floor beside the tub, his broad back braced against the creamy tile that went halfway up the wall. Lifting one knee to support a loosely bent arm, he settled a twinkling gaze on her.

She walked her fingertips down her thigh, stopping at her knee and then backtracking. When she glanced back up, he was tugging on his earlobe, a gesture she was fast coming to recognize as a nervous habit. "I honestly am sorry," he said huskily. "I don't know what possessed me to ask you such a thing. It's not really any of my business, and it was rude to pry."

She mulled that over for a moment. "I don't really mind your asking. I'm just not sure how to answer. It's sort of like living in town and owning a high-powered rifle. If you know you'll never have occasion to use it, you just lock it away somewhere safe and forget you've got it."

He smiled and nodded. "I can associate with that." He tugged on his ear again. "So . . . tell me about your family. You and Jake seem very close. Do you have the same kind of relationship with your other brothers?"

Happy to change the subject, Bethany launched into a brief description of her siblings. "In a large family like ours, it's never easy being the youngest, and I think it was especially difficult being the only girl. Too many protectors. Someone was always watching after me. It took a lot of maneuvering on my part to get away with anything."

"I'm sure your folks appreciated your brothers' efforts."

"Oh, yes. They never had to worry about me much. When Jake went away to college, there was Zeke to take up the slack, and after he left, the twins were always breathing down my neck."

"The veterinarians in progress."

She nodded. "Next oldest was Hank, twenty-eight to my twenty-six. He was just close enough to me in age to be more of a friend than a pain in the neck. Occasionally he even aided and abetted."

"And your folks? I've met your dad down at the store. He seems like a nice man. What's your mom like? I saw her from a distance last night. She looks like a sweetheart."

She is that." Bethany flattened a hand over her waist. "You have to know her to get the whole picture. She's— what are the words?—a plump nun in street clothes who just happens to be married and have six kids, all of whom she'll swear were magically dropped into Daddy's boot during the night while they were sleeping. Sometimes I almost think she believes it herself."

He laughed at the description. "I can tell by your expression that you love her a lot."

Bethany nodded. "She's a neat lady. Just a little naive. Daddy is from the old school, and he's always shielded her. Me, too, for that matter. He just wasn't quite as successful at the endeavor. If it had been left up to him, I would have been given information about the birds and the bees on a strictly need-to-know basis."

"That birds tweet and bees buzz?"

"Exactly. When we still had the ranch, he went to incredible pains to make sure I never saw the horses breeding." She flashed him a smile. "It caused me no end of difficulty."

"You sneaked to watch," he said with a knowing smile.

"Of *course*."

He shook his head. "Your poor dad. Raising you must have been a trial."

"For him or me? It can be incredibly stifling when you're daddy's little angel. If I had it to do over again, I would have been sexually active at twelve."

"Twelve? That terrifies me. Heidi's twelve."

"Who's Heidi?"

His eyes shimmered with fondness as he described Maggie's little sister. "She keeps asking me to wait until she's grown so she can marry me. She keeps me on my toes. I love her to death, and I don't want to wound her. At the same time, I don't want to encourage her, either. It's a fine line."

"She sounds darling."

"Yeah." The slash in his cheek deepened as he grinned. "Won't be long before the boys line up at the door. I'll have to go over to help Rafe kick butt."

"I was so crazy about horses as a teenager that I wasn't much interested in boys until I met Paul. Maybe Heidi will be like that."

"Maybe. She wants to barrel race."

"Really?" Bethany's interest was piqued, and she was about to pursue the topic when he broke in with, "Speaking of Paul. How did it happen that you tied up with a kid that age who didn't know squat about kissing?"

"We were young, for one, and Paul was a minister's son and very devout. We mostly just—" She felt suddenly embarrassed and wondered how they'd ever gotten off on such a subject. "We were waiting until we got married."

His mouth hardened. "Too bad he didn't keep his fly zipped with your little friend. What was her name?"

"Nan. How'd you know about her?"

Something dark flickered in his eyes again, and he suddenly became unaccountably interested in the ceiling. "Their marriage was announced in the newspaper as I recall. Not exactly a state secret. Right?"

Bethany's nape prickled. "Why do guys always stare at the ceiling when they lie?"

His gaze dropped back to hers. "You have too many brothers."

"Jake?" she whispered. It wasn't really a question.

Ryan sighed. "You're very lucky, you know. Having an older brother who loves you so much. He'd fight a mountain lion for you, bare-handed."

"He called to talk to you."

He sighed again and said, "Damn. Me and my big mouth. I never meant to rat on him." He shook his head. "And, no, he didn't call. He showed up here Saturday night. We had a nice, long chat."

"Nice? You and Jake?"

"Well, it wasn't nice initially. But he settled down once we talked, and I convinced him my intentions toward you are honorable."

"That we just want to be friends?"

He smiled slightly. "Yeah. The best of friends. He's okay with that. He meant no harm by coming out here, you know. He's just watching out for you. I admire him for that."

"Stick around. Soon your admiration for him will know no bounds."

"I plan to," he assured her.

"Plan to, what?"

"Stick around."

Lying before the fire with his wife clasped in his arms, Keefe felt the tension in her body. After the intense love-making they'd just shared, he felt confident her mood wasn't due to lack of sexual gratification.

"What's wrong, Annie mine?" he asked, smoothing a hand over her hair and kissing her brow.

"A guilty conscience," she confessed. "I should have gone over to Ryan's. Normally, not interfering would be all well and fine, but I keep thinking about that poor girl. If she had another woman to help her, she'd feel much better."

"Hmm."

"Do you think I should run over?"

"It's so nice, lying here. A snowmobile ride doesn't sound appealing."

"You don't have to go."

He sighed. "And risk letting my wife drive off in the lake in a snowstorm?"

"I won't drive off in the lake. I know the way blind-folded."

Keefe pushed up on his elbow. "If I stay here, I'll miss getting to meet my new daughter-in-law."

"He hasn't married her yet."

Keefe chuckled. "Yeah, well . . . Ryan always has been slow to do things. He'll get around to it."

"Slow? By whose standards?"

"Kendrick standards. Been me, I would've had her to Reno and back already. Never have understood that boy. He thinks every damned thing half to death before he does it."

Ann hugged his neck. "I'll let you go with me, under one condition."

"What's that?"

"Don't give him any advice."

Keefe scowled. "Why not?"

"Because he's managing just fine on his own, and I don't want him doing anything harebrained, like abducting her."

"I didn't abduct you."

"You pretended we were lost and kept me out in the wilderness for five days. If that's not abduction, what is it?"

"A damned smart move. By the time I got you home, you'd agreed to marry me. I saved myself weeks of frustra-tion." He winked and grinned. "I also did you a big favor. By the time I took you home, you knew that skinny little college boy wasn't so hot, after all. There was also no question in your mind that I could take care of you, regardless of the situation."

"Ah, yes." Ann rolled onto her back, chuckled, and closed her eyes. "You even started a fire with two sticks. Remember that? Later I found out you had a cigarette lighter in your pocket the entire time."

"I also had another blanket in my saddle pack."

"What?"

Keefe leaned over and kissed the end of her nose. "You heard me. I had two blankets."

Ann grabbed him by the ears. "You rotten, conniving scoundrel."

Relaxed from her bath, Bethany toasted in front of the fire while she waited for Ryan to return from the welding shop. From where she sat, she could gaze out the sliding glass doors at the falling snow, which created a pretty winter scene. The lake gleamed like polished black glass, its shores lined with thick stands of towering, snow-laden trees. Dusk had already descended, making everything look misty and ethereal near the ground, the shades of charcoal turning to soot against the sky.

Snuggling deeper in her chair, she savored the quietness, which gave her some thinking time to come to terms with her predicament. Not that this really qualified as a predicament. She'd had a wreck, and now she was stranded here for the night, a situation that had all the earmarks of a disaster for someone in a wheelchair. But so far, Ryan had seen to her every need and managed to do so in such a way that she felt cosseted rather than embarrassed.

Just as predicted, he had gotten her dressed with little difficulty. After lining her chair with a bath sheet, he had lifted her from the tub, set her on the terry, and left. She removed the wet T-shirt, dried off, and put on a fresh one. Then he had returned to help her into a pair of gray sweatpants with elasticized cuffs and a drawstring waist, which had gone on as easily as her skirt and panties had come off. Her oversize ensemble was complemented by a gigantic pair of gray wool socks with red triangular patches at toe and heel.

After getting her dressed, he had pushed her into the great room to sit near the fire, tucked a sofa throw around her shoulders, and then moved some of the furniture to create wider traffic paths. Before leaving for the welding shop, he had fixed her a cup of hot cocoa. Considering the dire circumstances she'd faced less than two hours ago, Bethany felt as if she were caught up in a lovely dream, where nothing was quite as it should be.

Ryan. Thinking of him brought a smile to her lips. How many men would have thought to use a clothespin to keep her T-shirt from floating up? He was so sweet and wonderful.

"Yo! It's me!" a deep voice called out.

Bethany jumped with a start, then turned to see Ryan in the entry. "That was fast."

She no sooner spoke than she realized it wasn't Ryan after all, but a stranger who looked enough like him to be his twin. The man froze in his boot tracks, clearly as surprised to see her as she was him. When he jerked off his black Stetson, the melting snow on its brim sent droplets flying.

"Howdy. You must be Bethany." He brushed at the flakes on the sleeve of his lined denim jacket. "Sorry for dripping on the floor. I tried to shake off outside, but more snow just blew in under the porch overhang."

"You must be . . ."

"Rafe. You met my wife Maggie last night."

Bethany nodded. "She's lovely."

"I think so." He finger-combed his hair, the gesture reminding her of Ryan. She'd heard that the Kendrick brothers closely resembled each other, but she hadn't realized until now that they were dead ringers. "I'm sorry for barging in on you." He glanced at her borrowed clothing. "I didn't know Ryan had company."

"Yes, well, it came as something of a surprise to Ryan as well." She quickly related the string of events that had led to her being there.

"You're not hurt, are you?"

"Not even a scratch. It really wasn't much of an accident. The worst of it was all the wrecks, making it difficult for anyone to come get me. Weather allowing, someone in my family will come collect me in the morning."

"I doubt Ryan's in any big hurry to get rid of you. More like, dancing to the snow gods."

"Pardon?"

A ruddy flush crept up his dark neck. He tugged on his ear, yet another gesture that reminded her of Ryan. "Nothing."

Cold air coming in the open doorway curled around Bethany's shoulders, and she drew the throw more snugly around her. Rafe snapped erect, reached to close the door, and then hesitated. "Do you care if I shut it?"

Bethany couldn't help but laugh. "No, please do. I've already been chilled to the bone once today."

"I'm sorry." He closed the door. "I just—well, you know—me being a stranger and all. I thought you might be leery. Leerious, as Sly would say."

Bethany laughed. "I'm not the leerious type."

Even with the jacket providing camouflage, she saw his shoulders relax. "No, I can see you're not. That's good. We don't stand much on ceremony."

"Most ranchers don't."

He grinned, the crooked twist of his mouth once again putting her strongly in mind of Ryan. "That's right. You're no stranger to cows, are you?"

"No, although it's been a long while since I've been around them. You look so much like Ryan, it's astounding."

"People do say we look a little alike."

"A little? You could pass for identical twins."

"Nah. I'm a lot better looking." The corners of his mouth twitched. "Maggie tells me so all the time."

"I'm sure she's speaking from the heart."

"And seeing through rose-colored glasses, to boot."

"We only chatted for a couple of minutes, but she left me with an impression of warmth and sincerity. I liked her immensely."

"I like her a lot myself."

He rested a shoulder against the door. Once again, the way he stood, with most of his weight on one long leg, reminded her of Ryan. He studied her for a moment, his gray-blue eyes seeming to miss nothing. Then he smiled slowly. "Where is Ryan, anyway? I'm surprised he's not joined to you at the hip."

"He's over at the welding shop, wherever that is."

"What's he doing over there?"

"He, um—" Bethany tried to think of a delicate way of putting it. "He's building bars."

"Bars?"

"For the bathroom."

She saw it click. He pushed away from the door, tapping his hat against his thigh. "Well, I guess I'll mosey over that way." He inclined his dark head. "Good meeting you. Maggie says you may come out for a visit. She gets lonely for female company, living so far from town, so I hope you'll do that soon."

"I'm looking forward to it."

He opened the door, started to step out, and then stopped. "I guess I won't mosey, after all. Here comes Ryan now."

Bethany heard male voices and boots crunching on the snow, along with what sounded like a snowmobile coming toward the house.

"Hey, Mom and Dad," she heard Ryan say. "What brings you over this way?"

"You said you needed help," a female voice rang out. "Your father offered to drive me over so I wouldn't end up in the lake."

"I've got it under control now."

"Really? Well, that's good," the woman replied. "We'll just come in and meet Bethany before we leave, if that's all right."

Ryan made a grunting sound and metal clanked. "It's not all right. She isn't dressed to meet a bunch of people, and I don't want her feeling—*Mom,* get back here."

Rafe flashed Bethany a grin and threw the door wide. "Hi, Mom." A petite blonde came stomping into the entry. She fluffed her hair with fine-boned hands to rid it of snow, then offered her cheek to Rafe for a kiss. "Hi, dear heart," she said cheerfully, her large gray eyes flicking past him to find Bethany in front of the brick hearth. "Johnny-jump-ups. No wonder he's been waxing poetic."

Bewildered by the comment, Bethany nodded in greeting. "Hello. You must be Ryan's mom."

"Ann," she corrected warmly as she crossed the room, her right hand extended in greeting. "And you're Bethany, of course. Ryan's told us so much about you."

"He has?"

"All of it good."

Ann Kendrick had a firm handshake and a steady, sincere gaze. Bethany liked her. No artifice, none of the distance that so often erected a wall between strangers. She was simply Ann, dressed in snug jeans, well-worn riding boots, and a denim jacket rubbed white at the elbows. Looking at her, Bethany never would have guessed she was one of the richest women in town. No diamonds, no gold. The only flashy thing about Ann Kendrick was her beautiful smile.

After the handshake, Ann linked fingers with Bethany and sat on the hearth. "You look none the worse for your experience today. I understand you had a wreck?"

"Not really a wreck, more just a fender bender with a huge rock." Bethany was beginning to feel like a stuck recording. "I wasn't hurt."

"That's good. Ryan said you got a bad chill."

Bethany explained how her coat and purse had been thrown to the floorboard upon impact. "I never realized before how much cold air seeps up through the floor of a vehicle until I was lying on one."

Ann sighed. "Well, I'm very glad you thought to call Ryan."

Just then a snow-encrusted Ryan came backing in the open doorway, wrestling and cursing a huge network of piping that refused to fit through the opening. Bethany gaped. How many bars did they think she needed, anyway?

"Dear God," Ann whispered. "He's built you a sky-scraper, honey."

Bethany stifled a giggle. It *did* look like a small sky-scraper, with a triangular pull-up bar dangling on a chain from the uppermost crossbar.

"Son of a *bitch*." Ryan popped a barked knuckle into his mouth.

"That'll be ten dollars," Ann called out. "I'm keeping track."

Ryan flashed her a glare and muttered under his breath.

"Bring her in through the sliding glass doors," Rafe suggested.

"And then what? If she won't fit through here, she sure as hell won't fit through the bathroom doorway," Ryan said.

A wiry old cowboy with a turkey neck and a face so baked and wrinkled by the sun it resembled a crumpled brown paper sack manned the opposite end of the sky-scraper. His droopy tan Stetson looked like an extension of his body, the camel shade of the battered, badly soiled felt almost the same color as his skin. With solemn eyes, he peered through the bars at Ryan. "You reckon she'd fit if we tipped her over?"

"Why is it," Ann mused softly, "that men automatically think that anything difficult is a female?"

Bethany nearly choked on a giggle. "I have no idea. In this case, I'm glad it's a she, though. I'll be getting up close and personal with that contraption."

Ann's eyes danced with merriment as she resumed watching the men.

Waving his injured hand, Ryan stepped back to regard the framework from all angles. The brim of his Stetson and the shoulders of his jacket were covered with snow, and his fresh jeans were wet to the knees. Observing him, Bethany couldn't help but recall that he'd said this would be no bother.

Just then an older gentleman who looked very like Ryan and Rafe appeared outside on the porch beside the wiry cowboy, whom Bethany guessed to be Sly. "What you got the girl figured for, son, a trapeze artist?"

"Enough, Dad. We didn't know how high to make the bars, so we made two. And Sly thought a pull bar would be nice, so we made it tall. Otherwise, all us guys would hit our heads every time—" He broke off and glanced at Bethany. "Every time we went to see a man about a dog," he finished.

Ryan's father grinned through the bars at Bethany. "I'm Keefe Kendrick, by the way. Ain't this a hell of a way to get acquainted with people?"

That was an understatement. She couldn't remember a time when her bathroom requirements had been the main topic of discussion among strangers.

Oddly, after the first wave of intense embarrassment passed, she was able to relax, mainly because everyone else was so matter-of-fact. They all got into the act, finally managed to get the contraption into the house, and then worked together as a team to fit it in the bathroom. The ribbing and laughter ran rampant, and soon Bethany was chuckling right along with everyone else.

"Ya-hoo!" Keefe Kendrick said in a booming voice when the job was finally completed. "Butter my ass and call me a biscuit. I think the damned thing might work, son. Let's have her give it a try."

Bethany threw a startled look at Ryan's father, half afraid he meant for her to try it out right then.

"Come on," he urged.

Oh, God, that was exactly what he had in mind.

"Not for real," Ryan assured her. "We just need to see if the bars are right. If not, I'll run get the portable welder, and we'll make some quick adjustments."

So it happened that Bethany first tried out her skyscraper while everyone looked on. The triangle pull-up bar proved to be a marvelous improvement on the bars she had at home. She was able to grab hold of it and swing from her chair so easily she whooped with delight. Her audience applauded, and Ryan and Sly beamed with pride for having devised something that worked so well.

"Ryan, this is *wonderful*!"

"You really like it?" he asked hopefully.

"Oh, I *love* it. When I leave, can I take it home with me?"

"No way. That monster is staying put. If you really like it, we'll build you another one for your place."

Bethany frowned. "You don't really mean to leave it here."

"It won't be so ugly if you paint it."

She gave him an incredulous look. "Paint it?"

He winked at her. "I'll spray paint it first, then you can paint little flowers and doodads here and there. It'll pretty right up."

"Painting it would take me days."

"Works for me."

Keefe, who stood in the doorway with an arm around his wife's shoulders, gave the skyscraper a long, narrow look.

To Bethany, he said, "If you don't want us fellas bitchin' like a bunch of women about the toilet seat, you'd best remember to wrap that chain around a sidebar after you use it, honey. Otherwise somebody's gonna get his pearly whites knocked down his throat."

Ann smiled serenely. "What are you going to name her, Bethany? Anything that big and homely needs a handle."

Still perched on her throne, Bethany thought for a moment and then swatted the pull bar. "I think I'll call her 'Sweet Revenge.'"

Chapter Eleven

E veryone had dinner at Ryan's, a family gathering made
complete when Rafe drove home to fetch Maggie, his
mother-in-law Helen, and the three kids. Only Becca, the
housekeeper-cum-nanny, who had the evening off, was unable to attend. After some good-natured bickering, spaghetti
was chosen as the main course with garlic bread, salad, and
green beans on the side.

Usually people assumed Bethany couldn't help with meal
preparations. In the Kendrick family, everyone was expected to help, including Sly, who was sent over to Ann's
house to fetch fresh garlic. Bethany was recruited to prepare
the bread. Ryan and his mom put on the spaghetti sauce.
Helen was in charge of setting the table, Maggie and Rafe
fixed the salad. Grandpa Keefe and Heidi were assigned
baby-sitting duty, a task they seemed to greatly enjoy.

The comradeship reminded Bethany of her own family,
and she settled into the Kendrick circle easily, smiling at
their teasing banter, laughing when the ragging was turned
on her. She found herself wishing that the evening wouldn't
end—or, more precisely, that the feeling of belonging didn't
have to end.

Ryan. Occasionally their gazes would lock, and the look
in his eyes made her heart catch. *You see?* he seemed to be
saying. *This can work. It will work, if only you'll give me a
chance.*

"Toes!" Bethany warned as she took the bread over to

slip it in the preheated oven. "I run over all feet that get in my way."

"You're just hoping to get out of drying dishes," Maggie said with a laugh. "No such luck, lady. We'll take our chances."

The baby awoke and started to cry just then. In the middle of reading a story to Jaimie, Keefe hollered from the great room. "Heidi's talking on the phone. Can someone take care of Amelia? Jaimie and I are to the good part."

"Bethany, can you take care of her? I'm on mop-up detail." Maggie dabbed at Rafe's cheeks with a towel. "Poor baby. Onions do it to you every time."

"I'm not good with babies," Bethany said. "I haven't been around them."

"No time like the present to start," Maggie replied cheerfully. "She may be wet. Her disposable diapers are in the bag there by the sofa."

Bethany went to the great room. Amelia was not a happy camper. Lying on the sofa with pillows plumped around her as bolsters, she was thrashing all her limbs and screaming. Sly stood to one side, gnarled hands at his hips, chin jutted, eyes crinkled as he peered down at her. Judging by the expression on his weathered face, he was more at home with cows. No help there.

'Have you ever changed a diaper?" Bethany asked hopefully.

"Never have much truck with kids 'til they can walk and wipe their noses."

Sly didn't run after making that pronouncement. A true cowboy sauntered, even if he was putting out a fire. Sly did, however, manage to saunter away with amazing speed.

Bethany lifted Amelia from the blankets. The baby's face went serene. She fixed Bethany with big brown eyes and smiled, showing off two tiny teeth.

"Hello," Bethany said softly. She felt inside the little girl's diaper, and sure enough, it was wet. Never having changed a diaper before, Bethany whispered, "Oh, boy. I'm not sure I'm ready for you, Amelia."

Keefe glanced up from the storybook. "There's nothing to it, honey. The diapers have tape tabs. They go on slicker than greased owl dung."

"We have no babies in our family yet, so my experience with them is nil."

"Amy isn't hard to please." He cuddled Jaimie closer and turned the page of the storybook. "If you don't do it exactly right, she won't give a rip."

Bethany's hands trembled as she dug in the bag for a diaper. She kept expecting the baby to start screaming with impatience, but Amelia only gurgled and smiled, as if all the stops and starts were loads of fun.

Heidi returned just as Bethany got the diaper off. She leaned over the back of the couch, her big brown eyes curious but friendly. "Ryan says you were an awesome barrel racer."

Bethany glanced up. "Not bad. I hear you're a barrel racer, yourself."

Heidi wrinkled her nose. She looked very like her older sister, Maggie, with the same delicate features and a wealth of dark brown hair. "I'm trying to be. Ryan said that maybe, if I asked you real nice, you'd come out to watch me race and give me some tips."

"Oh, gosh, I . . ."

"Please?" Heidi inserted. "He says you took state *three* times. That makes you an all-time great, practically a *legend.*"

"Not quite that good," Bethany said with an embarrassed laugh.

Heidi glanced down at the baby. "You're s'posed to wipe her off now."

"Oh." Bethany felt foolish, having a twelve-year-old give her instruction in diaper changing. There was no help for it. "What should I use to wipe her with?"

"A wipe." Heidi came around the end of the teal sofa to rifle through the bag. She finally located a slender white plastic case filled with disposable cloths. She plucked out one and handed it over. "Haven't you ever done this?"

"No." Bethany dabbed at Amelia's bare bum. "This is my first time."

"You're doing good," Heidi assured her. "You don't have to be so careful, though. Just wipe her off all over, making sure you get in the wrinkles. Otherwise Maggie says she gets all sore. Then you put on powder."

Bethany did as instructed, and soon Amelia was put back together again. The baby chortled happily and kicked her feet, her chubby legs churning beneath the ruffled hem of her cute little red-checked dress.

"We make a pretty good team," Bethany told Heidi as she gathered the baby onto her lap. "When the mud dries up, I suppose I could come out and watch you race the barrels some afternoon."

Heidi's eyes went wide. "You will? For true? *Wow.* Just wait 'til I tell Alice. She'll be green."

Bethany laughed again. "Alice? Another barrel racer, I presume?"

"Yeah, and she's a lot better than me. Now I'll have an edge."

"I don't know how much I can really help you," Bethany warned. "I can't get on a horse and show you anything. Advice can only help so much."

"It'll help me oodles. I just know it! And we don't have to wait for the mud to dry up. Ryan can figure out something."

"Ryan can figure out what?"

Bethany glanced up to see the topic of conversation walking toward them. He leaned down to rest his elbows on the sofa back. "You volunteering me for something, Heidi girl?"

"Only to figure out a way for Bethany to watch me race the barrels. She's worried about the mud."

Ryan smiled at Bethany. "She has a fixation about mud. Not a problem. I can lay out planks, if nothing else. Can you come out next Saturday? That'll be easier than trying to schedule a time after school."

"I have Saturdays off," Bethany agreed. "That would be a good day."

Heidi was so excited, she bounced up and down. "This is *so* cool." She took Bethany by surprise, leaning down to hug her and kiss her cheek. "I was so sure I just *totally* wouldn't like you. But you're so nice, I can't help myself."

Bethany was still laughing as the young girl went racing back to the bedroom to call her friend on Ryan's extension. "Why on earth was she so sure she wouldn't like me?"

Ryan chuckled. "I think she sees you as competition."

"Uh-oh."

He settled a twinkling gaze on her. "You're home free. In the order of importance, I rank well below barrel racing, thank God."

"I'm not a competitor for your affections, in any case."

"Nope. Not in any case," he agreed.

Story time over, Keefe set Jaimie down and watched him scamper away to the kitchen. The child was a pint-size replica of his grandfather, his dark hair and skin earmarking him as a Kendrick by blood.

Bethany's gaze shifted to Ryan. "He looks so much like you."

Ryan gazed after the child, his expression thoughtful. "Yeah, he does. I keep accusing Rafe of hiding in Maggie's woodpile three winters ago, but he swears he wasn't anywhere near Prior, Idaho, when the kid was conceived."

Bethany frowned and shot a startled glance after the little boy. "Pardon?"

"He isn't Rafe's biological son. He was a month old when my brother met Maggie. Not that it matters, one way or another." He held her gaze, his expression suddenly intense. "It's just something I figured you ought to know."

"Not Rafe's?" She shook her head. "I never would have guessed it. He looks so much like all of you guys, and you seem to love him so much."

"We do love him. Bloodlines are important in horses, not people. Jaimie is Rafe's son in every way that matters, and when he's old enough to understand, he'll never feel less a Kendrick than any of Rafe's biological kids. That's the way it is in our family. Right, Dad?"

Keefe tucked in the back of his chambray shirt with sharp jabs of his fingers. "Damn straight. I'd take a dozen more just like him."

As Keefe moved toward the kitchen, Bethany marked the lazy, loose-jointed way he moved, which was strongly reminiscent of his sons. Someday, when Jaimie grew older, would he walk with that same fluid grace, simply because he'd been raised by these men?

She flicked a wondering glance at Ryan. She'd been so sure he would never in a hundred years be content to adopt children.

A twinkle slipped into his eyes as he steadily returned her regard. She half expected him to say something. Instead he merely straightened and exited the room, leaving her alone with the baby and her confusing thoughts.

Amelia didn't allow Bethany to dwell on those thoughts. Well rested from her nap, she was ready to socialize, and she chortled and thrashed until Bethany focused full attention on her beaming little face. Big mistake. What a beautiful angel she was, all plump and soft and sweet-smelling. Holding her, touching her, and playing with her, Bethany couldn't help but wish for a child of her own. A child she could never have. The doctor who'd done her surgeries had been very clear on that. *Chances are, you'll never carry a child to term. In my opinion, that's a blessing. A woman in a wheelchair has no business having children.*

Remembering those words dealt Bethany a crushing blow to the heart even now. *A blessing*. Never had anyone said anything so cruel to her. She'd been nineteen years old when she had her third surgery. Only nineteen, and a doctor had all but said that she'd never be able to have a normal sex life or a family. When you boiled it all down, what was left? *Nothing*.

Staring down at Amelia's little face, Bethany struggled to shove these feelings away. This was stupid. What was more, it would be embarrassing if anyone saw her looking long in the face. It was just—oh, *God*. Being here in Ryan's home, getting to know his family . . . she wouldn't be human if the thought didn't seep into her mind that this could be *her* home and *her* family.

What was it about him that made her so soft in the head? Oh, sure. His brother had adopted a son, and right now, at this stage of his life, Ryan might think he would be content to do the same. Only it was different for Rafe. He'd already had another child of his own with Maggie, and chances were, he'd have others. Ryan would never be able to have a child of his own with Bethany.

How would he feel about that when he was fifty? A lot of men wanted to sire their own offspring. She suspected it was a man thing, somehow connected with their sense of self-esteem and virility. What Ryan might count as unimportant now could become a major concern later. He was a wealthy landowner with a family dynasty to pass on. When he grew old, wouldn't he want his heritage to go to children with Kendrick blood?

Besides, who was she kidding? As if her inability to have a child was the only problem. Not by a long shot. He spent the majority of each day outdoors, riding, roping, and climbing over rough terrain, and his leisure-time activities were centered on the outdoors as well. A couple was supposed to share a life, not exist in different stratospheres.

There was no way she could hope to share Ryan's reality.

If she were to go outside right now, she wouldn't get three feet before her chair wheels sank in mud and snow. Ryan would end up having to carry her and her chair wherever she needed to go. Was that what she wanted? To become a burden? *No.* She would want to be a contributing partner in a marriage, not an onlooker.

And on this ranch, an onlooker was all she could ever be.

Standing at the breakfast bar, Ryan glanced her way just then, and their gazes locked. For an instant, Bethany felt as if the world moved away, that they were the only two people in the room.

She was the one who averted her gaze first, and she did so with heartfelt finality. Maybe Ryan could accept her paralysis, but he'd never be able to accept all that came with it—or more to the point, all that didn't come with it, babies of his own and a physically active wife at the top of the list.

What was more, only a very selfish woman would ask it of him.

After a wonderfully congenial dinner around the kitchen table, Ryan put in a video, and everyone adjourned to the great room to watch the movie, a children's film about two dogs and a cat that embarked on a journey through the wilderness to return home. Bethany expected to sit in her chair as she did while watching movies with her own family, but Ryan had other ideas. He scooped her up, deposited her on the reclining love seat, and settled beside her.

After drawing an afghan over them both, he kicked up his footrest and slipped an arm around her shoulders. "Comfortable?"

She was more than just comfortable. It was lovely, being able to snuggle down on soft furniture like a normal person. "I'm perfect," she assured him.

"Yeah, you are," he agreed, his voice pitched low. Before Bethany could ask what he meant by that, he said, "Have you already seen the movie?"

"No. Have you?"

He glanced at the children, who were sitting at one end of the long sofa with Rafe and Maggie. Like ill-matched bookends, Sly and the delicate Helen sat elbow-to-elbow at the opposite end. "I'd say we've all watched it about twenty times. It's Jaimie's favorite. Sally Fields does the cat's voice and Michael J. Fox does the younger dog's."

"Really?" Bethany gazed at Maggie's mother, Helen, whose lovely brown eyes were fixed eagerly on the screen. If she'd already seen the movie that many times, Bethany wondered why she was so anxious to watch it again.

"Helen's one tier shy of a full cord," Ryan whispered.

Sly glanced over and frowned, making Bethany wonder if he had overheard the comment and took exception to it.

Bethany flashed Ryan an appalled look. "What do you mean?"

"Heart attack," he explained softly. "Oxygen deprivation to the brain. She's a darling, just a little childlike."

She gazed at Helen through new eyes. Over the course of the evening, she had noticed that Maggie's mother was strange in a very sweet sort of way. "She's still so young and pretty. What a tragedy."

"Depends on how you look at it, I guess. She'll think more or less like a ten-year-old for the rest of her life, but she's the happiest person you'll ever meet. Fifty-five years old, and she believes in Peter Pan."

Bethany studied Helen a moment longer and decided Ryan was right. The poor thing seemed happy, her eyes shimmering with delight as the movie began. She seemed to be as captivated as the children.

Bethany directed her gaze to the television, hoping to enjoy the movie herself. No easy task. To do so, she needed to block out the caress of Ryan's fingertips on her shoulder. He traced circles on her sleeve, the assault on her nerve-endings ceaseless. Her skin burned everywhere he touched.

Bethany nearly asked him to move his hand a dozen

times, only if she did, he would know his touch unsettled her. It was only innocent touching, after all—an absent-minded, repetitive movement of his fingertips on the cotton knit.

Watching the distracted frown that pleated Bethany's smooth brow, Ryan smiled to himself. He knew exactly what was causing that frown and continued to do it without a twinge of guilt. Any young woman who'd never even taken a solo flight was in dire need of a man's hands on her, and in this particular instance, not just any man's hands would do. When the time came, Ryan was determined it would be him who taught her to fly.

He looked across the room and winked at his mother, who was sitting on his dad's lap in the recliner. Ann Kendrick smiled sleepily and cuddled closer to her husband, resting her cheek on his shoulder.

When the movie was over, Bethany couldn't recall much of the plot.

"This has been lovely," Ann said as she rose from the chair. "But now it's time for this old lady to go home to her comfortable bed." She hugged Rafe and his family good night, then circled behind the love seat. After leaning down to kiss Ryan's cheek, she lay a hand on Bethany's shoulder. "It was lovely getting to meet you, Bethany. I hope I'll be seeing a lot of you from now on."

Bethany was trying to think of something to say in response when Keefe sleepily crossed the room to join his wife. He curled a strong arm around her. "Let's go home, Annie girl. You make that bed sound mighty good."

His salt-and-pepper hair gleaming like dark silver in the low light, Keefe dipped his head to nibble on his wife's neck and whisper something as they moved toward the door.

Ann reached up and thumped him on the top of his head with delicate knuckles. "Keefe Kendrick, you stop it. Our grandbabies are here."

"They're all asleep, Mom," Rafe called as he bent over

Heidi to stuff her arms down the sleeves of her parka. "And you can forget hurrying out of here like a couple of teenagers. I need help loading cargo."

Helen fluttered behind her son-in-law, nearly bumping into Sly as he lumbered to his feet. "Easy, there, honey," he said softly as he caught her from falling. "No point in wearin' yourself out standin' in one place."

Helen's cheeks turned a pretty pink, and she cast Sly a look as coquettish as any young girl's. The foreman gave her slender shoulder a gentle squeeze and pat, which made her blush even more.

"I just want to help," she explained.

"I'm sure Rafe can think of something for you to do," the foreman said pointedly. "Right, Rafe?"

Rafe smiled. "You can put her shoes on, Helen. That'd be a help."

Keefe reversed directions to assist his elder son. Ryan took that as his cue to get up and start helping as well. While Rafe commandeered the troops at the opposite side of the room, Ryan brought Jaimie over to the love seat and began trying to stick the child's limp fingers into winter gloves. Before long Bethany started trying to help, and within seconds they were both laughing.

"This is like trying to string boots with wet leather laces," Ryan complained. "Damn, Rafe, how come you don't just buy the kid mittens?"

Rafe peered over Ryan's shoulder. "He wants real gloves like mine."

Jaimie mewled in his sleep and snatched his small hand out of Ryan's grasp, which put them back to square one. "Oh, for Pete's sake," Ryan said.

Maggie walked up just then. Unable to help because she was carrying Amelia, she merely observed for a moment, then laughed and shook her head. "Rafe, just stick his gloves in his jacket pocket."

1 don't want his hands to get cold," Rafe insisted as he

knelt beside Ryan. "Come here, partner." He gathered his son in the crook of one arm. "Come on, Jaimie boy. Daddy needs you to wake up a little bit."

Jaimie burrowed against his father's chest. "Daddy," he murmured.

Leaving Rafe to handle the gloves, Ryan started trying to stuff Jaimie's feet into his cowboy boots. It quickly became apparent that this would be yet another difficult task. Bethany glanced at Maggie, who just smiled.

"They're overprotective," she said by way of explanation. "No cure for it, so I just let them go."

"I am not overprotective," Rafe informed her. "It's damned cold out there."

"Jaimie isn't very big, Maggie," Ryan put in. "Not much meat on him. And Rafe's right. It's colder than a well digger's ass out there tonight."

Keefe nudged his sons aside. "I swear, it's simple enough to dress a kid."

Everyone gathered around to watch Keefe struggle to dress the limp child. After managing to get one glove on, he rocked back on the heel of his boot, rubbed his jaw, and said, "How's about we just wrap him in a quilt?"

That suggestion was met with enthusiasm, and soon Ryan was seeing his family out. Before leaving, Keefe leaned over to give Bethany a hug. "Good night, little darlin'. You make a mean loaf of garlic bread. I think we'll keep you."

Bethany stared sightlessly at the blank television screen while Ryan was gone. She prayed he kept his distance now that they were going to be alone. If he didn't, she wasn't sure she'd be able to resist him.

When Ryan returned to the great room, he knew the instant he saw Bethany's face that she was tense. He stood near the fire, feet spread, arms folded over his chest. The way he saw it, she'd endured about all the sensual circling and feinting that she could handle. If he was smart, he'd back off. There would be all the time in the world to work on her later if he handled this situation right and made her feel comfortable about returning for future visits.

"You look exhausted," he observed. "I think I'd better get you headed in the direction of bed. Out this far from town, I never know when I'll have unexpected overnight guests, so I keep spare toothbrushes and stuff on hand."

"That's good. I'll be glad for a toothbrush."

He suddenly remembered that she was without her medication. "Damn. I don't remember you drinking much wine at dinner."

"I was afraid I'd get tipsy and embarrass myself in front of your family."

Ryan headed toward the kitchen. "Well, they're gone now. If you get tipsy around me, it's no big deal."

He quickly collected the half-full bottle of wine and two goblets from a cupboard. "You hungry for a bedtime snack?"

He heard the whir of her chair and glanced up to see her coming around the counter to join him. As he set himself to the task of forking pickles from a jar and slicing cheese on the cutting board, he asked, "How's that chair powered?"

"A rechargeable battery. I'll need to plug it into a wall socket overnight."

"Not a problem." He smiled as he popped a piece of cheese into her mouth and then handed her a full glass of wine. He'd happily charge this girl's batteries anytime. "Bottom's up. Two full glasses."

"You needn't tell me twice. I don't want to get any leg cramps."

For some reason, it had never occurred to Ryan that paraplegics might experience pain in their legs. In fact, he had assumed exactly the opposite, that they never felt anything at all, which made him question how many other of his assumptions were wrong. Searching her sweet face, which was smiling ninety-five percent of the time, he realized he was beginning to wonder about a lot of things now that he was coming to know Bethany better, namely how often she smiled when she really wanted to cry.

He remembered watching a movie called *Passion Fish* about a paraplegic woman. The scene that stuck in his mind was of the woman sitting in the kitchen, frustrated beyond bearing by her disability, and suddenly starting to scream. Pulling her hair and screaming at the top of her lungs, with only the walls to hear. Had there been a time when Bethany had wanted to pull her hair and scream? Probably. There were undoubtedly still times when she wanted to.

"Does massage help with the cramps?" he asked.

"I'd have to twist and strain so much to massage out a cramp that I'd end up with back spasms, which are even worse," she informed him with a laugh.

Ryan wouldn't have minded getting his hands on those pretty legs again to give her a massage, paying special attention to that live spot on the inside of her left thigh. That thought had him circling to another even more frustrating consideration, that Bethany might have at least partial sensation in her female parts. Maybe he was all washed up, but it seemed to him that her chances of being able to enjoy sex were good, possibly even excellent, if there were places where she had some feeling.

Thinking of the logistics had him reaching for his goblet. If he hoped to sleep tonight, he needed a good dose of wine himself. Sitting on the love seat with her for nearly two hours had cranked his libido up on high.

He focused his attention on the food and wine, determined not to let his gaze stray to her soft curves. After filling a plate for her, he began eating. Bethany picked up a dill pickle. Instead of biting into it, she touched the tip of her tongue to the end and sucked the juice. Ryan stared, a slice of forgotten cheese caught between his teeth. *Holy hell*. He was in trouble here. Watching her suck on that pickle was enough to send him running for an ice-cold dunk in the lake.

Pocketing the cheese in his cheek, he asked in a froggy voice, "You like pickles?"

"Mmm." She sucked and nipped at it, driving him insane every time she flicked the firm flesh with the tip of her tongue. "Do you?"

Ryan doubted he could taste a pickle. His pulse was slamming in his temples like shod hooves on concrete. "I sure enjoy seeing you eat one."

She went still, her eyes crossing slightly as she looked down her nose. Her cheeks turned a pretty pink, and she plucked the dill from her mouth.

Ryan grinned, experiencing a purely male sense of satisfaction that he'd managed to make her blush. She wasn't as unaffected by him as she tried to let on, and he made her just a little nervous, which was always an encouraging sign. "Don't stop. I find it refreshing to watch a woman enjoy her food." One of his pet peeves was females whose obsession with being thin ruled every aspect of their lives. "So many women are always on diets these days. Why is beyond me, but they act like eating is a cardinal sin. When I spring for filet mignon, I like a woman to dig in and enjoy eating it."

She met his gaze and took a huge bite out of the pickle. It was all Ryan could do not to flinch. He nearly laughed out loud, for he knew very well she'd done it on purpose, expressly to make him cringe. Her eyes danced with mischief. She was such a fascinating blend, he thought warmly, greatly lacking in actual experience with men, yet sharp as a tack and quick to read between the lines. He enjoyed sparring with her.

"I'm your lady, then," she informed him as she chewed, pickle puffing out one cheek. "I enjoy my food. Buy me filet mignon, and I'll devour every morsel."

He laughed at the impish twinkle that lingered in her eyes. "You're on. With what for dessert?"

She raised her finely drawn brows. "I'm surprised you have to ask."

"Chocolate?"

She got a dreamy look on her face. "The richer and more fattening, the better. I crave it like you wouldn't believe."

Ryan wondered if she knew that the ingredients in chocolate supposedly mimicked the feelings a woman had when she was in love. The question no sooner skittered through his mind than she said, "It's a great substitute for sex, you know. Scientifically proven fact."

This time, he did laugh. "You're doing your damnedest to shock me, aren't you?"

She smiled beatifically. "Just testing your mettle. With five brothers, I learned early that it's better to keep a guy on his toes than the other way around. Why? Does it worry you, having a sexually frustrated houseguest? You can always whip up a double batch of fudge."

Ryan Kendrick had a fail-proof cure for what ailed her, and it sure as hell wasn't chocolate.

Chapter Twelve

With two full glasses of wine to relax her, Bethany slept deeply and awoke the next morning well-rested but out of sorts. Some people sang in the shower and threw their arms wide to embrace the day. When she woke up, all she wanted was caffeine, solitude, and absolute silence until the grumpiness wore off. It had been that way ever since the accident, an awful trapped feeling coming over her the instant she opened her eyes and realized her lovely dreams would never again be possible. Dreams of walking and running . . . riding and dancing . . . of being released from the prison that her body had become.

Morning sunlight shafted through the windows, its brilliance nearly blinding because it reflected off snow. The ecru drapes did little to diffuse the glare. Bethany cracked open one eye, groaned, and angled an arm over her face. Even the crackle of the pillowcase linen seemed loud.

Hoping to adjust to the brightness slowly, she inched her arm down. The white walls were whiter than white. There was nothing to break up the monotony, no photos, pictures, or anything. The dresser and bureau were nearly bare, no knickknacks, no scarves or doilies. Motel rooms had more personality.

Men. How could they live like this? Her brothers were the same. Their idea of decorating was to hang a calendar on the wall the first part of January.

Bethany groaned and flopped her arms out from her body like a child about to make a snow angel. Staring at the ceiling, she tried to recall coming to bed. Blurry images circled through her mind. She remembered Ryan sitting beside her after she was settled in, but she couldn't recall what they had talked about. Her only sharp memory was of how his eyes had shimmered in the dim light, a gentle, silvery blue that had given her shivers each time he met her gaze.

Sprawled on her back, she silently cursed her leaden legs, wishing she could turn onto her side to ease the crick between her shoulders. No way. Rolling over required more work than it was worth, tugging and lifting and twisting. Better to just lie there like a beached whale and be content.

Drowsily she studied the patterns in the ceiling plaster, which was also painted a relentless white. How in heaven's name was she going to get out of bed? The door to her room was closed, and though she listened, she heard no sounds to indicate Ryan was up. First thing of a morning, she always needed to use the bathroom. Small problem. Without her bed sling, she was trapped here.

She hated to yell for help and wake him up. Pushing onto her elbows, she glared at her chair, which he'd placed against the wall near an electrical outlet to recharge the battery. It was only about six feet from her, but it may as well have been in the northern reaches of Canada for all the good it did her.

"Rats!" she said. "I *hate* this. Hate it, hate it, *hate* it!"

Seconds later a sharp rap came on her door. "You decent?"

Bethany jerked with a start and blinked. "Yeah. Come on in."

The door cracked open, and Ryan poked his head into the room. Still damp from the shower, his wavy jet-black hair glistened like polished obsidian, and his burnished jaw gleamed in the brilliant morning light, hinting that he'd just shaved. He looked wide awake and nauseatingly cheerful. She detested people who smiled this early in the morning. It made her want to smack them.

"Hi," he said, strong white teeth flashing in a grin. He pushed the door open more widely.

"How did you know I was awake?" she asked crossly.

He hooked a thumb over his shoulder at a white plastic box mounted on the wall near the door. Was everything in his house above floor level white? "Intercom. I've been having my morning coffee and waiting for you to stir." His teeth flashed at her again. "Sounds to me like you're a little grumpy."

Grumpy didn't say it by half. Getting out of bed took bloody forever. Then the drawn-out process of going to the bathroom followed. Like most people, she wanted a cup of coffee as soon as she opened her eyes, and it was generally a half hour before she even saw the kitchen.

He came to stand by the bed. Bethany gazed up at him, detesting the fact that she couldn't get up by herself and had to lie there, waiting for him to help her. "You have bare walls. Don't you get tired of looking at all this white plaster?"

He flicked a glance at the room. "I don't actually look at the walls much."

Like that was a news flash? "Well, you need to decorate. Your house says who you are."

"Uh-oh."

"Uh-oh is right. If your walls are an indication, you have no personality."

He laughed and said, "I'm working on getting a decorator."

"You don't need a decorator. You need—*things*."

"What kind of things?"

"I don't know. *Things*. You know, stuff that reflects who you are."

"I've got mirrors in the bathrooms. They reflect who I am."

"Very funny. Don't you have things that mean a lot to you?" She jerked at the sheet, the corner of which had gotten stuck under her rump. "You need to hang things on your walls to make a statement."

"What do I want to say?"

"That you're someone. That you've lived and had life experiences. Snapshots of your horses, maybe. Pictures of the people you love, at least."

"I got a pair of old boots I'm real fond of."

She glared at him, which made him chuckle.

"Are you like this every morning?" he asked pleasantly.

"Yes."

"Oh, boy." He bent over to tug back the covers, then lifted her into his arms.

She clutched his shirt, still not entirely at ease when he picked her up. "I don't accept any grievances before noon."

He settled her in her chair. "I'll be in the kitchen, sunshine. Coffee will be waiting."

When Bethany joined him at the front of the house a few minutes later, he gave her a wary look. "You cheered up any since I saw you last?"

She rolled to a stop near the counter and rubbed her eyes. Her hair was all tangled, her armpits smelled, and as near as she could tell, the man didn't own a brush, only combs that jerked her long hair out by the roots. She was a creature of habit, with morning rituals that began her day. Here, she didn't even have clean clothes to put on.

"Can I have some coffee?"

He hurried to the coffeemaker and filled a waiting mug. "How do you take it, honey?"

"Strong."

"No cream or sugar?"

"No. Black and straight into the vein will suit me fine."

He chuckled, which earned him another glare. "You want a nail to chew on?"

She ignored the jibe, took the cup of coffee, and went to sit by the kitchen hearth to stare mindlessly at the fire while she tried to wake up. After downing a mug of coffee, she started to feel a bit more human and a whole lot guilty for snapping at him.

"I'm sorry for being so cranky."

Ryan pushed up from the table and joined her at the hearth, resting a boot on the brick as he regarded her. "You weren't so bad that you need to apologize for it. Just a little bristly around the edges."

She struggled to suppress a smile. "You're being polite. Jake says he's seen badgers with sweeter dispositions than I have when I first wake up."

"Yeah?" He shrugged and sighed. "That's a brother for you. Always ready to tell you the unvarnished truth, whether you want to hear it or not."

Bethany burst out laughing.

Jake arrived thirty minutes later. Bethany had performed her morning ablutions as best she could and was enjoying a second mug of coffee when Ryan and her brother came striding into the house, talking and joking as if they were best friends.

Bethany was in no mood for a male bonding ritual. She gave her brother a narrow-eyed look and smiled sweetly. "My goodness, aren't you Johnny-on-the-spot? I'm surprised you found Ryan's house so easily."

Jake flicked a glance at Ryan. His gaze meandered around the room, coming to a halt on the ceiling. "I've had business out this way before."

Ryan cleared his throat and tried to signal Jake with a sidelong glance, which Jake totally missed because he was busy counting ceiling cracks and trying to look innocent.

"Really?" Bethany mused. "What kind of business?"

Jake scratched in front of his ear, glanced her way, and then abandoned his perusal of the ceiling to study Ryan's floor tile. "The Rocking K is always ordering stuff from the store. You know that."

"And that's why you were here before, to deliver an order?"

Jake looked relieved. "Yeah, exactly that. I came out here recently to give Ryan an order. Right, Ryan?"

Ryan shrugged and gave Bethany a wary look. "He gave me an order, all right."

Jake's brow pleated. He looked at Ryan, then at her. His mouth pursed, and a thoughtful expression entered his eyes. "You ratted on me," he said softly.

Ryan held up his hands. "It was an accident, partner. We were talking, and she picked up on something I said. When she asked me point-blank, I didn't want to lie to her."

Jake settled an apologetic gaze on Bethany. "It wasn't any big deal, Bethie. I just wanted to get a few things straight with Ryan. That's all."

"It is a big deal. You're *always* butting into my business. It has to stop."

He shrugged. "It has. I won't be doing it again."

"Why the sudden change of heart? Have I missed something?"

Jake smiled at her. "Nope. I've just realized you probably won't be needing me to watch out for you anymore."

Ryan suddenly leaped into motion. "How's about some coffee before you head back, Jake?"

"Sounds good."

Ryan grabbed a mug from the cupboard. "Nothing like a good cup of java on a snowy morning."

"Nope. Nothing to beat it." Jake joined Bethany at the table. "Am I allowed to ask if you're all right? Or will that be met with resentment, too?"

Bethany had a feeling both men were eager to change the subject, and since she felt she'd made her point, she relaxed. "No, it won't be met with resentment, and in answer to the question, I'm fine. Not even a bruise, and Ryan was the soul of hospitality last night." She filled Jake in on the evening. "He has a really nice family. They all went out of their way to make me feel welcome."

"That's good to know."

Ryan took a chair across from them. He seemed tense to Bethany, but for the life of her, she couldn't think why. It wasn't because Jake was there. Her brother had done an about-face and couldn't have been friendlier had he tried.

The men talked about cattle for a few minutes. Then the conversation drifted to horses, a topic Bethany found far more interesting. As if he sensed that, Jake pushed suddenly to his feet. "Well, sis? You about ready to roll?"

Bethany sighed. "There's no risk in my *talking* about horses, Jake."

Jake grinned. "If you get a bee in your bonnet about riding again, it's not gonna be my hide Dad takes after. I'll let Ryan take the heat."

"I'm not going to start riding again."

Jake met Ryan's gaze. "Never said you were."

Getting back home proved to be the least of her problems. Her specially equipped van was still sitting in a ditch. Jake told her not to worry, that they could do without her at the store until she had transportation again, but Bethany was concerned. She had bills to pay, and she was determined to earn her own way. It could take a day for the roads to clear enough for a wrecker to pull her van to a garage and heaven knew how long after that before the necessary repairs would be done.

Ryan phoned that afternoon and immediately guessed by Bethany's tone that she was upset. When she told him why, he tried to reassure her. "If you need to go somewhere, I can take you."

"No, no. It's just that I hate to miss work for however long it's going to take. It'll make a big dent in my paycheck."

"I can float you a small loan."

"It's not that. Jake will happily give me the money to make ends meet."

"Where's the problem, then?"

She sighed and twisted the phone cord around her finger. "That *is* the problem. Nothing would make my family happier than if I depended on them and didn't work at all. It makes me—" She broke off. "I know it sounds silly, but knowing I may miss work for a week or longer makes me feel panicky."

Long silence at his end. "Panicky about what, sweetheart? You'll be back to work sometime next week."

"And Jake will be standing there with money held out, happy as a clam to be taking care of me."

"What a jerk."

Bethany laughed and closed her eyes. "I know I'm being silly. It's just—I can't explain."

"Try."

"I've worked so hard not to need anybody. It's no big deal to other people, but to me, being independent, making my own way is everything. I know this sounds bad, but my family hovers like a bunch of vultures, just waiting for me to fail. My folks would love for me to move back home so Daddy could watch after me and Mama could pamper me. They'd be pleased if I never worked again, if I just let them do everything. The thought makes it hard for me to breathe."

"And not having your van may enable them."

"Exactly. Without it, I'll lose ground. They mean well. And I love them all so much. It's awful to feel this way, let alone say it aloud."

"I understand. We all need to feel self-sufficient."

"My folks want me back in the nest."

"Well, we won't let that happen, so stop fretting. If they try to put you back in the nest, I'll beat 'em off with a club. How's that?"

She smiled sadly. The very fact that he felt it necessary to offer his support made her feel like a lesser being. "Thank you, Ryan. You're a good friend."

After they broke the connection, Bethany went to a window and stared out at the snow. In Portland, she had never become stranded like this. When it snowed up there, the driving conditions weren't this bad. At least she'd never spun off into a ditch on some stupid mountain road.

She needed her van. It was her freedom. She couldn't even go to the grocery store for bread without it. Until she got it back, she would be a prisoner in her own house and dependent upon other people for everything.

It was nearly midnight that same evening when the peal of the doorbell jerked Bethany from a sound sleep. She fumbled with her sling to get out of bed, her heart pounding with fear. No one in her family would come calling this late unless something awful had happened. *Daddy.* Her first thought was that he'd had a heart attack. *Oh, God—oh, God.* Not her father.

"Damn it!" She jerked at the sling, hating the fact that she couldn't simply hop out of bed and run to the door. When the bell rang again, she wondered if it was one of her brothers. They all had keys to the dead bolts, just in case she ever fell. Why would they lean on the doorbell?

"Coming!" she yelled.

Minutes later she fumbled with the locks, and cracked the door open to peer out. She'd forgotten to flip on the light, and all she could see was a dark, hulking shadow of a man standing on the step. *Ryan?* She'd kill him. Was he out of his mind, coming to see her at this hour?

"You scared me out of ten years' growth."

"I'm sorry, honey. I couldn't get it here any earlier."

"Get *what* here?"

He dangled her car keys in front of her nose. "Your van. She's running again. We used liquid weld to patch the radiator up. Won't last, but it'll work until I can pick up another one at a junkyard this week."

A lump came into Bethany's throat. She opened the door wider to look out, and sure enough, there sat her van in the driveway. Behind it, a dark-colored four-wheel-drive idled, the parking lights casting an amber glow over the snow in her driveway.

"Sly helped me tow her to town." Ryan bent down and kissed her forehead. "Don't want to keep him waiting long, so I'll make tracks. Sorry for dragging you out of bed so late, but I figured you'd be glad to have your wheels first thing in the morning. Now you can go to work."

"Oh, Ryan . . ." Tears gathered in her eyes. "I don't know what to say. You didn't need to do this."

"It was no big thing. We just pulled her out of the ditch with a winch and took her back to my place for a quick fix."

It *was* a big thing. A very big thing. Now that her eyes were growing accustomed to the darkness, she could see how tired he looked. She guessed that he'd worked on the van for hours to get it running.

"I don't know how to thank you."

"Friends don't have to thank each other, honey. It's understood. When you come out Saturday to watch Heidi ride, Sly and I will stick a new radiator in for you. You'll have to go to a body shop to get the grill and hood fixed, but at least she'll run."

With that, he was walking away, and Bethany was left to

sit there, shivering in the icy draft, staring after him through tears. *Friends don't have to thank each other.* That man. That big, wonderful, *impossible* man. He was going to make her fall head over heels in love with him, whether she wanted to or not.

Chapter Thirteen

Just friends. Over the next few days, that became Bethany's mantra. She could never be the woman Ryan needed or deserved, not in bed or out of it. To allow herself to wish or entertain the notion that they could be more than friends would be sheer folly, she told herself firmly. As tempting as the thought might be, it wouldn't be fair to Ryan.

On the following Saturday when she went out to the ranch to watch Heidi ride, she was determined to set the tone of their relationship. The first part of the visit was a snap, for Ryan was busy somewhere else, working on her van. When the radiator was finally replaced and he rejoined her to watch Heidi ride, she reminded herself not to let gratitude weaken her resolve.

"Thank you, Ryan. What do I owe you?"

He turned a twinkling gaze on her. "Nothing. It was a junkyard special and only cost a few bucks. We have our own engine shop, so it wasn't even much work to slap it in, not with all the right tools to do the job."

"I really do want to pay you."

"Nah." He winked at her. "I'd rather just take it out in trade."

Bethany had heard that expression before. Her cheeks flooded with heat, and she averted her eyes, momentarily uncertain what to say. Then years of experience at verbal sparring with her brothers came to the rescue. "I really hate to rip off a friend. In a trade like that, you'd definitely get the short end of the stick."

He chuckled and said, "You can fix me dinner some night. How's that?"

"How do you know if I can cook?"

"Any woman who enjoys her food as much as you do has to know her way around a kitchen."

The tension between them dissipated then, and she was able to relax. It was easy to joke and laugh with a rancher who had a very spoiled pet bull, an equally spoiled and very plump dog, and was in the process of building a pen down at the lake to save orphaned ducklings from marauding carnivores. Ryan had a wonderful sense of humor, an appreciation of the absurd, and wasn't easily offended when she ribbed him about being such a softie.

When his bull made an appearance, he issued a warning to Bethany. "If T-bone ever starts bawling and slobbering all over the sliding glass door when you're up at the house alone, just toss him a carrot. Make sure you close the door fast, though, so he doesn't get inside."

"That bull gets in your *house*?" Bethany asked incredulously. "Good grief."

"He just wants in the bathroom," Ryan explained solemnly. "He got pneumonia as a baby, and I kept him in there under steam until he got well. He still remembers and can't seem to understand why he's not welcome inside anymore." He scratched his head and frowned. "A man's gotta draw the line somewhere."

A few minutes later T-bone pestered Ryan for a treat. Bethany laughed until tears streamed down her cheeks. The bull butted Ryan, and he nearly knocked him off his feet. In the end Ryan went to the house for a carrot. T-bone was in no mood to take no for an answer.

After Heidi's riding lesson was over and Bethany was making her way back along the planks Ryan had laid out to prevent her chair from getting stuck in the mud, he walked beside her. "You're a fantastic riding teacher," he told her. "Have you ever considered starting an academy?"

"When I can't ride myself?" she asked with a laugh.

"With the proper facilities and a special saddle, you could ride again. 'Never say cain't.'" He flashed her an amused look. "That's Sly's motto, and he brought me up believing in it. 'Ain't nothin' on earth ever gits done sayin' cain't, and that there's a fact.'"

Bethany sighed as she drew up near the van. "Well, not to contradict Sly, but I think we all must accept our limitations occasionally."

"You're a natural," he said softly. "You picked up on mistakes Heidi was making that I've never caught. And she's right, you know. Your name is almost legend in these parts. With some advertising to generate interest, you'd have young people signing up for classes and summer-camp seminars in droves. What's more, you'd love the work. What a waste, you sitting behind a computer."

Bethany smiled. "It's lovely to think about."

"That's a start." He stood aside as she got settled in her van. Then he hooked his folded arms over the edge of her door. "Thanks for coming out. You made Heidi's whole year."

"It was fun. I enjoyed every minute."

T-bone came ambling over just then to butt Ryan in the rump. He laughed and said, "If I bribe you with a barbecued *T-bone* steak, will you come out to watch her ride again sometime?"

"I'd love to." Bethany leaned out to pat the bull's broad head. "Don't listen to him, T-bone. He would never eat you."

Ryan grinned and scratched the bovine's ears. "I sure as hell would. Butt me one more time, and you're gonna be rump roast, T-bone. Makes my mouth water, just thinking about it."

Bethany was still smiling as she drove away. She had enjoyed the afternoon immensely and looked forward to doing it again. However, she didn't expect to see Ryan again any time soon. He owned a ranch some distance from town, she had a desk job, and their paths weren't likely to cross very often.

But Ryan had other ideas. He appeared on Bethany's doorstep that very evening, a boxed pizza balanced on one hand, two rented videos clutched in the other. Did she mind having some unexpected company? He was lonesome.

Bethany couldn't very well turn him away, so she opened the door, never guessing when she did that it wasn't only her home he meant to invade.

Ryan wanted to claim her heart, and set himself to that task. Corny B-grade movies set the mood. They spent the evening tearing apart the plots, criticizing the acting, and laughing at the absurdities while they munched pizza, sipped Coke, and snuggled together on the sofa under the afghan Bethany's grandmother had crocheted. *Just friends.* No searching looks, no kissing, no hint of anything of a sensual nature.

If Bethany's pulse raced when Ryan curled an arm around her, that was her secret. If her heart caught just a little when he brushed his fingertips over her sleeve, that was her problem—or so she told herself.

Actually that was Ryan's plan—to be the proverbial wolf in sheep's clothing.

He became a frequent caller at her house from that evening on. Some evenings he took her out for dinner and then to a movie. On two occasions he accompanied her and her mother to the "Y" on swim night and got soundly trounced when he challenged Bethany to a race in the pool. The girl swam like a porpoise, compensating for her lack of leg propulsion with strong, rhythmic arm strokes. Afterward Ryan was huffing, and he found himself looking at her with new respect, wondering what she must have been like before her accident. Competitive, surely, and incredibly determined. He wouldn't have wanted to enter a rodeo competition against her. She must have been hell on horseback, which explained why she'd been well on her way to the nationals and countrywide recognition as a barrel racer before fate had pitched her a curve ball.

Other nights they sat at her kitchen table and played games. She taught him how to play pinochle, which he'd actually been playing for years, but he pretended ignorance because it was cozier that way. He taught her how to play poker, which was also cozy—just not as cozy as it might have been if they'd been betting articles of clothing, which he didn't dare suggest. On the evenings in between, they played other games—Monopoly, Aggravation (he was aggravated, all right), Yahtzee, Trivia Pursuits, and Mexican dominoes. Whatever the activity, they had fun.

Ryan often gazed across the table at her sweet face and wondered how she could fail to see what was so glaringly apparent to him—that they were meant for each other. He loved the way she laughed, tipping her head back and just letting go, the sound almost musical. He loved her indomitable sense of humor. He liked the fact that she played to win and beamed when she outwitted him. God help him, he even enjoyed arguing with her. She had a quick mind and proved to be as stubborn in her convictions as a little Missouri mule, but she was also open to new ideas and conceded a point without any rancor if he was able to prove her wrong, which didn't happen often.

Ryan's favorite nights were when he arrived with videos to watch, whereupon he deposited Bethany on the sofa, snuggled her up under Grandma's afghan, and worked his ass off for two or three hours, trying to seduce her. Casual, seemingly innocent caresses were the ticket, he felt sure, all executed in such an offhand way she wouldn't guess what he was up to—until it was too late.

Ryan the wolf. It didn't take him long to discover a few of her most vulnerable spots, his favorites being the silken nape of her neck and the sensitive hollow beneath her ear, which he tortured mercilessly with feathery touches of his fingertips. He pretended to watch the movies while he waged his assault, of course, but in reality, he was observing Bethany from the corner of his eye and smiling—wolfishly.

When he touched her lightly just under her ear, he could see her pulse leap and then flutter in the hollow of her throat like the wings of a frightened bird. If he ever so casually trailed his fingertips down the slope of her neck and dipped them under the edge of her collar, a rosy blush flooded into her cheeks. He loved the sweet way her breath caught in response to him and how her lips parted on a silent little gasp, her lashes drooping low to veil eyes gone dark with desire. She often gave him searching looks that told him she was suspicious of his motives. He returned her steady regard with the well-practiced innocent look that had served him well with females most of his adult life.

Bethany, an absolutely fascinating combination of wide-eyed innocence and wisdom. Ryan often found himself looking into her startled, big blue eyes and feeling like a low-down skunk for deceiving her.

But he didn't let guilt stop him.

He wanted her—in his bed—in his life. One way or another, he intended to have her. When he wasn't with Bethany, he worked furiously out at the ranch, having his kitchen remodeled, building ramps, and pouring cement walkways until the property was networked, giving her wheelchair access even down to the lake, He also contacted her brother Jake and enlisted his help in tracking down Bethany's mare, Wink, so he could work a deal to buy her back.

When Bethany visited the ranch again, Ryan wanted all the construction to be finished and everything else close to perfect, his aim being to protest her every reservation and argument against marrying him. All his life, he'd heard that actions spoke more loudly than words, and he meant to show her, by the sweat of his brow, how much he loved her and that they could have a wonderful life together, if only she'd give him a chance.

Yet, while Ryan was busily revamping the ranch, Bethany was agonizing over how to break off their friendship. They'd been seeing each other practically every day for over a month now, and it was time for her to face facts. She couldn t make this work. Every time she was with Ryan, it became harder and harder to think of him as only a friend. She had tried—oh, how she had tried—and for a while she had been able to lie to herself. She just wished she could go on lying in order to continue seeing him. He was so much fun, and he always made her laugh, no matter what they were doing. No longer having him in her life was going to half kill her.

But her own needs and happiness weren't the issue. She had to do the right thing, and as difficult as it might be, the right thing was to let him go. It would only become more difficult as time wore on, she knew. With each passing day, her resolve weakened just a little more, making it easier and easier to believe she could fulfill all his needs, when in truth she could never be the wife he needed or deserved.

Foolish, pathetic Bethany. She'd feared from the first that this would happen, and now it had. She was head-over-heels, wildly, crazily in love with him, and she wasn't sure how much longer she could go on pretending differently.

It might have been all right—she might have continued to fool him and herself—if only Ryan had been the type to keep his distance, but he wasn't. He was a hands-on person and very affectionate, always hugging and rubbing and *touching*. Her hair. Her ear. Her neck. Her cheek. He was driving her absolutely mad. Sometimes after he left, she'd lie awake for hours, staring at the ceiling, wondering how it would have felt if he had kissed her in all those places.

Some mornings her brother Jake would stop by her office to ask, "So how's it going with you and Ryan?"

"There is no me and Ryan," she always replied. "We're just friends, Jake. Don't read anything into it that's not there."

Jake invariably grinned when she said that. "Okay, let me rephrase the question. How's it going with you and your *friend* Ryan?"

"Fine."

Jake would frown. "That's it? 'Fine?' "

"There's nothing else to say. We're friends. It's fine. He's very nice, and I enjoy his company, end of story."

On the morning Bethany decided that she had to stop seeing Ryan, Jake asked the same old question again, lingering in her office doorway sipping a cup of coffee:

"So, sis, how's it goin' with you and Ryan?"

Bethany was so depressed, she couldn't muster the energy to go through their usual routine. She just shrugged and said, "All right, I guess."

"Uh-oh. That doesn't sound good. Problems?"

"Not really," she replied, when in truth she wanted to weep every time she thought of how empty her life would be without Ryan in it. How on earth would she fill up her evenings without him? "Nothing I can't handle, anyway."

"Honey, are you feeling all right?" Jake stepped closer to peer at her face. "You've got circles under your eyes."

"I haven't been sleeping very well the last couple of weeks."

Cupping his coffee mug between his hands, Jake leaned a hip on the edge of her desk. "Is something troubling you?"

Bethany wondered what he would say if she told him what the problem was—that his beloved sister, whom he considered to be worthy of canonization, was sexually frustrated and about to lose her mind. "No. A bout of insomnia, is all. I'm sure it'll pass."

Frowning thoughtfully and narrowing his eyes against the steam, he raised his mug to his lips and took a slow sip. "If it continues, maybe you should see a doctor."

Bethany had seen enough doctors to last her a lifetime, and besides that, she really didn't think a doctor could help with her present problem. Given her physical complications, she wasn't even sure Ryan could. What if she was doomed to a lifelong itch, with no way to scratch? Just the thought made her want to scream. She sighed and cleared an erroneous entry on the computer with a vicious jab of her finger on the delete key.

Ryan was in the tack room, replacing a bridle bit, when his cell phone chirped. He sighed and grabbed his jacket off a wall-stud nail to fish the phone out of the pocket.

"Kendrick here," he barked.

"Ryan? Jake Coulter."

Ryan smiled and sank back against the saddler rack. "Hey, Jake. How's it goin'?"

"Not worth a tinker's damn. What the hell's going on between you and Bethany?"

Ryan moved the phone away from his ear. "Nothing." Much to his regret. "What are you talking about? I haven't laid a hand on her."

"I figured as much," Jake said. Long silence. Then he sighed. "Holy hell."

"What does that mean?" Ryan asked cautiously. Jake Coulter was not a man he wanted to tangle with if he could avoid it.

"She's not sleeping," Jake said. "This morning she looks like somebody slugged her in both eyes."

"Not sleeping?" Ryan's scrunched his brow in a worried frown. "She's not sick, is she?"

"Hello. Add it up. She can't sleep, and you say you haven't laid a hand on her. It doesn't take a genius to figure out the problem."

Ryan grinned like a fool. "You think?"

Jake sighed again. "Ryan," he said with exaggerated patience. "Do you remember our conversation when I came out to your place that night?"

"I remember."

"When are you planning to get to the wedding vows and forever-after part of our understanding?"

"I'm working on her."

"Well, if you love the girl, kick it in the ass."

Ryan raised his eyebrows. "Would you repeat that, just for clarification?"

"Don't press your luck. And for the record, you're a dead man if you don't marry her afterward. Clear?"

Ryan chuckled. "I read you. No worries, Jake."

Seducing a woman like Bethany called for careful planning. Ryan preferred to stage the seduction scene at his place. Less risk of being interrupted that way. He didn't want one of her brothers dropping in to check on her right in the middle of everything. He could warn his own family not to come over or telephone, threat of death.

He had hoped to put off bringing Bethany out to see the ranch for another week. Her saddle still hadn't arrived, and he didn't have her treadmill set up yet. But, oh, well. Desperate situations called for desperate measures. Circles under her eyes. Oh, yeah. He'd gotten under her skin. Now all that remained was to reap his reward.

That afternoon Ryan called the store and invited Bethany out to his place for dinner that night. She sounded distracted and weary, and for a moment, Ryan was afraid she was going to turn him down.

"There's something special I want to show you," he quickly inserted.

"Well . . . all right. I've been meaning to talk to you about something. Maybe it's just as well I do it there."

He didn't like the sound of that. "Hey," he said softly. "Is something wrong?"

"Not wrong, exactly. It's—complicated. I'll talk to you tonight. All right? Is six-thirty okay?"

"Six-thirty is fine."

Ryan frowned as he broke the connection. She'd been meaning to talk to him about something? That had "Dear John" written all over it. *Son of a bitch*. He rubbed his brow. The headache he'd been battling since Jake's phone call that morning was growing worse. No worries. He loved her, and he knew damned well she cared for him. If she was thinking about not seeing him anymore, he'd be able to talk her out of it.

He took some ibuprofen, gathered up all his dirty socks and the scattered newspapers in the family room, and then took two steaks out of the freezer to thaw. That done, he made for the shower.

With his aching head shoved under the jets of hot water, Ryan was able to think more clearly, and he began to plan his strategy. He definitely wanted to look sharp, but at the same time, he didn't want to overdo it. He'd be grilling the steaks himself. Nothing too fancy. He should dress accordingly. He decided to wear pressed black jeans, a long-sleeved black shirt, and a pair of black dress boots polished to shine like glass. Women went for black. Why he had no idea, but he wasn't about to mess with what worked. Not tonight.

Did all guys feel sort of sick before they popped the question? His stomach felt like a wet sock being turned inside out. He angled an arm over the tile and rested his aching head on the back of his wrist. He hadn't felt nervous like this over a female in years. After his green wore off and he'd gotten a little experience under his belt, he'd always just figured, "What the hell," and hadn't really worried about how he looked or what he should say.

Falling in love was a real bitch.

*　*　*

She was late. Ryan glanced at his watch. Six-thirty-two, and ticking. *Only two minutes late.* No big deal. It was a long drive from town, and people didn't always time it exactly right. She'd be here.

He paced. Through the kitchen, into the great room. Around the sofa. Past the slider. Quick stop to gaze out at the road. He'd be able to see her coming around the lake long before she got here. Back into the kitchen. He checked the steaks for the umpteenth time to make sure they were thawed. Opened the new low-profile refrigerator to stare at the salad he'd tossed. *Still there, still green.*

He sighed and stepped to the new universal-level sink to scrub the potatoes a little more. Looked out the window again. Where *was* she? *Damn.* His stomach squeezed. He passed a hand over his eyes. He went back over everything he could remember saying to her over the past few days. As far as he knew, he'd done nothing, *nothing,* to make her want to stop seeing him.

He glimpsed her gray van through the trees just then. His heart pitched and did a funny little dance in his chest, making him worry he was about to have a heart attack. He took a deep breath, realized he was sweating, and called himself a thousand kinds of idiot. *Never let them see you sweat.*

He'd wait inside, he decided. If he went out on the porch, he'd look too eager. He no sooner concluded that than he was stepping outside. So . . . he was eager. Big deal. He wanted to marry the girl. She was it for him. No harm in letting her know how he felt.

She parked on the cement pad he'd had poured between the stable and the house. Then she just sat there and stared. Ryan walked down the wheelchair ramp he'd added onto the kitchen porch, then moved along the walkway toward her, wearing a smile that felt carved into his face. He lifted a hand in greeting.

When she finally rolled down her window, he said, "Hi, there."

She fixed him with those huge blue eyes. Her face was so white it looked damned near bloodless. "Oh, Ryan, what have you *done*?" she cried.

Somehow, he didn't think she was any too happy. This wasn't the reaction he'd been hoping to get, to say the least. *Wow* would have been nice. He glanced around, swallowed. It was on the tip of his tongue to explain what he'd done, but then it struck him how stupid that would be. He had obviously built her wheelchair paths all over hell's creation.

"How do you like it?" he settled for asking. "You can even go down to the lake and follow the shore for quite a ways in either direction."

Her face went even paler, accentuating the dark circles under her eyes that Jake had mentioned. "Oh, *God*. What have you *done*?"

Ryan had had a few days in his life when he'd wondered if he wouldn't have been better off never getting out of bed. This was shaping up to be one of them. At the sound of her voice, a horse inside the stable started whinnying and screaming and kicking its stall. Ryan didn't have to go check to see which horse it was. *Hell*. He'd been hoping to surprise her with Wink a little later in the evening. There was such a thing as hitting someone with too much at once.

But, *no*. The horse recognized her voice. *Incredible*. It had been eight years. Eight frigging *years*. Most horses had long memories, but in his recollection, he'd never heard of one recognizing someone's voice after so long.

Bethany glanced bewilderedly toward the stable. "What on *earth* is the matter in there?"

It sounded like the stable was about to fold like a house of cards. Ryan followed her gaze and rubbed his jaw. "It's nothing." He hoped Sly was still around and would do something to settle Wink down. *Fast*. "We have a new mare in there. She gets a little—"

Wink grunted three times and whinnied excitedly. Ryan had never heard the horse make that particular succession of noises before, but he recognized horse love talk when he heard it. His stomach did a slow revolution, and he could only pray Bethany didn't make the connection.

"*Wink?*" she whispered. She started tearing at the driver's door to exit the van. "Wink!" She fixed a tear-filled, incredulous gaze on Ryan as she extended the lift. "That's my *horse!*"

Ryan thought, Well, hell . . . He puffed air into his cheeks. "Nothing like hitting you with all your surprises at once. I, um . . . bought her back for you."

She moved her chair out onto the platform, set the brake, and then lowered the lift to the pad. "You *what?*"

Just in case she hadn't heard him, he repeated himself.

"You what?" she said again.

Ryan wasn't going to say it a third time. She moved her chair off the lift onto the cement and took off like a shot for the stable. Ryan followed, almost wishing that he could stop her from going inside. But, no. He'd paved the way, so to speak.

At the entrance she braked to a sudden stop, stared for a moment at the wide asphalt alley that stretched, straight as a bullet, the length of the center aisle to the double, crossbuck doors that opened onto the riding arena. Before each stall, a lip of asphalt with a sloped edge extended out, making the hasp of the gate accessible to someone in a wheelchair.

"Oh, *Ryan,*" she whispered shakily.

Standing slightly back and to one side, he could see a tear rolling down her pale cheek. About halfway up the aisle, Wink thrust her head out over the stall gate, the whites showing around her eyes, her nostrils flared as she snorted the air. She made the three grunting sounds again and whinnied eagerly. It was clearly a greeting for Bethany alone. Gazing at the horse, Bethany made a low, keening sound, then covered her face with her hands.

"Oh, God, Ryan, why did you *do* this?" She dropped her

hands and whirled on him. "Just friends, you said. No risks, no expectations!" With every word, her voice grew shriller. "Jake sold Wink for twenty-five *thousand*. I know Hunsacker wouldn't have let her go for a cent less than that. How much did you pay for her?"

Ryan swiped a hand over his mouth, Instead of feeling like her hero, as he'd imagined he might, he felt like he'd committed a crime. "The money isn't important, honey."

"It *is* important! And don't call me *honey*!"

"Bethany, I—"

"How *much*?" she demanded.

"Thirtyish," he admitted. "That's peanuts, Bethany. I've paid over a hundred for a nice horse without batting an eye."

"Thirtyish?" She stared up at him in appalled amazement. "And what does the *ish* stand for?"

"Six.

"Thirty-six *thousand*?" She passed a hand over her eyes. She was shaking. Shaking horribly. "I can't believe you did this. I can't *believe* it! I can't ever pay it back. Not ever."

"I don't expect you to pay me back."

She stared at him with an accusing look in her eyes. Just stared at him as if she'd never seen him before. After what seemed like a small eternity, she spoke, her voice flat and hollow. "It's all been a lie from the very first, hasn't it? You never intended for us to be just friends. You lied so I'd continue to see you."

Ryan thought about lying again. At the moment that seemed like the wisest choice. Admitting the truth didn't strike him as a brilliant move. "Yeah," he said softly. "I sort of lied, I guess. Actually, it depends on how you define love and friendship, sweetheart. Can you really have one without the other?" He shrugged, doing his best to look reasonable. "I don't think so. An intimate relationship without a wonderful friendship isn't love or anything close to it. Been there, done that, and trust me, it has no meaning."

She hugged her waist and sat back in her chair, flinching

when Wink kicked her stall door again and shrieked. She closed her eyes, and the muscles in her face drew taut. "I told you from the first, Ryan. I didn't color it. We can never be more than friends. *Never.* And I planned to tell you tonight that even the friendship isn't working for me."

"Why, for God's sake?"

She lifted her lashes and fixed him with those beautiful blue eyes he'd loved since the moment he first looked into them. A deep, vivid blue so clear it could hide nothing, especially pain—the kind of pain that ran too deep for tears and hurt so much, it couldn't be expressed with words.

"I can't be what you need," she whispered.

She circled around him and headed for her van. Ryan gazed after her for a moment. Then he struck out after her. "Bethany, can we discuss this?"

"There's nothing to discuss."

He caught up with her just as she reached the lift. She rolled her chair up onto the ramp, raised it to move inside the van, and then positioned herself behind the steering wheel. He watched in silence as she hit the control to retract the chair lift and bent to fasten the restraints.

"So, you're just going to leave. Is that it?"

"Yes," she said softly, and shut the door.

Ryan hooked his arms over the edge of the window opening and leaned inside. "And I'm supposed to just let you go?"

"You don't have a choice."

When she reached to start the engine, he snaked out a hand and grabbed her wrist. "I outweigh you by a hundred and twenty pounds. That carries the vote."

She threw him a startled look. "Let go of me, Ryan."

"Not until I've said my piece," he bit out.

She twisted her arm free. "Nothing you say will change my mind."

Ryan knew he was about to lose his temper. At the back of his mind, warning bells went off. But he was past caring.

"Fine, then!" he bit out. "Run away, Bethany. It's what you're good at. Right? That's all you've done for the past eight years is bury your feelings and run away."

That got her attention. She turned to look at him, at least. Nose to nose with her, he glared back. "All this time, I figured you for having a backbone. I guess I was wrong. You didn't just lose the use of your legs in that riding accident. You lost your guts."

She flinched as if he slapped her. "That isn't fair."

"Fair? Are we playing fair, here? I'm sorry. I guess I missed it. I'm in love with you, damn it!" He swung his arm to encompass the ranch. "I've busted my ass for damned near a month, revamping my place to show you we can have a life together. Instead of being glad—instead of having the guts to at least give it a try—you're running! The truth is, I scare you to death. Good old Paul, back to haunt us. You're afraid of getting hurt, and you're too big a coward to take that chance."

"That *isn't* true!" she cried. "I'm doing this for you!" Tears rushed to her eyes. "You're just too blind to see it!" Her face twisted, and she cupped a shaking hand over her brow. "I *love* you."

"You have a hell of a way of showing it."

"It's the only way to show it! Do you think I don't want all this?" Her voice went thin. "That it's easy for me to turn my back on it? I want it so bad I can *taste* it! You're offering me *everything*! Everything I ever wanted, ever dreamed of, a life with you, being part of your world! Oh, *God*. Even *Wink*! You even bought my horse back!"

The agony in those words made Ryan's stomach drop. His flare of temper went out like a candlewick, dashed with a gallon of ice water. He was guilty as charged. He had tried to make all her dreams come true. He'd worked and planned and then worked some more, creating a world expressly for her—so she could go wherever she wanted, when she wanted—so she could be around horses and ride again—so she could visit the wilderness whenever she wished.

Looking at it all through her eyes, he tried to imagine how hard it would be to turn his back and drive away if he were in her shoes. He wasn't sure he'd be able to. He'd seen the yearning in her expression so many times—a bone-deep yearning for all the things she'd loved and lost—which was precisely why he'd tried so hard to give all those things back to her.

Yet she was prepared to leave . . . to simply turn her back on all of it, even on the horse that whinnied and called to her now—a horse that still remembered her and adored her after eight long years. It stood to reason that Bethany probably returned the animal's devotion in equal measure.

Yet she was still going to leave . . .

Ryan's throat closed off, and for a moment, he couldn't breathe. There was only one reason she would go when she yearned to stay. She honestly believed it was the best thing for *him*. This wasn't about her at all. It had never been about her. And she was right; he'd been too blind to see it.

"Oh, Bethany," he whispered. "I'm sorry." He hooked a hand over the back of her neck and drew her face to his shoulder. "I shouldn't have said any of that. I didn't mean it."

Her hands knotted on his shirt, and she shuddered as a sob tore up from deep within her. "I—can't—be—what you need, Ryan! No babies. Never any babies. M-maybe never any decent *sex*! I m-might die really young. And I c-can't be a g-good rancher's wife. I'd be a b-burden to you a-and everyone *else*!"

Ryan made a fist in her hair and drew her closer. "Sweetheart, no. Listen to me. Are you listening?"

She made a mewling sound and nearly choked, trying to hold back her sobs.

"I *love* you!" he said fiercely. "If we can't have babies, we'll adopt."

"It's not the s-*same*! Not for a man. And they might not approve me! You should have a f-family. You were *meant* to be a father. Just seeing y-you with T-bone, I knew that. You have so much love to give."

"Sweetheart, we'll have a family. You want a dozen kids? Fine. We can go through a private agency. I've already put out some feelers to find out which ones are reputable. And who says it's not the same? I'll love adopted children just as much as I would my own."

"You say that now. How will you f-feel when you're older?"

"The same. If I can't have babies with you, I'll never have them with anyone. I may be a single father and adopt kids without you, but there's never going to be another woman. You're it for me."

"That's s-silly. You don't mean it."

"Oh, but I do." Ryan turned his face against her hair. "I mean it, Bethany. With all my heart."

"Even if I can't give you good sex?"

"We won't know about that until we try. Maybe it'll be great, maybe it won't. We'll find a way, bottom line, some way that gives us both pleasure."

"Why should you s-settle for that?"

"Settle? Bethany, I *love* you. I've followed a hundred dead ends, searching for you. Not a single one of those women ever meant a hill of beans to me. Just you. I'm not settling, damn it. If I could rope the moon and have any woman on earth I wanted, I'd choose you."

"Aren't you hearing anything I've said? People like me live on borrowed time. Health risks, things we can't prevent! I could get a blood clot next week and die on you. There you'd be, with a dozen adopted kids and no wife to help raise them. *No*! I won't do that to you. I *won't*!"

Ryan tightened his hold on her, terrified in that moment that he'd lose her if he turned her loose. "Then, at least stay with me 'til next week," he whispered raggedly. "Let me have the seven days. Maybe I'll get lucky, and there'll be another week after that, and another week after that. Let me have what there is. Stay with me as long as you can. I'll let you go when God takes you, and I'll be thankful for every second He gives me, but I can't let you go like this."

"You're *crazy.*"

"Yeah. You got that right. Crazy about you. Give me what you can. No one has any guarantees, Bethany. No one. We all live on borrowed time. And you know what else?"

"No, what?" she asked shakily.

"You won't die on me. Forget that, lady. I won't let it happen. I'll watch your diet. I'll have you on a treadmill every blessed day, and I'll help you exercise your leg muscles in other ways to prevent blood clots. Plus I'll have you working on this ranch, staying active. You aren't going to die young, not on my watch."

She started to cry again, this time as if her heart were breaking. Ryan slipped his other arm inside the van to loop it around her, then hauled her close against him. He knew he'd won when she stopped resisting him and clung to his neck.

He simply held her for a while, allowing her to cry. He had a feeling these were tears that had been eight years in the making, that she'd held them back for far too long as it was. When at last her sobs began to subside, he ran a hand over her slender back and whispered, "I love you. You can't change that, Bethany. Done deal. And if you run from it, you're going to destroy my life. Can you live with that on your conscience?"

She laughed wetly, the sound muffled against his shirt.

"Give me right now," he urged. "No guarantees. I accept that, and I'll take my chances. Just give me the time you can. Will you do that? *Please?*"

"Oh, Ryan . . . how can I say no?"

"Now you're talkin'."

A shudder ran through her, and she sighed raggedly. "I

guess we can give it a try," she whispered. "At least until we see how the sex goes."

Red alert. Ryan tucked in his chin to look down at her. "No trial runs."

She raised her head to stare at him with huge, tear-drenched eyes that made him feel as if he was drowning in wet velvet. "But, Ryan, it might be *awful*. No promises. No commitments. Not until we know."

Though it was the most difficult thing he'd ever done in his life, Ryan grasped her by the shoulders and set her away from him. "No way, lady. If that's all you're offering me, I pass."

She blinked and rubbed at her cheeks. "What?"

"You heard me. All or nothing. No conditions. You either come into this for better or worse, or it's a deal breaker. I want you to marry me."

"But—"

"No buts. When people love each other, really love each other, they take the lemons and make lemonade. I won't settle for less. I want a woman who'll stand by me and stay with me, no matter what."

"You're the one who'll be stuck with a lemon!"

"How do you know? I could be the world's most rotten lover."

She swiped at her cheeks again, looking bewildered. "That's dumb."

"I've had a few complaints." He took a step back from the van. "Mostly not, but there you go. No telling how you'll feel about it. And what's the guarantee that things will remain status quo? Men get hurt and they get sick. A year from now, I could become impotent and unable to make love to you at all. You gonna hightail it then?" He backed up another step. "Thanks, but no thanks. I want promises, and I want commitments. If that's not what you're offering, I pass."

Her eyes turned a dark, stormy blue, and her brows drew

together in a scowl. "This is stupid, Ryan. I'm giving you an out."

"Thank you. That's very sweet, but I don't want an out." He braced his feet wide apart, folded his arms, and studied her, smiling slightly. "Well? You going or staying?" He glanced around them. "It's gonna be hell to pay if you go. I never will live all this down, and concrete's pretty damned hard to rip up."

She followed his gaze, finally really looking at the network of pathways he'd built for her. Her eyes filled with tears again, and her mouth started to tremble. "Oh, Ryan . . . I can't believe you did all this for me."

"Only for you, and everyone knows it. Turn me down, and I'll be a joke. The hired hands will be snickering behind my back for twenty years. Are you really gonna do that to me?"

She shook her head, her gaze shimmering as she looked out over the lake. "There are walkways going *everywhere*! I could go and go and *go*."

"Anywhere you want, honey. Just, please, don't go away."

She fixed him with worried blue eyes again and gnawed on her bottom lip. "I'm *scared*."

"Of what?"

"That someday not having your own babies will bother you. That you'll watch television sex and realize how *boring* I am and how much you're missing."

Television sex? He usually changed the channel. Ryan looked at her sweet face and knew he could study it for a hundred years and never get bored.

"You know that lady on the fabric softener commercial?" she asked in a squeaky voice. "The one that rolls over and bounces out of bed with a big smile and puts on her jogging outfit to go running?"

Ryan had absolutely no idea which commercial she was

talking about, or how that had anything to do with anything. "Yeah."

"Well, I can't roll over. I'm stuck the way I land. I have to pick up one leg and flop it, then the other leg and flop it. It's more trouble than it's worth."

He grinned. "In bed with me, rolling over will be a cinch. I'll just tuck you up against me, and we'll roll over together."

She wrinkled her nose. " I don't bounce out of bed, either. It's a big, major hassle every morning, and once I'm up, I'll never jog anywhere."

"Sweetheart, what's the point you're trying to make? If bouncing and jogging were real high on my list, would I be standing here?"

"I'm just afraid, Ryan. Someday you'll watch a commercial like that, and you'll feel like I've cheated you and hate me for ruining your life."

Ryan walked slowly back to the van. "Never. I swear it, honey. That'll never happen."

He opened the door of the van then and bent to unfasten the restraints on her chair to push her back from the steering wheel so he could lift her into his arms.

"What are you doing?" she cried.

"I'm making up your mind for you," he said as he swung her up against his chest.

She clutched his neck and gave a startled laugh. "I can make up my own mind, thank you very much."

"Nope. I've got it straight from Sly. 'Never stand around, waitin' for a woman to make up her mind, son. Not unless you're aimin' to put down tap roots.' "

"And what have you decided for me?"

"That you're staying," he whispered. "You're going to marry me, Bethany Ann Coulter. I'm not giving you any outs."

He bent his head to kiss her then, just as he'd yearned to

do and dreamed of doing since that first night in her entry-way.

He wasn't disappointed. Her mouth was every bit as sweet as he remembered. After her first shy withdrawal, she parted her lips and surrendered that sweetness to him, and just as before, he felt the jolt clear to his boot heels. *Holy hell*, was all he could think. No matter how the sex went, it wouldn't matter.

He could live on her kisses alone . . .

Chapter Fourteen

R yan carried Bethany halfway to the house before he came to a stop. Maybe some men could ignore the shrieks of that poor, damned horse, but he wasn't one of them. He glanced down and saw Bethany gazing over his shoulder at the stable. *U-turn.*

"I think you have some hellos you need to say."

Every step of the way to that horse stall, Ryan told himself there were some things more important than sex, and saying hello to a long-lost love had to be one of them. Wink had been just that to Bethany, one of the great loves of her life. *I would have slept with my horse if Daddy hadn't put his foot down,* she'd told him that first night. Ryan had lost a big chunk of his heart to her then—seeing the love shining in her eyes, sensing her sadness because an intrinsic part of who she was had been stolen from her.

This was important—a reunion after eight years of separation. He could make love to Bethany for the rest of their lives, but this special moment would pass, never to be reclaimed, not for Bethany or for Wink. Ryan had spent thirty-six thousand dollars so it could happen. He wanted both woman and horse to enjoy it. How else would he get his money's worth?

As they approached the stall, Wink started grunting again. Ryan had never heard a horse carry on so. "Listen to that. That's as close to talking as I've ever heard."

When he reached the stall, he thought the mare might

climb over the top to reach her mistress. Bethany threw both arms around the horse's neck, Wink swung her head, and the next thing Ryan knew, he was playing catch-as-catch-can to keep hold of his girl.

"Wink!" Bethany cried. "Oh, Wink!"

Clasping her waist to hold her back from the gate so her legs wouldn't be scraped or bruised, Ryan cried, "Bethany, for God's sake, turn loose!"

That wasn't happening. She'd locked onto the mare so tightly, it would have taken a pry bar to break her hold. It got really messy after that, the mare grunting and whickering, Bethany sobbing and raining kisses on Wink's nose. Ryan made a mental note to dunk Bethany in a trough and give her a good scrub before he locked lips with her again.

When the wettest part of the reunion had passed, he gently put Bethany over his shoulder, which made her screech, caught her behind the knees, and unlatched the gate. After carrying her inside, he carefully lowered her onto the fresh mound of hay in one corner of the stall.

"There," he said with a laugh. "Now you two can make happy for as long as you want without me being caught in the middle."

Wink walked over, grunting and making shrill little sounds of greeting. The mare snuffled Bethany from head to toe.

"Oh, Wink. My pretty lady! You're so beautiful." Bethany turned sparkling, red-rimmed eyes on Ryan. "Isn't she gorgeous, Ryan?" She had cried so much, she sounded as if she had a clip on her nose.

Ryan had already looked the horse over good. He raised one of the finest lines of quarter horses in the state and had seen nicer mares. "She's the most beautiful little mare I've ever clapped eyes on." He stepped close to run a hand over Wink's rump, then gave her a pat. "I can see why she was a champion."

"There, you see, Wink? Ryan's an expert, and even he

says you're the best." Bethany kissed the horse's muzzle again. To Ryan's horror, Wink rolled her lip back and wiggled it all over Bethany's face. "Kiss, kiss!" Bethany cried, giggling and making smacking noises. "I taught her to do this," she informed Ryan proudly. "She still remembers!"

Ryan sat down beside her. "All I gotta say is, you're washing your face, brushing your teeth, and gargling before I kiss you again."

Bethany rolled her eyes. "Wink doesn't have germs. Don't be such a priss." She grabbed Wink's halter strap and pushed the mare's head toward him. "Say, 'kiss, kiss.' She'll do it for anyone."

Ryan hiked up his arm to avoid the wiggling horse lip coming toward his face. "No, thanks. I draw the line at kissing a horse."

"It's a special trick," Bethany said, looking crushed.

It was special, all right. Ryan sighed, lowered his arm, and let the mare wiggle her lip all over his face. It wasn't quite as bad as he expected, but it wasn't one of his favorite experiences, either.

What a man wouldn't do for love.

An hour later, Ryan found himself eating steak sandwiches for supper in a horse stall. Wink's entrée was sliced apples, which Bethany fed her, piece by piece, as she ate her sandwich. Somehow, this wasn't quite what Ryan had envisioned as a romantic evening.

"This is the most wonderful night of my life," Bethany said with a glowing smile when she'd finished eating. She reached up to stroke her mare's neck. "I never thought I'd see her again, Ryan. Thank you so much."

"You can thank me by riding her again."

Bethany paled. "I'm a little scared."

"Your saddle won't come until next week. That'll give the two of you plenty of time to get reacquainted and bond again. If I were you, I'd probably feel a little shaky about riding her again myself."

"Oh, it isn't that." Bethany rested her cheek against the mare's velvety nose. "What happened wasn't Wink's fault. I've always known that, and I'd trust her with my life. If ever I get on another horse, it has to be her. It would break her heart if I rode someone else."

Ryan had to bite back a smile. She talked about Wink as if the horse were human. "Even though you were almost killed the last time you rode her?"

"Even though," she said with absolute certainty. "When I say it wasn't Wink's fault, I really mean it *wasn't*. Not at all." Her eyes got a distant look in them as she remembered the accident that had left her paralyzed. "She was racing her heart out for me, giving me everything she had to give. It wasn't her fault she stepped in a hole and fell. Afterward, I can't count the people who came by to see me at the hospital just to tell me I shouldn't blame Wink for what happened. They said that when she realized she couldn't stop, she shifted her weight to one side, trying her best not to fall on me. It wasn't her fault that the barrel tipped and threw me directly in her path."

Ryan watched her trail her fingertips along the horse's jaw, her touch so light and loving that she might have been caressing a child. "I don't suppose you can ask for more than that from anyone," he said softly, "not horse or person. Traveling at that kind of speed and stepping in a hole, she could have busted a leg. A lot of horses wouldn't have been watching out for their riders at a time like that."

"No." She smiled mistily. "And it would have been impossible for any horse to stop." She gave the mare another pat. "I know she tried her very best not to fall on me, and that's all I need to know. Why is it that people always want to place blame? Sometimes bad things just happen. The fairground maintenance crew raked the entire arena that morning and packed it with a roller. There shouldn't have been any holes. They're extremely careful about that because some very valuable horses compete in barrel racing events, and they don't want to be liable." She shrugged. "A ground squirrel tunneled up after the area was prepped. I won't say it was an act of God because I can't believe He wanted me to be paralyzed or that He orchestrated the accident, but I will say it was an act of nature — an unforeseeable one that couldn't be blamed on anyone." She wrinkled her nose. "Unless, of course, I want to blame the ground squirrel."

Ryan dusted some hay off his jeans. "Wanna go hunting? We've got ground squirrels aplenty around here that you can use for target practice."

She laughed and shook her head. "I appreciate the offer, but I worked through my anger years ago. I really don't think that poor little rodent tunneled a hole because he was out to get Bethany Ann Coulter."

Ryan grinned. "A very rational way to look at it. Not very satisfying, but rational."

"Looking at it rationally was the only way I stayed sane. Did you know that anger is the easiest emotion for human beings to feel, and when we lose our faculties, it's the last emotion to go? That's why people with dementia so frequently grow violent, because in the final stages, all they have left are unreasoning feelings of rage." Her smile faded, and she looked deeply into his eyes. "I was there once, feeling nothing but rage. I never want to feel that way again. Bitterness and anger affect every part of your life. I just want to be happy and make the most of things. We have to accept and move on. Feeling sorry for ourselves and casting blame only destroys what's left."

"I definitely want you to enjoy life," he agreed.

"For me, that means if I go riding again, it has to be on Wink. Anything less would be a cop-out. Riding her may bring back bad memories and frighten me, but it's something I'll have to do. Choosing to ride another horse would be a betrayal. I can't do that to her. I won't."

"I understand," he said huskily, and he honestly did understand, perhaps better than she realized. Bethany was no coward, and she didn't have it in her to take the easy way out, not when she thought it might hurt the horse that she loved so much. "I only have one question. Feeling the way you do about Wink—trusting her as you do—why are you so afraid to ride again?"

"Because I know I won't be able to use my legs and that it will never be the same. A part of me is afraid that it will be a huge disappointment—that maybe it would be better to dream about riding and tell myself how great it might be than to actually try and find out it isn't all great and never will be again. Does that make any sense?"

"It makes perfect sense. In dreams, there are no limitations. Reality seldom measures up to that. But, Bethany, look at the flip side. What if the reality turns out to be different from before, but just as wonderful in its own way? If you never dare to try, you'll be missing out on that."

"I know." She drew in a deep breath and slowly exhaled. Her eyes darkened with shadows as she met his gaze again. "I'm also really afraid that I may fall. Imagine being in the saddle and not being able to grip with your knees. The very thought ties my stomach in knots."

"You won't fall, honey. You'll be strapped on." Ryan reached out to brush a tendril of dark hair from her face. "We'll take it slow. The first few times, I'll lead you around the corral. You'll get used to it and soon love riding again."

"Oh, I hope so . . ."

"It'll happen."

Ryan meant to see that it did.

Bethany.

When Ryan suggested that they had spent enough time with Wink and should adjourn to the house, her cheeks turned as pretty a pink as June clover blossoms. En route to the van to collect her wheelchair, Ryan chuckled to himself over her shyness. Then he frowned, the realization suddenly striking him that he hadn't had much experience with virgins—as in none, period. Even in college, he'd sought out girls who knew the score. His father would have skinned him and hung his hide out to dry, otherwise.

Ryan sighed as he returned to the stable. Once in front of Wink's stall, he positioned the wheelchair and set the brake, then he stepped in to collect Bethany. She had straw in her hair, and as he got her settled in her chair, the hem of her ruffled blue skirt flipped up, revealing a rent in her hose. The jagged edges of the tear showcased a scrape on her knee.

Ryan hunkered down to examine the abrasion. She immediately started fussing with her skirt, tugging and tucking the folds around and between her legs. He glanced up. Big, wary blue eyes stared back at him. *Uh-oh.* He tried a harmless-looking grin. He never had been very talented at looking harmless.

"What?" he asked softly.

She shook her head. "Nothing."

Like hell. Ryan heaved an inward sigh, thinking that this was exactly why the traditional wedding night had been the butt of so many jokes. It was sort of like going to the dentist. If you thought about it too much beforehand, you got the jitters long before you sat in the chair.

"You feeling a little nervous?"

She shook her head no and then said, "Yes. A little."

Satisfied that the scrape on her leg was nothing to fret over, Ryan framed her face between his hands. Her cheekbones felt fragile under the pads of his thumbs—itty-bitty compared to his own. "You wanna just wait?"

"For what?"

His brain went blank. Good question. Except for marrying her, which he planned to do before the ink on the marriage license could dry, there was no real reason to wait. Unless, of course, he counted the worried look in her eyes. Which he did.

She curled her fine-boned hands over his wrists. "Oh, Ryan, I'm not nervous for the reason you're thinking. Not about making love with you. I've been—" She broke off, and the blush on her cheeks deepened. "I've thought about that part a lot, and I'm looking forward to it. It's just—"

"It's just what?" he pressed.

She smoothed a hand over the buttons of her blouse. "I, um—just sort of, you know, feel self-conscious. You're so . . ." Her gaze flitted over him. "You're so *perfect*. Handsome and superbly fit—the kind of man most women can only dream about."

Ryan's throat went tight. "Thank you. I think that's stretching it a bit, but it's a very nice compliment, and I'm flattered that you feel that way." He searched her expression. "Does that pose some kind of problem?"

"*No!* Not a problem, exactly. It's just that I'm not."

He mentally circled that pronouncement, not entirely sure what she meant. "You're not what?"

"Perfect," she replied, the word barely more than a whisper.

"Oh, honey." Ryan realized then that he'd been trying so hard to play the role of best friend convincingly that he'd failed to let her know how very much he desired her physically. He'd never even allowed his gaze to trail over her figure. Not when she might catch him at it, at any rate. "If you were any more beautiful, Miss Coulter, I'd have a critical case of pneumonia by now."

She looked bewildered. "Pneumonia?"

He chuckled. "From taking ice-cold showers."

She gave a startled laugh and said, "Oh. *Pneumonia*. Of course." A hopeful, slightly incredulous expression came into her beautiful eyes. "Did you really take cold showers?"

Seeing her incredulity made Ryan's heart hurt for her. To him, it seemed such a crime that someone so lovely could reach the age of twenty-six without ever being told how desirable she was. That was a state of affairs he meant to resolve in damned short order. "Dozens of cold showers," he assured her firmly. "I've wanted to make love to you ever since I first saw you. Every single time I was around you, I had to come home and stand under the cold water until I was numb enough to sleep."

He grinned and lowered his gaze to the lush roundness of her small but perfectly shaped breasts. Maybe it was only wishful thinking, but he could have sworn he saw her nipples tighten in response. Encouraged by that, he took visual measure of her tidy figure from there down, his hands itching to curl over her hips, his body aching to feel her softness pressed firmly against him.

When he returned his gaze to hers, her face was pink clear to her hairline, but there was a purely feminine sparkle in her eyes. He decided then and there that from now on he'd do plenty of ogling and make sure she caught him at it.

"I can't exercise certain parts of my body like other people," she confessed shakily. "In those places my muscles have atrophied, and I'm not well toned."

"Does that mean you're going to feel as soft and wonderful as you look?"

She sighed, conveying by her expression that this was no time for nonsense. "I'm just so afraid I'll disappoint you. That you might not like how I look and that I'll be a big disappointment in other ways as well, and that—"

He interrupted her by dipping his head to kiss her. Oh, God, how he loved her mouth, so soft and willing, yet uncertain and hesitant. He wanted to go on tasting her forever, wanted to spend the rest of his life pleasuring himself with her. He'd take this lady, horse slobber and all.

Forcing himself to end the kiss, he whispered, "Sweetheart, would you stop worrying? I think you're beautiful, and my opinion is the only one that counts. It's going to be all right between us. I have this gut feeling, and my gut feelings are seldom wrong."

"Oh, Ryan, I pray you're right. If we can at least have satisfying sex, I'll feel so much better about marrying you. If I can't feel anything, I think I'll *die*."

Wink nudged Ryan's shoulder. He reached up with one hand to rub the mare's neck. "Are you sure that's all you're worried about? You're not afraid I'll hurt you?" Just in case she was embarrassed to admit she felt uneasy on that score, he hastened to add, "This *is* your first time. That's a very natural concern for a woman to have, you know."

She laughed. "I *pray*."

"What?"

"I pray it hurts. That'll be good, Ryan. That'll be *great*."

The very thought made his guts clench. He would have happily hacked off an arm rather than cause her pain. But she was right. He should be praying it would hurt. In this instance, the more discomfort, the more cause to celebrate.

He returned Wink to her stall and battened the gate for the night. Then he pushed Bethany from the stable.

"You want to swing down by the lake?" he asked, thinking he needed to woo her just a bit. "It's beautiful down there at night. The stars twinkle on the water like thousands of diamonds."

"After," she said firmly. "We can go down later."

So much for that tack. When they reached the house, Ryan turned on only a couple of lights and grabbed the remote to flip on the stereo as he went into the kitchen to pour them each some wine. Bethany marveled over the changes in the kitchen, then sat at the opposite side of the counter, her big blue eyes following him nervously.

"Ryan?"

He broke off pouring to meet her gaze. "What?"

"Can we just—" She skittered her fingers down the front of her blouse, dragged in an unsteady breath, and then gulped. "You know—can we just—" She exhaled in a rush. "No big drawn-out thing. Please? I just want to—um—get to the important part. Just this time. I promise. I'm sorry for rushing you, but I need to know."

His heart caught at the shadows of anguish in her eyes. She was about to die of anxiety, and he was diddling around. He set the wine bottle aside, then circled the bar to scoop her up out of the chair.

"You won't have to issue that invitation twice."

As he swung her up against his chest, she wrapped both arms around his neck, pressed her face to the hollow just under his jaw, and whispered, "Tell me again, Ryan. I need to hear you say it one more time."

It wasn't necessary for her to clarify the request. He ducked his chin to press his lips to her temple. "I love you, Bethany, and I'll love you the rest of my life with every beat of my heart."

He carried her to the bedroom. When he set her on the edge of the bed, she bent her head so her hair fell forward to veil her face and then started unbuttoning her top with trembling fingers. She looked so forlorn, sitting there, with her pretty little feet turned all funny, one pointed inward, the other bent over at the ankle.

Ryan ran his hands down her calves, knowing she felt nothing when he touched her there, but allowing himself the pleasure anyway. Through the mesh of her hose, her skin felt cool and wonderfully soft, reminding him of how satiny she was. He kissed the scrape on her knee, which earned him a startled look from her, then he gently repositioned her feet.

When he glanced back up, she was struggling with a button. He pushed her hands away and relieved her of the task.

"Do you mind?" he asked. "I usually like to unwrap my own presents."

She flashed him a bewildered look, which he met with a smile.

"You are a gift, Bethany Coulter. The sweetest, most beautiful gift God's ever given me."

Her mouth went all funny, one corner turning down and quivering. "Oh, Ryan. I forgot to tell you one more really awful thing."

"What?" he asked, his heart catching because she looked so upset. "It can't be that bad. What, honey?"

"I have scars. Terrible ones."

His heart stuttered, then bumped back into rhythm. "Is that all?" He dispensed with the remaining buttons, then parted the front of her blouse and tugged the tails from the waistband of her skirt. "I'll bet your scars are nothing compared to mine. You want to see a scar, darlin'? I'll show you a *scar*."

He rocked back on one heel to unfasten his shirt, then jerked one side loose to reveal a jagged red scar on his rib cage. "I got it from a hay hook. Rafe and I got in a fight when we were kids. I threw something—can't even remember what now—and hit him on the back of the head. When he swung around to come after me, he accidentally gaffed me."

"Oh, *no*." She touched the mark with her fingertips. "Oh, Ryan, that must have hurt so much!"

He chuckled. "It hurt Rafe worse than it did me. He felt so bad, he cried. Dad felt so sorry for him, he didn't even give him a whipping."

Her eyes widened. "Did he whip you boys a lot?"

"Once a day and twice on Sunday, just to keep us in line." Ryan chuckled at the horrified look that came over her face. "Not really. Near as I remember, he took the strap to Rafe once, and that was way back in first grade when he smacked a girl. Kendrick code. No man worth his salt ever strikes a woman, including six-year-old boys."

"Did you ever get the strap?"

"Nope. The only time he ever took after me was when I was eighteen, and then he backhanded me across the mouth." Ryan rubbed his jaw. "Knocked me ass over tea kettle, too. The old man carries quite a punch."

"Why did he backhand you?"

Ryan chuckled, remembering. "You want a list? I drove home from town drunker than a lord. Mom took one look at me when I walked in the kitchen and jumped me about taking my life in my hands. I lied and said I hadn't been drinking, which was my second mistake. Then I called her a name in a roundabout way. I never finished the sentence before Dad decked me."

Bethany had clearly forgotten her partial state of undress, which suited him fine. "What on *earth* did you call her?"

Ryan grinned. "I didn't exactly call her anything. I just pointed out that other guys drank, and their moms didn't act like bitches when they got home. I never got much said after 'bitches.' Dad swung, I went down, and when I started to stand back up, he planted his boot in the middle of my chest to inform me there wasn't a man alive who'd ever called my mother a bitch and apologized to her on his feet. If I was smart, I'd talk first and stand up later."

Bethany giggled. "Oh, my. What did you do?"

"I lay there like the intelligent kid I was and told my mother I was sorry from a prone position. Afterward, Dad helped me up, checked my teeth, told Mom to put some ice on my lip, and left the kitchen. He never mentioned it again, and I sure as hell didn't." Ryan smiled, remembering. "I've never spoken to my mother since without showing the proper respect. Bitter lesson, good school. My father isn't a mean man, but he can be a hard one if you cross him, and the quickest way on earth to cross him is to get out of line with my mom."

He peeled her blouse down her arms, doing his damnedest to pretend he wasn't much interested in the view. She was such a pretty little thing, all creamy and soft, with pointy bones here and there for a man to nibble on,

"Where are those awful scars?" he asked, pretending to search for them as he took in the lacy cups of her bra and what they supported. Her breasts were as beautifully shaped as he had imagined and just large enough to fill his hands. Through the lace, he could see the rosy tips peeking out at him. They were hard and thrust against the cloth like little rivets. "I don't see a spot on you that's not perfect."

A flush of humiliation slashed her cheeks. "They're on my back. I had three surgeries, remember."

He started to lean around. "Please, don't look," she said. "I'm self-conscious about them. They're ugly."

Ryan narrowed an eye at her. "Well, there seems to be no help for it. I guess I'll have to drop my trousers and show you what a *real* scar looks like." He reached for his belt buckle. "Tangled with barbed wire. Another story. Rafe was behind that one, too."

She noticed he was about to unfasten his belt and shook her head. "No, no. I—believe you. You don't need to show me."

Ryan arched his eyebrows. "You need to show me yours. There's no room for secrets between us, and I don't want you worrying later that I might see them. Better to get it over with now. Agreed?"

She nodded, but judging by her expression, she was none too thrilled at the thought. He decided to get the misery over with quickly and leaned around to look at the scars along her spine. His guts clenched when he located them, not because the three marks were ugly, but because they represented all the pain she had endured. He wished she might have been spared that unnecessary suffering, yet he also accepted that he, too, would have encouraged her to have the operations on the off chance that the spinal repairs might have helped her to walk again.

Aware that she was waiting for his reaction, Ryan tried to think of something reassuring to say—that the scars weren't ugly, that they didn't bother him, that he would have barely noticed them when he made love to her. All of that was true, but for some reason, the words wouldn't come. So instead, he acted on impulse, bracing himself on one elbow to lean farther around, then slowly trailing his lips the length of each incision mark. Bethany stiffened and arched her spine.

"Oh, Ryan, *don't*."

He finished kissing each scar, then drew back to look up at her. "I love everything about you," he said softly. "Even the slightly imperfect parts. They just serve to remind me of how beautiful the rest of you is."

Her eyes misted with tears. "You don't think they're ugly?"

"Not at all. Nothing about you could ever come close to being ugly."

He grasped the edge of the mattress on either side of her and pushed forward until his nose touched hers. When he continued the advance, she gave a startled squeak and fell onto her back, which was right where he wanted her. He moved his hands beside her shoulders and followed her down. Her eyes crossed slightly as she gazed up at him along the dainty bridge of her nose. He couldn't resist kissing it, then following the slope in a slow ascent to her brow, where he traced the sable arches over her eyes with the tip of his tongue.

"My God, you are so beautiful," he whispered. "I could spend the whole night just tasting you."

She curled her hands over his upper arms, and he could feel her trembling. His heart caught. "Honey, you're not afraid of me, are you?"

"Oh, no."

He bit back a smile. She was so savvy and sassy much of the time that it was easy for him to forget she had absolutely no experience with men. *Down, boy.* Whether she wanted him to or not, he needed to take this slow.

Shifting his weight to lie beside her, he braced up on one elbow and traced the edge of her bra with a fingertip, beginning at one shoulder and taking a lazy journey across the swells of her breasts to reach the opposite strap.

"Do you have any idea how much I want you?"

"As much as I want you, I hope." She cupped a slender hand over his jaw, her dainty thumb trailing lightly along his cheek. Just feeling her touch him made his blood heat. "I tried so hard not to want you, but I couldn't seem to help it." She smiled dreamily. "It got so bad that I couldn't sleep. I just lay there, wide awake, thinking and wishing and wondering. I can hardly believe I'm here with you now and that I'll never have to imagine and wonder again."

Ryan searched her eyes and saw desire, turbulent and hot, eddying in those blue depths.

She nibbled on her lip, a sudden frown pleating her smooth brow. "I really appreciate your being so thoughtful. Going so slow and taking the time to say nice things. But I really don't need you to, if that's why you're doing it. I'm ready for you to—you know—*start*."

Ryan choked back a laugh. "I'm sorry. I don't mean to drag my feet."

"Oh, I'm not complaining! I just—"

"I understand," he whispered, cutting her off by bending his head to kiss her lightly. Against her lips he added, "But, honey, I have to get you ready."

"I'm ready," she assured him.

He settled a hand at her waist and deepened the kiss. *Sweet Christ.* She *was* ready. Her soft, yielding mouth opened hungrily, encouraging him to enter and take. Only a dead man could resist an invitation like that, and he was a long way from the grave.

Between kisses she whispered, "No secrets or games. Right? My body's been as ready as it'll ever get for over a month."

He reared back to search her face. "A *month*?"

She nodded. "All those nights on the sofa, while you were watching the movies? I was thinking about—well, you know—doing *this*."

Ryan struggled to keep a straight face. "You're kidding."

"No, really."

He unfastened the waistband of her skirt. Then he could no longer keep from grinning and started to chuckle as he bent his head to nibble on her neck. "When I was touching you here?" he asked as he nipped her skin. "And here?" He touched his tongue to the hollow under her ear. "And back here?" He leaned around, trying to reach her nape. "Damn, am I good, or what?"

She twisted to look at him. "You did it on purpose."

It wasn't really a question. Holding her gaze, he unzipped the side of her skirt. "Do bears live in the woods? Of course I did it on purpose. I was doing my damnedest to seduce you."

She giggled and closed her eyes. "When we're finished here, remind me to skin you with a dull knife. For now, though, rest assured that your efforts were successful. I insist that you start living up to all those unspoken promises you made to me."

"What promises?"

"That someday you were going to kiss me in all those places—and maybe in lots of other places as well. I've been wondering how it would feel for a whole month. Now I'm ready for you to put your money where your mouth is." She laughed again. "Or maybe I should say, put your mouth where your hands were."

Ryan was more than ready to make good on those unspoken promises. He just couldn't quite believe she was asking, or that he was the lucky man she'd chosen. He'd imagined having to ease her into this, thinking that she'd be shy and a little reluctant. Instead she was impatient, sweetly eager, and as hot as a little firecracker if her kisses were any indication.

Please, God. He wanted to make it perfect for her—an incredible night that would remain in her memory always. She was such a dear heart, He had no idea what she may have imagined while she lay staring at the ceiling in her lonely bed, but he wanted to make her every fantasy come true.

When he drew down her skirt, tights, and panties, she

squeezed her eyes closed in embarrassment, clearly afraid he might be disappointed with her. He skimmed his gaze from the lower edge of her lacy bra to the tips of her dainty toes, drinking in the wealth of milk white skin. Every inch of her was absolute perfection, her ribs forming a delicate ladder of descent to an incredibly slender waist that gave way to the ample flare of her hips. Unable to resist the urge, he bent to nibble on the jut of one small hipbone, which made her jerk, gasp, and open her eyes.

He grinned and hooked a fingertip under the edge of her bra. Tugging lightly, he said, "Everything off. I want to see all of you."

With trembling hands, she reached up to unhook the front clasp of the bra. As the lace fell away, her cheeks turned pink, and she studiously avoided looking up at him. "They're not very big. Do you like big ones?"

Ryan was so absorbed with looking his fill that he barely registered the question. The creamy globes of her breasts were small, but exquisitely shaped, each tipped with a delicate, rosy nipple that hardened and thrust eagerly up at him, as if titillated by the searing heat of his gaze. He wanted to touch his tongue to each sensitive peak, to learn the taste of her. But her question still hung between them, waiting to be answered.

He searched her eyes, realizing as he did that for her this was a momentous unveiling, the first time in her adult life that any man other than a doctor had ever seen her naked. Naturally she was unsure of herself. He hadn't had a surplus of self-confidence himself his first time.

"I prefer breasts on the small side," he finally found the presence of mind to tell her.

"You're not just saying that, are you?"

Ryan couldn't help but smile. "No, I'm not just saying that. And as soon as I get you fully on the bed, lady, I've got some promises I need to make good on."

When he leaned over her to turn back the sheets,

Bethany's stomach did flips. She didn't know why she felt so nervous, only that she did, and no matter how sternly she lectured herself, it didn't seem to help.

He slipped an arm around her waist, twisted to turn her on the bed, and then gently settled her back against the pillow. Gazing up at him, she thought she'd never seen anyone so handsome. In the dim light his skin looked as dark as teak, and his gray-blue eyes shimmered like moon-washed silver as they trailed slowly over her body.

She realized that her knees were parted and grabbed for the blankets to cover her sprawled legs. Grasping her wrist, Ryan stopped her from taking refuge under the blankets as he situated himself beside her.

"Don't," he whispered.

"But my legs are—"

"For tonight, they're *my* legs." Still wearing his unbuttoned shirt, he shifted his weight to better see her face, releasing her wrist to slide his palm up the inside of her left thigh. "I don't know what angle you've been looking at those legs from, honey, but from my point of view, they're absolutely gorgeous. Hasn't anyone ever told you that?"

"No." Bethany's breath caught again at the feel of his hard, warm palm on the sensitive skin of her inner thigh. "Not that I—oh, my."

"You've got dimples in your knees," he whispered huskily. "The cutest little dimples I've ever seen."

His dark face moved closer to hers—close enough that the warmth of his expelled breath wafted over her cheek as he spoke. He dipped his head to kiss where his breath had already started to make her skin tingle. His lips were silky and touched her like a whisper, blazing a fiery trail to her ear where the tip of his tongue came into play, licking at her lobe and electrifying her nerve endings.

Bethany's eyes drifted partway closed. She grasped his shoulders and dug in hard with her fingers, feeling as if his sturdiness was her only anchor in a world that was suddenly spinning. Oh, God. She loved the way his lips trailed over her skin, so lightly it was like being teased with butterfly wings. And, oh, how wonderful it was to feel his chest graze the tips of her breasts. With every pass, her heart leaped and her breathing hitched. The softness of his shirt was a flimsy barrier over hard, vibrant pads of warm muscle that rippled and flexed each time he moved. *Ryan*. She even loved the smell of him—a tantalizing blend of masculine scents that titillated her senses.

When he trailed his lips to her throat, she let her head fall back and arched, loving the sensations as he kissed and nibbled and suckled her skin. A hot tingling feeling ribboned through her to pool like liquid fire low in her belly, and the funny, achy sensation that had kept her awake countless nights grew so acute she wanted to arch against him like a cat. The inclination became more intense when he traced the shape of her collarbone with the tip of his tongue. Her breathing grew more uneven, the shallow little pants barely reaching her lungs. An unbidden whimper escaped her when she felt his lips moving lower.

A thousand times she had wondered how it must feel to be loved by a man, and a fair five hundred of those times had occurred over the last two months. In the darkness of her room, while she lay alone in her bed, she'd stared blindly into the blackness of night, and wondered, the ache of need inside her making her fantasize and *want*.

How would it feel to have Ryan's hands on her body?

How would it feel if he kissed her skin?

How would it feel to have him suckle her nipples?

Now he was finally about to do it, and she could barely stand the wait. She held her breath, yearning for the heat of his mouth on her breasts.

As he kissed his way downward, he kept to the center of her chest, following the line of her sternum to her cleavage. Bethany's heart started to pound—a resonant pounding that rang in her ears. Her nipples went all hard and were so sensitive that the slight movement of his shirt over the tips made all of her thoughts splinter. He kissed the inside swell of one breast, then he kissed the other. She wished he would just get over there where she so desperately wanted him to be, but he seemed bent on teasing her and building the suspense first.

He kissed little trails toward her nipples, then veered off course, mercilessly tormenting her until she felt sure she would go mad. Each time his jaw grazed her aureole, she jerked and thought about taking fistfuls of his hair to hold him fast.

When she couldn't stand the sweet torture any longer, she did just that, bracing her arms against him when he attempted to move away. He lifted his dark head and stared at the bare peak of her breast, his eyes turning dark and molten. He clearly knew what she wanted. And when he didn't give it to her, as she was praying he might, she could have wept with frustration.

"Oh, God, Bethany, you're beautiful," he whispered raggedly, his hot breath whispering across the throbbing peak to intensify her yearning. "You make me think of strawberries and cream, my favorite thing on earth."

She just wanted him to take a taste. "Ryan . . . ?"

He moved up to take her mouth in a long, deep kiss instead, which wasn't exactly what she wanted, but he kissed her until she couldn't quite remember what she'd been wanting, anyway.

Until his chest dragged over her breasts. Instant recall. "Ryan?"

"What, honey?"

"Would you—" Bethany gulped, wishing he would just get down to business. "Would you kiss me, please?"

He took her mouth again. A deep, tongue-tangling, whopper of a kiss that set her head to reeling. It was lovely. Beyond description. A fantastic, wonderful, soul-shaking kiss that made her heart pound. But it wasn't what she *wanted*.

When he finally broke away to grab for breath, she gulped and said, "Not my mouth. My breasts."

He searched her gaze for a long, pulse-hammering moment. Then he grinned and said, "The waiting is what makes it fun."

"I've had enough fun. Twenty-six years of it."

He chuckled, the sound wicked and laced with purely male satisfaction. "Got you beat. I've been waiting to kiss those breasts for thirty years, and I'm damned well going to enjoy the anticipation." He dipped his head to lap at the V of her collarbone. "I'm going to taste every sweet inch of you and save those beautiful breasts for last."

Bethany nearly groaned. She wanted him to kiss her there so badly that she was trembling. She kept a tight hold on his hair—or tried to, anyway—her mind splintering when the heat of his mouth zeroed in on the underside of her upraised arm and trailed slowly up to the bend of her elbow. She didn't know how he managed it, but he made the most ordinary parts of her body feel like supersensitive erogenous zones.

"Oh, *God*." She nearly sobbed when he shook her hand loose from his hair and attacked her palm, tracing the lines etched there as if he meant to commit each one to memory. When he drew the tip of her finger into his mouth and she felt that incredibly wet, soft heat drawing on her flesh, she did sob. "Ryan, enough. I can't bear it."

"Sure you can." He licked his way down her finger. "When I'm done with you, you won't remember your own name, and you'll be begging me to kiss those breasts. And when I finally do, the sensations will send you straight over the edge."

"Ah-ah-ahhhh" was all she could get out by way of response. He was nibbling on her wrist bone now. She felt like a smorgasbord laid out for his enjoyment.

He nipped his way back up to her elbow and sucked on it, laving her skin with his tongue. "I'll take your nipples between my teeth," he whispered raggedly, "just like *this*." He gave her a preview of the delights in store for her, nibbling gently on her arm. "And with each tug of my teeth, I'll make you think you're dying from the pleasure."

She was already dying. He ducked his head under her arm to nibble on her ribs, ascending the ladder of ridges to her underarm, which she might have found embarrassing if she'd still had a clear thought in her head.

"Ryan . . ." she murmured, dragging out each syllable of his name.

He grasped both of her wrists in one big hand, anchored her arms above her head, and then reared back to gaze down at her chest. "Lordy, girl, you're something." His eyes burned with the heat of passion when he met her gaze again. He smiled slightly—the smile of a man who knew exactly what he was about and was savoring every second of it.

"I'm going to kiss them now. Are you ready?"

She'd been ready for ten minutes. She managed to nod. He grinned and then, with an agonizing slowness that made her skin burn with anticipation, he bent his dark head. "Watch," he whispered.

The edict was entirely unnecessary. Her gaze was riveted to his mouth and followed its lazy descent. When his lips came to within an inch of her breast, her nipple went even harder, thrusting upward to meet him. He smiled and blew on the tip. The unexpected waft of steamy warmth followed by the coolness of the air made her spine arch and her breathing stop. She tried to wrest her hands free from his grip, but he tightened his hold.

"Oh, no, you don't. No interference while I do this, lady. For now, you're all mine."

He flicked out his tongue to circle her aureole. Dimly Bethany heard a shuddering pant interlaced with soft whimpers and realized it was her making the sound. He curled his tongue around her nipple. The shock of heat and the silken drag sent a jolt through her that shook the mattress. She sobbed at the white-hot surges of electrical sensation and arched her spine, craving more, *more,* her lungs so emptied of breath that she couldn't speak.

Ryan seemed to understand without her saying the words. He drew her into his mouth, the pull so unexpected and sharp that she cried out. Then he caught her throbbing flesh between his teeth. Red hazed her vision.

She sobbed and cried, "Oh, yes. *Yes.*" She felt him release her wrists, and she grabbed blindly for his shoulders, needing to feel him. She pushed in frustration at his shirt, her body feeling as if it was dissolving into molten liquid with every pull of his mouth. "Oh, Ryan, I love you, love you, *love* you." She tugged frantically at his shirt, finally found bare skin, and reveled in the feeling of touching him. "Yes. Oh, yes. Don't stop. Please, don't stop."

He chuckled and moved to nibble her throat. As he trailed more hot kisses south toward her breasts again, he whispered, "I'll never stop. But I will take occasional detours that will be just as good."

Nothing could compare to—his hot mouth was at her breast again, and whatever else she was about to think fled her mind. *Ryan.* Never in all her wildest fantasies had she imagined it might be this wonderful. Never.

He took one of those detours he'd just warned her about, trailing burning kisses to her navel, which he circled and nibbled, then invaded with his tongue. When he finally met her mesmerized gaze, he arched a wickedly dark eyebrow and asked, "Do you like this?"

She never would have believed that her belly button could be so sensitive, and she *loved* it. She just couldn't find her voice to tell him. There was something incredibly erotic about watching him kiss her there. As though he guessed her thoughts, he desisted his ministrations to look up at her again. His mouth tipped into that crooked grin she'd always found so devastating. It was far more devastating when the cleft of his chin was almost connecting with her navel.

He rose to his knees to finish stripping off his shirt. He was so handsome, he almost gave her a heart attack. She'd glimpsed Ryan's chest a couple of times, and earlier he'd drawn his shirt aside to show her the scar on his rib cage from the hay hook. But just seeing parts of him had in no way prepared her for the sight of Ryan Kendrick, naked from the waist up.

He was the epitome of masculine beauty, his arms, shoulders and chest burnished by the sun to a rich umber, every inch of him sculpted by hard physical labor. Until now, Bethany hadn't believed there was a man alive as muscular as her brothers. Ryan definitely was. His slightest movement set off a chain reaction of ripples. She could have spent hours just admiring the view.

He tossed the shirt on the floor, his grin growing broader as he braced his hands on the mattress on either side of her and moved so his face was above hers again. His gaze twinkling, he glanced at her breasts. "If ever there was a doubt in my mind, I can now say with absolute certainty that I vastly prefer small breasts," he whispered. "You are so beautiful, Bethany. I'm almost afraid to believe you're really here with me."

"Oh, Ryan, I feel the same way, like I'm having a wonderful dream."

He lowered himself beside her, bracing his weight on one arm. He curled a large palm over her ribs and bent to nibble at her lips. While he kissed her deeply, he skimmed his hand down, tracing the curves and hollows of her body, his fingertips setting her skin afire.

She was lost to sensation again, the sound of every breath she drew a muffled rush against her eardrums. Her belly knotted with yearning, the need spiraling down to center low in her belly, where it seemed to radiate heat clear through her. Building . . . building until something inside of her ached and quivered with every pass of his fingertips.

"Ryan?"

"I'm here," he assured her huskily.

His gaze resting on her face, he continued to caress her until she stretched and struggled to undulate her hips. Then he slid a hand down to her pelvis, where he pressed firmly with his palm and began a slow, circular rub that ignited her. She hiked her hips as best she could without the help of her legs, rising mindlessly against the press of his hand in a rhythm as old as man and womankind. Her breath quickened even more. Her heartbeat became a deafening thrum that made his whispery reassurances seem to come from a great distance. Not that she needed reassurance now. *Ryan.*

He moved his hand from her belly to the apex of her thighs. "Can you feel that, sweetheart?"

Bethany guessed that he was exploring the outer edges of her opening, which she'd already known was numb. The wonderful, dizzying heat of desire fell away, and her stomach knotted with anxiety. She stiffened. "I can't feel anything there, Ryan."

"Nothing?" he asked, his voice ringing with a disappointment so keen that it cut through her like a knife.

"No, nothing, I'm afraid." Her lungs suddenly felt as if they were being compressed by a leaden weight. "Up higher. I have some sensation there."

He touched her clitoris. As gentle as he was, Bethany jerked, startled by how supersensitive that place was. He rubbed the flange of flesh lightly with his thumb, and it felt as if her nerve endings were being abraded with sandpaper. She grabbed for his wrist.

"Oh, Ryan, don't. That sort of—hurts."

He lightened his touch, and when she still didn't release his wrist, he cursed under his breath. "Damn my rough hands. That's the problem."

His hands had felt marvelous on her skin. Hard and sandpapery with calluses, yes, but wonderfully warm and strong. She didn't think they were the problem. It felt more like her nerve endings down there had been damaged. They were so sensitive that even his lightest, most careful ministrations were uncomfortable. She didn't like the feeling but clenched her teeth, determined to make this work. Seconds later, she was hating her traitorous body and wishing she could scream. Instead she willed herself to respond normally to him.

"Easy . . . ," he whispered, and bent his head back down to tease her nipple while his fingertips toyed lightly below. "Just relax, sweetheart. You're so tense. When a woman's tense, this never works. You need to forget everything and just focus on the feelings and on me."

It was impossible for her to relax. The long awaited moment had arrived, and there was too much at stake. It seemed to her that everything was riding on her ability to enjoy this. Her whole future with this man, whom she had come to love so very much. If she failed him now—if she could feel nothing—she was afraid he might change his mind about marrying her. And who would blame him? No man wanted to spend his life with half a woman.

The next pass of his fingertips brought her shoulders off the mattress. She didn't experience pain, exactly, but it was close enough. "Stop, Ryan. Please. That doesn't feel right. I think the nerves there are damaged or something." She felt his hesitation and rushed to add, "Maybe I have feeling farther up inside of me. Let's just—you know—go ahead and see how it feels."

He resumed kissing her breasts. Bethany knew he was trying to arouse her again, but she was so upset, she couldn't get there again, no matter how desperately she tried.

She felt him tug off his pants and heard his boots hit the floor. The next instant, he rose over her, a dark blur of bronze and ebony. There was an odd crinkling sound, as if he were tearing open foil. Then she felt his hands grasping her hips, and she slid down the mattress slightly.

"I'll try not to hurt you, Bethany mine. Just tell me if you feel any pain, and I'll stop."

She felt the coarse hair on his leg brush against her inner left thigh, and he fleetingly touched her clitoris again, which was now so tender she gasped.

She braced herself, knowing that he was about to push in. *Please, God, let me feel it when he enters me. Please, please, please . . .* In that moment, she could think of nothing she'd ever wanted more. To *feel,* simply to *feel.* If God would grant her only that, she promised herself she'd never ask Him for anything else. For her, that would be everything.

She got an odd feeling—like pressure building way low inside of her. She blinked and brought Ryan's dark face back into focus. His beautiful steely-blue eyes were filled with question.

"Sweetheart, is it hurting?"

Bethany knew then. It was like being slugged right in the center of her chest, a staggering blow that emptied her lungs and made her want to weep.

He was inside her—and she felt nothing but an odd sense of fullness.

Absolutely nothing.

Chapter Fifteen

Ryan held Bethany in his arms until she fell asleep, and then he sneaked from bed to go walking on the lakeshore, his heart breaking a little with every step he took. *Please, God.* The words became a litany, the same words over and over and over. She was so dear, and, oh, how she shined. She was like gentle spring sunshine, his Bethany. Or like a fairy glow of moonlight on water, he thought as he gazed across the lake. Her bright smile. The sparkle in her eyes. She had brought light into his life, making everything seem golden.

"Please, God," he whispered as he reached his thinking spot on the knoll.

He sat beneath the overhanging pine boughs, finding no comfort tonight in the shadows that embraced him. When he gazed at the moon-silvered mountain peaks that loomed like specters over the forests that grew on the opposite lakeshore, all he could think about was Bethany. She'd been as eager for their lovemaking as he had been, responding so readily to every kiss and touch of his hands. She'd been shy at first, but she'd quickly set those feelings aside, giving herself to him so freely and completely, her trust in him glowing in her eyes. Then he had left her hanging.

He braced an elbow on his knee and cupped a hand over his face. He went to church almost every Sunday, and he considered himself to be a decent, God-fearing man, if not a pious and prayerful one. Countless times, he'd gone through the motions of prayer—kneeling, folding his hands, and bowing his head. But he realized now that all those times, he'd never really gone to his knees.

He was on his knees now. He loved that girl so very much. He would have done anything to make her happy. But for all of that, he couldn't give her the one simple thing she needed most, satisfaction in his arms.

Making love to her had been the most wonderful, fulfilling experience he'd ever had, making him feel complete in a way he couldn't begin to express. He'd taken so much, so very much, and in return, he'd been able to give her nothing. *Nothing*.

He'd felt the tension in her body afterward—the kind of tension that told a man he'd failed to bring a woman to completion. *If I can't feel anything, I think I'll die*. Oh, she'd tried to hide her disappointment, hugging him and burrowing her cheek against his shoulder, saying how lovely it had been. But he'd known, and he'd wanted to weep.

Now he was alone. If he cried, that would be his secret.

The tears felt like acid in his eyes. A sob built pressure in his chest until he couldn't breathe. That look in her eyes— oh, God—he doubted he'd ever forget it. Shock, disappointment, and then a terrible despair he hadn't been able to dispel.

His shoulders jerked, and the next instant, he was sobbing. *Please, God*. There in the darkness, Ryan cried like a child for the girl he'd left sleeping in his bed, and he prayed for a miracle, knowing in his heart that if God didn't make this right somehow, he might very well lose her.

The following morning Bethany lectured herself in the bathroom mirror. Time to count her blessings, and they were many. She was in love with the most fantastic man on earth, and he loved her back. That was an incredible blessing. And making love with him last night had been the most beautiful, indescribable experience of her whole life, all of it perfect and wonderful, right up until the last.

What more did she want? She'd enjoyed all of the touching and kissing. That was so much more than she had ever hoped to have. She would be foolish to let the wonder of that be tarnished by her inability to feel the last part.

No way. She would wear a bright smile, and she'd be grateful that God had chosen to give her this much. It was enough. It *was*. If she could grow old in Ryan's arms, she would count herself the luckiest woman alive, and she would not let herself wish for more or feel sorry for herself because there wasn't more.

When she reached the kitchen, he was at the table, nursing a mug of coffee. He pushed another mug toward her and smiled, his eyes lackluster as his gaze moved slowly over her. "Good morning, sunshine."

"Good morning!" she said brightly, which was totally uncharacteristic of her. She glanced out the window. "And it *is* a gorgeous one. Spring may come late in this country, but there's nothing more wonderful once it arrives."

Ryan rubbed his forehead. "Sweetheart, you don't have to do this."

Bethany's face felt so stiff that her smile hurt. "Do what?"

He kept his gaze fixed on his coffee. "Pretend everything's wonderful. I know you're upset—that it wasn't good for you last night, and I'm sorry it wasn't. We can work on it—make it better." He shrugged and flicked her a sad, hangdog look. "I'm sorry I didn't make it happen for you."

She felt as if two fists were twisting her heart in half, and an awful, frightened feeling tied her stomach into knots. Ryan might settle for less than perfect for himself, but it would eat at him like a cancer if he thought it was less than perfect for her.

Bethany didn't generally lie, and she found it particularly distasteful to think about lying to Ryan. But in this particular instance, she wondered if being completely honest wouldn't do more harm than good. Maybe she was lacking in practical experience, but she wasn't naive. Caring individuals, be they male or female, needed to know that their lovers truly enjoyed being intimate with them. Bethany couldn't imagine how awful she might be feeling right now if the tables had been turned—if it had been Ryan who hadn't found satisfaction in her arms last night instead of the other way around.

The twisting pain in her chest grew more acute, making it difficult for her to breathe. She couldn't bear the thought of losing him. Not now. Not after being with him. Before, as painful as it might have been, she could have turned away for his sake. But now she knew how much she'd be missing. So she hadn't achieved a climax. The rest had been so wonderful—so absolutely *perfect*. She couldn't go back to the empty existence she'd had before—to a life without Ryan. Oh, God, she just *couldn't*.

Not allowing herself to think about the right and wrong of it, Bethany made a snap decision. She'd lie. Before she was with him that way a second time, she'd watch *When Harry Met Sally* again and practice faking an orgasm until she could do it so convincingly that Ryan would never guess it was an act. He'd never look at her like this again, with his heart aching in his eyes. Never. She'd be the best lover he'd ever had, damn it. The very best. Last night, she'd been so caught up in her own pleasure, so overwhelmed by all the incredible sensations she'd never hoped to feel, that she'd given little thought to the things she might do to give him pleasure.

No more. She was no expert on sex, but what she didn't know, she could find out, even if it meant going to a sexual therapist and getting some how-to literature. She'd learn what turned men on, all the little tricks that drove them crazy in bed. No holds barred. Anything. She'd do *anything* to keep from losing him.

"Ryan, how can you say it wasn't good for me? That simply isn't *so*. It was wonderful for me."

He slumped back in his chair and met her gaze. "Sweetheart, let's not go there. All right? Honesty is our ace in the hole. Talking about it openly and working together to find a solution is our only hope. We'll find a way. I promise you. Somehow. It just may take some time." He winked and flashed her a grin that lacked its usual brilliance. "You know what they say. Practice makes perfect."

Bethany felt bile rise up her throat. As long as he felt guilty because she wasn't enjoying it at the end, it would spoil it for him. All along, her greatest fear had been that she wouldn't be able to give him pleasure. Now she knew she could. That, in and of itself, was a miracle. How it had been for her simply didn't matter, not in the overall scheme of things.

"Ryan, look at me." When he met her gaze again, she said, "It was fantastic for me, the most wondrous experience of my life." That much wasn't a lie. "It's true that I didn't feel anything at first. But I did later." She thought fast. "When you moved a little deeper, I *felt* you. What an incredible feeling it was."

Hope came into his eyes. "You did?"

"Oh, *yes*." She hugged her waist, praying he wouldn't notice how her hands were shaking. "I love you so much, Ryan. Being with you that way, it was so beautiful. And I'm so excited because I felt something, there at the end. I'm sure if we'd just kept going a few minutes more, it would have been fabulous."

"Deeper," he repeated. "You felt it when I went deeper? Bethany, that's wonderful." He sat straighter and shifted to face her. "How did it feel?"

Oh, God. She had no idea what a woman felt when a man entered her. She thought of the sensations when he'd kissed her breasts and grabbed for words. "An electrical, tingling feeling." She pressed a palm to her stomach. "Way deep, right here. It's hard to describe."

He laughed softly, and a joyous look came into his eyes. "That'll do." He came off his chair and went down on one knee beside her. After wrapping her in his arms, he buried his face against her hair and held her tightly for a moment. "That'll do, sweetheart," he said huskily. "I can work with that, and we'll get there."

Bethany clung to him and vowed that they would "get there" far sooner than he dreamed. "I love you, Ryan. Please, be happy. I am. So very happy."

Bethany propped her arms on her desk, ignoring the muted click and hum of the computer hard drive perched beside her. To heck with filling out purchase orders. She had more important fish to fry, namely learning all she could about giving a man great sex. There was no listing for a therapist in the yellow pages. Bethany ran her finger down the S's, praying to find *SEX* in all caps. She needed an expert, someone she could pump for information who wouldn't betray her confidence.

"Morning, sis."

Bethany slapped the phone book closed and glanced up from her desk to see Jake standing in her office doorway. "Jake!" She clamped a hand over her heart. "You startled me out of my skin."

He gave her a slow once-over. "How goes it with you and Ryan?"

"Fine. *Great*. He, um—we're doing fine." She was developing a headache that felt as if it might split her skull, but that was beside the point. "I, um . . . how are you?"

"Good." He nodded at the phone book. "Can I help you find something? You were looking pretty intense when I interrupted you. What's up?"

"Nothing. I was just—nothing's up."

He searched her gaze. Then, in a low, soft voice, he

asked, "You happy, Bethie? That's all I need to know, that he makes you happy."

There was no mistaking the knowing look in her brother's eyes. She'd told her family that she was going to Ryan's for dinner last night. Jake had probably tried to call her later in the evening to make sure she'd gotten home safely. When she didn't answer the phone, he must have concluded that she was spending the night at Ryan's place. Armed with that knowledge, it didn't take a genius to put two and two together. That was a little embarrassing. But if she meant to marry Ryan, she supposed she would have to get used to it.

"Yes, he makes me very happy," she finally replied. "So happy, Jake. I never thought—well, you know—that I could have a life with him. But he's convinced me I can. You know he bought Wink back for me."

Jake raised his eyebrows. "You're kidding! He did?"

Bethany might have been fooled by her brother's feigned surprise if Ryan hadn't told her that Jake had played a role in locating the mare. "It was so good to see her again, Jake. You just can't know. We spent half the evening in her stall. Ate dinner out there and everything."

"I'll bet Ryan loved that." Jake chuckled. "I'll let you tell Pop about Wink, by the way. He's going to burst a vessel."

Bethany sighed. "Yes, well—maybe I'll wait. Kind of hit him with one thing at a time. It'll probably be a big enough shock when I tell him I'm getting married."

"Oh?" Jake looked surprised again. "This is news."

"Liar. I know you've been talking with Ryan. He told me last night that you hooked him up with the contractors who remodeled his kitchen and that you helped him track down Hunsacker so he could buy Wink back for me."

Jake chuckled. "On that note, I'm heading downstairs to crack the whip."

"Without congratulating me?"

"Congratulations. Just understand, if he doesn't treat you right, you'll be a young widow."

Bethany was still shaking her head when he headed down the hall. She waited a moment, then reopened the phone book, turning back to the list of physicians. There had to be someplace she could go to talk straightforwardly with someone about sex.

"You seen the coffee filters?"

Bethany jumped, slapped the phone book closed again, and glanced up to see Kate, one of the store's employees, in the doorway, holding a coffeepot full of water in one hand. "We have extras filters here in the cabinet."

Bethany hurried over to open the metal door. While waiting, Kate stepped into the office and set the coffeepot on the edge of the desk. After locating the filters, Bethany grabbed a new package and turned to hold them out.

"Thanks," Kate said, reaching over the desk.

A tall, slender woman with lovely features and gleaming auburn hair that hung like a veil to her shoulders, she had always reminded Bethany a little of Cher—a very unpolished and shopworn version. Her heavily made-up brown eyes were bloodshot this morning, and she flashed a strained smile that had "hangover" written all over it. According to Jake, the woman drank heavily and slept with anything in trousers, but she was a good employee who showed up for her shift and came in on her days off when others called in sick. Bethany didn't usually work the floor, which made it difficult to cultivate friendships with the downstairs help, but she'd always liked Kate, sensing she was a warm, genuine person, for all her rough edges.

Kate retrieved the pot of water from the desk. "Too much happy last night," she said in a whiskey-and-smoke voice. "I need a good jolt of caffeine to jump-start the old bod."

"I know that feeling," Bethany said. "Only I don't need too much happy to make me feel that way. I wake up with a dead battery no matter what."

Kate spied the ashtray Bethany kept on her desk for any "no-smoking" offenders to snub out their cigarettes. She glanced over her shoulder at the open door. "Say?" she said conspiratorially. "Would it bother you if I closed that and sneaked a couple of drags? Jake's got a nose like a bloodhound."

"I suppose I can be your partner in crime for one cigarette."

Kate put the pot back on the desk, gave Bethany a grateful look, and closed the door. Smiling as she plucked a pack of Marlboros from her shirt pocket, she said, "You're okay. Thanks. I woke up late, you know? Didn't get my coffee, didn't get my smokes. I feel like I was rode hard and put away wet."

Kate looked that way too. Bethany bit back a smile, watching as the other woman fished in the hip pocket of her skintight blue jeans for her lighter. With a flick, she inhaled gratefully, then exhaled through her nose. "Man, I needed that."

Bethany enjoyed the smell of cigarettes while they were being smoked. It was the stench of stale smoke that turned her stomach. "I tried smoking once."

Kate raised her eyebrows. "I never figured you for the type."

Bethany sat back in her chair, about to launch into a comical account of her brief walk on the wild side in college— or in her case, her brief *roll* on the wild side—with a tight-knit group of female paraplegic friends. As they had all gone through school on special grants for the handicapped, they'd been short on money, so they'd had much more in common than just their physical limitations.

But before Bethany could speak, it hit her like a fist between the eyes that Kate was just the kind of person she'd been praying to find—an expert on sex. And here she was, standing right under Bethany's nose.

"Say, Kate?" Bethany thought quickly. "Are you busy today after work?"

"Why? You need something extra done? I gotta tell you, I have a bitch of a headache. Tomorrow would be a better day for me."

"No, no, nothing like that. I just thought—you know—that maybe we could go have coffee together someplace after work and chat for a while."

Kate frowned. "Have I screwed up? You're not gonna can me, are you?"

Bethany couldn't think of a reasonable explanation for the sudden friendliness so she decided the simple truth was best. "No, nothing like that. I haven't been here very long, and I haven't made many friends yet. Being stuck up here on the second floor most of the time, I can't even get to know the people who work here very well. I've got a problem right now that needs solving, and it's not the sort of thing I'd feel comfortable discussing with one of my brothers. It would be really nice to be able to talk it over with another woman, and I thought maybe you might have a few minutes to spare."

Kate glanced uneasily toward the door. "Jake know about this?"

"No. I'm twenty-six years old. I don't need permission from my brother to have coffee with a friend."

Kate raised her eyebrows. "I didn't figure you for that old." She shrugged. "Sure. Okay. You buyin'?"

Bethany laughed. "I'll even throw in a piece of pie."

"You're on. My stomach should handle pie by then."

After work that evening, Bethany waited in her van. When the other woman finally emerged from the store, she honked to get her attention. Kate waved and broke into a long-legged jog. Once in the van, she rolled down her window, lighted a cigarette, and said, "Way cool. I've never seen the inside of one of these jobbers. You're all set up to roll."

Bethany considered mentioning that no one was allowed to smoke in her van, but then she decided it was a fair trade-off for the information she needed. "Where sounds good? There's a Denny's restaurant a couple of blocks over."

Kate sighed. "I don't suppose I could work a trade, could I? A beer instead of coffee and pie."

"A beer?"

"Yeah. I know a quiet little place we can go."

Bethany would have preferred going to a restaurant. Because she had to adjust her daily dosage of anticoagulant if she drank much alcohol, she seldom imbibed. Kate also liked to party, and her definition of a quiet place might differ greatly from most people's. She hesitated.

"Come on," Kate urged. "Live a little."

Ten minutes later, Bethany was entering a seedy-looking place called Suds. A shotgun floor plan sported a bar along one darkly paneled wall, tables along the other, with two pool tables, end to end, at center stage. Kate pointed Bethany toward a table and stepped up to the bar as if she owned the joint.

"Two Buds, Mike! Hold the head."

"Gotcha!" the bartender called back.

Bethany scooted a chair out of her way and drew up to the table. After withdrawing her wallet, she set her purse on the floor at her feet. The next table over was occupied by two men wearing flannel work shirts and jeans, the sawdust on their clothing earmarking them as mill workers. Bethany paid them little notice as she watched Kate advance toward her with two full beer mugs clutched in her hands.

"I was supposed to buy," Bethany said as Kate set a mug in front of her.

"I'll let you get the next round," Kate assured her as she sat down.

The next round? Uh-oh. Bethany took a sip of beer and

smiled. "Mmm. This hits the spot. I didn't realize how thirsty I was."

Kate took a long pull from her glass. White foam mustached her upper lip when she finally came up for air. "God, I've been dying all day for some hair off the dog that bit me. You're a champ, Bethany. I know this isn't your thing."

"I don't know. It's rather nice, actually. I expected someplace a little livelier. You strike me as the type who enjoys large groups of people—with the ratio of males to females making it easy for an attractive single woman to score."

"God, do you have me pegged, or what?" Kate rubbed her temple and sighed. "I'm not feeling up to snuff today. Check in tomorrow night, and you'll see lively." After taking another swig of beer, she leaned forward over her mug as she lit another cigarette. "So—what's the problem you need to talk about?"

Bethany took a big gulp of beer for fortification. "Sex."

Kate shrugged, blew out smoke, and said, "Yeah. What about it?"

Bethany swallowed more beer. "Don't laugh. I'm really in need of some advice. I'm, um—how shall I put this?—a novice, I guess you might say." She patted the arm of her chair. "Wheels have a way of putting a damper on a woman's love life, and I'm only just now starting my first relationship."

Kate narrowed her eyes slightly, the exhaled smoke forming a blue cloud in front of her long, pretty face. "Jesus, honey. That's the saddest thing I've ever heard. Twenty-six years without sex? That sucks."

"Yes, well. I only count the years since puberty. It doesn't seem quite so pathetic that way."

"That's still a long dry spell."

Bethany took another sip of beer and smiled. "I've survived. It was lonely sometimes." She wrinkled her nose. "Oh, to heck with it. You're absolutely right. It sucked."

Kate chuckled. "Hey, without sex, what's it all about?"

"Exactly," Bethany agreed. "Which brings me to my problem. I enjoyed most of it immensely, but toward the end—" She broke off and flapped her hand. "For some paraplegics, the finale isn't all that it should be, and it seems that I'm one of them."

Kate studied her solemnly. "You can't get off?"

Bethany glanced around to be sure no one else could overhear. Then she stared into her beer for a long moment. After taking three huge gulps and wiping her mouth, she said, "Nope, I can't get off. And I really, really want to keep the guy. I love him a lot, and all the rest was really nice."

"Just no bang at the end." Kate sat back in her chair, took a deep drag from her cigarette, and then said, "Shit." She regarded Bethany for a moment. "Well, there's worse things. A lot of women don't get off. They go their whole lives faking orgasm, and they seem to get along fine."

Bethany smiled. "You settle for what life dishes out, I guess, and you learn to be happy with what you have. That's the way I look at it, anyway, and overall, I think I'm very lucky." She shrugged. "I just want to keep it that way. He's the best thing that's ever happened to me, and I don't want to lose him."

"Can't blame you there."

"During my lunch hour, I stopped by the video store and rented *When Harry Met Sally* so I can brush up on my— well, that part goes without saying. But movies and books fall a little short when it comes to giving detailed explanations of how a woman can give a man pleasure. I really, really want to be *good* in bed. As good as I can be, at any rate, given my physical limitations, and I thought you might know a few tricks you might share with me. Like what to wear, for instance. Or maybe some special tips about how to do things he'll really like. I need a crash course."

Kate pursed her lips. "Damn, honey, you don't ask for much. It's a little hard to share twenty years of experience over a few beers."

"I know I'm asking a lot. But I'm desperate. I understand the basics, but I need to take a giant leap from beginner to intermediate, *fast*. I want it to be as perfect and wonderful for him as I can make it. You know? With plenty of added pizzazz to compensate for my failings, so to speak."

Kate sighed. "Can you wear a garter belt and nylons? Most guys really go for those. Meet him at the door wearing that and a lacy black bra. If he's got blood flowing in his veins, his eyes will pop out of his head. If I walked in here dressed that way on a busy Saturday night, I'd have comers lined up out to the parking lot."

Bethany laughed. "That and nothing else?" She'd thought of wearing a lacy peignoir, but nylons and a garter belt had never entered her mind. This was *exactly* what she needed, pointers from a woman who knew the ropes. "I'd feel sort of silly."

"Not for long." Kate winked at her. "Try it, honey. Works like a charm. Guys are weird. If that doesn't work, fix dinner for him wearing nothing but an apron. Just remember to turn off all the burners when he decides he can't wait for dessert."

"Nothing but an *apron*?"

"High heels are a nice touch. Why guys love them, I haven't a clue. I once accidently nailed a fellow in the ass with a spike, believe it or not. He never even broke rhythm."

Bethany laughed so hard at the picture that came into her mind, she had to wipe tears from under her eyes. "Oh, Kate, you're wonderful. Unfortunately, I can't wear high heels."

"Sure you can. You don't have to parade around in them to get his motor purring. Just seeing them on your feet will do it."

Bethany leaned closer. "Another question. You watched *When Harry Met Sally,* right? In your opinion, was that a pretty accurate portrayal of how a woman looks and sounds when she's having an orgasm?"

Kate rolled her eyes. "You're really without a clue. He

won't grade your performance, honey. Lesson number one about men. They all want to believe they're God's gift to women. Fake it as best you can, then tell him he's fabulous. He'll walk on water for a week."

Bethany laughed again. She didn't know if it was the beer or if Kate was just funny.

Kate finished her drink and went to get another round. When she returned, Bethany drew a ten from her wallet and pushed it across the table. "The next one's on me."

"Thanks." Kate stabbed the bill with a fingertip, then walked it around in a circle. "I know this is a really personal question, but I'm going to ask. Are you totally—you know—numb down there?"

Heat crept up Bethany's neck, and she glanced over her shoulder again. The two mill workers appeared to be intent on their own conversation, and the bartender was busy cleaning the taps. "Not totally," she said softly. "I have some feeling here and there. It's just—well, spinal injuries are funny. If your nerve endings are impaired, as some of mine are, having sensation in a certain spot doesn't necessarily mean that part of the body will function normally. I have feeling in my buttocks, for instance, but not all the muscles there will flex."

"Hmm." Kate frowned. "How many times have you tried for the big whammy?"

Bethany remembered that horrible moment when Ryan had looked into her eyes and asked if it was hurting. To her dismay, she felt her chin wobble. She took several more gulps of beer. "Only once."

"Only *once*?" Kate rolled her eyes. "Bethany, lots of women don't get off the first few times."

"They don't?"

"Heck, no. I didn't, anyway. I was too uptight, worrying about this and that and feeling self-conscious. Tension and orgasm don't ride double. You know those romances where the couple gets in a huge fight, and the guy muscles the woman into bed when she's still spitting mad?" Kate shook her head. "He kisses her, and she swoons. That's bullshit. At least it doesn't work that way for me. Some guy tries that when I'm pissed, and he'll end up wishing he hadn't. Sex doesn't usually work that way for a woman."

"I really didn't feel that tense until the last when I started worrying about how it would feel. Or, more precisely, if I'd be able to feel it at all. I don't think tension was the problem." She took another long pull of beer. "Afterward—" She passed a shaky hand over her eyes. "I could tell he knew it didn't happen for me, and he was upset. I'm so afraid I'll lose him, Kate. That he won't want to be with me anymore if it isn't good for me at the last."

Kate nodded. "Yeah, that'll do it. Like I said, they got big egos. Most of them can't handle doing a gal who doesn't hit the finish rope. Not for a steady diet, anyway, and that's your aim. Right? To keep him hanging around."

"Right. Oh, Kate, thank you so much for talking to me. You're so *real*. Most people take one look at my wheelchair and freeze up. Sex? The word doesn't cross their lips. They immediately assume I'm a head."

"A what?"

"A *head*." Bethany waggled her fingers beside her ears. "I talk, I smile, I laugh. Anything below the collarbone is distasteful as a topic of conversation."

Kate grinned. "Maybe it's because you never asked them out for coffee to talk about sex. Hell, babe, sex is most people's favorite subject."

Bethany raised her mug. "Here, here. I love you."

Kate's brows drew together. "You drink much?"

"Not a lot. More than I ever have just recently." Bethany swung her mug back to her mouth.

"Well, hell. Who do you talk to?"

"Since moving here, no one. Occasionally with Jake, but not about anything like this. He'd have a coronary."

Kate winked. "I have a feelin' he packs a wallop when he

lets the starch out of his collar, but it ain't happenin' around you."

"Exactly. My whole world is starched. With creases." Bethany sighed woefully. "I should have asked you out for coffee a long time ago. Now, here I am with this *man*. Oh, God. He's all my dreams, stuffed into chambray and denim. Just looking at him almost gets me there. *Almost*. That's the story of my life, Kate, a long history of 'almosts.'"

Kate chuckled. "What's his name?"

"Ryan Kendrick."

Kate's eyes widened. "Good Christ. Repeat that. You've slept with *the* Ryan Kendrick?"

Bethany nodded mutely. Apparently, even Kate found it unbelievable that someone like Ryan was interested in her.

Kate grinned and then laughed. "Holy *shit*. You don't mess around, sweetie. Ryan Kendrick? As in so good-lookin', women fall over on their backs like bowling pins and cock up their toes? *That* Ryan Kendrick? The to-die-for *rich* hunk nobody can nail?"

"I never thought I'd be lucky enough to have someone like him fall in love with me. He's *wonderful*. If he isn't happy with me, I'll *die*."

Kate cupped a hand over her eyes, propped her elbow on the table, and laughed so hard her beer slopped. "No *wonder* you're so hooked. He's like—well, *dynamite*."

"Yeah." Bethany swallowed, fixed Kate with an imploring look, and said, "Only with no big bang at the end."

Kate rocked back in her chair and shook her head. "Well, we gotta get a leash on his collar, no question. Isn't just everybody that gets a crack at him." Her smile softened. "You got stars in your eyes, sweetie."

Bethany envisioned Ryan's face and nodded. "I love him so much. I don't care if it's all that fantastic in bed at the end. You know? The first part was a lot of fun. Like, *wow*."

"Been there a couple of times." Kate grew pensive and gave the ten spot another turn. "Bethany, another real per sonal question. I know the guy's got a reputation for having been around, but that isn't always an indication. You sure he knows what he's doing?"

"Oh, *yes*." Bethany drank more beer. "He's followed a hundred dead ends. A *hundred*. Can you imagine?"

"Ryan Kendrick? Oh, yeah. I can imagine. Poor man. He's like one of them targets at a shooting range. Everybody wants to take a crack. Poor guy has probably had a lot of nasty surprises halfway into relationships when women finally let their true selves shine through."

"Probably. No consolation to me. I about *fainted* when he told me he'd dated so many women. They all had to be better than me. Just the thought scares me half to death. Being compared and all. You know what I'm saying?"

Kate smiled. "You're not exactly dog meat. Not a guy in the store who hasn't looked your way and rubbed his fly a few times."

"Pardon?"

"Christ. Never mind. Like you'd know if Kendrick knows his stuff? I can't believe I asked." She stubbed out her cigarette and immediately lit another one. "You're a sweet kid. Funny. I figured you for being stuck-up."

"You did?"

"Jake acts like you shit golden eggs. Never saw a man so protective of his sister. Must be nice."

"Nice?" Bethany groaned and finished off her beer. She stared at the empty mug, feeling mildly surprised at how easily it had gone down. "You know—I think maybe I just found my poison."

"Holy mother. I can't drive that rig of yours. We'll have to call a cab."

Bethany giggled. "What are you saying?"

"That you're getting a buzz." Kate pushed to her feet, grabbed the ten, and said, "What the hell. We may as well. Only go around once."

When she returned with the beers, she said, "Okay, now

we're both relaxed. Got all the starch out of *our* collars.
Let's get down to the dirty."

Bethany took a huge gulp of beer and smiled when she
came up with a mustache, just like Kate's. "Go for it. I'm all
ears."

"Before we talk more about what guys like, let's talk a
few minutes about you. I've got a question. Did he try to get
you both ways?"

"Both ways? I'm not following."

Kate leaned closer. "You know. Some women can't get
off the conventional way. Did he try your hot line?"

Bethany pictured a huge, red phone and burst into giggles. "No, mine's probably been disconnected."

Kate sighed. "Your love button, sweetie. Did he try that?"

"I've never heard it called that before." Bethany sighed
and shook her head. "In answer to your question, yes, he
tried it. To be honest, I found it very—well, not really
painful, but uncomfortable, like all my nerves were exposed.
It's hard to describe. The same sort of feeling you get when
you bite down on a piece of tinfoil. It made me want to
clench my teeth and shudder."

"It can feel that way if you're not into it." Kate got a
knowing gleam in her eyes. "The important thing is, you
have feeling there."

"That doesn't mean it works properly. Trust me, it didn't."

"It could be that he didn't have the magic touch. Ever
think of that?"

Bethany remembered the magic in his touch everywhere
else and shook her head. "No. It's more a case of damaged
nerves, I think. That isn't his fault, and—"

Before Bethany could finish what she meant to say, the
man behind her turned on his chair and said, "If he doesn't
know his way around a love button, honey, trade him in for
a new model."

"Butt out, Dave," Kate said. "Who invited you into this
conversation?"

The man draped his arm over the back of his chair and twisted farther around to give Bethany a long, hard look. "Well, now, if you ain't purdy as a picture."

"Jack off," Kate said.

The man ignored her. He scooted back his chair and pressed his face closer to Bethany's. "Hi, honey. I couldn't help overhearing your conversation. My heart's breaking. Sounds like you've got yourself one hell of a problem."

Bethany blinked and inched her face back. "I'm a little distressed."

He nodded. "What you need is a real man to grease your gears. I'm packin'."

Kate came up off her chair. "Hey, asshole, get out your dictionary. I said, 'Jack off!' Leave the lady alone."

"I'm surprised you recognize one, Kate."

"Stuff it where it'll never again see sunlight." Kate planted her hands on the table and glared daggers at him. "Leave her alone. She's with me."

He gave Kate a long, hard look. "You can't help her. This little gal needs a real man to get her motor running." He returned his bleary gaze to Bethany. "How 'bout it, honey? I'll get you perkin', then you can go back to lover boy."

Bethany inched farther away. All she could think of to say was, "I need to use the bathroom."

That seemed to cool his jets. Bethany rolled her chair back and fumbled for her purse. She glanced at Kate as she returned her wallet to the side pocket. "Excuse me." The man blocked her path. "Please. I really need to go."

He sighed and said, "I'll be waiting. Give me an hour. Problem solved."

Bethany's heart was pounding. The effects of the beer had done a vanishing act. That man wasn't taking no for an answer. She cut right, following the signs. She found herself in a long, dark hallway with warped paneling. The ladies' room was the last door on the left.

She was about to reach for the knob when a big hand

closed over her shoulder. "My name's Dave, by the way," he said in a slimy voice. Then he leaned down, grabbed the arms of her chair, and turned her to face him. "No one will bother us back here. Let me have a go at that love button of yours."

Bethany stared up at him. His eyes were glassy and hard. He was breathing funny. The smell of his sweat filmed her nostrils, making her feel as if she was breathing olive oil. "Let go of me."

"Ain't touchin' you," he pointed out. "Just your chair. So, arrest me. You want to get off. I want to get off. Let's make some music together."

Before Bethany guessed what he meant to do, he clamped his foul-tasting mouth over hers and shoved a hand down the front of her blouse. She pushed frantically at his shoulders, taking him so off guard that he lost his balance and staggered back, ripping her blouse at the shoulder in the process.

"Fine by me," he said with a laugh. "You want rough? I'll deliver."

A loud, shattering sound of glass startled them both. Dave swung around, as surprised as Bethany. There stood Kate, holding the jagged end of a broken beer bottle in her right hand.

"Take your paws off that girl, you son of a bitch, or I'll make you sing soprano."

Bethany tried to dart into the bathroom, but her chair was just a little too wide to fit. The man's full attention was fixed on the broken bottle now, allowing her the time to get unstuck, back up, and try again. With the second advance, she hit the doorway going faster, and the force of her momentum pushed the chair on through. She swung the door shut, then backed up against it so no one could easily enter. She was shaking so badly that she could barely dig her cell phone out of her purse. She imagined Kate murdering good old Dave, with blood splattered all over the warped paneling. *Oh, God, oh, God*. She shakily punched in the number to the store.

Jake opened a thick parts manual. "I don't know where she went. If she isn't at home, no telling. Have you tried my folks?"

Ryan rested his arms on the parts counter. "I just—hell, I don't know. I figured she'd want to spend the evening with me. How long has she been off work?"

Jake ran a finger down the small print, muttering numbers under his breath. When he found what he was seeking, he glanced up. "About an hour, maybe an hour and a half. You been by her house?"

"I called there." Ryan sighed, unable to shake the feeling that something wasn't right. "I can't figure her just taking off somewhere."

Jake chuckled. "Maybe you weren't as good as you thought."

"Shut up." Ryan rubbed beside his nose. The jibe struck a little too close to home.

The phone rang just then. Without glancing up from the parts catalog, Jake snaked out a hand to answer it. "The Works. Jake Coulter speaking. How may I help you?" He lost his place in the catalog. "What? Where are you?"

Ryan heard a faint voice coming over the line. Shrill, hysterical. He would have recognized it anywhere. He jerked erect, pulse racing. "What's wrong?"

Jake held up a hand. "You're *what?*" He listened for a second. "You *stay* right there. Do you understand me, Bethany? No matter what happens. Get in a stall and lock the door if you have to. I'll be right over."

Jake slammed the phone back into its cradle and came around the counter at a run. "Bethany's in a bar. Some bastard has her cornered in the bathroom, and Kate's about to rip his guts out with a broken beer bottle."

*   *   *

Ryan hit the door of the place called Suds two steps ahead of Jake. As he staggered into the dim interior, he scanned the room for any sign of Bethany. The bartender, a potbellied, sandy-haired guy in a white apron, jerked his thumb toward the rear. "Back there. I done called the cops."

Ryan and Jake scrambled for the rest room sign. It was a toss-up which of them made better time, the only certainty being that they didn't fit abreast when they started down the hallway. Ryan took the lead with an elbow in Jake's gut. If some creep had Bethany cornered, he wanted the honor of killing him.

When Ryan reached the end of the hallway, the scene that greeted him was worse than he imagined. Some woman who looked as if she'd been used hard and smacked for her trouble had a man backed against the wall with a broken bottle shoved against his crotch. She looked prepared to castrate him.

Ryan didn't really give a shit if the guy came out of this with his balls. He tried the ladies' room door, but the damned thing wouldn't open. Jake arrived at almost the same instant. Breathing hard, he flattened his hands on the door.

"Bethany, honey? Open up. It's Jake and Ryan. You okay?"

"*Ryan?*" she cried from the other side of the door. "Why'd you bring *him?*"

Ryan fell back. If that wasn't a fine how-do-you-do. He was here to save her. She was *his*. Not Jake's. Certainly not that creep's, who was about to lose his reason for being alive. Any man worth his salt looked out for his lady.

Ryan rapped his knuckles on the wood. "Bethany? Open the damn door."

"Is that awful man gone yet?" she asked shrilly. "He ripped my *blouse*."

Ryan glanced over his shoulder. His gaze connected with bleary brown vulture eyes, and he suddenly wondered why the hell he was messing with a door. He turned, advanced, and said to the woman, "I'll handle him from here."

Kate moved back, and Ryan stepped up to take her place.

He might not have laid hands on the man. His mama had raised him civilized, after all. But the son of a bitch looked Ryan up and down, grinned cockily, and said, "Are you the pussy who couldn't get the little lady's rocks off?"

Ryan never remembered exactly what happened after that. Witnesses claimed he grabbed the jerk by his shirt, picked him up, and proceeded to ring his bell by repeatedly slamming him against the wall.

The next thing Ryan clearly recalled, he was in handcuffs. He wasn't sure *why* he was in handcuffs. His knuckles burned, and there was a man in custody holding his face, but Ryan had no recollection of hitting him.

It was all pretty much confusing, actually. The cops brought Bethany out of the bathroom, and every time she looked at Ryan, she wailed, "Oh, God! Oh, God! All I wanted to do was to talk. I never meant for this to happen."

Kate put an arm around her. "Calm down, sweetie. You're twenty-six years old. If you wanna go have a beer now and again, I guess you can."

Ryan decided he didn't like Kate. She was a bad influence. He knew all about bad influences. Over the years he'd gotten into a lot of sticky situations he never saw coming with his brother Rafe. It always started with, "You know what I'm thinking?" And it went downhill from there. Oh, yeah. Ryan knew how easily you could find yourself in a hell of a mess, just because of the company you kept. Not that his brother was bad company. Rafe had just been one of those kids whose nose led him straight into trouble, and being the younger brother, Ryan had always been tagging along right behind him.

Ryan was thinking about that, albeit a little fuzzily, when Jake, who was in no real trouble with the cops, stepped over to the bar. He gave the bartender a long, narrow-eyed look that Ryan immediately recognized as bad news.

In a low, sort of friendly voice, Jake said, "Are you the man who called the cops when he realized a girl in a wheelchair was trapped in the ladies' room with an amorous, unruly drunk trying to bust down the door?"

The bartender might have said yes and gotten away with it. Instead, he puffed out his chest. "What do you think I am, buster, a bouncer? The lady came in, started complainin' to her friend about her sex life, and some guy half my age offered to show her a good time. I ain't touchin' that with a ten-foot pole. Like she wasn't askin' for trouble? My wife likes my face just the way it is."

"She won't now," Jake said conversationally.

And then he hit him.

Shortly after that, Ryan was getting cozier with Jake Coulter than he'd ever wanted to be—in the back of a cop car.

The Crystal Falls city jail had never seen such a ruckus. Ryan could hear his dad yelling clear in the back cell block.

Clinging to the bars like a convicted felon, Jake gazed across the aisle at Ryan. "You think your dad's gonna spring us or join us?"

Ryan pressed his brow against one of the bars and rolled his head back and forth on the coolness. As a substitute for an ice pack, it totally sucked, but it was as close as he was going to get in this place. "My father's jailbird days are over. He hasn't had any brushes with the law since he married my mom."

Jake listened for a moment. "He sounds a little hot under the collar."

Jake no sooner stopped speaking than Ryan heard his father yell, "What the *hell* is this country comin' to? A girl gets accosted by a drunk, and you arrest her menfolk for takin'

up for her? Explain that to me. Used to be, when a man de-
fended a woman, people patted him on the back!"

A low-pitched voice replied, the sound a murmur Ryan
couldn't make out.

"He always like this?" Jake asked.

Ryan considered the question. "Nah. Only when he gets
royally pissed."

"Then, call the judge!" Keefe roared. "Get the damn bail
set! I'm not leaving my boys in the hoosegow all night! You
got that, partner?"

Ryan flashed a weak grin at Jake. "Congratulations. You
just got yourself a second daddy. Ain't he a dandy?"

They both heard a woman's voice rise over the din just
then. "No, Keefe, *please*! I'm all right."

Keefe yelled, "Don't push my wife, you cocky little jackass!"

"Keefe, *please*!" Ann cried again.

A loud crash followed. Jake raised his eyebrows, fixed an
alarmed look on Ryan, and whispered, "Holy hell, I think
your dad just punched a police officer."

Chapter Sixteen

Sly had noticed Bethany's gray van sitting out front when he entered the stable, so he wasn't surprised to hear her talking to her horse. However, he was surprised when he realized she was crying as if her heart would break. With all the Kendricks at city hall, he was a lone soldier at the moment. Sly didn't mix any too good with weepy females.

That being the case, he considered leaving. Turning around, walking out. It seemed like a good plan, but when he reached the doors, the sound of her sobs grabbed him by the scruff of his neck. He stopped and slowly turned back, not entirely sure what he meant to do, but feeling as if he had to do something.

Once he reached the stall gate, he wasn't sure how to let her know he was there. She sat with her back to him, her face pressed against her mare's chest. Sly rubbed his jaw and then said, "Kinda looks like rain. Don't it?"

She jumped as if he'd jabbed her with a cattle prod. Then she hurriedly rubbed her cheeks before turning to look at him. From the first, Sly had thought she was a pretty little gal, but he hadn't really seen why the boy was so taken with her. Now he did. Them eyes of hers were flat something, damned near as big as flapjacks and bluer than blue.

"Sly! I, um—you startled me. I didn't know anybody was here."

He rested an arm on top of the gate. "Just came over to feed the stock. Ryan ain't around to take care of it tonight."

"I know. He's—in *jail*." Her face crumpled. "And it's all *my* fault."

That wasn't the half of it. Could be she hadn't heard about Ryan's daddy yet, though, and Sly wasn't about to tell her. "Well, now, don't take too much blame. That boy's a scrapper, always has been. He come by it kinda natural. Ain't like he just up and caught a bad case of the orneries after he met you."

She wiped her cheeks. As soon as she finished, another big tear spilled out. She dabbed at her nose with a tattered tissue that had more holes than a noodle sieve. Sly dug in his hip pocket for his handkerchief. After checking to be sure it was clean, he opened the gate and stepped inside to hand it to her.

"Here, honey. It's a little dusty but otherwise clean."

"Oh, I—" She stared at the blue bandanna for a second. Then she hesitantly plucked it from his fingers. "Thank you."

Sly hunkered, sifting through the hay while she blew her nose. "I couldn't help but hear you when I came in. Is there anything I can do?"

She took a quivery breath. "I wish there was. I feel so bad, Sly." Her mouth trembled and twisted. "Ryan's mom and dad are going to hate me."

"Aw, now, that ain't likely. This is just one of them things. Been kind of borin' around here of late. You sure enough fixed that."

"I guess I have." She dabbed the corners of her eyes. "All I wanted to do was talk to another woman. What a *disaster*. I was hoping to solve a problem, not create a new one."

"That's how it happens sometimes. The hurrier you go, the behinder you get."

She smiled and nodded. "I definitely didn't solve any-thing, that's for sure."

Sly searched her face. She looked so lonely sitting there,

with only her horse for company. "Don't you have any friends, honey?"

She shrugged. "Dozens up in Portland, just not many here yet. I haven't been back very long, and until just recently, all my time was taken up helping my brother at the store. There's Ryan, of course." She blew her nose again. "I can't talk to *him*. If only Kate would have gone with me for coffee. But, oh, no. We had to go to a stupid bar."

Sly smoothed the hay in front of him. He couldn't help but feel bad for her. "If you got a particular problem that needs solvin', maybe I can help."

"Thank you, Sly. That's very sweet. But it's—well, of a delicate nature, a feminine concern. That's probably not your field of expertise."

"With a name like Sly Bob, there ain't much about females I ain't expert on," he informed her with a wink.

"Sly Bob?"

"Short for Sylvester Bob, last name Glass. Down home, I harkened to Sly Bob."

"Is Galias a Mexican-American surname?"

He cocked an eyebrow. "No, darlin', it's Glass, not Galias."

"I'm not detecting a difference in the pronunciations. How is that spelled?"

"Just like it sounds, G-L-A-S-S."

Flattening a dainty hand over her chest, she burst out laughing, tears spilling over her lower lashes when she scrunched her eyes almost closed. "Just lack it sigh-yoonds?" she repeated, shaking her head. "G-Ale-A-Ayus-Ayus?" When her mirth subsided, she said, "Oh, Sly." She dabbed at her cheeks. "Thank you for taking the time to talk with me. I feel better already."

"I'm glad I lightened your load."

She smiled. "Considerably. So, tell me, how did Sylvester Bob *Glass* get shortened to Sly Bob? Someone didn't like you, or what?"

"Nah. It was the way in them parts, shortenin' boys' names, oft times to the first and middle initials, and my mama didn't like folks callin' me by mine."

Her brow furrowed in a frown, then understanding dawned in her eyes and she nodded. "Ah. I can see why she might have taken exception."

"Anyhow, she took to callin' me Sly Bob, and it stuck. I got teased a lot, and somewhere along the way, I started livin' up to the handle. Bad decision on my part, but it led to lots of interestin' experiences until I was nigh onto forty."

"Then you settled down?"

"Nope. Just got tuckered. Women have a way of flat wearin' a man out."

She rewarded him with another smile. Sly was glad she had at least stopped crying. "I appreciate your offering to lend me an ear. But it's not the sort of thing I can talk to a man about. Especially not *you*. You might tell Ryan."

"I ain't given to talkin' out of school, not to Ryan or anybody else."

"I couldn't ask that of you. I know you're very close to him."

Watching her expressions, Sly got a funny, achy feeling at the base of his throat. There were all different kinds of lonely, and he had a feeling this girl had been nose to nose with most of them. She was also very troubled about something, and unless he missed his guess, it had to do with Ryan. Sly loved that boy like a son. "It won't be the first secret I ever kept from Ryan."

She blushed and shook her head. "No. I just—it's too personal. I'd just—no. I couldn't."

Sly thought for a minute. "You ain't the only one who could use a friend, you know. Here of late, I got me a problem of my own."

Her eyes filled with concern. "You do?"

"Yep. Cain't talk to anybody in the family about it." Sly

rubbed a hand over his mouth. "They get wind of this, and I'm liable to get my walkin' papers."

"The Kendricks would never fire you. You're like a member of the family."

"Just goes to show how bad a problem I got, I reckon." He met her gaze. "Tellin' secrets has gotta go two ways. You wanna do a swap?"

"Oh, I don't know. As I said, I'd feel funny, talking to you about mine."

Wink stepped over and began pestering Sly for a scratch between the ears. He absentmindedly obliged the mare as he said, "No call to feel funny talkin' to me, honey. There ain't nothin' that shocks this old man."

She went to twisting on the handkerchief, her fingers clenching so hard that her knuckles turned white. "Yes, well, this is about *sex*." She leaned closer to whisper that last word as if she feared someone else might overhear.

"Sex?" Sly chuckled. "Well, now, you are in luck. I might've scratched my head a little on some subjects, but I'm sure enough an expert on that one. I've hung my britches on so many bedposts, I once wore a post hole in the seat of my jeans."

Her eyes widened. "My goodness. Did you really?"

He narrowed an eye at her. "No, not for true. I did wear a white spot, though. Anything you wanna know on that subject, I'm the feller to ask."

"I suppose getting a man's viewpoint might be helpful."

"I qualify on that count. Definitely a man, last time I checked. So what do you say? Wanna swap problems?"

She smiled slightly, then took a bracing breath. "All right. But only if you share yours first."

"Do I got your word you won't never tell? Nary a soul."

"Nary a soul," she agreed.

Sly shoved Wink away and ran his finger under his shirt collar. Then he cleared his throat. His voice went gravelly as he said, "You met Helen, Maggie's mother."

"Yes."

"Well, her and me, we're being friendly on the sly, no pun intended. If anyone find's out, it could cost me my job at the Rocking K. Helen ain't quite normal, you see."

When he finished speaking, she stared at him in stunned silence for several seconds. "Oh, Sly. I don't know what to say."

"Ain't much you can say, I don't guess." He released a pent-up breath. "Unless it's to call me a lowdown polecat for triflin' with her."

"Never that, Sly. I think she's a very lucky lady."

"You don't think I'm doin' wrong?"

"Not if you truly care for her. If you were only using her, then, yes, I think it would be very wrong. But it doesn't sound to me as if that's the case."

"I feel powerful better, just gettin' it off my chest. They all trust me, you see, and in the thirty-odd years I've worked on this spread, I ain't never broken that trust. Keefe and me—we go way back. When he first started this place, I was his right-hand man, and I been here ever since. Stood up for him when he married Annie. Helped raise both them boys." He took off his hat to turn it in his hands. "I tried to keep my hands off her. I knowed she wasn't right and maybe looked at me through a child's eyes, so I tried my damnedest. But the sad fact is, a man don't always choose who he loves. It just up and bites him on the ass."

"Does she love you?"

A burning sensation washed over Sly's eyes. "She thinks I can rope the moon. Could be that's why I love her so. Been a lot of women. None to speak of recent like, but a goodly number in my younger days. Nobody's ever looked at me like that." He tried to think of a way to explain. "When I talk, she listens, all interested like. Follows on my heels like a lost puppy whenever I'm over at Rafe's place. I ain't got a whole lot of schoolin', and lots of folks think I'm dumb. She admires me and thinks I'm smart. That makes me feel real good, and seein' the shine in her eyes when she looks at me, I walk a mite taller in my boots."

Bethany leaned forward to touch his hand. "Oh, Sly. I think maybe you're underestimating Ryan. If I understand how you feel, don't you think he will? He's got a good heart."

Sly enclosed her dainty fingers in his. "He does, at that. But the Kendricks, they're peculiar about their womenfolk. Step over the line in that respect, and they get downright testy." He gave her hand a squeeze. "I don't like sneakin' around, but I cain't see no other way. If they find out, the shit'll hit the fan. I'd marry her, of course. Ain't no way I'll have my Helen hangin' her head. Maybe she ain't real bright no more, but she's as fine a lady as there is."

"Oh, Sly, it goes without saying that you'd marry her. Perhaps that's the solution to this dilemma. Have you considered that? The Kendricks hold you in high regard, and you'd make Helen a fine husband."

"They won't hold me in high regard when they find out I been cozyin' up to Helen. Them thinkin' she ain't right, they're all-fired protective. Chances are, they'll can me. That's the policy here, no messin' with the women. I'd be without a job. How could I care for her? A man's gotta have work in order to do right by a woman, and someone pretty and fine like Helen deserves pretty and fine things. She ain't stupid, you understand. Or retarded, like. She's just slower to get there than other folks."

Bethany bent her head, her dark hair falling forward to hide her face. "I'm glad you told me." She glanced up to smile. "I know my vote isn't worth much, but I think it's wonderful that the two of you have found each other, and I hope you find a way to be together the way you should be."

Sly's voice turned gruff. "Thank you for that. Your vote means a powerful lot to me."

"I'll tell you something else. Just because you have little

formal education, that doesn't mean you haven't been to school. It was simply a different kind."

He grinned and winked at her. "I'm beginnin' to see why that boy's been like a pup chasin' its tail since meetin' you. Always did figure him for smart. Just didn't know how smart."

"Thank you, Sly. That's a lovely compliment."

"Sincerely meant. Now, enough about my problem. You gonna tell me about yours?"

After a great deal of hemming and hawing, she managed to do that. Sly scratched his head, after all, and almost wished he hadn't struck this bargain. "Well, now, that there is a whopper. No feelin' at all, you say?"

"Some here and there, but nothing seems to work right," she said hollowly. "I really don't mind that. Just being with Ryan is enough for me. I'm just afraid it won't be enough for him."

"If he loves you, it will. If he don't, you're well out of it. No marriage can work without love, honey, and lots of it. There are always problems. You ain't alone in that."

"I just want to make him as happy as I can. That's all."

Sly could understand that. Nothing made him feel better than to make his Helen smile. "Makin' a man happy is a pretty simple thing. You just follow your nose and find out over time what he likes and what he don't like. As for the other, I can't say I ever seen a woman fake it, leastwise not so's it was obvious. But I can tell you how they go on when they're really likin' it."

She fixed him with a hopeful look. "Can you?"

Sly held up a finger. "I'll be right back."

He had a bad feeling this might call for more showing than telling. He did most things better when he was stone-cold sober, but going on like a woman having an orgasm wasn't going to be one of them. He hurried to the office, fetched his flask, and returned to the stall posthaste.

An hour later when Ryan got home, he spotted Bethany's van. As he walked across the paved yard, he heard what sounded like a coyote inside the stable, gearing up to howl at the moon. *What the hell?* The instant he entered the building, he heard Sly's drawl. He followed the noises to Wink's stall, where he found Bethany and the foreman howling and laughing like fools.

Ryan hung back for a moment. Sly, who looked snockered, sat with his back to the wall, one knee bent to provide himself with an armrest. The foreman watched Bethany throw her head back and make odd noises, then he chuckled, shook his head, and said, "Not like that, darlin'. He'll dose you with pectate."

"Oh, Sly," Bethany said with a discouraged sigh, "will I ever get it right?"

"We're gettin' there," he assured her.

Ryan had seen enough to get the gist of what was going on. It seemed that his failings as a lover had become a main topic of discussion today. If everyone in Crystal Falls hadn't heard the story by noon tomorrow, maybe Bethany could post an add in the *Examiner* to get the word out.

He leaned against the stall gate. "Is this a private party?"

Bethany jumped with a guilty start. "Ryan!" she cried. "You're home."

He nodded. "Rafe called an attorney. First sane thing anybody did all day. The judge finally set our bail. Jake is out, too."

Sly angled him a look. "And your daddy?"

"Nope. The judge said he could cool his heels in there for the night. Punching a cop doesn't go over real well at city hall."

A horrified gasp escaped Bethany. "Your father struck a cop?"

"The guy had it coming. He was going for Dad, and in order to reach him, he shoved my mother out of the way. She hit her hip on the corner of the desk. Bruised her up pretty bad. Dad cold-cocked the little creep."

"Oh, *no*. That's a serious offense, Ryan."

"They'll never make the charges stick. Rafe took Mom to the ER for X rays. The injury is documented, and your dad and two of your brothers were there as witnesses. The cop was out of line." Ryan shrugged. "He got off lucky. If that first punch hadn't knocked him out, Dad would have stomped him."

"That's your daddy," Sly agreed with a nod. "If he hits a man and he don't go down, I'm gonna check behind the son of a gun to see what's holdin' him up."

Ryan moved into the stall and sat beside Sly. He gave Bethany a long look. "Don't let me interrupt. Sounded like you were having a lot of fun."

"Oh, we were about finished. Weren't we, Sly?"

"Yep. I think we was about done, all right."

Ryan smiled. "I don't know which of you sounded the sickest. No offense, but I think you need a little more practice to get it down right, honey. You start that howling and panting around me, and I'm gonna call the paramedics."

Bethany threw an appalled glance at Sly. The foreman pushed to his feet and screwed the lid back on the flask. "Well, I reckon that's my cue to scat." He kissed her forehead. "G'night, honey. If this young whippersnapper gets his ornery up, don't pay him a whole lot of mind. He's all growl and no bite."

"Better that than all howl and no loyalty," Ryan inserted.

"Yep. His ornery's up." Sly slapped his hat on. "G'night."

"Good night, Sly," Bethany called. "Thank you for—" She broke off and glanced guiltily at Ryan. "For all your help," she finished softly.

"Yeah, Sly. Thanks a bunch," Ryan said. When the sound of the foreman's footsteps faded away, he met Bethany's gaze and said, "Start talking."

Her gaze chased away, and her cheeks went pink again. "About what?"

Ryan sighed. She'd been crying. The end of her nose was all red, and she held one of Sly's blue bandannas bunched in her hand. "We can start with the incident this afternoon. Can you explain to me why you chose to talk with some strange woman about our sex life in a public place? And in a *bar,* of all places?"

She fiddled with the handkerchief, tugging up a corner, then tucking it back into the wad. "She wasn't a stranger. Kate works for us. As for the bar, I asked her out for coffee, but she asked if we couldn't go to a quiet place for a beer. She had a hangover and wanted some hair off the dog that bit her."

"A hangover, huh? That should have been your first clue. A *quiet* place? You were damned near raped in that quiet place. I see you went home to change your blouse."

"That's why I didn't go straight to the station. By the time I changed and got there, your folks were inside." She pushed at her hair. "I was embarrassed to face them. It was all my fault—you being there and everything—and I just—" She shook her head. "Now your dad's in jail. Oh, *God.* They'll hate me forever."

"They won't hate you." Ryan drew up his knees to brace his arms. For a long moment he said nothing. "You know, Bethany, the number one requirement for a great relationship is being open with each other."

"No, it's not," she said thinly. "The number one thing is good sex."

"And you feel I didn't give you that."

She looked genuinely appalled to hear him say that. "No. Oh, Ryan, *no.* I'm the one who failed you, not the other way around."

He could see the pain in her eyes—dark, shifting shadows that made him want to hug her. "You didn't fail me, sweetheart. It was fabulous for me."

"No. Do you really think I'm that naive? I wasn't asleep when you got up last night. You were so upset because I felt nothing, you left the house."

Ryan puffed air into his cheeks while he mulled over the situation. "So rather than upset me again, you recruited Sly to tell you how to fake an orgasm?"

"No, of course not. I talked to Kate first. Running into Sly tonight was an accident."

"And after running into him, you asked him how to fake it," he inserted again. "Just how long did you think that would work, Bethany?"

"I don't know. Forever, I hoped." Her lower lip quivered. "I don't want to lose you. If I can't make you happy that way, I'll lose you."

He slapped some hay from his pant leg. "I was upset last night. I admit it. I wanted it to be good for you, and it was really difficult for me to accept when it wasn't."

She fixed him with an imploring gaze. "It *was* good for me. All the parts I could feel. You can't—" She broke off and gave the bandanna a vicious twist. "You can't compare me to other women. Up until you, I had never even been with anyone and had little hope I ever would be. The parts I could feel were wonderful. *You're* wonderful. If I can have just that much—if there's never anything more for the whole rest of my life—I'll feel like the luckiest woman alive." She groaned and lifted her hands. "I don't want to lose you. Please, try to understand. If my pretending to feel would have made it better for you, I was willing to pretend."

Ryan leaned his head against the wall. Wink was munching grain, the sound so familiar that he focused on it for calm. When he finally lowered his gaze back to Bethany, his anger had ebbed. "Promise me something."

"What?"

"That you'll never lie to me again, even if you think it's what I need to hear."

She squeezed her eyes closed. When she finally lifted her

lashes, her face had gone pale. "I'm sorry I lied. It's not something I do very often, and I don't blame you for being angry. But try to understand my side. All the wishing in the world won't change my body, and I could lose you over this. The thought terrifies me." She laughed shakily. "Isn't that ironic? One of the main reasons I refused to have a relationship with you in the first place was because I feared exactly this. Now it's happened. I feel nothing. Only it doesn't matter. I want you anyway. And I—if you leave me, I don't know what I'll do."

She bent her head. "I *swore* I'd never do this to you. Clinging and begging. Wanting to keep you, no matter what, even if being with me won't make you happy." Her voice went shrill. "I'm sorry."

Ryan twisted onto his knees and crawled over to her chair. "I'm not going to leave you, honey. And if you try to leave me, I'm going with you. You got it?" He put his arms around her, pressed his face against the curve of her neck, and just held her for a while. "What you said just now— about enjoying all the parts you can feel, about that being wonderful and more than you ever had. I'll remember that. The problem last night wasn't that you failed to make it good for me, Bethany. It was fantastic. So fantastic I felt guilty as hell. You gave me so much, and I couldn't give you anything back."

She clung to him almost frantically, as if she was dangling off the edge of a cliff and he was her only lifeline. "You gave me *everything*," she whispered fiercely. "It was so wonderful, Ryan. You gave me everything."

"Yeah?"

"Yeah."

He pressed a kiss just under her ear. "You willing to go another round? I've been thinking all day about what you said this morning—about me going deeper. Last night, what with it being the first time and all, I was so afraid of hurting you that I didn't go very deep. Who knows? Maybe if I do,

I'll find one beautiful little nerve ending that's still alive and kicking in there."

"If not, it doesn't matter. Just having your arms around me is enough, Ryan. Being with you is enough."

Ryan tightened his hold on her, knowing she was right. Never had he loved anyone so much, and if God gave them only this, if holding her and loving her was all he could ever have, it would be enough.

Because, to him, she was absolutely everything.

Chapter Seventeen

Moonlight filtered in through the bedroom window, washing everything in silver. Stretched out full length on the mattress with Bethany tucked under his arm, Ryan gazed at her face, thinking how very beautiful she was, her features so delicate they might have been made of porcelain. He traced the shape of her brows with his lips, then trailed kisses down her nose, loving the way her breath caught and how she tightened her hands over his shoulders. He moved to her shell-like ear, nibbling lightly at the lobe.

"What can I do to please you?" she suddenly asked, trying to turn her head and foil his attempt to kiss her on the mouth.

"You please me just by existing," he whispered. "By being here with me. That's all I want, all I need, more than I ever dreamed I might have."

He felt her nose wrinkle against his jaw, a facial gesture that was habitual and always made him want to smile. "Don't be evasive, Ryan. You know very well what I mean. I'm new at this, and you need to be open with me so I can do all the things that turn you on. Do you like garter belts and nylons?"

He smiled in the shadowy gloom. "Kate again?"

"She did mention it's a favorite thing of men."

"Hmm. I like garter belts all right, I guess. But I'm not hung up on them."

"What do you like, then? I really want to know, Ryan. It's important to me to please you."

He just wanted her to lie back and let him devour her. Somehow, though, he didn't think that was what she wanted to hear. "I like you. A *lot*."

She laughed and playfully slugged his arm. "What a cop-out. *Tell* me. There must be things that turn you on. Do you like high heels?"

"Not really. I can't say I like any one thing in particular." He found the hollow beneath her ear and savored the taste of her skin there, thinking to himself that she was as intoxicating as wine, the faint scent of her shampoo making his head spin. "You could make me drool wearing a burlap sack."

"You're impossible."

"I like tight jeans and western shirts," he confessed as he nuzzled the curls at her temple. "The kind with pearl snaps on the breast pockets? There's something about seeing those pearls winking at me that makes my mouth go bone dry."

She giggled and toyed lightly with the hair on his chest. "I'll go buy some immediately. Would you like me to wear just the shirt and nothing else?"

"Sweet Christ." He grew still for a moment. "Would you?"

"If you'd like me to."

"Like isn't the word. Can I go with you to pick them out myself? I like fringe at the yoke, too. That white, shiny fringe. It shimmers and shifts back and forth. That drives me wild."

"I'll definitely wiggle my fringe a lot," she said with a laugh. "Do you like a woman to cook, wearing nothing but an apron?"

"As long as I can untie the sash. Holy hell." He trailed his lips over her cheek, intent on claiming her mouth. "You're driving me crazy. Enough talk. I want you, Bethany. *Now*."

She held him off by pressing a palm to his chest. "Just a few more questions, I promise."

He sighed. "Only a few."

She looked up at him with those beautiful blue eyes that always made him feel a little short on oxygen. "Do you, um, like fellatio?" Her voice went husky and shy as she posed the question. "I haven't ever done it, but I think—"

Startled, Ryan reared back to stare at her. He'd been with more women than he cared to remember, and never once had he been asked that question in just this way. Only Bethany would call it by its proper name behind closed doors. He suppressed a grin, not wanting to embarrass her. "It's all right, I guess," he said cautiously, half afraid she might scoot under the covers if he gave a more enthusiastic response. "It's not one of my favorite things."

"Oh. Why not? I thought guys really liked it."

He bent to take her mouth in a long, deep kiss. As he broke the contact, he said, "I'd much rather perform that service for you."

She wrinkled her nose again. "I want to do things for you, not the other way around. I didn't do anything to make it nice for you last night."

She was clearly bent on pumping him for information, and Ryan had a feeling he'd better cooperate unless he wanted her to have another tête-à-tête with Kate, the sex guru. He sighed and settled himself beside her again, propping his head on his hand. After winding a lock of her hair around his finger, he said, "I enjoy touching and kissing you. Knowing it makes you feel good makes me feel good."

"I'm very glad because I loved everything you did last night," she whispered, "and I'm sure I always will, but it can't always be only you who tries to please me. I want to be a satisfying bed partner. I never want you to feel like you're missing out on anything."

"That'll never happen. Being with you, making love with you—that was the best it's ever been for me, Bethany. Incredible. *Beautiful*. You can't improve on perfection, not in my books."

"Oh, Ryan, do you really feel that way?"

"I really do. And there's nothing particular I want you to do." He leaned over to kiss the end of her nose. "Except stop talking." He released her hair to move his hand to her breast. After capturing her nipple between his thumb and finger, he gave it a roll, smiling when she gasped and arched at the shock of sensation. He dipped his head to tease the tip of captured flesh with flicks of his tongue, which made her moan and make fists in his hair. "I just want to love you," he whispered. "For as long as I want, however I want. Do you have a problem with that?"

Her only response was a breathless mewling sound. She drew his head closer to her breast, offering herself to him and silently encouraging him to take. It was a request he couldn't refuse.

Forearmed with the knowledge that foreplay might be the only part of this that she could really enjoy, he lingered over her, kissing and fondling every spot on her body where she did have sensation. He wanted to make the prelude as glorious as possible. If he couldn't give her satisfaction, he'd at least give her sensuality and show her how desperately he loved her with every touch of his hands and lips.

Slow, feather-light caresses. Barely perceptible kisses. He used all his experience at lovemaking, putting his own urgent needs on hold while he met hers. *Bethany.* She was so dear. He loved the breathless way she cooed when he found a sensitive place and teased it with the tip of his tongue . . . loved how she tried to press closer to him . . . how she clung to him and cried out his name. *Bethany.* God, how he adored her.

Ryan rolled her onto her belly and kissed a slow trail down her spine, lingering just below her shoulder blades where he knew women were sensitive. From there, he moved to the hollow just under her arm, making goose bumps rise on her satiny skin as he journeyed slowly down her delicate rib cage to her waist, then to her plump derriere.

Her buttocks quivered beneath his lips, telling him how intense the sensations were for her.

When he rolled her back over, the shaft of moonlight fell across her breasts and gilded the turgid, pink crests. Smiling, he lay next to her, using his free hand to gently caress her while he lingered over her nipples, tormenting them with light flicks until they throbbed against his tongue and stood at eager attention. Then suddenly laying siege, he nipped them gently with his teeth and drew sharply with his mouth.

"Ryan!" She sobbed his name and arched up. He stayed with her, tasting and suckling until she trembled and he could feel her stomach muscles jerking beneath his palm. At that point his own needs had grown until he ached with urgency. Sliding his hand to the juncture of her thighs, he curled his fingers over her nest of curls to be sure she was ready. His fingertips encountered a slick, wet heat, an age-old welcome to any man.

As he withdrew his hand, Ryan brushed his fingertips over her clitoris. Bethany jumped as if he'd jabbed her with a pin. He froze, his gaze fixed on her face. Last night, he'd failed miserably to give her an orgasm by touching her there, and because it had been her first time, he'd been reluctant to suggest that he try doing it another way for fear of embarrassing her. It was still a little soon to introduce her to that kind of intimacy, but since she'd been the one to mention it first, he decided he might at least bring up the possibility.

"Sweetheart, would you let me try kissing you there?"

She frowned. "You touched me there last night, and it was uncomfortable for me."

"I know, but my hands are like sandpaper. I could be much gentler with my mouth."

She cupped a slender hand over the back of his, as though to protect the spot. "Oh, I don't think—"

"If it's just that you're supersensitive there, doing it with my mouth might make all the difference," he murmured, bending to suckle a nipple as he spoke. Her breath caught at the contact, and she mewled softly again. Between teasing passes of his tongue, he urged, "Please, honey? Say yes. It would make me so happy to give you an orgasm."

She arched up to his mouth. "Will you stop if it's uncomfortable for me?"

"Of course."

"All right," she said breathlessly. "I don't think it will work, but if you want to try, I won't stop you. If you truly want to, that is."

Oh, he wanted to. That sweet, nerve-packed flange of flesh was already swelling beneath his fingertips without his doing anything. Maybe she did have nerve damage there, just as she suspected, and he was tilting at windmills. There was only one way to find out.

He twisted onto his knees and pushed her legs apart so he might kneel between them. She smiled and released his hand. Ryan grabbed the unused pillow next to her and shoved it under her bottom.

"What are you doing?" she asked in bewilderment.

"Just getting you in a better position."

He cocked her knees out so they rested on the ends of the pillow, leaving her open and vulnerable. She cupped her slender hands over the exposed area, clearly self-conscious. They couldn't have that. Ryan lowered himself over her and reached back to tug up the covers to better shield her modesty.

He did his best work under a blanket, anyway.

"I love you so much," he whispered. "Have I told you that recently?"

She giggled. "Not for at least three minutes, you heel."

He bent to take her mouth in a long kiss, smiling at how eagerly she melted into it. *His Bethany.* His heart twisted, and he sent up a silent prayer. *Please, God, let this work. Let me give her pleasure. I'll never miss church on Sunday again, and I'll say a blessing at every meal, and I'll be on*

my knees beside the bed each night. I'll be the most rever-
ent, faithful man you ever saw, I swear, and I'll give thanks
for the rest of my life. Just give me this one thing.

Not wishing to embarrass her, Ryan didn't head immediately for his mark. Instead he went through all the motions
again, kissing her mouth, then all the sensitive places on her
body, working his way south the entire while. She held nothing back from him, her response unconditional and given
without hesitation. In only a couple of minutes, he had her
mewling and quivering with need again.

When he settled his mouth over the spot he'd been aim-
ing to reach, her mewling changed to startled whimpers. He
flicked her lightly with his tongue, taking care not to apply
too much pressure for fear of hurting her. She made an odd
sound at the back of her throat and then gasped in surprise
and sighed with pleasure. *Oh, yes.*

He wanted so much to make this good for her. He felt that
beautiful little tuft of femininity begin to swell again under
the careful ministrations of his mouth, and soon the under-
lying hardness of her arousal was apparent with every pass
of his tongue. He could feel her heartbeat there—her pulse
pounding like a trip-hammer.

Ryan cautiously increased pressure then. When she didn't
shrink away or cry out, his heart soared and he went for the
finish with hard, circular drags of his tongue over the spot.
She jerked and arched her spine. She tried to hike her hips.
He felt the urgency building within her, and knowing he
almost had her there brought tears to his eyes.

"Ryan?" she cried throatily, her voice laced with panic.
"This is—I—oh, God, I need you to hold me."

He cupped her bottom in his palms, hooking his thumbs
under her hipbones and lifting her up to his mouth. Against
her secret place, he said, "It's all right, honey. I'm right here.
Trust me, and just let it happen."

"Oh, *God*. Ryan?"

He resumed his assault with renewed determination. Her

slender body quivered like a plucked bowstring, and then
she sobbed. The next instant she cried out, her muscles jerking and going into spasms as her first orgasm rocked her.

Hallelujah.

For the first time in his life, Ryan Kendrick wept as he
brought a woman to climax.

Bethany's bones had melted. She couldn't move, couldn't
think, and didn't care. She just lay there in a limp sprawl,
dimly aware of Ryan rising over her.

"You okay, honey?"

Her tongue was glued to the roof of her mouth. Her heart
was still pounding. He had obliterated her thoughts. Her
bones had turned to the consistency of runny pudding. And
he wanted to know if she was all right? There was a possibility that she'd died of heart failure and was now in heaven.

"Mmm" was all she could manage to say.

He laughed softly. Then she felt that odd sense of fullness
she'd experienced last night, which told her he'd just entered her. "Hold on, sweetheart. Arms around my neck.
Come on. I'm going to take you flying again."

Bethany blinked. Arms, go up, she silently commanded.
Instead of obeying, her appendages just lay there, limp and
useless, one flung above her head, the other out from her
body. Ryan's dark face came into focus. His teeth flashed in
a broad grin. He dipped his dark head toward hers.

"Come on. Grab hold."

With effort she finally managed to lift her arms and
loosely hug his neck.

"There's my girl," he whispered. He reached back to lift
each of her legs to vise her knees under his arms. "You ready
for takeoff?"

She nodded, wishing he'd just let her go to sleep now.
Having lain awake for over a month, she felt so deliciously
relaxed that she selfishly thought, I won't feel this part any-

way. However, she managed to croak, "Ready," before she yawned.

He chuckled and shifted his torso sharply forward, the velvety length of his shaft making firm contact with the one place that had a *lot* of feeling. *Zing.* Bethany's eyes flew wide, and she stared up at him. He flashed her another grin as he made his first, cautious thrust. She gasped and dug all ten fingernails into his shoulders.

"I can make you come this way," he whispered. "Feel that? I'm connecting with *thousands* of lively little nerve endings, honey. It won't be uncomfortable, I promise. Not now."

To her surprise, it wasn't uncomfortable. At least not yet. "Why is that?"

"Because you're aroused, and it's all swollen, which makes it a little less sensitive."

She knew little about that sort of thing and could only trust his word.

"Don't be tense. If it doesn't feel nice, I'll stop." He dipped forward to kiss her. When their mouths parted, he whispered, "Come fly with me."

Bethany expected the friction to be unpleasant. He'd been so careful, kissing her there, but this was different. She felt sure that the rub of all that hardness against her would hurt. Yet instead, his shaft felt like steel sheathed in velvet, and for some reason, wasn't uncomfortable at all. Her breath snagged at the back of her throat when he thrust forward again.

"Tell me if you start to feel tender," he whispered.

With that, he picked up speed, and before she could formulate a thought, let alone articulate it, she was lifting off with him. Her mind spun at the indescribable sensations that rocked her. With every thrust, he was now connecting directly with her clitoris, which sent electrical shocks shooting out every which way to ribbon through her.

"Ryan!" she cried.

"I'm here, honey." His voice had turned husky and clipped. "I'm gonna go deep now. All right? If it even sort of hurts, you tell me, and I'll back off."

He shoved sharply forward with his hips, burying himself to the hilt. Bethany cried out. He stiffened and drew back, his gaze glassy and riveted to her face. "Does it hurt?" he asked.

"No, but I—oh, Ryan, way deep, I can feel you."

"You can?"

She laughed tearfully and locked her hands over his upper arms, urging him forward again. "Oh, *yes*," she cried when he drove into her again. "Oh, Ryan! Yes, yes, *yes*! I can definitely feel that."

He established a hard, fast rhythm then that made further discussion not only impossible but unnecessary. Her moans and gasps of pleasure communicated her feelings with ab- solute clarity, she felt sure. *Flying*. He was taking her on a private tour of paradise. The building pleasure. The coiling need and urgency. Soaring ever higher. When she crested and plunged over the edge, he stiffened and she felt a white- hot surge pour through her, way down deep.

She arched up as best she could to meet him, her mind splintering as a violent orgasm rocked her body. Definitely paradise, she decided dizzily as the small aftershocks jolted through her.

Ryan Kendrick was the most wonderful man ever to draw breath.

He drew her into his arms and held her with fierce pos- sessiveness when it was all over—hugged her so fiercely that she could almost feel the intensity of his love for her.

"Oh, Ryan," she whispered. She smoothed her hands over his hair, wanting to comfort him. "It's all right. Every- thing's going to be all right now."

In response he only tightened his hold even more. In that moment Bethany realized just how tormented he'd been about his inability to satisfy her.

She pressed her face against his shoulder. "Oh, Ryan . . . I love you so."

He rested his jaw against her hair, a shudder racking his big body. After a long while, when his breathing evened out, he sighed and said, "Now I wish I'd gone ahead and kissed you there last night. It would have saved us twenty-four hours of sheer hell."

Bethany rubbed her cheek against his skin, loving the feeling of muscle over bone, hard yet forming a comfortable pillow for her head. "Maybe we needed to experience the hell to fully appreciate the heaven. I'm still not normal. I feel absolutely nothing when you first go inside of me."

"It doesn't matter, Bethany," he murmured. "Unless I've been misinformed, you've got feeling where it counts. If given a choice, I think most women would choose to have a clitoral orgasm over a vaginal one."

Bethany grinned against his shoulder. It had definitely been intense—indescribably intense. "I wonder why it didn't feel nice when you touched me there last night?"

He nuzzled her hair. "You were so tense, for one thing. And I think you're right about having nerve damage there, which makes you supersensitive until I get you really hot." He chuckled, the sound laced with male satisfaction. "That's all right. You asked what things I really like? Kissing you there is my all-time favorite. I think I'm already addicted."

"I'm glad. It was wonderful," she whispered.

"I've been told there's no other orgasm that compares to it."

"By whom?"

Silence. Then a cough. "Never mind. That's not really important, is it?"

"I guess not," she said with an impish grin she hid by keeping her face against his shoulder.

"By shifting forward while I make love to you, I can give you a clitoral orgasm and make you climax with me. *That's* the important thing. It's fantastic for me, knowing you're enjoying it, too."

It *had* been pretty fantastic. Feeling so content and satisfied she could barely keep her eyes open, Bethany pressed closer to him and sleepily whispered, "I love you, Ryan. That was the most fantastic experience of my whole life. Thank you so much."

He chuckled and drew her more firmly against him. "Prepare for a lifetime of fantastic, lady. I enjoyed it as much as you did."

Sometime in the darkest part of night, Bethany woke up, realized Ryan wasn't beside her in bed, and reared up on her elbow to glance around. She blinked bewilderedly when she saw him kneeling beside the bed, elbows resting on the mattress, his big, rough hands clasped in prayer before his bowed head.

"Ryan?" she whispered hoarsely. "Are you all right?"

He glanced up. "Never been better. I was just saying my prayers."

"Your prayers?" Bethany had never figured him for the type of man who got on his knees. Now she wondered why she'd been under that impression. Any man as kind as Ryan Kendrick probably had a deep, abiding faith that guided him through life. "I didn't mean to interrupt you. I'm sorry."

She lay back, intending to leave him to his meditations. But he lowered his hands and grinned at her. "No problem. I was done."

A carnal gleam had come into his eyes. He slipped his hands under the covers to lock them over her knees. The next thing Bethany knew, her bottom was skidding over the mattress toward him, the rest of her startled self following.

"What're you doing?"

"Nothin'." He gave her an innocent-looking smile as he positioned her legs, one on each side of him, then slid his hands to her hips to pull her the remainder of the way to him. "Yet, anyhow."

Her most private place bumped intimately against his hard belly. He hooked his arms under her knees, curling his hands over her uplifted thighs.

"Hi," he said softly.

Bethany cupped her fingers over that place he had just laid opened to his gaze. He glanced down at her splayed fingers. "You're gonna have to move those, sweetheart. I got business down there, and they're in my road."

She laughed. "You surely don't mean to—you know—do *that* right now."

He bent his head to kiss the sensitive place on her inner left thigh. Against her skin he rumbled, "Name me one good reason I shouldn't."

"Because my heart may not be able to take it twice in one night?"

His nibbled her skin. "Nah. You won't die from it."

Bethany tried to think of a way she might explain that this was all still new to her, and that she felt a little embarrassed. It had been different when she was aroused and already wanting him. She'd barely been able to think, let alone feel modest. "But, Ryan, you haven't even kissed me yet."

"Hmm." He angled her a look with eyes that were definitely glinting with lust. "You particular about what part of you I kiss first?"

She giggled. "A lady needs a little bit of foreplay to get in the mood."

He arched an imperious brow at her. "I'll tell you what," he said huskily. "Move your pretty little fingers out of my way and prop up on your elbows to watch. You'll get in the mood real fast."

"Oh, I don't think—I'm not going to *watch*."

"Why not?"

She couldn't readily think of a reason, and he didn't give

her any time to come up with one. She giggled again when he started nipping at her fingers to make her move them. "How can you switch from saying your prayers to doing this before you even get off your knees?"

"Because I believe with all my heart that the love we have is a sacred gift, and that anything we do to express that love is beautiful."

"Oh, Ryan . . ." Bethany's throat went tight, and she did push up on one elbow then. Being loved by him *was* beautiful—the most beautiful experience of her entire life. He'd kissed her scars. He touched her as if she were a priceless treasure. She felt content as she never had when he held her in his arms. What could be more beautiful or right than that? "I love you so much. So very, very much."

"Then, don't hold anything back from me," he whispered against her skin. "I know we've moved fast, but for us, it's the only way. I want to make love to you again, and I want it to be wonderful for you. I can be sure it will be, doing this. It's a miracle, Bethany mine, a gift from God."

It really was a miracle, Bethany thought. A beautiful, wondrous gift. It would be the height of stupidity to let modesty ruin it for her—or for him.

She moved her hand, watching as he kissed his way up her leg. For just an instant she wished she could feel the silky brush of his lips, but she quickly shoved the yearning aside. Seeing him kiss her inner thigh was just as erotic in its way, and it was so wonderful to know she would be able to feel every light brush of his lips when he finally reached his destination.

He finally got there and touched the tip of his tongue to her. Bethany gasped at the shock of hot delight that coursed through her. "Oh, *Ryan*. That—feels—so—*good*."

His hot, wet mouth closed over her, and his tongue flicked lightly at her flesh, gently teasing her sensitive nerve endings until her head was spinning and her blood started rushing.

"You okay?" he rumbled against her.

The movement of his mouth and the thrum of his voice vibrated through her, and she nearly died on the spot. She tried to answer him, but her throat was locked shut, the only sound she could make a soft panting noise.

That was evidently answer enough, for he resumed his gentle assault. He hiked her bottom off the mattress to situate her just so. Every muscle in her upper body snapped taut and jangled. Then she forgot everything. *Lightning bolts*. It was the only way to describe the sensations that jolted through her.

Somehow one of her hands became fisted in his black hair, and the next thing she knew, she was using his hair to pull herself up to a sitting position. He hunched lower to continue loving her. Then he moved up to kiss her breasts.

"Oh, Ryan."

"You dead yet?" he asked with a rumbling chuckle.

"Not yet."

He kissed his way back down to her navel. "Good. Stay with me, sweetheart. I'll take you flying again."

Ryan Kendrick was a man of his word.

She definitely soared.

Chapter Eighteen

When Bethany awakened, the morning was too gorgeous for her to greet it with a frown. Sunlight poured in Ryan's bedroom windows, gilding his hair and face with gold. They shared a pillow, which struck her as being symbolic of their lives together from this moment on. He slept with one arm angled up her front, his big hand curled loosely over her left breast. They were both naked, and she reveled in the feeling of all that delicious maleness curled around her.

She sighed, blissfully content. For the first time in eight years, she'd been able to roll over during the night. True to his word, Ryan had tucked her against him several times to switch sides, making it possible for her to snuggle against his back or be cuddled in his strong arms. It had been the most heavenly feeling.

He startled her by suddenly mumbling into her hair. "Will you eat breakfast with me like this?"

"In the kitchen?" She giggled. "Naked, you mean?"

"What kind of fantasy would it be if you weren't?"

"Only if you do the cooking. The oil always splatters when I fry eggs."

"Fruit and a bagel won't splatter." He flicked her nipple. "Imagine my mouth on you there after I've taken a sip of steaming hot coffee."

Bethany's stomach clenched at the thought.

"I'll smear low-fat cream cheese all over you and lick it

off," he said huskily. "You can sit naked in my kitchen, skim your teeth over your banana, and drive me out of my mind. You'll never make it out of the house before noon."

She laughed again. "I have to go to work."

"Stay home with me today." He nuzzled her ear. "Go with me to city hall. We'll break my dad out of jail and apply for a marriage license, all in one visit."

"Surely we don't need a license straightaway."

"Yep. I want a ring on your finger, darlin'."

She turned to kiss the bridge of his nose. "Oh, Ryan, you're so sweet."

"No sweet to it. If I don't marry you immediately, Jake'll kill me."

"Don't worry about Jake. I can handle him."

He intercepted her before she could kiss his nose again and settled his mouth over hers. Bethany's pulse started to race. When he came up for air, he replied, "No arguments. You're marrying me as soon as I can arrange it."

"I can't possibly. It takes time to plan a wedding."

His eyes came wide open. "I'd like to keep it simple. No fuss, no muss."

"I used to fantasize about being married at a high mountain lake."

"Now you're talking."

Her heart squeezed. "That's out of the question now."

He rose up to nibble on her throat. "I can get you to a wilderness lake. A beautiful one. In fact, that's how I want to spend our honeymoon, just you and me, at a high mountain lake."

"Ryan, I can't stay at a high mountain lake. I told you, I—"

He laid a finger across her mouth. "I ordered you an all-terrain chair. It's lightweight, so we can pack it in by horseback, and it's guaranteed to go over rocks and small logs. It's due here next week, same day as your saddle."

"You *what*?"

He moved his finger to dip his head and steal another kiss. "Don't frown. You'll get wrinkles."

Bethany scowled anyway. "Even with an all-terrain wheelchair, I'd need special facilities for my personal needs. It's just not feasible for me to—"

"I'm working on that. Mom helped me design an outhouse for you."

"An *outhouse*?"

"Yeah. My dad's been helping me, too. He's more experienced at welding aluminum. It'll be light, have bars, and it all comes apart for easy transport. We're using tent nylon for the top and walls. You'll have all the comforts of home."

She moved her head back to stare at him incredulously. "You're serious."

"Of course I'm serious. We're going on a wilderness ride for our honeymoon. Just you and me, at a gorgeous high mountain lake, just like you loved to do before you got hurt. We'll catch trout for our supper and cook them over an open flame. Make love under the stars. Then I'll tell you scary stories before bed so you'll snuggle up real close when we get in the tent, and I'll make love to you in the sleeping bag. We'll go swimming, too, and I'll make love to you in the water. There's a falls up there. It's so pretty, it'll take your breath, and I'll—"

She burst out laughing. "Make love to me under the spray?"

He grinned. "How'd you guess?"

Bethany relented and took the day off from work so she could be with Ryan. While she enjoyed a third cup of coffee, he went over to the stable to care for the stock. It was such a glorious morning that Bethany threw open the slider to let in fresh air. She was about to shut the screen when the phone rang. Circling Tripper, who snoozed near the end table, she grabbed up the portable.

"Hello?"

"Hey, sis. How are you this morning? Fully recovered from the mix-up yesterday, I hope."

"I'm great, Jake. Better than great, actually."

He sighed. "That's good to hear. I was a little worried when I got the message that you weren't coming in to work."

She explained that Ryan wanted to apply for their marriage license later.

"He doesn't waste any time," Jake observed. "You sure this is the right thing, Bethie? Marry in haste and all that. No need to get in a rush."

"I've never been surer about anything, Jake. I love him so much it hurts."

Long silence. Then Jake said, "Pardon me for bringing it up, but just yesterday weren't you blubbering in your beer, disappointed with the sex?"

"Where on earth did you get that idea?"

"From the bartender."

Bethany's face went hot. She drew the line at discussing the particulars of her love life with her brother. At the same time she understood that he was concerned and needed some reassurance so he wouldn't worry.

"I wasn't disappointed. I was afraid Ryan was." Bethany couldn't think how to explain. "But that's all behind us now. Everything is *marvelous*."

"Marvelous, huh? You sure, Bethany?"

"I'm positive. Please, don't be worried. I love him so much, and he loves—"

She heard something behind her and glanced guiltily over her shoulder. Ryan wouldn't be happy to hear her discussing their relationship with Jake.

Instead of Ryan, it was T-bone behind her. Bethany stared into the bull's vacuous brown eyes, not sure if she should scream or say hello. She glanced toward the sliding glass door, recalling Ryan's warning that T-bone barged in if it wasn't kept closed.

The bull let out a bellow just then that was so loud it seemed to vibrate the walls. "Holy hell, what was that?" Jake asked.

"A bull." Bethany imagined T-bone butting her as she'd seen him butt Ryan. This was no laughing matter. If her chair tipped over, the bull could very easily trample her. "I have to go, Jake. I'll call you back."

"Aren't you in the house?"

"I, um . . . yes," she admitted faintly.

"That sucker sounded close, like he was right on top of you."

He *was* right on top of her. Almost, at any rate. "I'm fine, Jake. I'll call you right back." Bethany broke the connection and tossed the phone on the sofa. "Hello, T-bone," she said shakily.

Long strings of drool hung like shoestrings from the bull's broad muzzle. He nudged Bethany's arm. She half expected him to send her flying with a hard shove, but almost as if he sensed she was different, he was very gentle instead. With a trembling hand, she scratched behind his ears as she'd seen Ryan do.

"I suppose you'd like a carrot. You stay right here, and I'll run fetch you one." And throw it outside, she thought, gulping down terror.

She hurried toward the kitchen. T-bone followed docilely. Once at the refrigerator, she endured wet snuffles while she dug through the vegetable drawer. The bull seemed to like her perfume and the smell of her shampoo. He kept sniffing her ear and hair. She plucked out two carrots and gave him one, hoping to get around him while he ate it.

No such luck. The bull blocked her way, trapping her in the kitchen with him while he enjoyed his treat. When it was gone, he mooed for another. Bethany shivered in the cold draft coming from the open refrigerator as she fed him the second carrot then dug in the drawer for more. Her heart caught when she saw there were only three left. T-bone would devour those in no time at all. What would he do when she had nothing more to feed him?

It wasn't long before Bethany found out. "That's all," she said in a quaking voice. "Time to go now, big guy."

T-bone nuzzled the front of her blouse. When he discovered her armpit and dove his nose in to sniff, she gave a startled laugh. "There's no food in there. That's deodorant, you goofy animal."

T-bone sniffed her chest, giving her breasts gentle nudges. Bethany began to relax. He gave no indication that he meant to butt her. He was only curious. She sighed and began petting him. "Do you like fruit, you big clown?" She moved to the bar and plucked an apple from the bowl. "Here. *Bon appétit.*"

T-bone ate the apple whole. He seemed to love it. Bethany quickly handed him another one, which he also devoured in a couple of chomps. She started to laugh. "How do you feel about bagels and low-fat cream cheese?"

As if she'd rung a dinner bell, Tripper woke up and hurried in. The fat golden lab sat next to the bull, tongue lolling, brown eyes fixed imploringly on her. She grabbed the bag of bagels and gave the dog one of those. T-bone sniffed the bread but politely turned it down. He loved bananas, however, and ate three.

That was how Ryan found Bethany a few minutes later, holding court in his kitchen with his bull and dog in attendance. T-bone had discovered the marvel of Bethany's skirt and was attempting to learn what was under it. She giggled and shoved at his massive head.

"What is it with the guys around here?" she asked the bovine with a tinkling laugh. "*No,* T-bone."

Ryan leaned his elbows on the breakfast bar and watched her for a moment, trying to imagine the reaction of any other woman he'd ever dated had she been cornered in his kitchen by a bull. Hysteria, surely, and screams to rattle the windows. But here was Bethany, in a wheelchair, calmly petting the huge galoot, as if finding a bull in the house was an everyday occurrence. Ryan had never been more certain that she was the only lady in the world for him.

"Are you spoiling my critters?" he finally asked.

She jumped with a start, then laughed when she saw him there. "Ryan. I'm glad you're back. I have this little problem."

"That's eight hundred pounds of problem, darlin', nothing little about him. I was hoping he'd find himself a love interest and stop hanging around so close to the house. Instead, he's up here trying to make time with my lady the first moment my back is turned."

She flashed him a beaming smile. "No worries. Your lady has eyes only for you. I was afraid at first, but it's almost as if he knows I'm different."

The bull chose that moment to try to get under her skirt from another angle. "He's noting the differences, all right. He's seen Mom a few times, but otherwise, he's never been around ladies much."

"I mean different in that I'm handicapped. You wouldn't believe how careful he's been."

"That's good to hear. I'd hate like hell to have to shoot him."

"Oh, no!" She looked horrified at the suggestion. "Please, don't even *think* it. I'd feel so awful. Just look at how gentle he's being."

Ryan had to admit the bull was being uncharacteristically gentle. He smiled slightly, wondering if those big blue eyes of hers worked on bulls just as they did on men. Over at the stable a moment ago, he'd encountered Sly, who had gone on and on about how special this young lady was. "One look into them big blue eyes, and my old heart flat melted," Sly had told him.

Ryan smiled, recalling the sappy grin on Sly's weathered

face. "He sure seems to be taken with you," he told Bethany, not entirely sure if he was talking about the foreman or the bull. "How'd he get in the house, anyway?"

She rolled her eyes. "I forgot and left the slider standing open."

Ryan sighed. "Dumb critter." He stepped around the counter and gave his bull a gentle swat on the rump to get his attention. "Come on, T-bone. Time to go back outside before you decide to take a dump on my floor."

Bethany wrinkled her nose and shuddered. "What a thought."

Ryan got the bull turned, then shooed him outside by brandishing his Stetson. He shut the sliding glass door, feeling sad. Now that Bethany would be around all the time, something would have to be done about T-bone. Ryan couldn't take a chance that the bull might hurt her. Next time, T-bone might get ornery with her. By nature, he was an unpredictable creature.

"Don't even think about it," she said.

Ryan turned to find her sitting behind him. Her big eyes searched his.

"I mean it," she said shakily. "It was my fault he got in, but he was a perfect gentleman. If he's gone the next time I visit, I'll never forgive myself."

Ryan slapped his hat against his leg. "I'm afraid he'll hurt you."

She gazed past him at the bull that still stood on the deck. "You owe him the chance to prove he won't. I'll be careful around him, Ryan. If he gets obnoxious a single time, I promise to tell you immediately. How's that?"

Ryan glanced through the glass, remembering T-bone as a baby. It was a damn fool thing, a rancher turning bulls into pets. He'd named T-bone after a cut of steak, hoping it would serve as a reminder of that, but T-bone had been sickly, forcing Ryan to care for him, and in no time, he'd started to love the puny critter.

"I'll think on it," he said softly.

"Are you going to be one of those husbands who thinks it's his right to make all the decisions, no matter how I feel or what I say?"

Ryan shot her a bewildered look. "Of course not. This is different."

"That's what they all say." She lifted her stubborn little chin—a feature he'd noticed the very first time he saw her. "If you shoot that bull without just cause, I'll never forgive you. Am I making myself perfectly clear?"

He chuckled. "Are you going to be one of those wives who pokes her nose into my business and offers an opinion whether it's wanted or not?"

She hesitated. Then that chin came up again. "Probably. I was raised on a ranch. It's not as if I know nothing about raising cattle and horses."

"I was hoping you'd say that." He sent his hat sailing toward the coat tree. The Stetson hit the hook, spun, and then settled, pretty as could be. "So when are you going to quit that desk job and help me run this place?"

"You want me to quit my job at the store?"

"If Jake can figure out a way to get along without you, I could really use your help here. There aren't enough hours in the day for me to get everything done. I need a partner, someone I know I can trust. You'd be a damn good stable manager. You know your horses and love them as much as I do."

A gleam of interest entered her eyes. "I couldn't manage the stables, Ryan. I'm in a wheelchair."

"Not a place over there you can't reach now," he reminded her. "I'll have you riding as of next week. You can keep books, give orders, oversee the help, and handle business over the phone, same as I do. Name me one thing you can't do just because you're in a wheelchair."

"I can't do any of the actual work."

"That's not part of the job description. The hands will do

the work. Managers manage. That's why they're called *managers*. Even if you weren't in a wheelchair, I'd paddle your fanny if I caught you doing any heavy work. Not my wife. Now that the ranch is doing so well, we hire able-bodied men to help with all that, which is a much better setup. My dad hated it when he had no choice but to count on my mom to do a man's job, and as much as she loves ranching, you'll never see her at the business end of a pitch-fork anymore."

"A man's job."

Ryan saw a glint of feminine pride in her eyes, and he rushed to clarify that statement. "You know what I mean. Very few women have the muscle to safely buck hay or lift a struggling calf. It ate at Dad to see Mom doing things that he was afraid might injure her back. She's not a whole lot big-ger than you are. It was never a question of respect or equal-ity. She has always been his equal here on the Rocking K, but no matter how you slice it, she's put together differently, with a more delicate bone structure and less muscle to sup-port it. That's all I meant."

A twinkle of laughter replaced the glint in her eyes. "I'll accept that so long as you'll concede that a woman has the brains to figure out a way to compensate for her lack of strength to get the job done if it's necessary."

He grinned. "I won't argue that point. But it's never nec-essary now."

She relaxed and smiled wistfully. "It's a very tempting thought. I'd love to be a part of all this." She glanced out the slider at the stable. "But what if a mare went into labor?"

"You'd call the vet out, same as I do."

She laughed and rolled her eyes. "You have an answer for everything. The sad fact is, even if I can start riding occa-sionally with you, I'll be unable to mount or dismount a horse without help. A stable manager who can't ride? I don't think so."

Ryan kept his gaze fixed on hers and struggled not to

smile. "We've about got a sling finished for you. All electric."

"What?"

He stepped over and leaned down, bracing his hands on the arms of her chair. "A sling. The seat is made of nylon, and it's tailored to fit. Once you're in the saddle, it unhooks from the pulley ropes, and you can wear it while you ride. When you get back to the stable, you just reattach it to the hooks, and it'll lift you off the horse and onto the chair again."

She stared blankly at him for a long moment. "A sling," she repeated expressionlessly, as if she'd never heard the word. "For the stable?"

"Designed especially for you. It wasn't that difficult. We already have electric slings for the horses. We modified one. My grandpa was a machinist, and Dad inherited his knack for designing gadgets. Mom made the sling seat for you on her sewing machine. All of us ride, and we love it. We know what a joy it'll be if you can get on a horse any time you want."

"Oh, Ryan."

"It was no big thing," he said, half afraid she was getting upset.

She glanced past him at the door. "It's in this stable?"

"Mom's still putting on the finishing touches. It'll be done before your saddle gets here."

"And it works?" she asked softly. "How can you know if it works?"

Ryan realized then that she was afraid to believe him, that it meant even more to her than he'd imagined it might, and she didn't want to get her hopes up, only to have them dashed. "That was Maggie's contribution. She's about your size. Mom fitted the seat to her, and she was our guinea pig. It lifts her on and off a horse, no problem. She made sure not to use her legs, tried to pretend she couldn't. Got her in the saddle, slick as a whistle."

A smile moved slowly over Bethany's trembling mouth. "Can I see it?"

Ryan heaved a silent sigh of relief. "Sure. Right now, if you'd like."

"I'd like."

Bethany couldn't believe her eyes when Ryan demonstrated how the sling worked a few minutes later. She stared up at the ceiling tracks attached to the rafters. She was dreaming, surely. Paralyzed women couldn't buzz out to the stable and hop on a horse to go riding like a normal person.

Ryan Kendrick didn't seem to understand that. Instead he looked at a problem from all angles, recruited his wonderful family to help him, and devised some crazy way to make the impossible happen. She imagined Keefe and Ann Kendrick, along with Rafe, Maggie, and Ryan, all gathered in this stall, puzzling and working, trying to make a small miracle happen for her.

Never say cain't. Ryan had told her he believed in that motto, but this was beyond her wildest imaginings. A stable lift, her ticket to freedom. She'd be able to get on Wink any old time she liked and feel the wind on her face again.

She searched Ryan's beautiful, steel-blue eyes. The love for her that shone in them was impossible to miss.

"I hoped it'd make you happy," he said.

"I'm speechless. This is—well, it's incredible, Ryan. I think I'm dreaming. I'm afraid someone will pinch me awake, and you'll vanish in a puff of smoke."

"Nope," he assured her. "I'm real, and you're stuck with me."

"Oh, I hope so. Forever will suit me fine."

He rubbed his jaw and gazed at the lift. "It just occurred to me that maybe I'm throwing too much at you at once."

"Oh, Ryan, *no*. Aside from Wink, this is the most wonderful gift anyone's ever given me."

"I don't want to push you. We Kendricks—that's a fault

we have with the women we love. I don't mean to come over you like a high wind. It's just—well, it sort of runs in my blood, I guess. My dad, with my mom. And you wouldn't believe how Rafe was with Maggie. We Kendricks tend to be a little pushy."

"A little?" Sly poked his head in through the doorway. "Son, you Kendricks are like bulldozers. When you set your sights on a lady, she don't have a chance." He winked at Bethany. "Mornin', darlin'. How you doin' this bright and sunny day?"

Bethany wished she could step over and hug him. Instead she looked him straight in the eye, trying to tell him with her eyes what she couldn't say aloud, that she would never forget last night and that she'd treasure his friendship. "I'm wonderful, Sly. And you?"

"Ain't never been better." His eyes twinkled as he glanced from her to Ryan. "Looks like he got over his orneries, and you lived through the experience. Knew you would, of course. Just like his daddy, that boy. Strike a match to his temper, and he may tear hell out of everything around you, but when the dust settles, ain't a hair on your head gonna be mussed."

Bethany smiled. "He got a little lippy, but I just slapped him up alongside the head and told him to behave himself."

Sly nodded. "Good for you, darlin'. Only way to handle him."

Ryan muttered something under his breath and gave the foreman a narrow-eyed look. "You need something, Sly?"

"Nope." Sly chuckled and winked at Bethany. "I best stop makin' eyes at you. Now his jealous is gettin' up." He started to leave, then stopped and turned back. "Rafe went to get your daddy, by the way. He said if we was to wait 'til you pried yourself away, your daddy would be so het up, he'd act like a rabid badger all the way home."

Ryan chuckled. "We could've sent Mom. She can handle him."

Sly winked at Bethany. "You hear that, darlin'? You watch Annie in action. She'll teach you all you need to know."

Bethany laughed. "Is that right?"

Sly's weathered, sunbaked face creased in a smile. "Damn straight. Ain't a man alive with the guts or where-withal to tangle with Keefe when he's in a stir. But our Annie will go toe-to-toe with him, one hand tied behind her back."

Bethany raised her eyebrows. "Really? And who wins?"

"Annie," Sly said with a wry chuckle. "Hands down, no contest. Keefe give up on fightin' with her some twenty years back. He just shakes his head and lets her go. Most times, she's right anyhow, so it works out good."

Ryan sighed. "Sly, do me a favor and just shut up. Don't go putting ideas into her head."

"I hate to tell you this, son. She was born with ideas in her head. She don't need me to put 'em there."

Sly left then. Ryan gazed after him for a moment, then laughed and gouged the dirt with his boot heel. "Is he ornery, or what?"

"He's wonderful," Bethany said, and she meant it with all her heart.

When Ryan met her gaze, there was a silent message in his eyes. "You'll never find a better friend. I was sort of upset with him last night, but I'm glad he was here to talk to you."

"He loves you. Do you realize how much?"

Ryan's eyes darkened. "He'd lay his life down for me. Never a doubt."

"Just you remember that," she said softly. "If the time ever comes that he needs you to stand up for him, Ryan, just you remember that."

A bewildered expression crossed his face. "I guess I will. He's like a second father to me." He searched her gaze. "Why do you say that?"

Bethany smiled and shrugged. "No particular reason."

"There is a reason. I know you. Is Sly in some kind of trouble?"

Bethany wanted so badly to betray Sly's confidence then. She believed with all her heart that Ryan would understand the old foreman's feelings for Helen, just as she did, and that he'd fight the whole family on Sly's behalf if need be. But it wasn't her place to open that can of worms.

"Just remember this moment. If ever you doubt him—if ever his honor is called into question—remember this moment and shove your doubts aside. Stand up for him. That's all I'm saying. He's earned that, hasn't he?"

Ryan gazed at the spot where Sly had last stood. "Damn straight. A thousand times over."

Bethany knew then that everything would be all right, that when the moment came, Ryan would stand shoulder to shoulder with Sly and defend him. That was all she needed to know.

Chapter Nineteen

L ater that morning while Ryan did chores, Bethany drove to town to feed and water Cleo. Before returning to the ranch, she stopped by her parents' house. It was time to tell them about the unexpected turn her life had taken. If she waited, her folks were bound to hear about her relationship with Ryan from another source, and she felt they deserved more consideration from her.

Harv Coulter wasn't exactly supportive when he learned that his paraplegic daughter planned to marry a man she'd known for less than two months.

"You're going to what?" he asked when Bethany told him.

Never more than in that moment had Bethany been able to see the resemblance between her father and Jake. Big, dark, and *glowering* pretty much described the pair of them.

She bent her head and fiddled with the gathers in her burgundy skirt, which had been far easier to put on this morning without her dressing sling. She could have asked Ryan to help her dress, of course, and he would have happily obliged her, but her determination to be self sufficient aside, she'd been afraid such a request might have ended with him putting off his chores again. Every time he touched her intimately, they seemed to gravitate toward the bedroom, which was delightful but not very productive when stock was waiting to be fed. As soon as Ryan got all her equipment moved to his place, she would start dressing the part of a rancher's wife, she promised herself, wearing those snug jeans and fringed western shirts that he liked so much.

When she glanced back up, she was smiling and had to jerk her thoughts back to the issue at hand. She fleetingly met her mother's gaze. Mary Coulter smiled and laid a hand on her husband's shoulder. "Harv, our girl has never been flighty. Hear her out, and remember she's always shown good judgment."

Harv settled a worried gaze on Bethany. "Ryan Kendrick is a scalawag. He flits from woman to woman, never making a commitment. What are you thinking, that you're going to tame him? Marry him, and you'll rue the day."

"He isn't like that, Daddy. Maybe he has flitted a little. He'd be the first person to admit that, actually. What else is a man to do when he's searching for the right person? Jake flits, and you don't call him a scalawag."

Harv tapped the salt shaker on the tabletop. Then he looked helplessly at his wife. "Mary, talk to her."

Bethany's mother looked discomfited. "And say what?"

"Talk sense to her. Tell her how insane it is to tie up with some"—Harv waved his hand—"*scalawag* like Ryan Kendrick!"

"But, Harv," Mary said softly, "Bethany's right. If failure to settle down is an indicator, even our Jake is a bit of a scalawag. And so were you. My parents had a fit when I started going out with you. Remember? Daddy said you were no good, that you'd break my heart. You never did."

Harv propped his elbows on the table and rested his head in his hands. "Holy hell, Mary. That was different, and you know it. I admit, I did a little skirt flipping, but I was looking for you under every single one of them."

Mary beamed and fixed a guileless gaze on her daughter. "Has your Ryan been flipping all the wrong skirts, honey?"

Harv groaned. Bethany swallowed back a horrified

laugh. *Finally,* her mother was actually admitting that conception occurred under skirts instead of in boots. She should record this day in the family Bible. "Yes, Mama," she managed to say solemnly. She glanced at her father, who was still holding his head. "I don't know how many skirts Daddy flipped, but Ryan had to flip a number of them before he finally found me."

"Holy hell," Harv whispered again.

"Now, now." Mary bent over her husband and whispered something that made his ears turn red. As she straightened, she patted Harv's hand, then sat down to search Bethany's gaze. "Does he love you, Bethie? When he looks at you, do you feel like he'd wade through a den of rattlesnakes for you?"

"Mama, I think he'd lie down and sleep with rattlesnakes for me."

Mary nodded and squeezed Bethany's hands. "He's the one, then. A woman just knows. Life is riddled with trials. If you know, without a doubt, that he'll stand fast and protect you from any kind of threat, he's the right man."

Bethany nodded. "He'd die for me, Mama. He's so wonderful."

Mary's eyes sparkled. "When are you going to bring him to meet us?"

"I've already met him," Harv said, forcing out the words between clenched teeth. "He's a sweet talkin', good lookin', spoiled little rich boy who's been playing fast and loose for so long he's forgotten the meaning of honor."

"That is *not* true," Bethany declared. "He is as honorable as any of my brothers!"

Harv leveled a finger at her nose. "Your brothers would never make promises to a girl they didn't intend to keep. The day I put your hand in Ryan Kendrick's, and he says, 'I do,' I'll eat my jock shorts."

*   *   *

After speaking to her parents, Bethany went by the store to talk to Jake. Her brother was swamped, trying to wait on customers while he filled out an inventory order. Nevertheless he smiled when he saw her.

"I was hoping you might spare me a few minutes to chat," Bethany said with a laugh. "I guess not."

Jake held up a finger for her to wait. He finished helping a customer, asked an employee to cover for him, and then walked with Bethany to the elevator. Once upstairs, they went to his office.

Jake dropped onto a castor chair and propped his boots on the edge of his desk. "It's been one of those mornings. You never phoned me back, twerp. I was a little worried. It sounded like that bull was inside the house."

Bethany smiled. "It was." She went on to explain about T-bone. "Ryan was pretty upset, but I think I've convinced him to see how things go."

Jake sighed and frowned. "Can't blame him for being worried. Bulls can be ornery."

"T-bone is an exception. He's big and clumsy, but he was so gentle with me. We'll see."

Jake glanced at the clock. "So what do you want to talk with me about?"

Bethany gazed at a snapshot of his horses that he had pinned to the wall. *Jake, the horse whisperer.* She knew he hoped to one day purchase a ranch, that it wasn't his plan to run a supply store for the rest of his life. If anyone would understand what she was about to say, Jake would. "I want to talk to you about two things."

"You seem upset."

"Not upset, exactly. I'm feeling a little guilty about a decision I've made. If this will put you in a bind, Jake, please don't hesitate to tell me. All right?"

He lowered his feet to the floor and shifted forward on the chair. "Ryan's asked you to quit the job."

"If you need me here to take up the slack, I won't leave

you in the lurch. It's just—well, Ryan's fixed it so I can really be a help on the ranch, and the opportunity is . . ." Her voice trailed away. She'd been about to say it was a dream come true, but that didn't seem fair. Jake had dreams of his own, but he was here, running the family business instead of pursuing them.

"The opportunity is too sweet to resist?" Jake finished for her. He sighed and spent a moment straightening some papers on his desk. "I can do some juggling and get by without you. If that's what you came to ask, consider it done."

"I don't want to be selfish and unfair to you. I'm a member of this family, too."

Jake smiled and glanced around the office. "Thank you for that. But the truth is, I'm helping myself as much as I'm helping Dad. When the doctor told him he had to start taking it easy, he was going to sell the store. It's a going concern, and there are always interested parties. But I asked him to hold off."

"You did? I thought you wanted to buy a ranch."

"I do." Jake grinned and tapped a pen on his desk pad. "And I will. But saving for a few more months will get me better set. I have a good down payment tucked away. Now I'm trying to gather up some working capital. Running the store is allowing me to do that. Dad takes out a monthly income. A certain percentage of the profits are automatically set aside to build the business. The rest is mine, just as if I owned the place. How much goes in my pocket depends solely on how hard I'm willing to work. Most months, I've done well."

Bethany stared at him. "So you asked me to quit my Portland job and move home, knowing you only meant to keep this place a few more months?"

He chuckled. "Before I ever made the decision to call you, Zeke decided to take over the store after I leave. You have a job here for as long as you want one." His smile grew tender. "Those first few months, you helped me hold this place together. Things have smoothed out now. I can get by without you."

"Oh, Jake, are you sure?"

"Go live your life, Bethie. Ryan's offering you the much sweeter deal. When the time comes, I won't hesitate to follow my dream. Why should you?"

"I just don't want to leave if you need me."

He tossed down the pen. "Well, I don't, so pack up and hit the road."

"I'm afraid you're saying that because you think it's what I want to hear."

A suspicious shine came into his eyes. "Eight years ago, I sat beside your bed, night after night. I'd get off work and go directly to the hospital. Remember that?"

She nodded.

"I always laughed and talked and pretended everything would be fine," he said thickly. "You needed me to be strong for you. But lots of times after you fell asleep, I sat there beside your bed and cried like a baby, begging God to give us a miracle. You were only eighteen, and your life had been destroyed."

Bethany lowered her gaze to her lap, her chest squeezing with an awful pain. *Jake.* She hadn't always been asleep when he had cried.

"God didn't see fit to make you walk again, and until now, I was afraid you might never get married and have a normal life. Now, bingo, along comes Ryan Kendrick. He seems to adore you. He's offering you a life I know you're going to love. How do you think I feel about that?"

"Glad?" she whispered.

He nodded. "So glad, Bethie. You've got this wonderful chance to be happy. Really, really happy. *Go.* Don't look back. There's nobody who deserves this more than you."

"Oh, Jake . . . How did I ever get so lucky? Of all the brothers in the world, you're the best."

"Let's not get any sappier than we have to. What was the second thing you wanted to ask me?"

Bethany hauled in a cleansing breath. "I was wondering if you'd mind talking to Daddy for me. He's not at all happy about me marrying—"

Jake burst out laughing. "This is where I play rotten brother. No way."

"But—"

"No." Jake pushed up from the chair. "Dad is Ryan's problem. If he's half the man I think he is, he'll go see our father and do his own talking."

"That's just it. I don't want him to know Daddy's frothing at the mouth. His family has accepted me with open arms."

"And why wouldn't they? Ryan's damn lucky to get you."

"In your opinion. On the flip side, aren't I just as lucky to get him?"

Jake laughed again. "Maybe so, but let Ryan convince Dad of it. My last word, end of subject. I'm not getting in the middle of it."

As she drove back to the Rocking K, Bethany tried not to let her father's reaction spoil her happiness. *Ryan*. She loved him so very much. Jake had just set her free to go dream chasing. She had every reason to be rejoicing.

Nevertheless, when she got to the ranch and parked the van, her heart felt heavy. Her dad was the best. He'd been there for her all her life, and it hurt that he wasn't standing behind her now.

"What's wrong?" Ryan asked when he saw her face. "Is Cleo all right?"

"Cleo's fine." Bethany gazed past him at the lake, wishing she didn't have to tell him this. But if she kept it under her hat, she'd be setting him up for a nasty surprise when he saw her father. "Oh, Ryan. I went by to see my parents."

He hunkered down in front of her. "Uh-oh. I hope you didn't take it upon yourself to tell them I've asked you to marry me."

"Take it upon myself? They're my parents. Of course I told them."

Ryan shoved his hat back. "Sweetheart, if your dad's anything at all like mine, he's pretty old-fashioned."

"A little. So what?"

"Old-fashioned fathers have set ideas about how things like this should be done. I'm supposed to go see your dad and ask him for your hand. That gives him an opportunity to grill me for a while and make me squirm. If I say the right things, he feels good about the situation. If I don't, he tells me to take a hike."

Bethany gulped. "What happens if he tells you to take a hike?"

Ryan winked at her. "He won't. I'm a slick talker."

"That's one of the things he doesn't like about you."

He threw back his head and barked with laughter. When his mirth subsided, he assured her, "I can handle him, honey. Don't worry. All right? He'll think I'm the greatest thing since the invention of popcorn."

After applying for their marriage license that afternoon, Ryan dropped Bethany off at her house. While she packed some clothes, he drove over to see her father. After a two-minute conversation, Ryan stood on the Coulters' front porch, wondering how in the hell things had gone so wrong.

The man's shouts were still ringing in Ryan's ears as he started toward his truck. *A no-account scalawag?* Nobody said "no-account scalawag" these days. *Damn.* The guy was living in the Dark Ages.

Once in his truck, Ryan envisioned the dejected expression on Bethany's face when he told her how badly this had gone. He slammed his fist against the steering wheel and glared through the windshield at her parents' house, thinking he could buy a thousand just like it and still make change. Who the hell did that old codger think he was?

Ryan nearly started the truck and drove away. But, no, damn it. Instead he climbed back out, slammed the door, and stomped along the walkway to the porch. Up the flipping steps he went, boiling mad. The man was Bethany's father, and for that reason, Ryan would show him respect. But he wasn't about to crawl away with his tail tucked between his legs.

He rapped his knuckles on the door, swearing under his breath. Expecting Bethany's mother to answer as she had before, he strove to school his expression. Then the door flew open, and he found himself standing nose to nose with the old man. Blue eyes like Bethany's shot sparks at him.

"Mr. Coulter, I'd appreciate it if you'd at least hear me out," Ryan began.

"You've got nothing to say that I'm interested in hearing. If my daughter marries you, it'll be against my wishes. That's my last word."

Ryan lost his temper. "No 'if' to it. I *will* marry your daughter. Nothing you can say or do is going to stop me. We're both consenting adults, and it's our decision to make. I'm here only as a courtesy, Mr. Coulter, more for her sake than yours. Your approval is very important to her."

"In one breath you ask for my blessing, and in the next, you inform me you don't really give a rat's ass if you get it. You call that a courtesy?" Harv's face flushed an angry red. "Get off my porch."

"You can make me leave, sir, but what good will that do?

First thing you know, I'll be back, asking for her hand again."

"And I'll be saying no, *again*. You're not good enough for her."

"There's not a man on earth good enough for her."

"Amen."

"That established, will you at least give me the benefit of the doubt and trust that I'll do my damnedest to be *half* the man she deserves?"

"Harrumph."

Ryan sighed. "Look, Mr. Coulter, I understand how you feel."

"No, damn it, you don't understand how I feel. And pray God you never do. My daughter isn't like other young women. I don't want to see her go through any more heartache, and you've got heartache written all over you."

Ryan grabbed for patience. "I understand Bethany's got some very special problems and that it's going to take a special man with a lot of staying power to make her happy. I know you're not sure if I've got what it takes. I'm telling you I do, and I give you my word I'll never hurt her."

"I appreciate that. But I've got no way of knowing if your word is good. I know your father, and he's a fine man. But that's no indication you are."

"He raised me, didn't he? It's true I've never stayed in a relationship. I admit that. But it's only because I never found the right woman until now."

"Look, son. It's nothing personal. All right? Our Bethany—if she were like other women, I might be a whole lot more relaxed about this. But she isn't. How are you going to feel a year down the road when the shine has worn off and you're stuck with a wife in a wheelchair? What'll happen to my little girl then?"

"So instead of taking a chance on me, you'll break her

heart now? That's what you're doing, you know, breaking her heart."

Harv blinked. "Say what?"

"It's true. She wants you to be glad for her, and knowing you aren't is ruining what should be the happiest time of her life." Ryan met the older man's gaze. "I don't blame you for loving her and being afraid for her. But if she's going to have a normal life, you have to turn loose and let her live it. You can't shield her from everything, not without being the man who hurts her the most."

"I'd never do anything to hurt that girl."

"Then, give us your blessing," Ryan said evenly.

Bethany's mother appeared in the doorway beside her husband. She smiled at Ryan. "Consider it given. Tell Bethany her daddy is as happy as a clam, and that her wedding day will be the proudest day of his life."

"Mary," Harv said warningly.

"Go," Mary urged Ryan. "Give her a hug from me." She linked arms with her husband. "I'll take care of the situation here."

"Mary!" Harv said again.

Ryan figured Mary Coulter could handle her husband with no help from him, so he took her advice and headed for his truck. Halfway there, Harv bellowed, "Just understand one thing, Kendrick! The day I find out you've made my little girl cry will be the sorriest day of your life!"

Ryan was laughing when he started the Dodge. He'd never been threatened so much in his life since the day he'd met Bethany. First Jake, now her father. What the hell. He only had four more brothers to go. He shook his head. These folks were so cantankerous, they made the Kendricks seem mild tempered.

Standing in Bethany's bedroom, Ryan peeked in a sack she had just stuffed full of clothing. He plucked out a flannel nightgown. Next he found a Snoopy nightshirt. As soon as possible, he had to take her shopping for lingerie, he decided. Lacy see-through stuff was more to his taste.

She turned from the dresser drawer and caught him frowning. "What's wrong?" she asked with an impish smile. "Don't you like my Snoopy shirt?"

"I'm crazy about Snoopy." He stuffed the shirt back in the sack. "I was thinking about something else."

"You were scowling." A worried look came over her face. "Was there a problem with Daddy you didn't tell me about?"

"He got a little prickly. Nothing I couldn't handle. We have his blessing. That's all that matters. Right?"

"Right." She sighed and glanced around the room. "I have enough stuff to do me. Except for my bathroom sling. Would you mind taking it to your truck?"

"You won't be needing it out there."

"How on earth will I take a bath?"

He grinned and waggled his eyebrows at her. "One guess."

Her cheeks turned a pretty pink. "It's sweet of you to offer, but I'd feel far more comfortable with my sling."

"What fun would that be?" He dipped his voice low and whispery. "When I'm done lathering you up, you'll be so clean, you'll squeak."

Her gaze flitted away from his. "As fun as that might be, I like to do things for myself, and I don't want to depend on you for my baths."

"I ordered you a better one."

Her gaze came chasing back to his. "*Ryan*. What all have you bought me that I don't know about yet?"

"Not all that much."

"What, exactly?"

"You want to be here all night?"

"I'm starting to feel really bad."

"Why?"

"Because you've spent so much money on me. I

mean—on the one hand, I know we're going to get married, and I shouldn't feel that way. But on the other, I feel indebted."

"Works for me."

"What does?"

He winked at her. "You feeling indebted. I can think of some fantastic ways for you to work off the debt."

"As your stable manager?"

"Nope. The corporation will pay you a wage for that." He glanced at her bed. "I'm thinking of something more interesting."

She giggled when he started toward her. "Forget it."

"Why?"

"Someone might come. My brothers all have keys."

That stopped him in his tracks. He hooked his thumbs over his belt and slowly skimmed his gaze over her. "We're not even married yet, and already I have in-law-itis. But that's okay. This is Thursday. I have plans for you later."

"What's Thursday got to do with anything?"

A gleam warmed his eyes. "It's your swim night. I have an indoor, heated pool off the back of the house. I'll give you some swimming lessons."

"I already know how to swim. I creamed you doing laps."

"You've never seen my version of the 'breaststroke'."

She giggled again.

"You'll also find ceiling watching a lot more entertaining in there. It's all skylights. When I set you on the side of the pool after I teach you the breast stroke, you'll be able to gaze at the stars while I—"

Cleo began rubbing against his pant leg just then. Ryan broke off to glance down. When he saw who had interrupted him, he bent to scoop her up in one hand. "Damn cat. I was on a roll."

"She's been lonesome. I've never left her alone this much."

"Let's take the pest home with us, then," he suggested.

"I sort of had the impression you weren't very fond of cats."

"I'm not. I hate cats. Did you know she'll eat you if you die?"

"No, sir! Who told you such an awful thing?"

Cleo narrowed her green eyes at him. Ryan squinted back at her. "I know it for a fact. When I was a kid, my grandmother's neighbor lady died, and her cats had almost polished her off before someone found her."

"Maybe the poor things got hungry because there was no one to feed them."

"She fed them." The thought gave him the shudders. "You ever wondered what she's thinking when she squints at you like that? I think she's thinking about having me for lunch with a little A-1 on the side."

"She is not. She's probably just afraid you're going to hurt her. She likes gourmet cat food. No offense, but you probably wouldn't appeal to her."

"You would." He winked at her. "You definitely appeal to my taste buds."

Her cheeks went pink again. "Is that all you think about?"

"Mostly. They say the normal male thinks about it every four minutes."

"You're kidding. You don't, do you?"

"Nah. I think I'm a little undersexed. I go as long as ten minutes sometimes without ever thinking about it." He winked at her again. "You about ready? I can carry greeneyes and one sack if you can get the other one."

"Actually, Ryan, I was thinking I might give Cleo to my mom. Cat's are sensitive. She needs a home where she'll be loved and understood."

Ryan stared into the cat's slightly crossed eyes, thinking the poor thing looked a little retarded. "We understand each other, honey." Cleo understood he didn't like her, and he understood she didn't like him. The only reason she rubbed against his leg was to shed on his pants. "And I'll learn to love her, I promise." With his luck, the damn critter would live until she was twenty. "I pretty much like all animals." Except cats.

"I don't know. She's never been around a dog. I'm afraid she won't like Tripper."

Ryan tucked the damned cat under his arm. "She and Tripper will get along fine. He's good with the barn cats over at Rafe's place."

A half hour later, after a harrowing ride from town with Cleo hanging upside down from the truck ceiling for much of the trip, Ryan finally got the squirming, scratching cat into his house. When he turned her loose in the great room, Tripper came waddling over to make friends. Accustomed to barn cats, who weren't afraid of dogs, the lab never saw the calico's claws coming. He took a swat squarely on the end of his nose, yipped and howled, then ran for the bedroom. Cleo fled in the other direction, leaped at the vertical blinds, and scaled them to gain a perch atop the wood valance, where she arched her back, raised all her bristles, and hissed, looking for all the world like a Halloween decoration.

"Well," Ryan said, "we're off to a great start."

Bethany whirred down the hall toward the master bedroom. "Tripper? Come here, sweetie. Let me look at your nose." From the bedroom, she yelled, "Ryan, he's not in here."

Unless the dog had broken out a window, he had to be somewhere in there. Ryan joined Bethany and executed a search. He finally found the lab hiding in the bathtub.

"If you aren't the sorriest excuse for a dog I ever saw," Ryan said. "I can't believe you, Tripper. You outweigh that kitty by a hundred pounds."

"Oh, Ryan, his nose is bleeding." Bethany parked sideways to the tub and leaned over to examine the dog's nose. "Poor baby. She really got you good."

Ryan checked the injury. "He'll live. It just smarts a little."

Bethany fixed him with a worried look. "I hope this is no indication of how our life is going to go."

"Don't even *think* that way. Our life is going to be absolutely perfect, sweetheart. Cleo will settle in, and before we know it, she and Tripper will be snuggling together on the sofa."

"Oh, do you think so? She's so easily excited. I worry she'll never like it here. Before I lived in an apartment, and she never went outside. In town, I kept her indoors, too. Now here she is on a horse and cattle ranch."

"She'll be fine. Cats are very adaptable."

A few minutes later, when Ryan tried to pluck Cleo off the valance, the cat yowled, leaped, and dug all four sets of claws into the front of his shirt. "Son of a"—Ryan caught himself just in time, and finished with—"biscuit maker!"

The cat catapulted off of him, hit the floor at a run, and sent stuff flying as she scaled the front of the entertainment center. Once on top of it, she glared at Ryan with gleaming green eyes and hissed.

"I don't think she's adapting very well," Bethany observed.

Ryan smiled. "Sweetheart, she'll be fine. She may sense that you're upset. Ever think of that? If you relax and ignore her, maybe she'll relax, too."

He removed his hat and sent it sailing toward the coat tree. The Stetson missed the hook and fell crown first on the floor. That was not a good omen.

"Oh, *no*!" Bethany cried.

Ryan spun around. "What?"

He followed her horrified gaze to the top of the entertainment center, where Cleo was scratching at the oak as if to cover something up. The hair on his nape prickled. "What the hell is she doing?"

"I think she already did it."

Ryan forgot all about having to donate ten dollars to the college fund and said, "Son of a-aaa-a *bitch!*"

Chapter Twenty

T he wedding date was set for Saturday, weekend after next, and the intervening eight days were the most glorious of Bethany's life. *Ryan*. He insisted that she remain with him on the Rocking K, and from the moment she opened her eyes in the morning until he kissed them closed for the last time each night, she had fun. The most wondrous aspect of that, in her opinion, was that even the silly, unimportant things turned out to be unexpectedly wonderful.

The crazy mix of Ryan's household pets, for example. Who would have thought that a very spoiled seventeen-pound feline and an equally spoiled, eight hundred–pound bull would become bosom buddies? Certainly not Bethany. But the following morning was the beginning of what promised to be a lifelong friendship between the two animals.

After having coffee with Bethany, Ryan grabbed his Stetson to head over to the stable to feed the stock. When he opened the door to step out, he paused to flash her a teasing grin. "On the Rocking K, even my wife has to earn her keep, you know. If you want to eat regular, no lady of leisure stuff for you. You'd best show up over there in a couple of minutes, ready to make yourself useful."

Bethany was about to reply when Cleo darted between Ryan's feet to escape outdoors. "Oh, *no*!" she cried.

Ryan dashed out after the cat, Tripper barking excitedly at his boot heels. Bethany hurried out onto the porch. *Cleo*.

The poor kitty had seldom been outdoors, and then it had always been in town. She would be terrified out here. Bethany envisioned her small pet dashing off into the woods and getting lost. Cleo was just the right size to become some large, hungry carnivore's lunch.

"Here, cat!" Ryan called in a big, male voice.

Bethany anxiously scanned the yard, looking for a splotch of mottled fur. She didn't see poor Cleo anywhere. "Don't call her like *that*. You'll frighten her."

Ryan shot her a disgruntled look. "How should I call her then?"

In a shrill voice, Bethany called, "Here, Cleo! Here, kitty-kitty!"

Ryan swore under his breath, stomped onto the cement pad, and began calling Cleo in an off-key alto. As much as Bethany appreciated his attempt to achieve the right tone, she thought he sounded like a 220-pound cat killer on the prowl. T-bone came to the summons, bawling stupidly with every step. Bethany felt fairly sure that Cleo would never show herself now.

She wasn't counting on Tripper to join in the search. The plump golden lab clearly had a score to settle, and now Cleo was on *his* turf. He put his nose to the ground, zigzagged across the yard to a stack of firewood, and began wagging his tail excitedly.

"Ah-hah! She's in the woodpile!" Ryan stomped over. "Here, kitty!" he rumbled as he began moving pieces of wood. With every other breath, he muttered, "Damn cat."

Bethany zoomed down the ramp and hurried over to rescue her poor kitty before Ryan unearthed her. Unfortunately she didn't get there in time. Ryan moved a piece of wood, and there huddled poor Cleo. The frightened feline hissed and yowled, then eluded Ryan's reaching hands by diving between his legs. Bad mistake. She ran straight into Tripper, who was barking excitedly.

When threatened, most cats head for the highest perch

available, and Cleo was no exception. It just so happened that, except for Ryan, T-bone was the tallest thing in the immediate vicinity. The cat leaped on the bull's back. Startled to have an uninvited and very prickly creature clinging to his shoulders, T-bone did what any not-very-bright bull would do.

He ran.

Determined to save Bethany's stupid cat, Ryan pursued the unlikely duo, but every time he got close enough to grab Cleo, the cat became frightened and dug in with her claws, which made T-bone run again.

After thirty minutes of fruitless chase, Ryan returned to Bethany, slapping his Stetson against his leg with every step. "I can't get her, honey."

Bethany gazed down toward the lake, where T-bone stood forlornly on the shore with Cleo clinging to his back. The pair looked so silly that Bethany burst out laughing. "I think she's going to stay there. T-bone is the perfect kitty scooter!"

Ryan began chuckling as well. "He's all terrain, too, and goes at a fast clip in high gear." He had worked up a sweat, chasing the bull. He touched a shirtsleeve to his brow. "I'm sorry I couldn't catch her, honey. Now you'll worry all day."

Bethany sighed. "Well, she's safe enough on T-bone's back. Not that she'll stay up there for long."

Famous last words. Come noon, the cat was still riding the bull's broad back while he grazed. Bethany studied the pair, smiling and shaking her head. She wasn't close enough to tell for sure, but it looked as if Cleo was having a nap. Since T-bone had apparently accepted the cat's presence, there was nothing to do but wait for Cleo to get down and come back on her own.

As if he guessed Bethany's thoughts, Ryan said, "She'll get hungry. When she does, she'll come to the house."

No such luck. That night, Bethany had Ryan set out food for Cleo on the woodpile. At some point during the night, the cat must have dismounted the bull in order to eat, for the food was gone in the morning. But when Bethany went out to find her kitty, Cleo was nowhere around.

"She's still riding T-bone," Ryan informed her a few minutes later when she entered the stable. "Sly says the bull came in for breakfast a bit ago, and Cleo was still curled up on his back, pretty as you please. She gave herself a bath while T-bone ate his grain."

Bethany shook her head. "Maybe T-bone's her answer to ranch life. She feels safe on him. Everything here must seem really scary to her. He's big and solid." She smiled up at Ryan. "Sort of like you. I can associate."

Ryan's eyes started to twinkle—which Bethany was quickly coming to realize meant trouble. "Oh, yeah?" He glanced around to make sure they were alone, then leaned down to kiss her. A long, heated kiss that made her head swim. "I want you," he whispered.

Bethany could associate with that as well, which struck her as slightly amazing. After the poolside exploit last night, two more sessions in bed, and a wake-up round that morning, both of them should have been completely sated. "Be good," she whispered. "Sly's here somewhere. We'll get caught."

Ryan flicked the white fringe on the blue western shirt she'd purchased especially for him. "You don't really think I can ignore the way that fringe shifts back and forth over your nipples, do you?" He grazed an already hardened tip and chuckled. "No way, lady."

Since she'd worn the shirt expressly for him, Bethany could only smile smugly, pleased that her efforts had been noticed. Nevertheless, she was startled when Ryan suddenly scooped her from her chair. She shrieked and grabbed hold of his neck. "Not in the *stable*."

"I'll find a private place."

He carried her to the tack room, locked the door, and laid her out on a hay bale. This morning, she wore the shirt and snug blue jeans. He attacked the buttons of her top, saying, "This is where I eat my lunch most days. Tomorrow can you come to work wearing plastic wrap?"

She giggled and then gasped with pleasure when he bent his head to nip gently at her nipple through the lace of her bra. "Ryan, I'm afraid I'll forget where we are and make noise. Sly may hear me."

He grabbed for a length of leather hanging from a nail above them. Still nibbling at her flesh and sending shocks of delight coursing through her, he whispered, "Bite down on that."

She giggled again, and then she moaned, every thought in her head slipping away as he unhooked her bra and touched his hot, wonderful mouth to her bare breast. When he shifted to give her other breast the attention it craved, the cool morning air washed over her moist nipple, making it turn rock hard, which seemed to inflame him when he took it in his mouth again. June sunlight poured in the tack room window to play over them. Ryan mumbled something about barely ripe strawberries, making her whimper mindlessly as he unfastened her jeans. "I'm starving for you. I promise this won't take long."

It took about forty minutes, and she loved every second.

Ryan. She was quickly coming to realize that he was going to be an impulsive, unpredictable, and insatiable lover, the kind of man who could be working intently one moment and then be totally focused on making love to her the next, the only uncertainty being where he might grab her.

After the tack room episode, Bethany didn't really expect to make love again until that night, if then. Ryan had other ideas. Later that morning in the stable office while he was showing her how he kept the books, the phone rang, and Bethany automatically answered because she was sitting closer to it. It was Jake, calling during his mid-morning break to check on her.

Bethany no sooner greeted her brother than Ryan grinned wickedly and started unfastening her blouse. She pushed at his shoulder. When he moved in to kiss her collarbone, she braced the heel of her hand on his forehead, trying to hold him at bay. It was like trying to keep water from rushing downhill.

"This shirt drives me wild," he whispered. "Why should I let this fringe have all the fun?" He drew the cloth apart, unfastened the front clasp of her bra, cupped her breasts in his big hands, and proceeded to drive her half crazy with his fabulous mouth while she tried to carry on an intelligent conversation with her brother.

When Ryan started tugging at her nipples with his teeth, Bethany had to ask Jake to repeat a question. She glanced worriedly toward the door. Ryan chuckled and whispered. "I always plan ahead. It's locked."

That made her feel marginally better—until he pushed her breasts together so he could tease both throbbing nipples at once. The gentle squeeze made blood rush to the tips. Ryan leaned back to observe the swelling process with some interest, his gunmetal blue eyes glinting with mischief. In that moment Bethany wondered how his mother had survived his childhood.

Over the weekend Ryan's parents came to visit. Ann was limping from the bruise on her hip. "The doctor says it'll be a while healing, that I'm lucky I didn't break it. I'm getting too old for bouncing off the corners of desks."

Keefe, who was sporting barked knuckles on one big hand, put an arm around his wife's narrow shoulders and said, "The little son of a bitch will think twice before he pushes a lady again." He winked at Bethany. "He dropped the charges against me yesterday. Got to thinking how it'd look on the front page of the paper and decided his behavior toward my wife had been inexcusable."

"I wonder who put that thought in his head," Ryan

mused. "You didn't threaten to call the newspaper, did you, Dad?"

Ann smiled. "Your father is far too direct a man to be that conniving. *I* threatened to call the newspaper." She glanced adoringly at her husband and held out a hand. "My hero. That'll be ten dollars, please, you ornery old curmudgeon."

Keefe muttered and scowled, but he plucked a ten from his pocket and handed it over. Ann slipped it in her shirt and smiled at Bethany. "Not to worry. I won't let a little bruise keep me from being at the wedding."

This wasn't the first time Bethany had seen the men on the Rocking K getting ten-dollar bills out of their clips or wallets. She looked bewilderedly at Ryan, who quickly explained about the no-cussing rule on the ranch. Bethany thought it was a marvelous idea. By the time she and Ryan were able to adopt, the women would have all the men trained.

On Monday her saddle arrived. Ryan no sooner removed it from the crate than he started putting it on Wink. Bethany's stomach got nervous jitters when she realized he meant for her to go riding straightaway. When he turned and caught her expression, he knelt beside her chair, searched her gaze for a long moment, and then hooked a finger under her chin to lift her face.

"Sweetheart, you don't have to get on her. If all you want is to love Wink and be with her every day, that's fine by me."

Bethany stared at the horse for a long, heart-pounding moment. Memories flashed in her mind of her riding accident, and sweat filmed her face. It had happened so quickly in reality, yet in her mind the events leading up to that split second played out in slow motion. She yearned to ride Wink again. The wanting was so intense, her bones ached. But she was also terrified. No one who'd never experienced what she had could possibly understand how the fear grabbed her by the throat.

"I—um . . ." She squeezed her eyes closed. "Oh, Ryan, I want to so *much*. But I'm scared. So scared."

He caught her face between his hands. "I can get you to the lake for the wedding on a four-wheeler, honey. Don't even think about this as a have-to thing. All right?"

The wedding. Oh, God. Everyone planned to ride horses in to the lake to see them be married. A cold feeling washed over her. She felt all shivery when she met Ryan's gaze.

He swore under his breath and started raining kisses all over her face. "I'm sorry. Jesus, sweet Jesus. I need to be horsewhipped for being such a blockhead. Forgive me."

Bethany curled her hands over her wrists. "I *want* to ride again, Ryan."

He stared hard into her eyes.

"I want to ride again," she repeated. "I just have to gather the courage."

Fifteen minutes later Bethany was strapped onto her horse. She also sweated so badly that it dripped off of her, and she felt nauseous. Terror and bagels didn't mix.

Ryan held the reins. "You don't have to do this. Let's get you down."

"*No.*" Bethany realized she was clinging to the saddle horn like a child. *Oh, God.* The ground looked a hundred miles away. She imagined Wink stumbling and coming down on top of her. She gulped convulsively. "I need to do this. Even if I never go riding outside a corral, I need to do this, Ryan."

He just stood there, holding her horse and staring up at her. "Bethany, honey, please. This is all my fault. Let's get you down."

"No!" She didn't mean to scream at him, but she did. *Screamed.* As if he were her enemy. "Would you stop standing there and do something to *help* me?"

He stroked Wink's neck, trying to calm the mare because her rider was doing just the opposite. In some part of her brain, Bethany knew she needed to get hold of herself. "I need you to help me do this," she repeated shakily.

"What do you need, Bethany? Tell me, and I'll do it."

"*Talk* to me. Make me so I'm not nervous."

The next thing Bethany knew, he was behind her on the horse. The instant his arm came around her, she could breathe again. "I'm right here, sweetheart. Right here with you."

She leaned against his chest and twisted to press her face against his neck. *Ryan*. She felt safe when he was holding her. Absolutely safe. Rationally, she knew he could do nothing to protect her if the horse came tumbling down on top of them. But that didn't matter. Her fear wasn't rational.

She started blabbering. About the accident. How it had happened. How she'd leaned forward and shifted her weight as Wink went into the turn. How they'd been beating their best time, racing with the wind. Then the sudden lurch. The dizzying sensation of flying through the air. *Pain*. A flash of pain so excruciating her brain exploded and went black.

"When I woke up, I couldn't feel my toes. Isn't it crazy that I remember that over everything?" She tipped her chin back as far as it would go and stared at the blue sky above them. "It wasn't my legs I was worried about. I couldn't feel my toes. I remember staring at the sheet and trying to wiggle them. Trying as hard as I could. And—realizing. *Realizing*. My mom and dad were there. Jake grabbed my arms and pinned them to the bed. I remember looking into his eyes and screaming. They didn't even have to tell me. I knew when I couldn't wiggle my toes."

Ryan let Wink's reins fall and wrapped both arms around her. "Forgive me, Bethany. Please, forgive me. You never have to get on a horse again. You can enjoy Wink just as much without riding her."

"That's just it," she whispered against his neck. "I need to ride. I *need* to, Ryan, like I need air to breathe. Don't let me get off. I'll never have the courage to get back on. Keep me on her until this stops."

"Oh, Jesus," he whispered.

"Please," she begged him. "Don't let it end like this. Don't take me down. Just make it better. Please?"

Ryan splayed a hand over her midriff and retrieved the reins. "Sly!" he yelled.

"Yo?" The ranch foreman came into the exercise area. "Whatcha need?"

"Throw open the gate," Ryan ordered.

Bethany watched Sly unlatch the gate and pull it open. Ryan drew Wink around and lunged her out of the corral. Bethany's heart flew into her throat. The ground looked as if it might leap up and smack her in the face. Ryan veered the horse toward the lake. Even though he reined the mare to a walk, the panic she felt was indescribable. She was going to die. Her heart was going to stop. Only it kept beating, and Wink kept going.

After a bit Ryan slowed the mare's pace even more. The breeze that blew in off the lake to kiss Bethany's face was laden with rich, wonderful scents—spring grass and budding wildflowers, pine and fir, and a crispness to the air that came in off the mountains. She relaxed against his hard chest, letting her body undulate with the horse and him.

"Oh, Ryan . . ."

He pressed his face against her hair. "You know, honey, the way I see it, there's only two ways to live life. One way is to protect yourself from all danger as best you can, existing in a safe little bubble. Even then, chances are you could end up getting run over by a bus or contracting some terrible disease."

"What's the other option?" she asked with a shaky laugh.

"You can grab hold of life with both hands, enjoy every blessed minute of it, and take a chance that you may get hurt or killed while you're doing something you love."

She laughed again, the sound still quivery. "No halfway

measures, like having a little bit of fun while you play it safe?"

He nibbled her neck. "That'd be like making love and never having an orgasm. Big-time frustrating."

"Been there, done that. I don't want to live my life that way."

"Then, grab hold with both hands," he whispered, and the next thing she knew, she was alone on the horse. He reached up to give her the reins. His beautiful eyes held hers for a long moment. "Live happy, darlin'. You're strapped on, so you can't fall. The only way you can get hurt is if Wink stumbles, and the ground squirrels don't dig burrows along the lakeshore. They stay in the fields where food is plentiful. She seems like a surefooted little lady to me."

Bethany nodded. "She's only fallen with me once, and that wasn't her fault." Even so, once was all it had taken. She closed her eyes and hauled in a bracing breath.

"I'm walking back," he told her. "This being your first time out, it would probably be best if you came up and rode near the stable, where I can keep an eye on you."

Bethany stared straight ahead, so terrified she was trembling. "I, um . . . it's nice, even ground for as far as I can see. Wink responds to voice commands. I'm sure I'll be fine, and—" She broke off and swallowed to steady her voice. "I need to do this, Ryan. First time out, I need to do it by myself for a bit."

She heard him sigh. She didn't dare look at him for fear she'd lose her nerve. "All right," he said. "Go, then. It's flat ground all the way around the lake. I don't recommend that you go too far the first day, but I'll leave that up to you."

Bethany nodded, resisting the urge to ask him to saddle his horse and go with her. It was stupid to feel afraid. The likelihood that Wink might stumble was minuscule. "I, um . . . I won't go too far."

"When you're done, I'll be in the stable. Just ride in and holler. I'll help you off."

Bethany nodded, still staring straight ahead. "If I—um—don't come back in thirty minutes, come find me. Okay?"

"Honey, that goes without saying."

She felt better, knowing he'd come after her if she didn't return in a specified period of time. Heart in throat, she urged Wink forward.

Ryan waited at the stable in a sweat, worrying every second Bethany was gone. When twenty minutes had passed, he saddled up his sorrel gelding and went to find her. She was clear at the opposite end of the lake near his parents' place when he caught up with her. At the sound of his approach, she twisted at the waist and waved, her face beaming, her eyes glowing.

"Oh, Ryan, thank you . . . thank you. This is so wonderful. So *freeing*. I can go places that are impossible in my wheelchair. You've opened up a whole new world for me."

He slowed his horse to a walk beside hers. His heart hurt to see her so happy. "Pretty special day?"

"Oh, *yes*. I don't feel so afraid now. Not entirely at ease yet. But not terrified, either."

"That's good. How's Wink doing?"

"Fabulously. I used to run her a lot, and she loved it. But today she seems content to walk." She leaned forward to stroke the horse's neck. "Maybe we're both just getting old. I think she's enjoying the slow pace."

"Nothing wrong with a slow pace. You can enjoy the scenery."

"That's true. It's so beautiful here, Ryan. You have no idea how very lucky you are to have all this in your backyard. The lake, the forests, and that incredible view of the mountains looming against the sky. It's *heaven*."

"It's your backyard now, too, you know."

She lifted her face to the gentle sunlight. "It *is*, isn't it."

"We're getting married in five days," he reminded her.

"Only five days." She smiled at him. "You getting cold feet yet?"

"Nope. Are you?"

She shook her head. "I've never felt so sure about anything."

He hated to be a wet blanket, but he was worried about her riding for too long. "It'd be best not to overdo the first day. You haven't been on a horse in eight years, and you can't feel what it's doing to your legs."

"Just a while longer. It's so wonderful, I don't want it to end."

Ryan considered their location. "You want to ride all the way around? We've gone so far, I don't think it'll be all that much closer if we double back."

"I'd love it!"

It took half an hour to circle back to Ryan's place. Shortly after their return to the stable, Bethany's legs started to cramp. Ryan carried her to the house. When he jerked off her shoes and jeans, he saw that her feet were bent nearly double in muscle spasms and that the tendons were knotted in her calves and thighs. She lay forward at the waist with her teeth clenched.

As Ryan tried to straighten her legs, she couldn't stifle a scream. He rushed to the phone to call Dr. Kirsch, the Kendrick family physician. The kindly old doctor drove out to the Rocking K. After examining Bethany, he gave her an injection to help relax her muscles.

When the shot started to take effect, Kirsch sat on the side of the bed, holding her hand. "From now on, take it one step at a time, young lady. Tomorrow, no riding. The following day, you can ride for ten minutes. If that goes well, you can add a few minutes to your riding time each day. You have to build up to this slowly, and chances are, even when you've been back in the saddle for a while, you'll still need to take frequent breaks when you go for long jaunts."

"But we're supposed to get married at a mountain lake on Saturday. Ryan planned for us to ride in."

The doctor fixed a questioning gaze on Ryan. "How far is the lake, Rye?"

"About three hours by horseback."

The doctor shook his head. "She won't be ready. Postpone for at least another week, and even then, you'll have to break up the trip, going half the distance one day and half the next."

"We can do that," Ryan said. "Bethany and I can head up on Thursday, go halfway, and camp for the night. It'll be fun."

She angled an arm over her eyes. "I'm sorry, Ryan. I was so excited about being on Wink again, I never even thought about getting leg cramps. I should have had better sense."

The doctor patted her hand. "It's easy to overdo. I don't ride all winter, and the first time I go riding in the spring, I hobble around for days afterward. Every single time, I swear I'll never be so stupid again, but I always am."

"You ride?"

Kirsch chuckled and winked at Ryan. "Why else do you think this bunch out here likes me so well? Keefe doesn't really trust a man unless he smells like a horse every once in a while." He turned back to Ryan. "When you ride in to the lake, take along a pint of distilled white vinegar. If she gets cramps, have her drink two shots, straight. It'll fix her right up."

"Yuck." Bethany shuddered at the thought.

"Nasty tasting and a little acidic on the tummy, but it works in a pinch."

Kirsch went on to carefully question Bethany about her accident and the resultant paralysis. When she'd answered his questions, he said, "Well, young lady, I'll look forward to seeing you again soon. I've delivered all the Kendrick babies. If Ryan has a say, I'll probably be delivering yours as well."

Bethany's face grew pale. She flicked a pained glance at Ryan. "It's very unlikely I'll be able to carry a child to term,

Dr. Kirsch. Ryan and I want to try, of course, and we'll hope for the best. But my chances aren't good."

The doctor looked surprised to hear that. Very surprised. "I see," he said. "And why is that? Did you sustain internal injuries I'm unaware of?"

"I, um . . . no. I was badly bruised, of course, but there was no permanent damage. When I had my last checkup, the gynecologist said I was fine."

"Ah. So who said you might not be able to carry a baby to term?"

"The spinal specialist who did my surgeries. He felt my risk of urinary tract and kidney infections would be extremely high, which can lead to miscarriage or preterm labor. There's also a very dangerous condition—I can't remember the name—that he said I might get."

Dr. Kirch mulled that over. Ryan wondered why he was frowning so. "Have you had a history of urinary tract infections?"

Bethany shook her head.

"I see." Kirsch rubbed his chin. "The condition the doctor warned you about was probably autonomic dysreflexia."

"That might've been it," she said. "It's been a long time, but I remember it was a name like that. It sounded really awful when he described it to me."

"It *is* pretty awful," he agreed. "It can cause serious complications at any time during pregnancy or come on during labor. However, it commonly occurs in women with an injury at or above the seventh thoracic vertebra."

"Mine's at L2. But he said there was a chance I might get it."

"What's this condition do to you?" Ryan asked.

"There can be a sharp rise in blood pressure, a severe escalation or drop in heart rate, and there's a risk of convulsions and enlargement of the heart. All in all, it's nothing to mess around with," Dr. Kirsch said solemnly. "There are ways to control it, but sometimes they fail."

"*Sweet Jesus,*" Ryan whispered. "Something like that could kill her." He searched Bethany's face. "It's just not worth it, honey. Not with the risk of another blood clot on top of it. I'd rather we simply never try."

"What's this about a blood clot?"

Ryan quickly recounted to the doctor what Jake had told him.

"There's nothing to say I'll get the dysreflexia stuff," Bethany argued. "And I can be really careful while I'm pregnant not to get a clot. I can stay in bed most of the time with my legs up." She fixed Ryan with an accusing look. "Is that why you've been using protection every time, because of what Jake told you?"

Ryan sighed. "I don't want to take any chances, Bethany. A blood clot might kill you. Jake feels it's unwise for you to get pregnant, and so do I."

She gave him a look that promised she would have a great deal to say about that decision once they were alone.

Ryan glanced at the doctor, then back at her. "We'll settle this later. All right?"

"Just remember what you said about living in a bubble or grabbing hold of life with both hands. That's how I feel about this—that trying is worth the risk."

Cold sweat popped out on Ryan's face. He stared down at her, thinking how dearly he loved her and how devastated he'd be if anything happened to her. He sure as hell didn't want a baby of their own so much that he would put her life in danger.

"I'd like to speak with your surgeon," Dr. Kirsch said. "Do I have your permission to contact him, Bethany?"

"I don't mind if you speak to him, Dr. Kirsch, but I'm sure he'll tell you exactly what he told me—that I shouldn't have children." Her eyes darkened. "He even went so far as to say he felt it was a blessing because a woman in a wheelchair has no business having babies, anyway."

"Hmm." Kirsch shook his head. "What's this doctor's name?"

"Dr. Reicherton. He's up in Portland. You probably don't know him."

"As a matter of fact, I do. We doctors run into each other more often than you might think. Medical conventions and such. Benson Reicherton." He smiled and nodded. "He's a competent surgeon, one of the best on the West Coast."

"Daddy wanted the best," she said. "He was told we couldn't find better than Dr. Reicherton. I never liked him, but he seemed to know his stuff."

Again Kirsch nodded. "Ben's very good. If I had a spinal cord injury and surgery was recommended, I wouldn't hesitate to have him as my doctor. I'd walk a mile to avoid having him as a golfing buddy, though."

Bethany laughed and then suddenly yawned. "You *do* know him."

Dr. Kirsch smiled and winked at her. "I do, at that." He pushed to his feet and collected his bag. "I see that the shot is making you drowsy, young lady, so I'll take my leave and let you rest." He leveled a finger at her nose. "No riding tomorrow. I have a ten o'clock tee time, and if this overprotective fellow of yours calls me off the course over leg cramps, I'll be cranky as a bear."

Ryan followed the doctor from the bedroom. Once at the front of the house, Kirsch scratched his balding gray head. His silver eyebrows drew together in a thoughtful frown. "Something about this doesn't add up. Let me check into it. I'll try to get in touch with Reicherton when I get back to the office."

"You think she can have babies, don't you?"

The doctor glanced toward the hallway. "I don't advise you to tell her that, not until I'm sure. I wouldn't want to give her false hope and then disappoint her. I'm certainly no spinal specialist."

"You're a damned good doctor, though, and I trust your opinion."

The physician smiled. "Thank you. In answer to your question, for what my opinion's worth, this damned good doctor thinks the young lady either misunderstood what she was told or Reicherton gave her incorrect information. Paralysis doesn't generally affect a woman's ability to carry a child, especially not in a case like hers, where the nerve damage is incomplete."

It seemed pretty damned complete to Ryan. "How do you mean?"

"It's a term we use for a spinal cord injury that kills or impairs only some of the nerves. You can take a dozen individuals with a spinal cord injury at the same level and see a dozen different results. Some people may have partial use of their limbs or have feeling where others don't. With an L2 injury like hers . . ." His voice trailed away. "I don't think it should have any bearing on her ability to have children, and unless I'm completely misinformed, there's little or no risk of autonomic dysreflexia. But let me check into it. Could be I'm just an old country doctor who doesn't know beans." He lifted his hand in farewell and stepped out onto the porch. "I'll be in touch."

"What about the blood clot thing?" Ryan asked anxiously.

Kirsch sighed. "I think we can work around that problem. They have some very nice wheelchairs now with adjustable, comfortably cushioned leg rests, kind of like small recliners on wheels, enabling the user to put her feet up whenever the chair is stationary. I also think we can keep the blood thin enough to reduce the danger of clotting without harming the baby."

After bidding the physician farewell and closing the door, Ryan went to check on Bethany. The muscle relaxant had indeed made her drowsy, and she was already asleep. He sat beside her for a while, gazing at her sweet face. The drug had put her so deeply under that her mouth was lax, and a bead of drool glistened on her bottom lip. He smiled and thumbed it away, his heart squeezing at the thought of anything happening to her.

An hour later when Doctor Kirsch phoned back, Ryan took the call in the kitchen. "What did Reicherton say, Doc?"

"A lot of nothing. Basically, this is my take. No doctor can guarantee even a perfectly healthy young woman that she'll be able to bear children. The chance that she'll have problems may be minuscule, but it always exists. The odds against her successfully carrying a child increase substantially if she has special problems or the propensity to have them. That being the case, I won't go so far as to say that Reicherton actually lied to Bethany. However, I do believe he mentioned unlikely complications for a woman with an L2 injury."

"*Why*?" Ryan whispered. "Sweet Lord, *why*?"

"That's a very good question. I keep circling back to his comment to her—that a woman in a wheelchair has no business having babies. I've known Ben for a number of years. I distinctly recall his telling me once that he went into his field because his mother was a quadriplegic."

"How does that relate to what he told Bethany?"

"I'm walking a very fine line here, Ryan. I don't want to speculate and malign the man's professional reputation. As we were speaking on the phone, it occurred to me that perhaps—and I stress the word *perhaps*—his childhood was a difficult one because his mother was severely handicapped. Maybe he hates to see any woman in a wheelchair try to raise children. I only know he said nothing over the phone to justify what Bethany claims he told her. He hemmed and hawed. He pointed out that it's been a number of years, and he didn't have her file in front of him. But essentially he agreed with my prognosis, that unless there are other complications, a woman with an injury at L2 who is continent and has no history of urinary tract infections should be able to bear children without difficulty. Worst case, she may have to deliver by C-section."

A picture of Bethany sobbing her heart out in the van the other night flashed through Ryan's mind, and he closed his eyes, feeling sick. *Never any babies,* she'd cried. Why in God's name had the doctor told her such a vicious lie? Granted, maybe some handicapped women were unable to be good mothers because of their disabilities, but each case was different, and it hadn't been Reicherton's call to make.

"Ryan? You still there?"

"I'm here," Ryan said softly. "Just trying to absorb this. That's all. That girl in there has gone for eight years believing she might never have children. It makes me want to drive nonstop to Portland and rearrange Reicherton's face."

"I'm only guessing. Bear that in mind. And forgive me if it sounds pompous, but I think belated anger over something we can never prove would be fruitless. Why ruin what should be a happy time for both of you? You obviously adore this girl. Enjoy this very special time in your lives."

Ryan nodded and smiled. "You're right. After I wring her neck for not telling me about the autonomic dysreflexia, I'll do exactly that."

The physician laughed. "Now, now. If I were to tell you that having sex might kill you, what would you do?"

"Die a happy man."

"There you are. Don't blame her for making the same choice."

"That's entirely different. She can have safe sex. Having our own baby isn't important enough to put her health at risk."

"In your opinion. Women feel differently sometimes. Having a baby is the most important thing in the world to some of them."

Ryan rested his elbows on the counter. "I hear you, Doc.

Maybe instead of wringing her neck, I'll just yell at her for a while."

"Ah, now."

Ryan grinned. "You're invited to the wedding, by the way."

"I'll be there, then. Oh, and Ryan, I want to see the bride in my office. No rush. Call in the morning and set up an appointment for sometime after the honeymoon. I should give her a good going over, get a baseline established for reference during prenatal care."

"I'll get her in to see you, then." Ryan straightened and quickly added, "Hey, Doc? You think, just to be safe, that I should continue to use protection until after you see her?"

Kirsch chuckled again. "Well, now, that all depends. You going to pull a long face if you're hitting the floor for three o'clock feedings in nine months?"

"Hell, no."

"Then, grab hold of life with both hands, as she put it. I honestly don't believe she's at any great risk. I'll take good care of her. Judging by the mutinous expression I saw on that girl's face, you may play heck getting near her again if she so much as glimpses a prophylactic."

"You may be right."

Kirsch cleared his throat. "If I thought there was a need to be cautious, I'd tell you so. I honestly don't. Give the young lady a baby."

Ryan was still grinning when he hung up the phone. He returned to the bedroom, lay down beside Bethany, and drew her into his arms. *A baby.* He'd meant it when he told her he'd be perfectly happy to adopt. But deep in his heart, the thought of making a child of their own had a very special appeal. To see her with a big tummy and know she was carrying his child. To be with her when she gave birth. To watch her cradle a dark, downy head to her breast for the very first time. No matter how much love they might feel, adoptive parents missed out on some of the magic.

Ryan pressed a kiss to her hair and then closed his eyes to dream with her of raising Kendrick sons and daughters on the land where he'd grown up himself. He'd teach them to love these mountains just as he did, he thought sleepily, and one day, they'd take over in his stead to operate the Rocking K.

The thought filled him with a sense of purpose that had been lacking in his life before meeting her. He remembered back to the morning when he'd told Rafe how lost and horribly alone he often felt, that his pets were all that kept him sane on long winter evenings. He no longer felt that way.

How could a man feel lonely or lost when he held heaven in his arms?

Chapter Twenty-one

T he day after next, Ryan was working in the stable office doing books when it occurred to him that it was nearly eleven and Bethany still hadn't joined him for her daily training session. Not that they usually got much accomplished by way of work. She was proving to have an insatiable hunger for him, just as he did for her, and whenever they were alone in here, they ended up making love at least once, sometimes twice, before lunch.

Remembering the last time, Ryan thought of how beautiful she'd looked, lying naked on his desk, and he burned with a sudden yearning to see her there again. He was about to abandon the books to go find her when he heard Sly shout his name. He leaped to his feet, knowing before he made it as far as the door that something bad had happened.

"Down here!" Sly yelled as Ryan exited the office.

Ryan turned to see the foreman disappear into the stall where they'd connected Bethany's sling. He raced along the center aisle, the thump of his boots on the asphalt only slightly faster than the pounding of his heart. He knew without being told that something had happened to Bethany.

When he reached the open stall and saw her lying crumpled on the dirt beside her horse, Ryan thought his heart might stop. With a quick glance, he determined that she'd attempted to mount the mare by herself, utilizing the sling.

"Jesus Christ!" He pushed Sly out of the way and dropped to his knees beside her, so frightened he didn't know if he was cursing or praying. "Bethany? Oh, dear God."

"I'm all right, Ryan." She suffered his probing hands, telling him over and over that she wasn't seriously hurt. "I just slipped off the saddle, is all. It wasn't far to the ground."

Ryan's fear turned to anger. "What the bloody hell were you doing?" He shot a scathing glance at the foreman. "If she wanted to use the sling, you should have called me."

Sly held up his hands. "Don't jump all over me, son. I didn't know a thing about this until I found her in here."

"It was my fault, Ryan. I wanted to do it by myself."

Ryan wanted to shake her until her teeth rattled. Instead he finished checking her for injuries and then gathered her into his arms, shaking so badly the vibrations made the fringe on her new western shirt jiggle. "Never again," he said fiercely. "Promise me you'll never try to mount her alone again."

She drew her head back to fix him with a mutinous look. "That was the entire point of building the sling, so I could go riding without help."

"That was before. This is now, and if you ever risk breaking your neck again, I'll warm your fanny until you can't sit for a week."

Bethany pushed away to sit up and straighten her shirt. "Don't be silly," she said, brushing straw from her sleeve. She flashed him a bright smile. "I almost did it, Ryan. All by myself. Next time, I'll know not to unfasten the hooks before I get my leg sheathes buckled. I wouldn't have fallen but for my own stupidity."

Ryan gathered her up in his arms, pushed to his feet, and

started to leave the stall to take her to the office. She stopped him by pressing a slender hand to his chest. "Not yet. I want to try again. Just put me in my chair and leave, please. This is something I have to do."

"Over my dead body."

She held his gaze with hers. "I won't fall again."

"You can't know that." He imagined her breaking one of her legs or being accidentally stepped on by the horse. The very thought made his blood go icy. "I meant what I said. Take a chance like that again, and I'll—"

She touched a finger to his lips. "I know I frightened you, and I'm sorry for that. I was afraid of falling myself, which made me so nervous I didn't think everything through clearly." She smiled again. "But now it's happened, and it wasn't as awful as I thought. I fall quite nicely, half of me being limp. It didn't even hurt all that much. Just knocked the wind out of me for a second."

Ryan thought of possible bruises on her legs that she wouldn't be able to feel. His heart squeezed at the flame of pride he saw burning deep in her eyes. *Sweet Jesus, help me.* He knew this was something she wanted and needed to do without anyone's help, that being self-sufficient was one of the most important things in the world to her. But at what price? There was such a thing as carrying pride too far.

"Please, Ryan? Try to understand. I *have* to do this without you. I have to."

He glanced at her wheelchair, which in that moment represented all the reasons why she shouldn't. He almost wished he'd never had his family help him build the damned sling. But, no. He'd built it for just this reason, so she could be free of the chair and all the other constraints in her life. He just hadn't counted on her being so stubborn and taking this do-or-die approach.

Do or die. From the first, he'd always loved the stubborn lift of her small chin. This was who she was. How else could she have become a champion barrel racer? She had probably taken a do-or-die approach to that as well, pushing herself beyond her limits until she became the best. Recalling how she'd trounced him in the swimming race, he suspected she did everything full out. Since that was one of the things about her that he loved, did he really want to change her?

Feeling as if he'd just swallowed ground glass, Ryan said, "Will you let me do just one thing before you try to mount her again?"

"That depends on what it is."

"You'll see soon enough." He forced himself to lower her into her chair. After glancing at the remote control tucked into the waistband of her jeans, he said, "Promise me you won't move until I get back?"

She heaved a sigh. "Don't take very long. The longer I wait to try again, the more nervous I'll get."

Ryan glanced at Sly, who lingered in the open doorway. "Can you lend me a hand real quick, Sly?"

The foreman nodded and followed Ryan down the center aisle to the bunk room, where they sometimes slept when a mare was due to foal. A few seconds later, when both men returned to the stall carrying cot mattresses, Bethany burst out laughing.

"Those should make my landing a little less jarring," she observed.

Ryan smiled weakly as he positioned one mattress beside the mare. As he relieved Sly of the other one, he said, "That's the general idea—to keep you from breaking your stubborn little neck."

"Thank you," she said softly after the padding was in place. "I'll feel better knowing it's there." Then she looked expectantly at both men. "You can leave now." When they hesitated, she smiled. "I won't fall again, I promise. Now, go!"

Ryan gestured for the foreman to follow him, and he left. He only went approximately three feet. Sly drew up beside him. They stared worriedly at the open stall doorway. The hair on the back of Ryan's neck curled when he heard the sling motor start to hum. Where was the harm in her accepting just a little help this first time? he wondered. Once she got the hang of it, he'd happily leave her to do it alone.

He started to step toward the stall. Sly snaked out a hand to grasp Ryan's arm. "Don't," he said softly. "This is something she needs to do by herself, son. You built the damned sling just so's this could happen. Don't spoil it for her."

Ryan knew the foreman was right, but, damn, it was hard to just stand there. Those mattresses weren't that wide. If she fell and missed one of them, she could be hurt. His heart felt as if it was going to pound its way out of his chest. What was happening? Was she on the horse yet? He strained to listen, but he couldn't tell anything by the sounds.

"I *did* it!" she suddenly cried. "I did it, Ryan! Come and just *look* at me. All by myself! I'm ready to ride!"

Ryan and Sly almost ran each other down to reach the doorway. Then Ryan forgot everything but the sight of Bethany. She wheeled Wink around to face them, her eyes glowing, her cheeks flushed with joy. In that moment Ryan caught a glimpse of the feisty, dauntless girl she'd been before the accident. Her hair was a wild tumble of dark, silky curls around her small face. She sat erect in the saddle, looking perfectly capable.

For the moment she was gloriously free, the wheelchair forgotten. The look on her face reminded him of the night that he had waltzed with her behind the grange, and a lump came to his throat. *This* was why he'd bought back her horse, ordered the saddle, and fashioned the sling. So he could see that inexpressible joy in her eyes. He wouldn't spoil the moment for her now by trying to coddle her.

He glanced at his watch. "The doctor said no more than ten minutes today. You're wasting precious seconds."

She snapped the reins and clucked her tongue to get the mare moving. "Out of my way, gentlemen! I'm going for a ride."

Ryan watched her take off down the center aisle. "Take it easy crossing that cement!" He couldn't resist yelling after her. He glanced at Sly. "Christ! I never knew love was such a pain in the ass. Am I going to live through this?"

Sly sighed and shook his head. "Same with kids. You gotta let 'em go. I remember the first time you went riding by yourself. Damn near gave me a heart attack. It ain't easy to turn loose, son, but you have to do it. That's life."

Ryan nodded. He'd told Bethany's father almost exactly the same thing. People had been wrapping her in cotton for far too long. He suspected that was the main reason she'd stayed in Portland, to escape the well-intended but stifling love of her family. He didn't want her to feel that way about him.

Eleven minutes later, Ryan wanted to saddle up Bucky to go find her. Sly stopped him. "She's only running a minute over. Give her a few more to get back. It'll ruin it for her if you go charging to her rescue like the dad-blamed cavalry."

The longest two minutes of Ryan's life passed before he heard the clop of Wink's shoes on the cement outside. He hurried over to grab a bucket from a hook, trying to look busy so she wouldn't know he'd been standing there sweating the entire time she was gone. Sly grabbed a feed bucket as well. Then the two men looked questioningly at each other, wondering what they meant to do next. It wasn't time to grain the horses.

"Hi!" Bethany called gaily as she rode the mare through the front entrance. "It was fantastic! You just can't *know*. And I did it, start to finish, all by myself, you guys. Isn't that phenomenal?"

She wasn't down off the damned horse yet. Ryan swallowed to stop himself from pointing that out.

"I'm so proud of myself." She rode Wink into the stall

where her sling awaited. Then as if she had eyes in the back of her head, she stopped both Ryan and Sly dead in their tracks by saying, "Stay out of here. I'll get off of her by myself."

Ryan glanced at the foreman. Sweating as if he'd been hard at work, Sly took off his hat to wipe his forehead with his sleeve. Ryan sympathized. The hum of the sling motor made his guts knot. He bit down hard on the inside of his cheek to keep from calling out precautions.

Seconds passed that felt like multiple eternities strung endlessly together. Finally she yelled, "Okay! I'm off. You can come fuss over me now."

Ryan's knees felt a little weak as he covered the distance to the stall doorway. Bethany was in her wheelchair again and was tugging at the sling girdle to get it off. She glanced up and smiled as the nylon pulled free from under her rump. "We should patent this gadget. We'd become millionaires."

"I'm already a millionaire," Ryan reminded her grumpily. It irritated him no end that she could be so cheerful when she'd just scared him so badly. "When we're married, half of that money will be yours."

"I ain't rich," Sly pointed out. "Maybe I'll patent the thing. If I had me a big, fat bank account, I just might get myself hitched."

Ryan cast the foreman an amazed look. "To who? Are you seeing someone I don't know about?"

Sly cocked a gray eyebrow, scratched his ear, and then said, "What if I am? I'm of age and then some. I reckon it's not just young fellers who can git bit by the lovebug."

Ryan was so startled by the revelation that he nearly forgot his concerns about Bethany. "I never said it was. I think that's great, Sly. Who's the lucky woman?"

The foreman smiled. "That's for me to know and you to find out. Just know when you finally do that I love the lady."

With that, the wiry foreman left the stall. Ryan turned a

bewildered gaze on Bethany. She smiled and sighed. "Isn't that romantic? Sly is in love with someone."

Ryan frowned. "He makes damned good money working for us. He doesn't need millions to get married."

Bethany turned toward the doorway and wheeled out into the aisle. "Come on, Wink. Time to put you back in your stall."

The mare followed her mistress like a dog trained to heel. Ryan stared after the pair for a moment, then hollered for Charlie, one of the stable hands, to come unsaddle and walk Wink to cool her down.

En route to the office a few minutes later, Bethany flashed him a teasing smile over her shoulder. Once inside the small room, she was the one who locked and bolted the door this time. She turned, gave him a sultry look, and flicked the fringe on her shirt with a fingertip. "Hi, cowboy. Did you miss me while I was riding?"

Ryan's pulse hadn't returned to normal yet. As happy as he was that the sling episode had ended well, he still couldn't get that picture of her on the ground at the mare's feet out of his head. "I'm not really in the mood for that right now."

She only smiled and started unsnapping her shirt. "I'm sorry for giving you such a scare. I won't make the mistake of unfastening the hooks until I'm secured to the saddle again. I promise."

Ryan averted his gaze, determined not to get sidetracked. "I think we need to talk about wise choices and the necessity of taking the proper precautions."

He heard cloth rustle, and his eyes were drawn back to her as if they were metal shavings attracted by a magnet. *Two magnets*. God help him. Her bra was unfastened, and both breasts were trying to spill out. One rose pink nipple peeked around the scalloped edge of lace at him. At the sight, the insides of his cheeks sucked fast to his teeth. He couldn't have spit if she'd yelled, "Stable fire!"

"Please don't be mad," she said softly. As she spoke, she grazed her dainty fingertips over the hardening tip of her now bare breast, her eyes beckoning to him. "Come here and let me make you feel better."

Holy hell. She'd gotten a late start at sex, but she was a fast learner. Ryan was across the office before he realized he'd moved. He quickly forgot all about being upset with her. How could a man hold onto a rational thought?

By the following Thursday when they began their trip to Bear Creek Lake for the wedding, Bethany had conditioned herself daily to the saddle and was ready for an hour and a half ride. She was feeling so happy and optimistic about her future with Ryan that it almost frightened her. Cleo had settled in at the ranch as if she'd been born there, spending her days on T-bone's shoulders and her nights in the house, snuggled in her kitty bed. Bethany had used her new stable sling regularly, mounting and dismounting Wink without any help. Ryan was talking about her opening a riding academy in the near future, not only to train aspiring barrel racers like Heidi, but to work with paraplegic youngsters as well.

It all sounded too good to be true. A handsome, loving, wonderful husband. Being able to have babies. Working full-time with horses. Being free to wander the pathways that networked the property. She felt as if her world had been magnified to gigantic proportions, and she sometimes felt almost giddy. Surely no one could be this happy without something happening to spoil it.

When she confessed her fear to Ryan, he fell back to ride abreast of her, looking so incredibly handsome in the saddle with June sunlight glinting off his breeze-tousled black hair that he made her heart sing. The jingling, almost musical sounds of their camping paraphernalia on the packhorse mingled with the clop of hooves striking rock as they rode along.

"Sweetheart, that's silly," he said. "You *deserve* to be happy. Nothing's going to happen to spoil this for us. *Nothing*."

Bethany let her head fall back to gaze at the sky. "I know I'm being silly. It's just—oh, Ryan, I'm *so* happy. You know what I'm saying? I've lived so long, always telling myself to be practical, always scolding myself for wanting what I could no longer have. And now, all of a sudden, I'm getting every single thing I ever wished for. Nobody should be this happy. It has to be a sin or something."

He chuckled and leaned sideways on his horse to steal a quick kiss. "Bethany Ann, I can't imagine you committing a real sin, and I'm sure God would agree with me. I've never known a person with a purer heart. I think He sent me an angel."

Her eyes danced with mischief, and she plucked a pinecone from a tree bough to chuck at him. "Angels don't think about what I'm thinking about right now. Let's stop and take a rest under a tree."

Ryan knew what that warm gleam in her eyes meant, and he was sorely tempted to stop. But if they lingered along the trail for too long, it would spoil his plans.

He sighed and reached over to ruffle her hair. "As much as it pains me, I have to pass."

She frowned and pouted her bottom lip. "We're not even married yet, and you're already tired of me."

"Not a chance. There's just something special I want to do this afternoon. When we stop and get our camp set up, will you do me the honor of becoming my wife?"

She threw him a bewildered look. "Today? How can we do that? The minister won't be coming up until Saturday."

"We don't need a minister," he assured her. "Remember telling me that for you, the wilderness was your church? Let's say our private vows today. Just you and me, on a mountain ridge, making our wedding promises to each other with only God as our witness. Who else really counts?"

After thinking about it for a moment, she nodded and flashed him a smile. "I'd love that. I think it would be even more meaningful than the official ceremony."

Two hours later Ryan knelt at the feet of a dark-haired angel in a wheelchair and vowed to love, honor, and cherish her for the rest of his life. As he said the words, he looked into those beautiful pansy-blue eyes of hers and knew that loving her was what he'd been born to do.

When he finished saying his vows, she tremulously followed suit, her eyes sparkling as she whispered each word, promising to love him forever. *Bethany.* She was surely a gift from heaven. To himself, Ryan vowed to be the man she deserved, to spend the remainder of his days protecting her and trying to make her happy. If anyone on earth deserved to be happy, it had to be this woman.

He drew their rings from his shirt pocket. Before he slipped hers on her finger, he held it up to the sunlight. "They say a ring is a symbol of eternity—of pure and everlasting love. I think a lot of people forget that. I never will. I promise you that." He slipped the ring on her finger and then bent to kiss it. "With this ring, I thee wed."

She smiled as she gazed down at the ring on her finger. Then, after hauling in a deep, shaky breath, she held up his ring to the sunlight. "Whenever you look at this ring," she whispered, "remember I'll spend the rest of my life trying to love you more than I love myself. Because you are who you are, I don't think that will be a tall order." She leaned forward to kiss him. As she drew away, tears sparkled on her cheeks like diamonds. With his help she slipped the ring onto his finger. "With this ring, I thee wed."

Ryan framed her face between his hands as he bent to settle his mouth over hers. A burning desire flowed through him, setting his blood afire. "Now for the best part of a private, mountain ridge ceremony," he whispered as he drew back. "Instead of just kissing my bride, I can seal our vows by making love to her."

Her eyes widened. *"Here?"*

Ryan glanced around and chuckled. "One nice thing about mountain ridges, the neighbors mind their own business and aren't given to gossip." He pushed to his feet, lifted her into his arms, and carried her to a sun-dappled grassy place under a pine tree. After clearing away the needles with the side of his boot, he carefully laid her down and made passionate love to her in the golden sunlight, giving the squirrels something to chatter about.

Afterglow . . . Ryan had heard the term hundreds of times, but the feeling itself was incredible. He held his wife close to his heart, too exhausted to move. Sunshine played over their nude bodies in a warm caress that felt so good he wanted to remain just as they were. Only a fear that Bethany's sensitive skin might burn finally prodded him to move.

The late afternoon and evening played out perfectly. They caught trout for supper from a nearby stream and dined like royalty by a crackling campfire. Ryan was able to find a deep place farther downstream, and just before dusk, they went down to bathe. Big problem. The instant he saw Bethany's bare breasts bobbing so sweetly on the surface of the water, he grabbed her high in his arms, waded to the bank, and made love to her again. They were both a little chilled by the time they finally got out of the water. Ryan dried off his bride, carried her to camp, bundled her in a blanket, and sat with her in his arms by the fire until she felt warm to the touch again. *Touching.* For some reason, that invariably led to more, and he found himself making love to her again, this time on the blanket by the fire. He couldn't get enough of her, and she seemed to share the feeling, always turning eagerly into his arms when he kissed her.

"Listen," she whispered urgently after they got settled for the night in their tent.

Ryan cocked an ear. A moment later he heard coyotes howling.

"Isn't that the most *beautiful* sound?" she said. "Oh, Ryan, just *listen*. The wind whispering in the trees and whining over the ridge. The call of the coyotes to the moon. I never thought I'd hear any of it again. *Never*. Have you any idea how much this means to me, or what a beautiful gift you've given me?"

Ryan personally felt that she was the gift, he the recipient. "I just feel lucky to have found a wife who loves it as much as I do," he told her. "Not everyone does, you know."

She lay on her side, facing him. A coyote howled again. As the sound trailed to them through the mountain darkness, she pressed a kiss to his mouth. Then she sat up suddenly, shoving back the sleeping bag to smooth a hand over his bare flank. "Roll onto your back," she whispered, "I want to make love to you while they call to the moon."

That was a request he couldn't refuse. He turned onto his back. She braced one arm on the sleeping bag beneath them to support her weight. Then she bent her head to trail kisses down his chest toward the triangle of dark hair below his navel. With the light from the fire shining through the nylon wall of the tent, he could see her clearly and guessed her intent. Maybe he was impossibly old-fashioned, but this was something he'd chosen never to let another woman do, feeling it was far too intimate an act to engage in with someone he didn't love. He'd never gone down on a woman until Bethany, either, always choosing instead to use his hand.

His erection was as prominent as a flagpole. All it lacked was Old Glory, flapping in the wind. He smoothed a lock of dark hair back from her cheek. "Sweetheart, you don't have to—"

"Shush," she whispered, and then proceeded to lap at him as she might an ice-cream cone.

It was the most erotic experience of his life. He couldn't say it felt all that wonderful because his shaft wasn't as sensitive as she obviously believed. She was mimicking his technique, which didn't quite cut it for a man. But that didn't matter. Just seeing her love him that way nearly made him lose control.

Ryan caught her by the chin, as pleased with her as he'd never dreamed he might be with anyone. Because she loved him so. Because she would clearly do anything, just to make him happy with her. What she failed to understand was that she was all his dreams, rolled into one, without trying.

"I'm sorry," she said softly. "I don't really know how to do it. Won't you tell me so I can make it nice for you? With practice, I'll get better."

Ryan nearly groaned. *Practice*. One more lap from that quick little tongue of hers, and he would embarrass himself. "I don't know how it's done," he lied. He did know, of course. He had a general idea, at any rate. "No woman's ever done that to me."

Even in the dim light, he saw her eyes fill with bewilderment. "Never?"

"And you're the first I ever kissed there," he said, catching her around the waist to haul her higher on his chest. "That's something special, and I saved it for you."

"Oh, Ryan." She was clearly touched and found that romantic. "For a rank beginner, you're very good at it."

He only smiled. "Thank you. It's important to me to please you."

"So you can understand my wanting to please you."

"You have, honey. If you'd done it any better, I'd be finished right now and snoring. What fun would that be?"

She grinned and relaxed her weight on his chest. What a

sweet burden she was, every inch of her so soft and silken. "Liked it, did you?"

He chuckled at the feminine purr in her voice. "So much that I couldn't take any more." He glanced at her mouth and folded his arms under his head. "Kiss my mouth instead." Sensing that she wanted to be the one in control this time, and that she wanted to do things to please him, he whispered, "While you kiss me, rub the tips of your breasts over my chest."

She did exactly as he instructed, and when he felt her nipples turn hard, he forgot about letting her take the lead. *Bethany.* He grabbed her close, rolled to get on top, and made love to her to the forlorn accompaniment of the howling coyotes . . .

Bethany awakened him at dawn. In the time since she'd been staying with him at the ranch, she'd stopped being cranky upon rising, but on that morning he marveled at the drastic change. After he helped her into her chair, she literally threw her arms wide to embrace the morning, tipped back her head to gaze at the treetops, and laughed with gay abandon.

"I feel *alive!*" she cried. "Not just here, not just breathing. I feel so alive!"

Her mood prevailed throughout the morning. When they were once again on the trail, she sang silly songs, reminding Ryan that she wasn't completely perfect, after all. The girl couldn't carry a tune for squat. He was forced to join in just to make it easier on his ears.

"Sixty-seven bottles of beer on the wall! Sixty-seven bottles of beer! You take one down, and you pass it around, sixty—"

"Four bottles of beer on the wall!" he inserted.

"Huh-uh. Sixty-six!"

Ryan was laughing when he heard a large animal tearing through the brush to the left of the trail and spotted a flash of Hereford red between the trees. Seeing cattle up here wasn't a rare occurrence. The Rocking K herds enjoyed an open range and wandered all over these mountains, foraging. But Ryan seldom saw one at a dead run like that.

He reined in his sorrel and listened to the crashing sounds as they grew more distant. "What the hell?"

Bethany had stopped her horse just behind the pack animal. "I wonder what lit a fire under her?"

Ryan frowned thoughtfully. "I don't know. Something tells me I should mosey over and have a look, though. A couple of weeks back, a rancher on up the highway lost two head to poachers." He turned his gelding Bucky and rode back to hand Bethany the lead on the packhorse. "Sit tight for a minute, honey. I'll be right back."

It took Ryan only a couple of minutes to ride through the trees and locate the cow's hoofprints. Following her tracks with his gaze, he spotted a glistening patch of wetness on the low-hanging bough of a fir tree. He swung off his horse to go check it out. When he touched the feathery fir needles, fresh blood came off on his fingertips. He followed the cow's trail on foot for a bit, and sure enough, he soon saw blood on the ground as well. The animal was badly injured.

When Ryan got back to Bethany, he told her what he'd found. "Some idiot must have shot her," he said. "Damn fools. If they can't shoot straighter than that, they've got no business packing a rifle."

Bethany twisted at the waist to gaze behind them. Concern filled her eyes. "Oh, Ryan, how *sad*. If the poor thing's been wounded and she doesn't bleed to death, she's liable to die slowly and horribly from infection or something. We can't just leave her like that."

Ryan agreed. "I can track her," he said. "It's pretty rough terrain once you get off the trail, though. I don't think you should go with me."

"No problem. I'll just wait here."

Ryan smiled. "I think I can do better than this. There's a pretty little meadow just a ways on up the trail. How's about if I let you wait for me there?"

"With food?" she asked.

He laughed and nodded. "I suppose I can dig you out a few snacks."

"That sounds lovely. I could use a little rest, anyway. This way I won't be overtired when we get to the lake."

A few minutes later when Ryan had her comfortably settled in her chair under a tall pine growing at the edge of the meadow, she grinned up at him. "I feel like a princess! All I lack is a soft drink and those snacks you promised me."

He chuckled and went to get a can of pop out of the small cooler on the packhorse, then grabbed the picnic basket, which was brimming with goodies. When he returned to set the provisions at the base of the tree, Bethany said, "Yum." She opened the basket and plucked out the salami and cheese. "It sucks to be you. What a shame you can't join me."

He unstrapped his holster from his hips and handed it down to her. "Just in case," he said. "You know how to use a revolver, I hope."

She accepted the .22, her eyes dancing with devilment. "This isn't a revolver. It's a popgun. And, yes, I know how to use it. I can shoot an acorn off a limb at fifty yards. Is that satisfactory?"

"With or without a rest?"

She raised her small chin. "Without, of course. What do you think I am, a city girl or something?" She glanced around the peaceful clearing. "Why, exactly, do I need the gun? Are the squirrels up here bloodthirsty?"

He chuckled and headed for his horse. "I was thinking more about snakes. I carry it for the occasional timber rattler."

She shuddered and rubbed her arms. "I detest snakes."

Ryan swung up on his horse, watched her rifle through

the basket for a knife to slice the cheese, and then said, "Save some of that salami and cheese for me, lady. I may work up an appetite."

"I will." Her expression became more serious. "I hope you find her, Ryan. Good luck."

"Hey, you're lookin' at one of the best trackers this side of the Pecos, lady. What do you think I am, some city boy?"

She pursed her lips. "Where *is* the Pecos, exactly?"

"Beats the hell out of me. But this side of it, I'm the best." He winked at her and grinned as he checked to be sure the magazine in his rifle was loaded. "She was bleeding heavily. It'll be fairly easy to track her. If she's beyond help, I'll finish her off. If not, I'll contact Rafe and give him her location." He patted the cell phone on his belt. "With smoke signals, of course."

She was laughing as he rode away. "Be careful, Tex!"

"Not to worry."

Rather than meander along the trail, he decided to go as a crow flew and save time. As he wove his gelding through the brush that grew in wild profusion off the beaten path, he kept an eye out for sign, hoping to spot where the cow had been shot. She'd been running from somewhere up here, he felt sure.

He hadn't ridden far when the hair on his nape started to prickle. Drawing his horse to a halt, he listened and sniffed the air. The woods had gone eerily silent. Even the wind seemed to be holding its breath. Ryan had been riding in these mountains on a regular basis all his life. He knew every ridge and gully like the back of his hand. When something wasn't right, he sensed it.

And something wasn't right.

At that moment, he was mightily tempted to head back to the meadow and Bethany. He couldn't say why. A part of him thought he was being silly. But another big part of him had the willies.

Then he smelled it. *Blood*. He'd straddled the top rail of

a slaughter chute too many times not to recognize the scent of freshly killed cattle. He nudged Bucky forward, his ire rising. What the hell? Had some kids come up here with rifles and used their cows for target practice?

Not far up ahead, there was a water hole—a place where the winter floodwater of Bear Creek had long since wallowed out a wide hollow in the shale and formed a small gorge that was nearly boxed off at one end. In the summer the cattle favored it as a gathering place because trees grew along the lips of the ravine, providing deep pockets of shade below on the banks of the stream.

If some cows had bunched up in that wash, they would have been like ducks in a shooting gallery, easy to pick off with a rifle. With one end of the area almost boxed off, they wouldn't have been able to escape quickly.

Ryan headed straight for the spot. The scent of blood grew stronger. A *lot* of blood. An awful, coppery taste coated his tongue. As he crested the last rise above the water hole, he was prepared to see a number of slaughtered cows. He didn't look forward to it, but he'd looked death in the eye so many times, he didn't expect it to come as a shock, either.

When he saw the carnage, bile crawled up the back of his throat.

Dear God. The cows had bunched up in the gorge, just as he'd guessed. But it hadn't been a sniper that killed them. Never in all his life had Ryan seen such gore. At least ten cows lay dead, some in the stream, others on the banks. The creek flowed red with blood from the mangled bodies.

Something had mauled them.

From a distance, Ryan couldn't tell what kind of animal had killed them. The concentration of cougars was heavy in these mountains because of legislation that had been passed a few years ago, prohibiting the use of hunting dogs. But a cougar didn't usually go on a killing rampage. It snapped the neck of its prey upon impact, then dragged the dead animal off somewhere to eat it.

Ryan dismounted, tethered Bucky to a stump, and slipped his 30.06 pump-action Remington from the saddle boot. The way down to the stream was steep. He slid partway in the loose shale, barely managing to stay on his feet. Once in the gorge, he wasted no time in examining the slaughtered cows. The animal tracks he found in the soft earth near the dead cattle were unmistakably those of a bear.

Ryan could scarcely credit his eyes. Black bears didn't do this sort of thing. They were carnivores, yes, and occasionally killed for sustenance, but as a general rule they tended to be opportunistic creatures, more likely to dine on already dead animals, wood worms, or vegetation, such as berries. Over the years Ryan had heard of bears killing a cow now and again, but never more than one at a time, and always for food.

Yet there was no denying the evidence. Judging by the tracks, this was a large bear. The rare renegade black bear usually turned out to be a young male. An older male seldom attacked without provocation, and a sow generally only got ornery when her cubs were threatened.

A chill trickled down Ryan's spine. That injured cow they'd seen running for her life through the woods had undoubtedly escaped from here. That had been no more than twenty minutes ago. This was all fresh kill, and it wasn't the act of a hungry carnivore, attacking for food. The bear hadn't eaten on any of the corpses. No. It had been in a killing frenzy and had slaughtered these animals for the sheer joy of it.

The thought sent Ryan scrambling back up the bank. *Bethany.* He'd left her sitting in that meadow without any means of defending herself. That .22 caliber revolver would only piss off a charging bear. It certainly wouldn't drop it.

He was panting from exertion and in a cold sweat by the

time he reached his horse. Because he knew he had to ride hard to get back to Bethany, he returned the rifle to the boot so he'd have both hands free.

Bethany. She'd been slicing salami and cheese when he left her. A bear could smell food from well over a mile away.

Ryan kicked Bucky hard in the flanks, urging him into a flat-out run. It was rough terrain, and Ryan knew he could very easily injure the horse, riding at such a reckless speed. But he had to. If it came to a choice between the gelding and his wife, he'd sacrifice the horse in a heartbeat.

Please, God. The silent prayer circled dizzily through his mind. He urged Bucky to an even faster pace, terrified that the bear might circle around to the meadow. Bethany was so helpless. She couldn't even try to run.

When Ryan reached the edge of the meadow, he'd never felt such relief in his life. There sat Bethany, beneath the pine right where he'd left her. She spotted him and waved. Ryan slowed his horse. She was fine, thank God. He was close enough now to pick off a bear with his rifle before it could get near her.

As he drew closer, Bethany saw how hard his horse was blowing and called, "Did you find her? Is everything all right?"

"No, I didn't go after her." Ryan scanned the hillsides that encircled the meadow. He didn't want to frighten her, but he didn't want to lie to her, either. "It was a bear, honey. You need to put all the food back in the containers. Seal it up tight. I don't want any uninvited picnic guests to come calling."

"You saw a bear?" She looked delighted. "Way cool. Maybe we'll spot it again. I haven't seen a black bear in aeons."

"Their population has increased substantially over the last few years. They got lumped in on the bill to protect cougars and can no longer be trapped." He drew Bucky to a stop beside Wink and the packhorse. As soon as he dismounted, he drew his rifle from the boot as a safety precaution. He sure as hell didn't want to get caught with his guard down. "I didn't actually see the bear. Just lots of really fresh sign."

When she saw him walking toward her with the rifle cradled in one arm, her smile faded. Her gaze became riveted to his. After a long moment of searching eye contact, she said, "Oh, Ryan . . . what is it?"

He scanned the hillsides again. "I don't want to scare you, honey. But this is no ordinary bear. He's gone berserk."

"What?" Her voice was thin and shaky with incredulous laughter. "How do you mean? Berserk in what way?"

Ryan shifted his gaze back to hers. "You know that cow we saw? She'd been attacked." He gestured with his head. "About a mile east, there's a creek ravine where the cows like to water. Steep shale walls on both sides. Not a box canyon, but almost, making it difficult for them to get out of there fast. The bear must have caught them by surprise. I didn't take time to count heads, but I'd say at least ten are dead."

"*What?* You think a black bear killed ten cows? That's crazy, Ryan. Black bears don't do that. A grizzly, maybe, but not an Oregon black bear."

The hair on Ryan's nape started to prickle again. "He's a big old boy. People go berserk. Why not a black bear?" He leaned his rifle against the tree beside her. "You as good with a pump action as you are with a revolver?"

She was looking over her shoulder at the hillsides. "It's been a long time. I used to be a fair shot with a rifle. No guarantee I can hit anything now."

Ryan nodded toward the weapon. "Keep your eyes peeled while I saddle Wink. We're getting out of here." He glanced at the basket. She'd lain the pistol and holster on the closed end. "Get that salami sealed up in a container. A bear can smell food for a mighty long way. I don't want him coming in on us."

Ryan hurriedly saddled Wink. When he went back to get Bethany, he had to smile. She was doing exactly as he had asked, keeping her eyes glued to the hillsides, one hand curled loosely over the rifle stock in case she had to shoot. She might not be able to walk, Ryan thought, but there was no one on earth he would have trusted more to guard his back.

He bent to lift her from the chair. "I'll get you in the saddle, then come back for the rifle and other stuff."

She hugged his neck as he carried her toward her horse. "You're really worried."

"I've never seen anything like it," Ryan admitted. "It made my blood run cold and scared the hell out of me. The whole way back here, I was praying you were safe."

"Oh, Ryan. I had the .22. I was fine."

He narrowed an eye at her. "That pistol wouldn't have stopped that big old boy. Trust me on—"

"Mrrrhaw!"

The sound came from behind them. Only halfway to the horses, Ryan whirled to see what in the hell it was. When he saw the bear charging across the flat toward them, his heart stuttered to a stop and felt as if it just hung in his chest like a chunk of ice. The animal was huge, and it ran with incredible speed—its fat and fur jolting with every impact of its paws on the earth.

"Mrrrhaw!"

"Oh, my God," Bethany cried. "Oh, my *God!*"

Ryan glanced frantically at the rifle leaning against the pine only a few feet away where he'd left it in order to carry Bethany. If he put her down, he might be able to reach the weapon before the bear caught him. Big problem. There was every chance the animal would stay on course, charging blindly. If so, it would be on Bethany before Ryan could get off a shot. There might also be lag time after he fired. Bears were notorious for taking lead and not going down immediately.

Bethany could be killed.

Ryan had to make a decision, and the way he saw it, he had no real choice. He lay Bethany on the grass right where they were and faced the bear without a weapon.

In those split seconds before the huge animal reached them, his mind spun with disjointed bits of information he'd heard over the years about charging black bears, the most pertinent being that they would sometimes back down if you made yourself look as large as possible and behaved aggressively. He put himself between Bethany and the bear, flung his arms wide, and yelled as loudly as he could. But the bear kept coming.

"Get out of here!" Ryan yelled again. This time he took a couple of steps forward, wondering even as he did if he'd totally lost his mind. "Rrrhaw!" he cried, trying to emulate the bear's ferocious growl.

"Ryan!" Bethany screamed. "Run! Get away!"

The bear was on him then. Ryan felt as if a locomotive plowed into him. His feet came clear off the ground, and both he and the bear went airborne. Dimly he could hear Bethany screaming. *Pain*. His mind washed red with it.

"The rifle!" he managed to yell. "Sweet Christ, the rifle!"

All Ryan's life, he'd been told to play dead in the event of a bear attack. He felt the son of a bitch biting his hip. Felt his bones splintering like chalk under the force of its jaws. How could a man play dead when his body was exploding with such agony? Ryan screamed. There was no holding it back. He screamed as if he were on a torture rack and being ripped apart.

Perhaps he was being ripped apart . . . Pictures flashed through his mind of the mangled cows. *Bethany*. The bear would go for her next. Blind with pain, Ryan forced his body to go limp and rolled onto his stomach, groping for the knife scabbard on his belt. It would be a little like jab-

bing a hippo with a toothpick, but it was the only weapon
he had.

The rifle. The rifle. The rifle.

Bethany dragged herself toward the tree, her gaze fixed
on the weapon. She heard Ryan screaming. *Oh, God*. He
could have saved himself by running for the gun. But, no.
He'd stepped between her and the bear, and now—oh,
God—oh, God—now he was dying for her.

No, no, no, no, noooo! She clawed wildly at the grass,
dragging herself over the ground one agonizingly slow inch
at a time. Useless. She was absolutely *useless*. Dying. Ryan
was dying. And she was inching along like a slug on her
belly, unable to do anything to help him.

When she finally reached the tree, Bethany felt as if a
thousand eternities had passed. She grabbed the gun, managed to sit up, and braced her back against the trunk.
Breathing in . . . breathing out. The sound of her lungs
echoed against her eardrums. Every swish of her blood
was an explosion inside her brain. *Ryan*. She flicked the
rifle off safety, jacked in a shell, and threw the butt to her
shoulder.

The bear was mauling Ryan. Tossing him around as if he
were a rag doll. Every time Bethany started to shoot, she lost
her nerve, terrified she might hit Ryan. *Please, God*. She
needed a clear shot.

It never came. The bear was in a frenzy. Bethany realized
she absolutely had to shoot. She got a bead on the bear, re-
fusing to think about Ryan getting in her line of fire. She
hauled in a breath, held it, and squeezed the trigger. *Ka-
boom*. The kick of the rifle slammed her spine against the
tree trunk.

The bear screamed in rage and turned toward her, going
up on its back legs. *Mrrrhaw!* The cry was horrible and
sounded almost human. Bethany jacked in another shell,

sighted in. Before she could fire, the bear took off at a dead run.

Sobbing and calling Ryan's name, Bethany dragged herself toward him. *Blood*. Oh, dear God. She'd never seen so much blood. He was surely dead. She pushed the rifle ahead of her over the ground, knowing she'd need the weapon if the bear circled back. *Ryan*. She loved him so much. Please, God. He couldn't be dead.

When she finally reached him, he mumbled something and opened his eyes. Blue spheres, surrounded by crimson streaks. He smiled at her. "You hit the son of a bitch?"

"I don't know," she sobbed. "Oh, my God, Ryan. You're hurt. You're badly hurt."

"No shit. He got my hip." He blinked and stared hard at her for a moment. "Bethany, I'm—" His throat worked. "Keep the gun close, darlin'. Don't let the bastard hurt you."

That was all he said, and then he lost consciousness.

Praying mindlessly, Bethany managed to sit up. She began checking Ryan, knowing she had to find the worst of his injuries and somehow stop the bleeding. She looked at his hip first. Nearly vomited. Started to cry, then gave herself a hard mental slap. No hysterics. She had to keep her head. Do what had to be done.

She ripped off her shoes to get at her socks. Then she peeled off her blouse and bra. Padding. She had to pad the wounds and tightly wrap them to staunch the bleeding.

While she worked, she prayed, bargaining mindlessly with God. *Just please let him live, and I swear, I'll never come out like this again. My fault. I had no business coming with him into a wilderness area. He would have run for the rifle if it hadn't been for me. Please, just let him live. Please, please, please.*

When she'd done all she could to stop the bleeding, Bethany tugged the cell phone from his belt. She almost lost it when she saw that the case had been crushed. The bear had mangled it while biting Ryan's hip. She tried to dial out anyway. The phone didn't work. It was as useless as she was.

No time to blubber. She had to get help. Use her head. She gazed at the horses. There was no way she could get on one of the animals by herself, let alone lift a wounded man onto a saddle. But those horses were still their only hope.

Keeping the rifle with her, just as Ryan had told her to do, Bethany dragged herself toward their mounts. All three animals were terrified and pranced nervously. As she got closer, she stared at their hooves, praying they wouldn't trample her. *No matter.* She had to get help up here for Ryan. He'd die if she didn't.

Bucky was their best chance, Bethany decided. The packhorse was too loaded down to make good time, and Wink hadn't been on the Rocking K very long. Bucky had probably covered these mountain trails with Ryan many a time, and if set free, he'd know the way home.

Miraculously the gelding stopped prancing the instant Bethany got close to his hooves. Tears nearly blinded her. "You're a good boy," she told him shakily. Before she untied the horse's reins, Bethany sat up and rubbed her bloody arms on his chest, praying whoever found the horse would notice the smears of crimson on his sorrel coat. "I need you to go home, Bucky. Run as fast as you can, boy. Go home."

She jerked his reins free from the stump.

"Go!" she yelled. "Ha! Ha! Out of here. Go on!" She slapped the gelding's chest. "Ha, I said!"

Already terrified from the recent bear attack, the horse was skittish anyway, and that was all it took. He wheeled and bolted. As she gazed after the gelding, Bethany sent up a silent prayer that Bucky would head straight for the ranch and that someone would be over at Ryan's place to see him when he got there.

*   *   *

The instant Sly saw Ryan's horse come wandering into the stable without a rider, he knew something was wrong. He immediately contacted Rafe.

"We got trouble, son. You best get over here."

Rafe was there within five minutes. He looked Bucky over, saw what appeared to be blood on the horse's chest, and swore under his breath. "Something happened. One of them is badly hurt."

Sly had already deduced that much and had started saddling horses. "You want I should call Bethany's brothers? We're gonna need all the men we can get if we gotta track 'em."

Rafe nodded. "I'll call them, Sly. If you'd finish getting the horses saddled, I'd much appreciate it."

"How many?" Sly asked as Rafe turned toward the stable office.

"She's got three brothers living here in town. My guess is they'll all come. Five mounts for us, I reckon, and a spare for Ryan, since his is here." Rafe stopped and sent Sly a hollow-eyed look. "Just pray to God he's alive to need a horse. That's a lot of blood on Bucky."

"Think positive, son. Ryan's a smart boy. Knows them mountains like the palms of his hands. He's okay."

Rafe nodded and opened the door to the office.

The howls of coyotes weren't so beautiful when you were alone in the dark, praying with every breath that the man you loved could hang onto life a while longer. Bethany sat with Ryan's head on her lap. He had regained consciousness a few times. Only briefly. A few lucid moments to break up an eternity of aloneness . . .

Each time, all he seemed concerned about was her.

"Bethany," he croaked the first time. "Honey, keep the rifle close and don't go to sleep. One bullet probably didn't kill the bastard, and he may come back."

"I won't sleep, Ryan. Don't worry. I promise you, I won't sleep."

He slipped away from her again. The second time he awoke, he seemed calmer. Or was it only that he was weaker? Bethany's heart twisted, and she wanted to cry as she looked into his shimmering eyes.

"There's a song," he whispered. "Garth Brooks, I th-think. A man wondering if she knows—wondering if he's done enough."

Bethany touched her fingers to his lips and sobbed, unable to imagine what a song had to do with anything. "Save your strength. Don't try to talk."

"Got to. Important." He gulped and stared at the sky. "If I don't wake up, I need to know that you know."

"Know what?"

"How much I—" He closed his eyes. "How much I love you."

He passed out again then. Bethany sobbed and hugged him close, rocking wildly. "I know, Ryan. How could I not? I know . . ."

The next time he regained consciousness, he said, "They'll circle back. Sometimes, they circle back. Keep the gun close and the safety off."

"I will. It's right here beside me. I'll shoot the son of a bitch. Trust me."

His teeth flashed in a weak grin, his face pallid and eerie looking in the moonlight, streaked with dry blood. "I've never heard you cuss. I'll be damned."

"Right now, I could teach you a few dirty words."

He smiled again. "You already taught me a lot, darlin'." He gazed up at her. Then his eyes seemed to lose focus. "It's been good," he whispered. "It was—everything. Understand?"

She nodded. "I know, Ryan. I know how much you love me. Almost as much as I love you, I think."

His face contorted with pain. His lashes fluttered closed. "Bethany?" he whispered weakly.

"What?" she squeezed out.

"I don't think—" He gulped and grabbed for a painful breath. "I don't think I can hold on much longer."

"I'll hold on for you. Rest, Ryan. I love you so. You can't leave me."

The next time he came to, he was weaker. He wasted no time on unnecessary words. "Rafe. My folks. You tell them. We made vows. I want you to have the place."

As if she cared. Tears streamed down Bethany's cheeks. "I don't give a shit about your money, Ryan. Don't even think about that."

"Not the money," he forced out. "The *place*. Heaven in your backyard. You stay, Bethany. You and Wink. With my family. Promise me?"

"You're going to make it, Ryan. You have to. Do you understand? I sent Bucky back. Help will be here soon. Just hold on a little longer."

"Can't," he whispered. "Promise me. You'll stay. Gotta know."

"I promise. I'll stay there, Ryan. With heaven in my backyard. I promise."

He lost consciousness for a long time then.

Bethany kept checking his pulse. It was weak. So horribly feeble. The beats had become so faint, she could barely feel them, and they were spaced an eternity apart. He was losing his strength, his life's blood slowly seeping away.

A terrible stillness came over her as she cradled his head to her bare breasts. *Ryan*. Had it all been a dream, then? A beautiful dream doomed to end, as all dreams did?

The moon was at its zenith when Bethany thought she heard Jake's voice calling her name. She jerked her head up and stared stupidly through the moon-silvery gloom, wondering if she'd nodded off and been dreaming.

"Bethaneeeeeee! Bethaneeeeee!"

Her heart soared with hope. "Jake? We're here! Over here! Jake?"

She saw lights. *Flashlights*. What appeared to be dozens of them, bouncing wildly in the darkness. She hugged Ryan's limp shoulders and rained kisses over his face.

"You made it! They came. Just in time, but they *came*. You made it!"

Even as Bethany said the words, she wondered if she was lying to herself. He was so horribly weak now. As much as she loved him, sometimes love simply wasn't enough.

Nightmares. Bethany dreamed of helicopters. Totally weird. Of Ryan and helicopters? He'd mentioned once that the Rocking K had an airstrip, but he'd never said anything about owning a helicopter. Nevertheless, she dreamed they were flying. She smiled as she struggled toward consciousness. She and Ryan, flying. Just the two of them, lifting off together. Darkness. Confusing lights all around them. The deafening whir of helicopter blades.

In her dreams, Jake was there and so were Ryan's brother and dad. She kept trying to remind them that it was a ten-dollar fine for every cussword, but somehow she couldn't get her brain and mouth to work.

"It's all right, Bethie," she heard Jake whisper. "You did good, honey. It's going to be all right."

Bethany was freezing, yet she felt as if her skin was on fire. She drifted in and out of blackness, deep in an exhausted sleep one moment, jerking awake the next to see swimming faces. Her mom and dad, Jake, and her other four brothers. Everyone she loved seemed to be there.

Everyone except Ryan.

When Bethany finally awakened, rested and lucid, in the middle of the night, only Jake sat by her hospital bed. She gazed solemnly at his dark face for a long moment, remembering all the many times he'd sat with her in just this way eight years ago. Back then, he'd always been the one to tell her the most recent bad news—that she was still paralyzed after her last surgery and she'd probably never walk again. Poor Jake, always chosen to be the bearer of bad tidings. Bethany prayed that wasn't the case now.

"Ryan? Please tell me he's all right," she whispered.

Jake's eyes ached with sadness. "He's still alive," he told her.

Still alive? Not that he was fine. Not even that he was doing fairly well. "What's that mean?" She struggled up onto her elbows and immediately cried out at the pain. Her torso burned at the slightest movement. "Oh, God!"

"You've got a bad burn from sitting all that time in the sun, honey. No clothing to protect your skin. When we found you, you were cooked and flirting with hypothermia as well."

Bethany filed away the information for later and pushed the pain aside. That was a trick she'd learned long ago, how to ignore pain. When it was a part of everyday life for a long while, you had no choice but to live with it. "Ryan. Tell me how he is, Jake. Don't color it. I have to know how he is."

Jake sighed and ran a hand over his rumpled dark hair. "Not good. A crushed hip, three broken ribs, and some very serious wounds, Bethany. He lost a lot of blood. They did a direct transfusion, using Rafe's blood."

Terror washed through her. "But he's—he's here in the hospital now. Right? They'll fix him up, and he'll be fine."

Jake closed his eyes for a moment. When he opened them again, Bethany knew the awful truth before he said it out loud. "He's hanging on, honey. Been a rough night. Touch and go. The doctors " He shrugged and swallowed hard.

The sight of him struggling to control his emotions told Bethany just how grave Ryan's condition was and made her all the more afraid. "He put himself between me and the bear. He could have run. Tried to save himself. But he protected me."

Jake nodded. "I figured."

"He can't—die. He *can't*. Not now that he's in the hospital." Her voice rose in volume. "He can't *die*. Don't even tell me that! Don't *even*!"

"I'm sorry, sweetie. I'm so sorry. They've done all they can. He's too weak right now to undergo surgery. They have him in ICU. The doctors say if he makes it through the night, he'll be out of the woods."

"If?" Bethany began pushing at the blankets. "Take me to him."

"Bethany, honey . . . you're not in great shape yourself. You shouldn't—"

"Take me to him!"

Evidently Jake saw she meant business. He lifted her from the bed into a hospital wheelchair, covered her legs with a blanket, and pushed her to ICU.

Three days later, Bethany sat by Ryan's hospital bed, staring at his lax features. Still heavily drugged for pain, he slept deeply, unaware of what went on around him. A jagged, angry red cut angled over one of his sunken cheeks. She knew it would leave a scar on his beautiful face, every line of which had been engraved on her heart. Oh, how she wished she could kiss him. Touch him. But she was trapped in her wheelchair and couldn't reach him.

The doctors said he would live, that the danger was past. He'd undergone surgery on his hip. His other wounds would heal with time. He might always have a limp. But he was going to live.

Bethany was so glad. So very, very glad. Over the last twenty-four hours, she had cried enough to cause a major flood.

Ann Kendrick came into the room just then. She stepped around to stand at the opposite side of her son's bed. After touching his forehead in that universal way of all moms, she fixed sad gray eyes on Bethany.

"He'll never understand, you know. It'll break his heart, Bethany, and he may never forgive you. I know my son."

Bethany stared hard at her lap. She hadn't told Ann or anyone else of her decision, but it didn't surprise her that Ryan's mother had guessed. She seemed to be an intuitive lady.

Bethany found the strength to meet her gaze. "Do you understand, Ann?"

Ann's eyes took on a suspicious shine. She stared for a long moment at Ryan. "Yes, I understand," she admitted softly. "He'll probably never forgive me for telling you that. I should probably deny it with my last breath, but, yes, I do understand." She smoothed his black hair with a trembling hand. "If I were in your place, I might do the same thing myself. Kendrick men make wonderful husbands. They love passionately with their whole heart and soul, and they treat a woman like a queen. But as wonderful as it is, being loved that fiercely places a burden of responsibility on a woman's shoulders as well, especially for someone like you."

"A terrible burden," Bethany agreed.

"I wish I could tell you he would never again throw himself in the path of danger for you. I know this is as heartbreaking for you as it will be for him. But sadly, I can't. No telling what it would be next time. A frightened horse or a loco steer." She shrugged and smiled tearfully. "On a ranch, you just never know, the only certainty being that he'd jump in to protect you and might get hurt."

Bethany was so relieved that it wasn't necessary to explain her reasons. "Oh, Ann, thank you. For understanding, I mean. It's so hard for me to go."

"It's hard for me to let you go without arguing his case, given the fact that he's unable to speak for himself right now." Ann trailed a fingertip over the tray beside Ryan's bed. "If he were awake, he'd tell you how very much he loves you, and that he'd rather be dead than live without you."

Bethany closed her eyes. She knew that was exactly what Ryan would probably say, but hearing Ann say it aloud was worse than merely hearing it in her mind.

"Loving him as you do, Bethany, I hope you've considered the problem from every angle and know with absolute certainty that there's no way to work it out. I meant it when I said he may never forgive you. This will hurt him so much. I'm sure you know that." She sighed and shook her head. "Forgive me for butting in. It's your decision to make, and I should just let you make it. It's just that I'm not sure he'll take you back if you should change your mind later. It wouldn't be fair if I let you leave without telling you that."

"I won't change my mind." Bethany tried not to look at Ryan. "The day before it happened, we, um . . . we exchanged wedding vows on Bear Creek Ridge. Just he and I, with only God to hear. One of my promises was that I would try to love him more than I love myself. I'm trying to keep that promise right now."

"Oh, sweetie . . ."

"If I stay on the ranch, the only way I can avoid putting him at risk again is to stay completely away from the animals. That wouldn't be a marriage, Ann. He needs someone to share his life with him, someone who can work beside him and dream with him."

"I know," Ann agreed hollowly.

"All of you tried so hard to make that possible for me," Bethany whispered raggedly. "You'll never know how grateful I am. But I just can't do it. I just—can't. All the trying in the world won't make me whole again, and my selfishness almost killed him."

"Oh, Bethany . . ." Ann took a bracing breath. "You're still very upset, honey, and you may not be thinking clearly. Can you give it a few more days? You need time to distance yourself from what happened up there. Time to let the horror of it become less vivid. Maybe then you'll feel calmer and see things a little differently."

Bethany shook her head and wheeled from the room. Ann followed, her riding boots tapping sharply on the well-waxed tile. "If I wait, I won't go," Bethany told her. "I love him so much. It would be so easy to start lying to myself and thinking up reasons to stay. And in the end, I wouldn't go."

"Exactly," Ann said with a humorless laugh. "That's my hope."

Bethany braked to a stop. "Is it really? You weren't on the mountain. You didn't see the bear attack. You're thinking clearly right now. Look me in the eye and tell me you won't blame me if Ryan ends up dead trying to protect me from a danger I might have avoided. Can you tell me that?" Bethany waited a beat. "The truth, and please don't answer lightly. Imagine yourself, standing over his grave. How will you feel when you look at me, Ann?"

Ann's face drained of color. She said nothing, but it was all the answer Bethany needed.

She left Ann Kendrick standing in the hallway and didn't look back. A few minutes later when she exited the hospital, she had never in her life felt so alone.

Chapter Twenty-two

Six weeks later, Ryan parked his dusty pickup next to a corral over at Rafe's place. When he exited the vehicle and started pulling on soiled leather work gloves, his father waved from inside the small enclosure where he, Rafe, and Sly were dehorning a hogtied steer.

"Looks to me like you're fixin' to go to work!" Keefe called. "You sure you're ready for this?"

"Can't sit around forever," Ryan hollered back as he limped toward the fence. "I'm getting damned tired of staring at bare walls. Time to rejoin the world of the living."

Keefe strode over to the fence, watching as Ryan struggled to climb up and over the rails. "Still a little sore, I see."

"Nothing that won't get better with use." Ryan swung down inside the corral to stand beside his dad. "Too pretty a day to be inside, that's for sure."

Keefe smiled and squinted at the sky. "Nothing like a summer morning to get the blood to perking. Can't believe it's damned near August. The snows will come before we know it."

Ryan forced a laugh. These days, strained laughter was all he could manage. His heart just wasn't in it. But that would pass. Bethany's four younger brothers had tracked down the renegade bear and killed it. The surgery to repair the damage to his hip had gone very well, and in time, he'd have only a slight limp as a reminder of that day. As for the mess his life was in, the Kendricks were survivors. In time, the pain would subside.

Yep. To hell with her. To hell with everything. He'd move on. Eventually her face would blur in his memory, and he'd forget the color of her eyes. In time, he'd stop hurting.

Time. That was all he needed, a little more time.

"Your mother says you're packing up a bunch of stuff to ship to Bethany," his dad said.

Ryan's guts knotted at the sound of her name. "Yeah. That treadmill, the all-terrain wheelchair, and a couple of other things I've got no use for. She may as well have them."

"Must've been hard, reaching that decision. A final step, cutting her out of your life."

Ryan shrugged. "I don't want to look at the shit. I figure sending it to her is another step toward healing for me."

"Probably wise thinking." Keefe sighed. "I'm sorry, son. I know you're hurting."

"It hurts to cut out cancer, too." Ryan hauled in a deep, cleansing breath.

"That's mighty harsh," Keefe said softly.

"Yea, well, it's how I feel. I'm well rid of her. For better or worse, that was our bargain. First spot of trouble, and she ran out on me. Without a word, Dad. I damned near died for her. I think she owed me a face-to-face good-bye. Don't you? At least a note or something. Screw it. I don't need the aggravation or the heartache. I've come through the worst part without her. I'll get through the rest and be better off in the long run for the loss."

"I hear you." Keefe gazed off at the mountains. His mouth twitched at one corner. "The little bitch."

Ryan stiffened. He stared at the ground for a long moment. "I don't love her anymore," he said evenly. "But that doesn't give you license to call her names."

Keefe's eyes started to twinkle, and he nodded almost imperceptibly. "You're right. It's the daddy coming out in me. She doesn't have that coming. I apologize, son."

Ryan shrugged. "No skin off my nose, I don't guess. If it flips your skirt, go for it."

Keefe rubbed the back of his fist over his mouth. "Nah. I was out of line. She's a sweet little thing. Never did anything to warrant any name-calling."

"Nope."

"Too bad it all came out the way it did."

Ryan shrugged again. Keefe watched Rafe and Sly work for a moment, his eyes still twinkling.

"Take heart, son. You'll find the right woman someday."

"I found her. It didn't work out. That's it for me."

"You'll change your mind when you clap eyes on the right girl."

"Nope."

That was all Ryan said, but the word was a vow.

"You know, son, not that I'm defendin' her or anything, but your mother seems to think she had sound reasons. Listening to her, I can damned near believe it myself. Women." Keefe shook his head. "Sometimes they see things inside out and ass backward, but their hearts are in the right place. They just need a man to get their heads on straight."

Ryan shot his father a glare. "Don't start, Dad. If you're going to switch sides, keep your thoughts to yourself. I don't want to hear it."

"I'm not switching sides. I'll always be on your side. You know that. It's just—"

"That Mom's been working on you?" Ryan finished for him. "I know she feels bad for me and that she hopes I'll go chasing after her. News bulletin. It ain't happening. She made her decision. The day I go chasing off to Portland to kiss her ass and beg her to come back, hell will freeze over. End of subject."

Rafe finished with the bull. As he shooed the animal into an adjoining pen, he spotted his brother and waved. A moment later Rafe sauntered across the enclosure. "Howdy. You're lookin' spry and ready to tangle."

Keefe slipped the cigarettes he seldom smoked from his shirt pocket. He tapped out a Winston, his eyes narrowing as he watched his elder son approach. "His mood just took a downward turn. All it takes is sayin' her name, and he gets prickly as a porcupine."

"Uh-oh." Rafe fixed an amused gaze on Ryan's scowling face. "He's probably just feeling better and getting horny. There's a cure for that, little brother. You can be on her doorstep in less than three hours if you break all the speed limits to get there."

"Jesus Christ." Ryan snatched the pack of cigarettes and lighter out of his dad's hands. The other two men watched him in stunned surprise as he lit up and inhaled. "Back off." He handed back the cigarettes and lighter. "Both of you. I don't need this shit."

Rafe chuckled. "He's hangin' on by a thread to his willpower when he grabs for smokes. Won't be long now."

Ryan had had enough. "Rafe, you're my brother, and I love you. But I swear to God, if you don't shut up, you're going to eat this cigarette, fire and all. Do I make myself clear?"

Sly strolled over. He smiled wryly as he opened his can of snuff and tucked a wad of chew inside his bottom lip. "You sound like a grizzly with a sore paw, boy."

Ryan took another drag from the cigarette, then tossed it on the ground and smothered it out under his heel. "Let's get to work," he said with a snarl.

"You sure you're ready for wrestlin' them steers?" Sly asked. "Next one up is one that slipped past us last year. He's a big old boy."

"I'm here, aren't I?" Ryan threw the adjoining gate wide to shoo in the next victim, a large black steer with wild-looking eyes. Recently brought in off open range, the critter was nervous around humans and ran a circle around the pen, looking for a bolt hole. Ryan settled his hat back on his head. "Well, boys?" he said to the other three men. "You gonna work or stand around with your thumbs up your asses all day?"

Everyone sighed as they resumed work. Sly roped the steer in short order. Rafe jumped in to help handle the huge creature, which didn't take kindly to having a noose around its neck. Nothing out of the ordinary. Half-wild steers never took kindly to being handled.

Ryan grabbed the dehorner. Because he wasn't back to full speed yet after his surgery, he meant to stand aside until his brother and the ranch foreman got the steer hogtied. Unfortunately, the steer had other ideas. It lunged, Sly lost his grip on the rope, and the next thing Ryan knew, the huge animal was charging right for him.

Ryan dropped the dehorner clamp and tried to spring out of the way, but his hip was still weak and it gave under the force of his weight. He staggered and fell. When he tried to scramble back to his feet, he moved too slowly.

"Ha!" Keefe yelled.

With growing alarm, Ryan watched his father jump between him and the charging steer. Keefe waved his Stetson to head off the huge animal. The steer lowered its head and just kept coming.

"Dad!" Ryan hollered. "Get the hell out of the way!"

Keefe stood his ground.

In the horrible seconds that followed, Ryan's brain seemed to assimilate the transpiring events in slow motion. He screamed again for his father to move, scrambling as he did to get out of the way himself. Then it happened. The steer rammed Keefe in the midriff and just kept charging, lifting Ryan's father off his feet and slamming him violently against the corral fence.

In reality it all probably took place in less than a second, but to Ryan, it seemed to take forever. The steer bawled and veered away. Keefe crumpled to the ground, his face ashen, his eyes bulging. He grabbed his chest and fought to breathe.

Sweet Lord. Ryan crawled to his father's side. Frantically, he checked for blood, thinking his dad might have been gored. When he found no blood, he could only deduce that maybe his father's ribs were broken. Keefe was still grabbing futilely for breath. His lips were turning blue.

Rafe and Sly reached them. Rafe fell to his knees beside Ryan. "Dad? Oh, Jesus. Sweet Jesus. His heart. Dad, is it your heart?" Rafe started fishing in Keefe's pockets for his nitroglycerin tablets. When he found the small vial, he tapped a tiny pill onto his palm, then stuck it under their father's tongue. "Try to relax, Dad. Just try to relax."

Ryan moved around to put their father's head on his lap. He imagined Keefe dying. They were so far from town. If the old man was having a heart attack, they'd never get him to a hospital in time. Oh, God. His fault. All his fault. He should never have been in the corral. He knew he wasn't completely back to normal yet. He had no business putting himself in dangerous situations and forcing the people who loved him to take up the slack. Now his dad had jumped in to protect him and could end up dying.

Sly kept the steer away from them while they hovered over Keefe. It seemed as if an eternity passed before the older man finally managed to catch his breath, and then he simply lay there for another eternity, replenishing his oxygen.

"Not my heart," he grated out. "Just knocked the breath out of me."

Relief made Ryan's bones feel watery. He hung his head and spent a moment grabbing for some much-needed oxygen himself. *Damn.* Seeing his dad get rammed like that—it had been the most awful moment of his life. Knowing he'd been the cause of it. Thinking his father might die. Ryan never wanted to experience such feelings again. That awful sense of crushing guilt and a clawing fear that had turned his blood to ice.

When it was all over and Keefe was back on his feet,

Ryan was still shaken. He left the corral and went to his truck, unable to stop thinking of how much worse it could have been. The steer might have gored his dad or broken his ribs, puncturing a lung.

Ryan leaned against the fender of his Dodge, shoulders hunched, head hanging, mind racing with so many horrible possibilities. Rafe walked up and laid a hand on his shoulder. "Hey, bro. All's well that ends well."

"He could be dead," Ryan bit out. "And it would have been my fault. I had no business going in the pen. I should have known better than to put other men at risk that way. If you can't cut the mustard, you keep the hell out of the way."

Rafe sighed and patted Ryan's back. "Life is full of risks. Sly's never lost his grip on a rope in all the years I've known him. It was just one of those things. Probably never happen again. We're lucky it didn't go worse than it did."

"Christ," Ryan whispered. "I can't stop shaking, and I think I'm gonna puke."

"It's a bad feeling, I know," Rafe said softly. "Nothing worse than feeling responsible when someone you love gets hurt. Is there?"

"You've got that right," Ryan agreed in a quivery voice that sounded nothing like his own.

Rafe rested his folded arms on the fender beside Ryan's. "Strange how a front-row seat can give you a different perspective on something. Now you have an inkling of how Bethany must have felt."

That brought Ryan's head up. He glared at his brother. "How the hell do you figure?"

Rafe gazed off across the fields. "Nah. You're right. There's no comparison, is there? Five minutes later, and Dad's up walking around, fit as a fiddle. She undoubtedly felt a million times worse." Rafe cut Ryan a hard look. "Probably still does. You damned near died. She kept you hanging on for hours. Imagine it, Ryan. Sitting there all that time, praying you'd live. Naked from the waist up, except for all your blood. Got so cooked from the sun, they had to knock her out with a shot for the pain. While she was holding you, getting baked, I wonder how many times she thought she'd puke? And you know the real kicker? You can look forward to getting better. The hip will heal. You'll get your strength back. You may never be good as new, but you'll come close, and the day will come when you can resume all your former activities without putting anyone at risk. Bethany can't look forward to that. She'll be paralyzed for the rest of her life."

Rafe pushed away from the truck. He didn't say another word. He didn't need to.

Two nights later at precisely half past six, Bethany's doorbell rang. In her pre-Ryan days, she might have felt excited, thinking it was one of her friends coming to invite her to join in an activity. Now she only sighed dejectedly, unable to work up any enthusiasm for company. She didn't want to do something fun. She didn't even want to see a friendly face. She just wanted to be left alone to wallow in her misery.

She hurried through the apartment, which was no easy task because she still wasn't finished unpacking, and she had moving boxes everywhere. She wrestled with the dead bolt, finally got it disengaged, and opened the door until the sturdy safety chain Jake had installed earlier in the week caught hold. Through the crack, she glimpsed a tall, dark-haired man in neatly pressed chinos and a brown sport coat.

"Yes? May I help you?" Though she hadn't yet seen his face, he looked respectable enough, definitely not a punk-with-purple-hair type who might rob her at gunpoint. Even so, she was reluctant to unfasten the security guard. "I'm really not interested in buying anything. Sorry. I just moved in here and—"

The man shifted so she could see his face. She broke off and stared incredulously into twinkling, gunmetal blue eyes.

"Hi, darlin'."

"Ryan?" With shaking hands, she unhooked the chain and backed away to open the door.

Hands in his trouser pockets, his body deceptively relaxed, he rested a slip-on Italian loafer on the threshold and leaned his shoulder against the door frame. Whether he meant to or not, he'd very effectively prevented her from shutting the door again. "You really do need a peephole. It'd save you from opening up to fellows you'd rather avoid."

"Ryan," she said again, her voice shaky.

He looked so different she almost didn't recognize him. Gone were the faded jeans and dusty boots. Every dark hair on his hatless head was perfectly styled. The sexy cowboy had vanished, and a successful-looking city slicker had taken his place.

"If you're here to try and convince me to go back to the ranch, you've wasted the trip."

"Nope. That's not my aim. I never want you to touch a wheel back on the Rocking K."

Her heart sank with disappointment. Stupid of her. Even though she had no intention of relenting, a part of her wished he might at least attempt to get her back. She tried to moisten her lips with a tongue that felt as dry as cotton.

"I'm moving in," he said.

"Oh." Bethany gazed blankly at him for a moment. "What?"

"You heard me. Do I really need to repeat myself?"

Bethany stared hard into his eyes. "I told you, Ryan. It's over. I'm not—"

"Forever," he interrupted. "That's what you told me." He pushed his way on in. "You're mine. No reneging on the bargain. If you don't have a double bed, we'll make do for tonight and I'll buy one tomorrow."

He limped slightly, she noticed. He didn't move as fluidly as he once had, either. He turned to shut the door, then he engaged the dead bolt and the chain. When he faced her again, he flashed that wonderful crooked grin that had always made her heart do flips. The jagged scar on his cheek was still an angry pink, but it in no way detracted from his rugged good looks. Instead it only lent that drop-dead gorgeous face more character.

"I'm not going back with you to the ranch, Ryan. Not ever. If you think by coming here you can convince me, you're wrong."

"I'm not asking you to go back. I understand why you feel we can't live there. Not a problem. We'll live here."

She laughed tremulously. "Right. You're leaving the ranch. Uh-huh. And where's the bridge from Brooklyn you'd like to sell me?"

"No bridge." He rested his hands on his hips. "Where you go, I go."

"No way. You'd shrivel up and die, living in the city. You're a rancher to the marrow of your bones. It'd never work."

"I'll make it work." He moved into her living room and glanced around at the boxes. "It's just as well you aren't unpacked completely. I want to get a house with a couple of acres. Someplace where we can at least keep Wink and Bucky and have a yard for Tripper."

Bethany hugged her waist. "A house? You want to buy a house here?"

He turned to regard her with a no-nonsense glint in his eyes. "Bethany Ann, we can do this the easy way, or we can do it the hard way. I'm here, I'm staying. Nothing you say or do will change my mind. Why don't you just accept what you can't change, and feed me. I'm hungry."

She'd known he loved her. No question. But the realization that he would leave the Rocking K , simply to be with her, nearly broke her heart. "I can't let you do this, Ryan. You'll never be happy in the city. You know that. I know that. You'd die an inch at a time."

He shrugged. "If I stay on the ranch without you, I'll die

an inch at a time, too. I'd rather die up here with you." He wandered into the kitchen and opened her refrigerator. "Where's the food?"

"I haven't gotten all that many groceries yet."

He sighed and shut the door. Then he eyed her with a speculative gleam. "I'm not really all that hungry for food, anyway. I'd much rather have you."

She held up a hand. "We're not going to hop into bed until we settle this."

"It's already settled." He grasped the lapels of his sport coat to show her his dress shirt. "I even bought new clothes. Decision made. I'm here. I'm staying." He released his hold on the jacket and moved slowly toward her, managing to do the cowboy saunter even in chinos and loafers. When he settled his hands on the arms of her chair, he dipped his head to look deeply into her eyes. "I love you so much, Bethany. Wherever you are—that's where I belong, and that's where I'll be happy. I'll make this work. Just give me a chance to show you."

She could barely see him now through her tears. "Oh, Ryan. You can't *do* this. You were born and raised on that land. It's where your heart is, where your heart will always be. I can't take you away from there."

"You already have," he whispered, and lifted her into his arms.

He swore when he straightened, cursing his bad hip. "I'm still not a hundred percent recovered. But I'm getting there."

"Don't hurt yourself, you big, stubborn blockhead." She hugged his neck, scarcely able to believe how very wonderful it felt to have his arms around her again. She'd lain awake countless nights, longing to feel his embrace, aching with sadness because she hadn't believed she ever would again. "Oh, Ryan. I love you. I love you."

"I know you do," he informed her huskily.

And then he carried her to the bedroom to show her how much he had missed her.

Afterward Bethany lay in his arms, gazing thoughtfully at the ceiling while he toyed with her hair. He honestly meant to stay, she realized. This wasn't a ploy to manipulate her. He simply loved her so much, he had to be with her, and if that meant living in Portland, he was willing to do that. He had absolutely no intention of trying to convince her that she should return to the ranch.

Yet that was exactly what he'd managed to do.

She recalled the promise she'd made to him, about always trying to love him more than she loved herself. How ironic that in the end, it was Ryan who was showing her the true meaning of that vow by loving her so selflessly. Oh, God. He made her feel so miserably misguided and small.

"I'll go home with you," she whispered tremulously. "If you can make it work here, then I can surely figure out a way to make it work there."

"Nope," he said stubbornly.

They spent several minutes arguing. Then they both started laughing. When his mirth subsided, Ryan told her about the incident with the steer. "I understood then, honey. How you felt during the bear attack and why you left me afterward. I'm not in a wheelchair, but in a way, I am physically handicapped right now. I got a very slight taste of how it feels. You aren't afraid for yourself. You're afraid for me, because you know I'll jump in and possibly get hurt again if anything threatens your safety. We can't live like that."

"We can't live like this, either. You aren't cut out for city living, Ryan."

"Sure I am. I've got two bachelor degrees, for God's sake. I can find some sort of work that challenges me. It doesn't even have to pay all that well. We've got all the money we'll ever need."

They argued a bit more. Then he got up to order some pizza. After the food was delivered, they ate until they were replete, and then he made love to her again. Bethany fell asleep in his arms with a troubled frown pleating her brow, for in her heart she knew that no matter how hard he tried, he'd never be happy living in the city.

The following morning, Ryan woke up to find the bed empty beside him. He stared hard at the sling Bethany had used to sneak out on him and made a mental note to get rid of the damned thing.

Yawning and rubbing his eyes, he bumped his toes on boxes all the way to the kitchen. Next to the coffeepot, he found a note from his runaway bride.

> Dear Ryan:
> I can't think how to tell you this, so I'll cut right to the chase. I've left you again. This is never going to work. I lay awake half the night, agonizing over our dilemma. I've decided I'd much rather lose you suddenly while you're doing some damned fool thing to protect me than to watch you slowly lose all your enthusiasm for life, which is exactly what will happen if you stay up here.
> Anyway, dear heart, I've gone home. Sorry for doing it this way, but you are being so obstinate, I know talking to you will get us nowhere. Please try not to be too angry with me.
> Love, Bethany

Ryan swore when he finished reading the note. Then he went back to the bedroom to throw on his clothes.

It was shortly after noon when Ryan reached the ranch, and sure enough, there was Bethany's van in front of the stable. His temper didn't improve when he discovered she wasn't in the house or any of the outbuildings, which forced him to walk all the wheelchair paths to find her. As chance would have it, he finally found her on the very last path he chose to take, the one that led to his thinking spot on the knoll.

He saw her sitting in her wheelchair under the pine tree

long before he reached her. Just sitting there, gazing off across the lake at the mountain peaks with a wistful look on her upturned face. He wanted to be irritated with her. He'd just chased her halfway across the state and back, after all. And this latest shenanigan of hers resolved nothing. He couldn't make her stay someplace where she'd feel afraid all the time, either for herself or for him.

Only how could he stay angry with someone who looked so damned sweet?

"Bethany Ann!" he barked. A guy had his pride, after all. "What the hell do you think you're doing down here? I specifically told you last night that I wasn't coming back here, that we could never make this work."

She didn't even have the good grace to jump. She only smiled slightly and waited for him to reach her. With a bad hip, it was a little difficult to stomp with every step, but he gave it his best shot.

"I've a good mind to turn you over my knee. You run off to Portland, and I follow you. Then you run off and come home when you know very well it's against my wishes. Who in the hell's wearing the pants in this family?"

She glanced at his prissy city-slicker chinos. "Neither of us at the moment."

He swatted his trouser leg. "Don't let the cut of these britches fool you. It's not the damned clothes that make the man. I told you last night that I'd thought it over and decided we'd live outside Portland."

"I've just changed your mind for you."

"You can't make up your own mind, lady. Don't go screwing with mine."

She just smiled serenely. "You know what Sly says. Stand around waiting for a woman to make up her mind, and you'll put down taproots. Your roots are here, Ryan, and they run deep, so this is where we're staying. I was wrong. I realize that now. We're staying here on Kendrick land, and that's final."

Ryan wanted to give her a good, hard shake. Instead he planted his hands on his hips. "You'll be miserable if I make you stay here." He swung a hand to encompass the ranch. "Everywhere you look, there are dangers of one kind or another."

"There are just as many dangers in the city, only different kinds. Remember what you said to me, Ryan? About our having two choices in how we live life—in a safe little bubble where we'll eventually die anyway—or grabbing hold with both hands, enjoying every single second?"

"I remember."

"This is your everything," she said softly. Then she turned shimmering blue eyes to his and tremulously added, "And it's my everything as well. I was wrong to leave. It was a stupid mistake. I thought I was doing the right thing, and I continued to think that until last night when you showed up on my doorstep. It took that for me to realize that there are many different ways to die. Some death isn't of the flesh, but of the heart and soul."

"Oh, honey."

She held up a hand so he'd let her finish. "I was dying inside before I met you. I was slowly suffocating with every breath I took. How can you think that I could be happy in Portland, watching you feel the same way?"

All Ryan's anger dissipated. "I guess maybe you couldn't," he said thickly.

Tears spilled over her lower lashes onto her cheeks. "None of us know how long we've got. That being the case, we shouldn't waste a single day. I want to live every moment we have together as fully as we can. And the only place on earth either of us can do that is right here."

He closed the distance between them. When he leaned down to meet her gaze, she looked up at him with big Johnny-jump-up blue eyes all filled with tears and said, "I want my scalawag cowboy back."

"Your what?"

She smoothed her hands over the shoulder seams of his sport coat. "Don't get me wrong. You make a very handsome city fellow, but I think you're a lot sexier in faded jeans and dusty boots with a Stetson cocked over your eyes. I want my scalawag cowboy back."

Ryan swept her from the chair into his arms. "You got him, darlin'."

He kissed her until both of them felt a little dizzy. Then he turned to carry her up the slope.

"What are you doing? You can't carry me to the house."

"Why not?"

"Because it's silly. Your hip! Just put me in my chair and—"

"What kind of a beginning would that be? I want to carry you over the threshold when we get home."

She laughed in spite of herself. "Has anyone ever told you you're just a little bit crazy?"

"A few people have made noises to that effect. I just ignored them."

With every labored step he took, Bethany gazed back at the lake and the trees and the majestic mountain peaks. She was so glad to be back. So very glad.

Home, he'd said. And he was so very right. Kendrick land, under Kendrick skies. Her man had roots here that ran far deeper than he knew. She'd made the right decision, not just for him, but for herself.

Home. What a beautiful word that was.

Epilogue

I n the Kendrick family Bible, it is now recorded that Ryan Kendrick, son of Ann and Keefe Kendrick, took to wife Bethany Ann Coulter on August 31, in the year of our Lord 2000. What the entry fails to note is that the wedding took place on the shore of Bear Creek Lake that beautiful summer day and was in fact a double ceremony. Also joined in holy wedlock that afternoon were Sylvester Bob Glass and Helen Marie Boyle. The entry in the Bible also fails to note that the younger bride had just discovered she was pregnant and was beaming with happiness.

Present to witness the weddings was a dusty, denim-clad assortment of guests, all of whom rode three hours from Ryan's ranch house to reach the lake by horseback. The Coulter family was well represented, with Bethany's father and all five of her strapping brothers glowering at her groom until he said, "I do."

No bears or cougars made an appearance. Halfway through the ceremony, however, a certain bull named T-bone showed up to witness the marriage. Wary of so many strangers, he stopped a respectful distance away and only mooed once to let his master know he'd found him. Upon the bull's broad shoulders sat a plump calico cat who chose that moment to have a bath.

After the ceremony Mary Coulter smiled sweetly up at her husband and handed him a neatly folded pair of his jockey shorts. Harv laughed, eyed them speculatively, and asked, "Did you think to bring any salt and pepper? I like my crow well-seasoned."

Mary smiled and put her arm around his waist. Zeke, the musician in the Coulter family, struck up a slow, lilting melody on his fiddle. Bethany's parents watched as her new husband lifted her from her wheelchair to sweep her around the sun-dappled clearing in a waltz that was all the more heartbreakingly beautiful because the bride's feet never touched the ground.

"I was wrong about him," Harv admitted. "I can see the love shining in that young man's eyes every time he looks at her."

"And in hers every time she looks at him," Mary whispered. "If it's any consolation, I was wrong as well. Did you see how she looked, riding in today? That girl was born to ride, and because of me, she was denied the pleasure for far too long. I feel so badly about that."

Harv gave her a loving jostle. "We love her, and we were terrified she might get hurt again if we let her ride. She understood that."

"There's such a thing as loving too much," Mary whispered. "I'm glad Ryan came into her life and had the wisdom to see what we couldn't. It's better to let her take risks and enjoy life than to be safe and unhappy."

"Maybe so," Harv whispered. "Just look at how she glows."

Bethany was indeed looking at her husband with love shining in her eyes. Ryan saw it as he turned with her in his arms. She leaned her head back and smiled, putting him in mind of the look on her face when he made love to her.

God, how he adored her. So much that he couldn't begin to express it.

Ryan stopped dancing long enough to tell her in the only way he knew, with a long, deep kiss that probably made the guests wonder if their welcome had run out. He didn't care. Since he and his bride intended to stay at the lake for a week to celebrate their honeymoon, he didn't want anyone to hang around for too long after the ceremony.

"What are you thinking?" she asked.

"That I'm the luckiest man alive."

"Oh, Ryan, I love you so."

Ryan knew she meant it with all her heart. He also knew she couldn't possibly love him as much as he loved her.

He began dancing again. Great swirling steps with his world in his arms, so happy that he wasn't entirely sure if his own feet were touching the ground.

Flying . . . together. In that moment, gazing into Bethany's pansy-blue eyes, Ryan knew the magic would always be there between them, a beautiful, special something that would never die. Some great love stories didn't end happily because there was no ending. They just went on and on, into eternity.

It would be that way for them, a great love story that never ended.

Photo by Athena Lonsdale

Catherine Anderson is the author of more than thirty *New York Times* bestselling and award-winning historical and contemporary romances, including the Harrigan Family series, the Coulter Family series, the Comanche series, and the Mystic Creek series. She lives in the pristine woodlands of Montana.

CONNECT ONLINE

catherineanderson.com

f catherineandersonbooks

NEW YORK TIMES BESTSELLING AUTHOR

Catherine Anderson

"One of the finest writers of romance."
—Debbie Macomber

For a complete list of titles,
please visit prh.com/catherineanderson